Mixed Opinions

"You were at the games, Pierce, you saw what went on. Rome is a psychotic society and we're not helping it. Thousands are dying every day of curable diseases, millions are slaves, and they get their kicks out of mass sadism."

Pierce held up his hands. "They give us—"

"A few hundred kids a year, I know. Eventually thousands. Meanwhile they're affecting us with their vices—ever see the videotapes of the games Domitian gave last year? A big hit uptime. I ever find who made those tapes, I'll put *him* in the goddam arena."

"I'll pass your views on, Robinetti. I presume you'll keep an investigation going until you find out who killed Domitian?"

"Sure. Otherwise how could I give them a medal?"

By Crawford Kilian
Published by Ballantine Books:

The Chronoplane Wars

THE EMPIRE OF TIME
THE FALL OF THE REPUBLIC
ROGUE EMPEROR

Rogue Emperor

A Novel of the Chronoplane Wars

Crawford Kilian

A Del Rey Book

BALLANTINE BOOKS ● **NEW YORK**

For Ernie and Judy Fladell,
with love

A Del Rey Book
Published by Ballantine Books

Copyright © 1988 by Crawford Kilian

Library of Congress Catalog Card Number: 88-91961

ISBN 0-345-35078-2

Printed in Canada

First Edition: September 1988

Cover Art by Stephen Hickman

If a man were called upon to fix the period in the history of the world when the condition of the human race was most happy and prosperous, he would, without hesitation, name that which elapsed from the death of Domitian to the accession of Commodus.

—Gibbon, *The Decline and Fall of the Roman Empire*

"Can't repeat the past?" he cried incredulously. "Why of course you can!"

—Fitzgerald, *The Great Gatsby*

One:

Late in the afternoon of May 22, A.D. 100, Gerald Pierce sat four rows up from the arena in Rome's new Flavian Amphitheater, the stadium later to be known as the Colosseum. The emperor Domitian himself was presiding as *editor* over the day's show. Sixty men had been killed so far, not counting the lunchtime execution in the arena of fifteen *noxii*, condemned criminals unworthy of a gladiator's death. Pierce was obviously a foreigner from the awkward way he wore his toga, and as such he should have found a seat up near the top of the vast stadium. But he had trusted his height and effrontery, and had marched into the seats reserved for Romans of the senatorial order. No one had objected.

While Pierce was beckoning to a vendor of honey-dipped buns, a flash of light flooded his peripheral vision. As he turned back toward the arena, the concussion crashed over him and the sixty thousand other spectators.

Pierce had been Briefed and Conditioned, enhancing his sensory input synthesis and reaction time. With perfect clarity, he saw bodies flying from the *pulvinar*, the broad terrace just above the arena where the emperor and his party had been watching the games.

Pigeons fluttered into the spring sky. Shrapnel sliced through the enormous mustard-yellow awning that shaded the seats, and a cloud of oily black smoke rose from the *pulvinar*. Pierce recognized the characteristics of the explosion: it had probably been caused by an antitank missile.

The musicians stopped playing their horns and drums, and the choir fell silent. So, for a stunned moment, did the crowd. Some wounded survivor cried out, and the spectators answered in a great wordless shriek and began to scramble for the exits.

Springing to his feet along with everyone else, Pierce shoved aside the well-dressed men who tried to trample over him. He threw off his cumbersome toga, revealing a coarse wool knee-length tunic. As the crowd began to thin in the lower seats, he shouldered his way down to the railing that fenced off the seats from the arena. Without hesitating, he vaulted over it to the sand four meters below. The moment of free fall and the sudden shock of landing were exquisite to his enhanced senses.

Between the stands and the arena itself was a two-meter iron fence, intended to keep animals and gladiators out of the seats and the spectators off the sand. A couple of dozen soldiers patrolled the narrow corridor, and one was close by.

"Get back up there, fool!" The soldier rushed him, sword in hand. Pierce stepped aside, pivoted, and struck a one-knuckle karate punch against the side of the soldier's exposed neck. The force of the blow threw the man against the rusty iron bars. Pierce used the soldier's body to boost himself up over the fence.

He had not seen the trajectory of the missile; now, with no one blocking his line of sight, Pierce tried to find the launch point. It had probably been fairly low, perhaps from one of the gates opening directly onto the sand. The assassins must have carried the missile in a crate or a roll of fabric. Setup and launch would have taken under ten seconds, and the team was doubtless working its way anonymously through the tunnels under the stadium.

A gladiator, reaching only to Pierce's shoulder but half again as heavy, waddled menacingly toward him. He was a *myrmillo*, carrying a big rectangular shield and a short sword; his protective faceplate was shadowed by the broad wings of his bronze helmet. Across the arena the gladiator's opponent, a *retiarius* armed with net and trident, stood gaping up at the turmoil in the stands.

"Peace be with you, brother," Pierce called out in Latin to the *myrmillo*, but his voice was lost in the uproar. He jogged across the sand, away from the gladiator, with his eyes downcast. Outside the shade of the awning, the sun was surprisingly warm, and Pierce's wool tunic was damp with sweat. Thousands of flies swarmed around him, and clustered, shining, on every lump of bloodstained sand.

—*There* was the wire: almost as fine as a human hair, visible only as a thin black line lying in gentle loops across the sand. Pierce bent, picked it up, tugged it. It was much too tough to break, of course, but he could tell from the matte-black insulation that the missile had indeed been a T-60, an old-fashioned TOW weapon based on an even older Soviet model. The Spanish had made thousands of them in the bad old days; they were the equivalent of the Saturday-night specials of Pierce's American boyhood. But none, Pierce was certain, had been exported to this chronoplane—and certainly not to anyone in Rome.

The *myrmillo* had clumped off, ignoring both his opponent and the other spectators who preferred the arena to the deadly jams in the exit tunnels. The African boys who raked the sand after each combat had come out to watch the confusion in the stands, along with the black-clad, horned Charons who finished off the dying gladiators and the Mercurys who dragged the bodies out. A couple of trainers stood amid the growing crowd in the arena, one of them still holding the red-hot poker he had used to encourage the *retiarius* to fight.

Pierce looked up at the emperor's terrace on the north side of the arena. The smoke had cleared somewhat. Scores of soldiers had posted themselves on the edges of the shattered *pulvinar*, their throwing spears gripped like lances to keep the mob at a distance. A couple of senior officers, recognizable by their plumed helmets, moved cautiously around the terrace inspecting the bodies. Furniture and hangings were on fire, and many spectators seemed to have become casualties of the shrapnel. Some lay writhing on the stone seats; others were being carried toward the exits by their friends. From the very top of the stands, where the women were segregated, a high keening cut through the noise.

Holding the wire lightly in his left hand, Pierce walked across the sand. It led him to an abandoned launcher just inside the gate through which the dead were dragged, the *Porta Libitinensis*. The sand in the gate entrance was a blur of footprints and gritty clots of blood. Pierce smiled at himself: what had he expected, the prints of twenty-first-century Adidas? Or the assassins themselves?

Spectators and attendants hurried past him into the dark tunnel, hoping to find a way out of the stadium that hadn't been clogged with people. Pierce followed them, ducking his head under the low arched ceiling and stepping hesitantly.

Within a few meters of the gate, the tunnel was almost black. It ran into a labyrinth of rooms and passages under the stands. A couple of small oil lamps burned smokily in sconces. Farther ahead, more lamps gleamed. Voices echoed off the stone walls, but it was quieter here than out in the arena. The air stank of urine and excrement, human and animal. Caged lions coughed and roared in the darkness, and were answered by a bear. Pierce's sense of smell, almost as keen as a dog's, caught other scents as well: pheromone signatures of men and women, fresh blood and rotting meat, and the easily identified pungency of the AB-4 solid propellant of the missile.

People who knew how to handle that missile had also known how to make their way through this labyrinth of tunnels and cells beneath the stands, and had known that Domitian would have just returned to his seat after finishing the midday meal. The timing had been more than excellent; it had been politically brilliant. The assassination of the emperor had been witnessed by sixty thousand Romans who had never before seen an explosive weapon.

Pierce wished he had a flashlight and a firearm. He was under heavy cover, not even staying in the Agency's villa on the Esquiline Hill. Technically he had no connection with what the Romans called the Hesperian embassy; he was a Gaulish wine merchant on a working holiday in Rome, and wearing only what such a man would wear. His tunic was plain but of good quality, with a wide leather belt that also held a small pouch and a scabbarded dagger. Strapped inside the tunic was a money belt holding a few *denarii* and a medallion, stamped with Domitian's profile, that would get him past the guards at the embassy gate.

Pulling one of the oil lamps from its sconce, Pierce cast about, seeking some trace of the hit team. The fleeing spectators had already obscured any footprints in the fine dust of the tunnel floor. Perhaps the team had found some quiet hole rather than getting away from the Amphitheater at once. He looked into a couple of small cubicles, finding nothing but crates. But at the second cubicle he paused, catching the scent of unburned AB-4 mixed with gun oil. Looking closer, he found a crate had been recently disturbed, leaving a dustless patch exposed on the crate below it. Pierce stepped into the room, crouched under its low ceiling.

Behind the crates was a roll of coarse material something like burlap, wrapped around a thin, hard cylinder. Pierce carefully lifted the roll and unwrapped it.

The backup weapon, a Spanish T-60 wire-guided anti-tank missile as long as his arm, was painted in flat mottled gray and black. Where the serial number should have been, just behind the warhead, was a raspy patch of filed metal. A launcher, its sights and joystick folded flat, was clamped to the missile.

Pierce wrapped the T-60, replaced it, and put the crates back to conceal it. Perhaps the embassy could send someone to retrieve it later; a careful inspection might reveal its provenance, though Pierce doubted it. The hit team had been professional enough to bring a backup. They would have been professional enough to leave no fingerprints or other clues.

Back in the tunnel, the lamp held before him, Pierce slipped and stumbled through the darkness. Around him men and women cried out in terror, called on gods, and collided with one another. The lions roared again, very close by.

Lights burned in another room, larger but low-ceilinged. Pierce stepped in and found himself in the *spoliarium*, the gladiators' mortuary. On crude stretchers, piled three and four deep along the walls, lay the corpses of the gladiators who had fought earlier in the day. Their wide eyes caught the light of Pierce's lamp and sent back brief gleams; their mouths gaped in silent cries.

Beside one of them a girl stood weeping, stroking the bloodsoaked hair of her dead lover. She was small, wiry, and beautiful, a gladiatrix dressed in leather armor over a coarse tunic. She was oblivious to the people a few steps away who were squeezing corpses' wounds to fill little glass jars with gladiators' blood—a famous remedy for impotence and infertility. Pierce reached out and touched her shoulder in sympathy; she looked up at him in surprise and then turned away.

The spectators packed the corridor by now; Pierce used his height and weight to shove through. He smelled fresh air, followed the scent, and was out under the stands in a narrow board-walled corridor like a cattle chute. This was where the animals were dragged down into the holding pens before going into the arena to their deaths. Now it was full of men hurrying out toward the sunlight.

Somewhere within a few hundred meters were the assassins, but he knew he had no chance of finding them. For a moment he hesitated.

Rome was without an emperor; the next few hours would be dangerous. He could go back to his inn and wait there until it was time to enter the Hesperian embassy tonight for the I-Screen jump back to Earth. Technically the assassination was none of his business. He had been sent to get rid of a general in Transalpine Gaul who'd been interfering with the local recruiting team. The mission was finished, the general dead along with his unlucky boy lover. The embassy didn't know Pierce, had had no contact with him apart from receiving him through the I-Screen and slipping him past Domitian's spies into Rome.

But Wigner would want a complete report on Domitian's death, including the reactions of the embassy staff. Pierce would have to get into the embassy, tell them what he'd seen, and try to find out whatever the Hesperians might know.

As he strode into the plaza around the Colosseum, Pierce smiled without humor. The shopkeepers were quickly shuttering their doors, and the thousands of spectators seemed to clog the streets as far as he could see. The plaza itself was almost deserted except for the Colossus itself—the immense bronze statue of Nero which the emperor Vespasian had transformed into one of Apollo by the simple expedient of installing a new head. The Colosseum itself must be empty by now: even the largest crowd, leaving through the building's eighty exits, could be outside in three minutes flat.

The Amphitheater and its surrounding plaza stood in a shallow depression between the Esquiline and Palatine hills. To avoid the worst of the crowds, Pierce ran west across the plaza, past the Temple of Venus and Rome, and up the Sacra Via, around the Arch of Titus and past the Temple of Vesta. Hundreds of others were running with him, some shouting at bystanders. Pierce squinted against the glare of sun on stucco and marble.

The Forum was boiling with people; two or three stood on the Rostra at the west end, trying to make themselves heard over the uproar. Pierce saw four members of the urban cohorts, the city police, laying about with heavy clubs as they tried to make their way through the crowds. Aware that his height made him conspicuous, Pierce moved to his right, into the shaded colonnade, and slowed his pace to a dignified amble.

Beyond the Forum the crowds had almost disappeared. Pierce turned north into the Via Lata; here the great official buildings and temples gave way to crowded tenements and little marketplaces. This was the Subura, a filthy and dangerous slum. It was a neighborhood of *insulae*, huge apartment buildings that each filled a whole block and rose five or six stories above the narrow streets. Normally each *insula* would be swarming with people; now they were still. One man called down to him:

"Have the oracles been fulfilled?"

Pierce looked up, thought of speaking, and then shrugged silently in reply. Oracles? Had Domitian's death been predicted?

He strode on to the Via Tiburtina, which would lead him back east to the Esquiline Hill. The streets were little more than sunless footpaths between the *insulae*, so narrow that he could easily touch the walls on either side with his outstretched hands. Sometimes the streets were paved, but more often they were plain dirt and always thick with mud and excrement. Idlers competed for space with hundreds of merchants, artisans, and whores. Wherever the plaster still clung to the brick walls of the *insulae*, graffiti and crude sketches had been scratched or painted.

Glancing up, Pierce saw more people looking down from windows and balconies. Many called to one another, their voices shrill with excitement. He caught an occasional word: *oracle, dead, Domitian.*

The smells of putrefaction mingled with those of frying olive oil, baking bread, and charcoal smoke; he reveled in them while still seeking some scent that didn't belong, perhaps a whiff of AB-4 blown from someone's clothes.

In a marketplace, fruit and vegetable vendors squatted under their awnings or in the shade of their carts. One grizzled old man beckoned to Pierce.

"Big fellow! What's this about a thunderbolt from a clear sky?" Pierce barely understood his hoarse peasant's dialect.

"In the Flavian Amphitheater. The emperor and many others were slain."

The old man nodded, scratching his beard. "We heard warnings these three days now. Omens have been seen."

"What omens? I've heard nothing."

"You're a northerner, a German down from the mountains by the sound of you."

"A Gaul. Yes—I came to Rome just yesterday."

"Marketplace has been full of rumors. The mysteries

have foretold great changes, a new emperor and a new order. Tell me, did you see the thunderbolt?"

"I saw what it did."

"And Domitian is dead, is he?"

"With a great many others."

The old peasant could not restrain a sardonic grin. "Well, well. Strange times we live in. Not like the good old days. Here, would you like to buy some dried apples, friend? Best quality, from Campania."

Pierce bought a double handful of dried apple slices and walked on, savoring the strange sweetness of the fruit. With tripled sensory input synthesis and enhanced reflexes, he was always hungry even though most food tasted metallic and bitter. At least Campanian dried apples were edible; he almost turned back to buy more.

The blocks of tenements, five and six stories tall, seemed to go on forever. Some of the shops that filled the tenements' street frontage were still open, and a few merchants were besieged with customers—slaves buying extra loaves of bread or handfuls of vegetables, amphorae of wine, jugs of olive oil. Their masters must be planning to spend a few days discreetly indoors until the imperial succession was decided. Poorer Romans, crammed into tiny apartments with no way to cook, would have to continue to come out to whatever cookshops stayed open.

At the intersections, men in togas stood talking solemnly, oblivious to the jostling crowds of slaves around them. A few looked curiously at Pierce—he was a head taller than most—but no one spoke to him. He overheard fragments of conversations, but could scarcely follow the rapid urban slang. His Latin was good, but far from colloquial. Agency personnel assigned to Rome were taught Latin based on what the Advance Survey teams had learned. The teams, composed largely of classical scholars, had studied the dialect of the upper classes; street Latin was almost another language. Pierce suspected he sounded more like a pretentious hick than a Gaulish merchant: he had the vocabulary, but the musical lilt of upper-class Latin was beyond him.

He passed into a little square where a fountain splashed water from a bronze lion's head. On the west side of the square was a high wall topped with sharp spikes, with trees and a brick tower beyond: the palace of the Hesperian embassy. Four foot-soldiers of the Praetorian Guard stood sentry duty outside the tall double doors of the palace gate. A two-story private house on the east side of the square was used, Pierce knew, by Domitian's spies; they kept the embassy gates under constant observation.

Well, they could make a note in their little waxed tablets that a Gaulish-looking man had entered the palace; perhaps in a few days they would realize he had not re-emerged. That was no concern of Pierce's. He reached into his tunic and pulled out the medallion.

One of the sentries intercepted him as Pierce approached.

"I hold a pass to enter."

The guard glanced at the upheld medallion and shook his head.

"No one allowed in without special permission today."

"I have business in the embassy."

"Go talk to the people in the house across the square." The soldier waved toward the surveillance house. "If they give you a pass, you can enter. Otherwise, no."

Pierce paused for a second only, debating whether to force the gate. The four soldiers would be no real problem, not with his reflexes, but the repercussions would be awkward—especially today. He nodded and turned across the square, walked to the surveillance house, and tried the door. When it refused to open he thumped it. A dog barked furiously.

"Who's there?" someone called over the dog's roars.

"Alaricus Rufus, a Gaul. I need permission to enter the Hesperian embassy."

"Go away. No one's allowed in there today. Orders of the Praetorian Guard."

Pierce pounded again, improvising. "Urgent message from the Flavian Amphitheater. The emperor's slain."

"What!"

A bolt slid back and the door opened. A sandy-haired man in a coarse tunic stood staring at him. He held a short sword with the point aimed at Pierce's throat; the dog, looking like an underfed German shepherd, strained at the leather leash the man gripped in his other hand.

"Who are you?"

"I gave you my name. Where's your commander here?"

"Tell me who you are."

Pierce gave him the cold glare of an officer annoyed by an enlisted man. "Fool! Will you let me in or will you be crucified?"

Hesitantly the man stepped back and lowered his sword. Pierce strode into the atrium beyond. A gap in the red-tiled roof, the *compluvium*, admitted light that reflected from the shallow pool in the center of the atrium. Through a short corridor Pierce could see more light: the garden.

"Is he in there?"

"He's asleep. A little nap after *cena*. He's not to be disturbed—but of course this is an exception," the man added hastily.

"And who else is in the house?"

"Two other Praetorians. Some serving maids and the cook, and a couple of male slaves."

"Tell them nothing. Lead on."

The sandy-haired man guided him into the peristyle and along the colonnaded walk that rimmed it. Pierce looked about with interest. The house was large and well built, doubtless once the home of some wealthy senator or businessman who had fallen foul of Domitian. Now it was the property of the emperor, his window on the comings and goings of the mysterious Hesperians. The Praetorian surveillance team had neglected the place: the peristyle garden was weed-infested and unwatered except for a few pots where the cooks grew herbs. The walls were painted with murals that would have brought a fortune uptime on

Earth, even with the recent graffiti scrawled across them by bored soldiers.

A door stood slightly ajar; the sandy-haired man tapped timidly.

"Master? Master? Urgent news. The emperor—"

"I'll tell him myself," Pierce interrupted. He gripped the sandy-haired man by one arm and propelled him into the room. Against the opposite wall a balding man sat up in a narrow bed. He looked at Pierce with dangerous intelligence and reached for the sword leaning against the bedstead.

"Not so fast, friend. The emperor is dead. I'm ordered into the Hesperian embassy at once."

"At whose order?"

"Need you ask?"

Still suspicious, the balding man swung his feet to the floor.

"I don't trust those Hesperians for a moment. They're not foreigners, they're some mystery cult. Sorcerers."

"You may well be right. I trust them no more myself. But I have my orders. Give me a written pass, and quickly—I have no time to waste."

"I don't know you, and you speak like a cursed German. Identify yourself or I'll put you under arrest and we'll torture your name out of you."

"Alaricus Rufus," Pierce said. "I'm a Gaul, not a German. And I must be inside that accursed wall at once."

The balding man reached into a wooden box and pulled out a scrap of papyrus. With a lump of charcoal he scrawled a few letters on it, then handed it brusquely to Pierce.

"The emperor is truly dead?"

"I saw him die myself. Like a thunderbolt from the clear sky."

"The oracles were right. A thunderbolt from a clear sky." He smiled uncertainly at Pierce. "We chose wisely, didn't we?"

Pierce grunted ambiguously. "I must go."

"In nomine patris, et filius, et spiritus sanctus."

The farewell struck Pierce like a club. Fighting to keep the surprise from his face, Pierce turned with a choppy wave and hurried out of the room, back across the peristyle toward the door and the square and the guarded gate back to the twenty-first century.

Two:

The cover story had been a compromise between those who wanted Rome left completely alone and those who wanted to take it over as a protectorate. One night in A.D. 94 an enormous sailing ship had appeared in the harbor at Ostia, twenty kilometers down the Tiber from the capital. The crew all spoke Latin and Greek, and informed the port officials that they were from the land of Hesperia, far to the west across the Ocean. They were descendants of Romans whose ships had been blown off course during the Punic Wars. Making landfall in a rich and unknown country, the castaways had flourished; yet they had not forgotten their Roman heritage, and always dreamed of returning to the *patria*, the fatherland.

Like any embassy, the Hesperians sought a patron who could introduce them to the senate and help them negotiate. That patron would of course be the emperor himself, Domitian. When he saw what the foreigners had to offer in trade, the emperor commanded the embassy to attend him in Rome at once.

The Hesperians had any number of useful gadgets: flashlights, bicycles, and razor blades were especially popular. They also brought new foods and spices: corn, potatoes, chile, cinnamon. Their fabrics were sometimes usefully stout and sometimes scandalously thin and transparent.

Most important from Domitian's point of view, the Hesperians brought enormous quantities of beautifully stamped silver coins, each with the head of one of the

Hesperian *praesidentes* and mottos in Latin. The ambassadors were willing to pay cash for what they wanted.

At first they had wanted mostly art, and their taste had been good: they wanted Greek works, or the very best of the Roman imitations. The emperor had grown rich as the intermediary in these transactions, and had sold them one of his palaces as a permanent embassy.

The Hesperian ship sailed away a year later, and Domitian's own ships failed to trace it to its home. Only one Roman vessel returned, with a few shivering brown-skinned slaves taken from a sweltering island far off west of the Pillars of Hercules. But a few months later the Hesperians returned with still more goods.

They also advised the emperor that his wife and slaves were plotting against him, and supplied proof enough to oblige him to execute all the conspirators. In gratitude the emperor was happy to give the Hesperians what they next asked for: permission to take a certain small number of Roman youths back to Hesperia for advanced education. Thereafter, each ship that left Ostia for Hesperia carried a hundred more young men and women. (That had perplexed the Romans: why trouble to educate women? They would be priestesses needed for the most arcane and powerful ceremonies, the Hesperians blandly replied.)

So far none of the young people had returned, and Domitian had had to silence a few rumormongers who warned that the Hesperians were feeding a Minotaur just as the Cretans had done with the flower of Athens' youth. Meanwhile the empire flourished, and the emperor more than any.

But now the emperor was dead.

The embassy was a sprawling palace set in ornate gardens and orchards covering over five hectares. Two Hesperian attendants, dressed in white linen tunics, met Pierce inside the gates. Both were short men, no taller than the average Roman but thickset and muscular.

They didn't know Pierce, and looked at him suspiciously. Pierce knew them very well through his Briefing.

He stood very still and spoke quietly. Either one, un-armed, could have disabled all four of the Praetorians out on the street; together, they might even be a match for Pierce.

"Hi, Fred. Hi, Howie. I need to see Robinetti."

"Who the hell are you?" asked Fred.

"An old college buddy. Let's go."

"He's busy."

"Not as busy as he's going to be. Somebody killed Domitian about an hour and a half ago."

The two men did not respond, but fell in on either side of Pierce to escort him down the winding path past fruit trees and an ornamental fish pond to the palace. A few gardeners, all uptimers, watched them go. Looking at the spring colors of the garden, Pierce reflected that it had been built on an ancient graveyard: beneath the beauty was old horror and corruption.

Two more attendants at the palace doors admitted them; these two had seen Pierce on his way out two weeks earlier, and made no objection. Inside, Pierce looked appreciatively around at the polished mosaic floors and muraled walls. Maecenas himself had built this palace and its gardens during the reign of Augustus, and his taste had been excellent.

The building had once been on the same plan as the surveillance house across the square, only on a far greater scale and with a fifteen-meter belvedere tower commanding a view of the gardens and the city beyond. Now the original plan was marred by new wings that extended almost to the far west wall of the estate.

Pierce and his escort crossed the peristyle garden, which was adorned with fountains, fruit trees, and a life-size statue of Domitian. At a small doorway at the end of the colonnade, Fred inserted a small plastic key in the door's electronic lock. It swung silently open, revealing a bare corridor. When the door behind them closed, another opened at the end of the corridor; beyond was the familiar glow of fluorescent lights.

The men stepped through and sighed with the pleasure

of clean, cool air that smelled of uptime. Printers hummed behind an office door, and Pierce's enhanced hearing picked up a holotaped hockey game playing down the corridor in a recreation area. He smelled coffee, roast beef, french fries, and the lingering scent of someone's Old Spice aftershave. A minute later he was in Pete Robinetti's office—as windowless as every other room in the wing—and Fred and Howie had been dismissed back to their post.

Robinetti's hair was cropped short and brushed forward, like most Romans', but he wore jeans and a sports shirt. He was twenty-one, Trainable of course, and intelligent as well; Trainability and brains didn't always go together. He sat behind a beautifully inlaid table that held nothing but a few microfiches and a flickerscreen computer. Pierce politely stood until Robinetti waved him into an uncomfortable Roman chair.

"So Domitian's dead at last." Robinetti shook his head and pursed his lips. "Tell me what happened."

Pierce did, in the elliptical manner of Trainables talking together.

"What were you doing in the Colosseum?"

"Absorbing local culture."

"I only went once."

"It's an acquired taste."

"Pray to God you don't acquire it. I'm serious."

Pierce smiled vaguely and nodded. "What's your assessment of the situation now?"

"Bad," Robinetti growled. "We're going to be crawling with people from uptime. Snooping around, upsetting the natives. This'll really cheer up the Trajanists." On Earth, Domitian had been succeeded by old Nerva and then by Trajan, one of the greatest of the emperors. Here Trajan was still just the general holding the German frontier, but he had his uptime supporters.

"Can you blame them?"

Robinetti shrugged. "Domitian wasn't Mr. Likable."

"We're not running popularity contests," Pierce said. "He let us recruit. That made him our boy."

"Mr. Pierce, I don't know you, or where you stand with the powers that be. Fairly high, I suspect. When you go through, would you please tell them for me that someone's done us a huge favor? Now maybe we can back someone who isn't totally bananas."

"I'll be glad to pass your views on."

"You know how he spent his first year in power? Sitting in his palace, catching flies and stabbing them with his stylus. Did his pinhead get it, too?"

He meant the microcephalic that Domitian kept as a pet. The boy—a young man now—had accompanied the emperor everywhere, listening vacantly to his master's rambling monologues. "Yes. So did Domitian's new wife and a couple of dozen other people."

Robinetti rubbed his palms together. "That's too bad. Even so, this is the best chance we've got to bring our Rome policy into line with reality."

"First we need to find who killed the emperor."

"Of course. A T-60. God. But the important thing is to get our relationship with this culture on a sounder footing."

Pierce's eyebrows lifted slightly, encouraging Robinetti to go on.

"You were at the games; you saw what went on. This is a psychotic society, and we're not helping it. Thousands are dying every day of curable diseases, millions are slaves, and they get their kicks out of mass sadism."

Pierce held up his hands, palms out. "They give us—"

"A few hundred kids a year, I know. Eventually, thousands. Meanwhile they're infecting us with their vices."

"Carnography?"

"Among other things. Ever see any of those videotapes of the games Domitian gave last year? A big hit uptime. I ever find who made those tapes, I'll put *him* in the goddamn arena. Plus I hear the Roman mysteries are even making converts on Earth."

"You can't blame the Romans. We've got culties getting ideas from everywhere, not just here."

Robinetti nodded irritably. "Fine, but Rome is *my* desk.

I want their Trainables, too, but these people deserve better than they're getting."

"Agreed. I'll pass your views on. Now, I've got to go through when the I-Screen comes on tonight, but I presume you'll keep an investigation going until you find out who did this."

"Sure. Otherwise how could I give them a medal?" Robinetti rolled his eyes at Pierce's pained expression. "Of course, of course we'll investigate. But God knows how. We've got about a hundred base staff here, all of them with too much work, and another hundred on recruiting teams. Maybe somebody heard a rumor, or knows what this oracle business is all about."

"You'd heard nothing about an oracle, nothing about omens?"

"No, and that's surprising, too. Everybody here is always seeing portents or hearing about prophecies. Domitian was sure he was going to get killed back in 96. All the soothsayers were predicting it, and of course we predicted it, too, but we did something to stop it. If someone was planning to kill him now, they'd probably have planted more predictions; and he would've got wind of them again. Then he'd have come to us asking for help."

"And he didn't."

"Not a whisper."

"Any reports of knotholers?"

"Constantly, but we haven't caught any yet."

Roman art, like that of the Cro-Magnons and medieval Byzantines, was immensely popular uptime. Illegal I-Screens, called knotholes, were often opened—sometimes by would-be traders, more often by smash-and-grab teams. With the illicit trade in Roman art alone running at well over a hundred million International Federation dollars a year, knotholing was highly profitable.

"So getting here wouldn't be a problem."

"Nor getting away uptime again."

Pierce sighed and stood up. He was hungry. "If any illegal uptimer is found here, I want him held until we can pick him up. We'll give him deep interrogation and get to the bottom of this."

Robinetti snorted. "If we catch an artlegger, he'll probably be working for somebody in the Federation Cabinet. Or am I being too cynical?"

"No. But if he's working for someone in the Cabinet, we can certainly arrange a shuffle." He extended his hand. "Thanks for your time. I'm going to go find some dinner and grab a nap before the I-Screen comes on."

A few years before, as a boy growing up in Taos, New Mexico, Pierce had made an easy choice. The economy was collapsing. The draft had been revived, and American soldiers were dying in Venezuela and two or three other places. When he left high school he could expect to be drafted at once; if he wasn't sent overseas, he'd be helping police some American city, making sure the food shipments weren't ripped off too badly and sometimes chasing the private armies like the White American Brotherhood and the People's Action Front.

Dodging the draft was out of the question: he simply couldn't afford the bribes. His stepfather, a highway patrolman, had been killed on duty a year earlier, and he and his mother were living on a pension barely enough for one. Pierce would have no chance for a civilian job, least of all a draft-exempted one.

"Why don't you try this new Training Test?" one of the school counselors had suggested. "At least if you pass, you'll go in the service as an officer."

Training was new then, a half-experimental mix of drugs and electronics. It was based on a perception aptitude that usually emerged in mid-adolescence. A Trainable, once Trained, could read a closely printed page in a tenth of a second or less and recall it perfectly. About twelve percent of all people were Trainable, but if the procedure was delayed too long the opportunity vanished; by age nineteen, Trainability degenerated into an ability to speed-read, and nothing more.

Pierce Tested out as an Alpha-18; probably not more

than a couple of hundred people in the country were faster. The army took him into a basic training program that lasted six hours, and then gave him a week's worth of graduate school. He emerged as a T-Major with many new abilities and one incapacity: he could no longer see movement in motion pictures, which now seemed like awkward slide shows.

A Trainable and a decent computer could process enormous quantities of data, see patterns, and act quickly on the results. One girl turned five hundred dollars into a couple of million on the commodities market; a boy reviewed the total current literature on cancer and identified twelve crucial factors in carcinogenesis. But the chief function of Trainables, in those last hard years of the twentieth century, was to try to hold things together.

The world economy was in ruins; even in the U.S., barter and robbery were the chief means of distributing wealth in most of the country. The Trainables kept things working a little better than they would have otherwise: a little more food could be grown, a few more bandits could be arrested; a few more schools kept open.

Pierce himself had known it couldn't last. Even with the powers he enjoyed during the Emergency, when the Constitution had been suspended and he had been the de facto ruler of Idaho and eastern Oregon, he had realized that total collapse could be only postponed.

Then in 1998 a young graduate student at Fermilab, Richard Ishizawa, accidentally built a time machine.

It was a hypermagnetic field, intended only to focus particle beams intensely. Instead, on the night he first turned it on in Cave 9 of the Superconducting Supercollider, the field had opened up. On the other side was a forest in the Illinois of a different world, a world in the year 1787.

Ishizawa, a lover of the poetry of William Blake, had named his beautiful new world Beulah. After some cautious exploration, he and his colleagues secretly announced the discovery to a handful of major scientists and administrators.

The implications were understood at once. Beulah was not Earth; interference in events on Beulah created no paradoxes on Earth. But all the resources that Earth had squandered were still there on Beulah: the same oil fields, the same gold deposits, unimaginable expanses of fertile, unpolluted soil and seas teeming with fish.

Soon Ishizawa and others found more worlds still further back in time: Eden in the twelfth century, Ahania in the first, and others stretching back through the ice ages of prehistory to Tharmas at almost 71,000 years B.C. These chronoplanes, as they were called, eventually totaled eleven—each a clean, beautiful world ripe and empty of all but a few "endochronic" natives. At the worst moment in modern history, humanity had found an escape hatch for its starving, angry billions.

Pierce had followed events closely, and was one of the first to learn of Ishizawa's sudden death when he opened up a chronoplane in the future.

This time the field had opened onto an airless world burning under the sun in a black sky. Ishizawa and everyone else in his laboratory had been sucked through to die in vacuum.

Other researchers set up their own fields (now called I-Screens) and probed ahead to the dead world called Ulro. Before long they realized that it had suffered a catastrophic death on April 22, 2089. On that day a beam of energy had struck the Earth at the equator. For perhaps seventeen days the beam had stayed focused while the Earth revolved beneath it. The oceans had boiled away into superheated steam, and then the atmosphere itself had either been blown into space or combined with the glowing rock of the planet's surface. Relieved of the burden of water and air, the crust was rebounding in a geological convulsion that would go on for millions of years.

A few months later another future chronoplane was discovered. Like Ulro, Urizen was dead. Volcanic outgassing had given it a little atmosphere, and a few hardy fungi grew here and there. But the causes of its death were as unknown as those of Ulro.

The prospect of Doomsday within a century spurred the creation of the International Federation, a world government that directed exploitation of the downtime chronoplanes while trying to find the reason for the impending disaster.

One ground for hope was the knowledge that neither uptime world had known about the chronoplanes. On both worlds economic and social collapse in the early twenty-first century had proceeded as the Trainables had foreseen. The population had fallen in a couple of decades from six billion to one billion. The survivors lived in regimented, technically advanced societies governed by Trainables. Those societies had had no inkling of their doom.

The phenomenon of the "Heisenberg cascade" had turned Ishizawa's field generator into a door between worlds. The Ishizawas on Ulro and Urizen had performed their experiments, gone on to other work, and died in food riots in 2007. But on Earth a few subatomic particles had chosen to behave slightly differently; that had triggered still more variant behavior until a genuine difference evolved between Earth and the two uptime chronoplanes: the failure of a microcircuit in Ishizawa's apparatus. Obviously such a difference would not stave off a major catastrophe like Doomsday, but at least humanity on Earth knew it was coming and could take steps.

The IF had established the Agency for Intertemporal Development to deal with the Doomsday problem. AID supervised the migration of millions to downtime chronoplanes. Meanwhile it Tested endochronic children; those who could be Trained were moved uptime to Earth for their education. Every Trainable was needed: for research, for administration, for communications.

Sixteen-year-old Stone Age savages were PhDs by age seventeen, and working as engineers, scientists, and synthesists. Not all wanted to go uptime; not all unTrainables wanted them to go either. Political resistance to AID policy was sometimes intense. Pierce's job was to remove that resistance.

He loved his work. The Agency made sure of that.

The Polymath in Eric Wigner's office signaled that information was coming in, urgent and high priority. Wigner put it on the screen and it began to flash at him at the steady rate of ten pages per second.

An anti-emigration riot in Singapore: ten thousand Thai refugees didn't want to go downtime to Luvah. Some ecological congress complaining because starlings had become established in North America on Orc. An anthropologist protesting in the media that his pet Neanderthal community on Tharmas had been wiped out by Milan flu. A report from Albion that a cultie group, the Church Militant, had apparently abandoned its colony site in Yugoslavia and taken off into the woods. (Blessings in disguise, thought Wigner: the Church Militant had been a real nuisance before its deportation. Its many enemies had referred to it as "Christian Jihad." With any luck at all, they had massacred most of themselves.) Violent demonstrations in Edmonton and Dallas by unemployed oil workers; they wouldn't go downtime to work in the new fields, and all the oil left on Earth was too expensive to take out of the ground.

As permanent deputy for operations, Wigner was responsible for the Agency's handling of all these concerns and more. In a sense, these troubles were the side effects of the greatest mass migrations in history: billions of men, women, and children from scores of nations and hundreds of cultures, moving out of the exhausted twenty-first century and back into the clean wealth of the downtime chronoplanes. Most went willingly, eager to carve out empires for themselves and to raise their children in greater prosperity than they had ever dreamed of.

Some, like the Church Militant and many other cult groups, went under compulsion. So did most criminals.

The International Federation, struggling to fend off Doomsday, had no time to rehabilitate or even to punish; it simply deported those who refused to cooperate, and let them take their chances in the wilds of some Ice Age chronoplane. Sometimes the results were brutal, not only for the deportees but for the poor Stone Age savages who encountered them; that was unfortunate, in Wigner's view, but an acceptable price to preserve humanity's future.

"Eric, I have an override from Piggly Wiggly," said the computer.

Good old Jerry Pierce. Wigner leaned back and rubbed his eyes, grateful for the interruption. "Put him through, Polly." Pierce's face appeared on the screen: hard-faced, cheeks covered in red stubble, still in his Gaulish tunic. "Hi, old son. What's new in Rome?"

Pierce explained tersely.

"An antitank missile? Who?"

Wigner glanced around the austere office: the plain, crowded bookshelves, the Polymath computer, the Robert Bateman print of a Labrador retriever in a field of yellow summer grass.

"Hang on a second, Jerry. Polly!"

The cartoon figure of a little girl appeared in the lower right corner of the computer screen. She smiled at him. "Yes, Eric."

"Get me the Rome/Ahania files for the last six weeks, but don't run them just yet."

"Sure, Eric."

"And copy the following conversation."

"I'll be glad to."

"Thanks. Okay, Jerry, tell me the whole story."

Pierce did so. Wigner asked:

"You were in the stadium, just killing time? What did you think of the fighting?"

"Amateurish." Pierce sounded annoyed. "I'll spare you the detailed review. What's more important is the Praetorian officer's password."

"Yes, that's very interesting. You're lucky he didn't want some password from you as well."

"Christians have no business being in the Praetorian Guard at this point, much less being involved in plots against the emperor. The last I heard, the Praetorians were solidly behind Domitian."

"Old son, that problem is so bizarre I propose to ignore it for the time being. We'll get to the bottom of it, but first we've got to get a new emperor in position."

"Trajan?"

"Don't know who else. Ideally I'd like one of our Roman Trainables, but they're too young and none of 'em has the right connections to please the army. Besides, their experience with us could make them suspect."

"We'll have to move fast. Whoever killed Domitian must have an agenda, and it's not ours."

"This is probably true, old son. Any guesses?"

"Rome is full of knotholers. The art trade. And carnography."

"Indeed."

"Or something completely different."

"Want to track it down?"

"I've been Briefed and Conditioned for over two weeks. I'd like to come down and rest for a while."

"B&C is no fun. Trouble is, Jerry, we're barely coping with the routine stuff, never mind assassinations. You're on the scene; we could send you back, get some news, and take it from there. You can take along some Pentasyn to handle the B&C backlash. Shouldn't take you more than a few days."

Pierce swore. Wigner looked pained.

"All right, then, a compromise? Do a quick report for me, a situation assessment. Then catch a plane up to Geneva and get deBriefed. We'll keep an eye on Ahania; if everything settles down, you can take a holiday. If it doesn't, we're all in trouble and we'll throw you back in without even apologizing."

"If I go back, I'll need more help than a bottle of pills. A Roman Trainable."

"You can take your pick. I'm not sure about their conditioning, however. Amazing how culture-dependent the whole process is."

"Are you doubting their loyalty?"

"Let's just say it hasn't been tested yet. But we'd certainly set you up with a good, smart kid."

"All right. You'll have your report tonight. Then I'm logging out."

"That's my lad. Talk to you soon."

When Pierce had hung up, Wigner ordered his computer to do a voice analysis. The conclusions were as he had suspected: Pierce had been under B&C too long. Ideally he should be deBriefed and put out to pasture for six months or a year. But this was not an ideal world.

He ran through the Rome/Ahania file: nothing. A few anti-Hesperian murmurs in the senate, the murder of a couple of Jewish scholars in Alexandria, a nasty outbreak of what was probably uptime measles in Athens and Corinth. Routine problems.

Wigner sighed, smiled, and went back to work. Life was good.

Three:

Wherever the International Federation established an I-Screen, it founded a Transferpoint to serve it: usually a single large building with warehouses, machine shops, offices, and apartments for those who oversaw the orderly transfer of people and material from one chronoplane to another.

The Rome Transferpoint, like an *insula*, covered an entire city block, but it rose ten stories. The site of Maecenas's estate, in the early twenty-first century, overlooked the church of Santa Maria Maggiore and an almost-depopulated city. On this crisp autumn day in 2005 the air was clear and sweet; few vehicles were about, except in the vicinity of the Transferpoint. Over half of Rome's people had moved downtime—not to Ahania, but to much earlier chronoplanes where Italy divided the Mediterranean into two huge lakes, and snow never left the Apennines, and Sicily was a vast forest.

Pierce prowled about in his transient's apartment on the eighth floor, eating dried apples that tasted bad compared to those the Campanian peasant had sold him. He was showered and shaved, his sensitized skin reveling in cleanliness and stinging from every razor nick; his tunic had been exchanged for casual slacks, a cotton shirt without necktie, and a light sportcoat. Despite his comfort he was impatient and irritable.

Wigner's reaction to the news from Ahania had been all too typical these days: Ahanian Rome was a political embarrassment, but otherwise of no special concern. Beset with hundreds of urgent demands, AID set priorities in its own interest. Wigner could not be expected to grasp at once the significance of Domitian's assassination.

Still, it seemed unfair to be stuck with the job of sorting things out when he was frayed and exhausted by two weeks of B&C. The thought of going back into the stink and squalor of ancient Rome was not appealing. He had had to be deloused immediately after coming through the I-Screen.

The phone rang. "Your cab has arrived, Signor Pierce."

"Grazie." He left the apartment with relief, glad to be moving. Because of his sensory enhancement, the deliberately bland decor of the apartment bored and angered him.

The cab was a sleek new Fiat; Pierce chatted in Croatian with the Yugoslav driver as they drove across town to the Accadèmia della Federazióne Internazionale.

"Rome is a dull place these days," the driver said. "Just as well. Back before the Federazióne, the gunmen were everywhere. My uncle was shot by the Brigati. Now it's all peaceful and quiet."

"Do you ever think of emigrating downtime?"

"Oh, maybe—when they get things just like here. Tell me, sir, are you interested in art?"

Pierce's eyebrows rose a little. "Of course. I'm especially fond of classical art."

"I know a fellow you might like to meet. He has some statuettes from ancient Rome, you know? Erotica. Very lovely. And very cheap."

"I thought such stuff was illegal," Pierce said with a chuckle. He admired the driver's gall: after all, his passenger was going to an Agency institution, and the Agency enforced intertemporal law.

The cabdriver shrugged. "Legal, illegal—it's here, it's beautiful, someone will enjoy it. If not you, then the next fellow."

"Give me your phone number. Perhaps you can introduce me to your friend after I've run my errand to the Accadèmia."

"A pleasure."

At the gateway to the Accadèmia the cabdriver waved a cheerful farewell; Pierce waved back and turned to go through the checkpoint. Four guards in pale-blue Agency uniforms scrutinized his identification and then escorted him through the tank traps to the main door. Doubtless excessive security: the anti-Trainable riots were over a decade in the past, back in the bad old days before the I-Screen. Trainables were still unpopular, but ordinary people were too distracted to worry about them.

A young Trainable secretary, no more than sixteen but very poised, welcomed Pierce in the marble foyer.

"A pleasure, Mr. Pierce. Welcome to the Accadèmia," he said.

"Thank you. I believe the director knows I'm coming."

"Right this way."

The building dated to the fifteenth century, but its interior had been utterly transformed. Beyond the foyer lay a labyrinth of corridors and cubicles that reminded Pierce of the windowless wing of the Hesperian embassy. Down each corridor, at intervals of three meters, solid doors stood firmly shut. Behind them were apprentice Trainables: some developing the skills, some already using them to gain encyclopedic knowledge.

"We are almost at the end of a Training cycle," the secretary said quietly. "Each cohort now takes only three weeks from orientation to first assignment."

"Remarkable." Pierce thought of the urban cohorts clubbing their way through the mob in the Forum; the new Trainables' jobs would be roughly similar.

The director, an owlish young man named Claudio Grossi, rose from his flickerscreen to welcome Pierce. He wore old-fashioned glasses, an affectation Pierce disliked, and offered a slim, cool hand without strength.

"Mr. Pierce. A pleasure to meet you. The Agency said you'd be coming. Please sit down. Coffee?"

"Water will be fine." Coffee only worsened his metabolic tension. Pierce settled himself in a fine armchair and looked around. The office was large but austere, its walls adorned only by a small wooden crucifix doubtless made on Eden. On one side of the office, French doors opened onto a pleasant garden.

For a moment Pierce thought a nude young woman was standing in a bed of chrysanthemums. Then he looked again and realized it was an Ahanian statue of Venus, painted in flesh tones and with gilded pubic hair. She stood leaning against a pillar as she undid a sandal.

"You like our little Venus?"

"A very popular subject."

"She's very elegant, don't you think?"

"Mm. And expensive."

Grossi smiled faintly. "I am fortunate to have private means. She was worth it. Well. I understand you need one of our live Ahanians."

"Yes, for a few days. Someone who hasn't been uptime very long."

Grossi spoke quickly in Italian to his computer, which chirped back at him and then printed out a narrow strip of film about ten cm long. Grossi held it out to Pierce.

"Shall I project it for you, or—?"

"I have a flickreader, thank you." Pierce slid the reader over his eyes; it looked like opaque brown spectacles. He slipped the film into the little aperture by the right temple, and spent a minute scanning the dossiers of sixty-two Roman Trainables.

"Why so few?"

Grossi shrugged. "We have a lot of medieval Italians from Eden at the moment. Most of the current cohort of Romans are Training at Naples, or Vienna, a few even in London. Are these candidates inadequate? We can look at—"

"Thank you. They will do. I'd like to talk to Gaius Aquilius Faber."

"Of course." He nodded to the secretary, who had been standing discreetly by the door; the secretary murmured into a ringmike for a moment.

"Perhaps you would like to meet him in the garden," Grossi suggested. "A bit more congenial than this room."

"Of course. A good idea."

Carrying his glass of water, Pierce walked out into the garden. The air was cool, the sky a deeper blue than that of Ahanian Rome with its eternal charcoal smog. The garden, quiet and secure behind a high wall, was a tidy arrangement of greens and oranges, ivy and chrysanthemums; gravel walks divided it neatly. Pierce found a marble bench and sat down to drink his water. It helped dilute the metallic taste in his mouth, for a moment.

"Mr. Pierce?" called a voice in English.

The young man who strode toward him down the path was short and dark-haired, with a clear olive complexion a little faded after three months spent mostly indoors. He wore the usual Trainee's rig, loose trousers and a long pullover sweater: quite a concession for a Roman who probably regarded trousers as hopelessly barbarian. Pierce admired the boy's graceful walk, a kind of glide, and the impassive alertness in his eyes. Pierce remembered a similar alertness in the eyes of the little catamite who had died with his general a week before, in a tent in the Alps. But Gaius Aquilius Faber was neither effeminate nor proletarian. He displayed the sober gravity of a young aristocrat, deepened already by his Training.

"Good afternoon, Aquilius." As a new acquaintance, Pierce would not presume to use the *praenomen* Gaius, nor to condescend by speaking Latin. He shook the young man's hand, pleased by the hard strength in it. "I have a task for you."

"Yes?"

They began to walk about the garden in slow, measured steps.

"I have just returned from your Rome. The emperor Domitian has been killed."

Aquilius said nothing.

"Your family has had its conflicts with the emperor, I believe."

"Many families of the *nobilitas* have disagreed with one emperor or another." He spoke English well, but with a strong trace of the lilting, almost singsong intonation of a well-bred Roman's Latin.

"Before you came uptime, were you aware of any plots against the emperor?"

The young man's intelligent eyes met his for a moment and slid away. "I would hesitate to answer that question even if my father put it to me."

Pierce smiled. "I may well put you in danger, but I will not betray you. I repeat my question."

"No. Since the emperor's wife was executed, no one has dared stand in his way."

"Someone has dared now. With a wire-guided missile."

Aquilius looked unsurprised. "Then it was done by the Hesperians."

"It was not. We are deeply alarmed by the killing. Someone else is on Ahania, and we don't know who. Tell me this: you have a cousin in the Praetorian Guard, Gnaeus Rufus Flaccus. Had you seen anything of him in the weeks before you came uptime?"

"Flaccus... But he gave no hint of any conspiracy."

"Did he talk about Christianity?"

Aquilius's black eyebrows rose. "That would be most unusual. The Christians are still only a cult, as you well know."

Pierce allowed himself to be mildly amused. The boy already understood that it was an insult for a Trainable to mention what ought to be known.

"Nonetheless," he said, "a Praetorian officer blessed me in the name of the Father, the Son, and the Holy Ghost."

"I hope it did you some good."

Pierce burst into laughter. "Sit down, sit down."

They sat on a marble bench, looking at the gaudy Venus.

"I think I have some understanding of what you have gone through in the last three months, Aquilius. You left your family, embarked on a ship, and two days later you went through the I-Screen on Sardinia and flew back here. You had a glimpse of your own city in ruins, overgrown by a monstrous new city, and then you learned your empire's future as just a part of our past. We've recruited you into a struggle no one dreamed of a few years ago, and you've joined us with no choice in the matter. Your life will be utterly different from anything you might have imagined, and you will never feel at home anywhere—not here, not in your own Rome."

"I understand that very well."

"You were born and bred to serve the empire. If Domitian had sent you to Numidia, or to fight the Parthians or Picts, you would have gone without a murmur and given your life as your ancestors did. That much, at least, has not changed for you."

"I understand that also."

"You are still a man, and a Roman. You can still demonstrate *virtus* and emulate your ancestors."

Aquilius looked at him without speaking.

"I know," said Pierce. "I am not a Roman, and *virtus* is a Roman trait."

"Part of me still thinks that," Aquilius agreed. "And yet now I know how men of many nations have acquitted themselves. Some of them showed *virtus* also."

"It is the achievement of glorious deeds for the benefit of the nation, is it not?"

"Yes—and emulation of one's ancestors' deeds."

"Would it be *virtus* to achieve some great deed that exposed your mother and sisters to shame and death?"

"Of course not."

"But a deed which saved them from shame and death . . ."

"Yes, that would be *virtus*."

"I need you for just such deeds, Gaius Aquilius. Someone on Ahania is planning some great evil against Rome. Not just a simple deception like the myth of Hesperia, but a betrayal of the *patria*. My masters are sending me back there to find out what this plot is, and to try to foil it. I need you with me."

"Why?"

"I have spared you my Latin; I speak it badly. Worse, I

am a stranger in Rome. How well would I do, blundering about asking questions of passersby? Even if they answered me truly, would I understand their real meaning? Alone, I would be blind and deaf. With you—"

"You would have a guide dog."

Pierce frowned. "Sarcasm is for the vulgar. I expect better from a son of *nobilitas*. If you have an objection to what I ask of you, speak it clearly."

The young man's face hardened; he glared at the gravel path beneath his feet. "I left Rome the mistress of the world; I would return to a shabby little client state, of less concern to this world than some tribe of Dacians would be to us. I would be working with you to ensure that Rome continues as a client, and an ignorant one. For all I know, those who killed Domitian have Rome's true interests at heart."

"The enemy of your enemy is not always your friend. Tell me—what do you see as the role we have cast you in?"

"This world will be destroyed in eighty-four years, as Ulro and Urizen were when they passed through Doomsday. But they did not know it was coming, as we do. So the nations of this chronoplane are gathering the resources of all the chronoplanes, as we would build an outpost against invaders. The noncombatants we send to the rear, to the downtime worlds. The soldiers we recruit and train."

"And you and I are soldiers."

"Soldiers with no idea who will invade."

"All the more reason to ensure that our forces are as strong as possible. If we cannot recruit more Trainables like yourself from Rome, we will be that much weaker. And whoever killed Domitian has endangered our recruiting."

Aquilius shrugged. "Perhaps they will be glad to allow recruiting, as long as they rule Rome."

"No. Our policy was to support Domitian."

"Your policy is to support whoever allows recruiting. Why should you care if someone else is emperor?"

Pierce felt both embarrassed and cheered. The boy was bright.

"The International Federation would not tolerate a usurper," Pierce said. "We need unity and cooperation, but on our own terms. We're not going to help just anyone who manages to seize power. My own country, America, destroyed itself in half a century by siding with whatever brigands ruled our client states."

Aquilius nodded. "Realpolitik easily turns to political self-deception."

Pierce smiled. "You've been reading Karalis's *Decline of American Hegemony*."

"I've been reading the history of three thousand years."

"Will you come with me?"

Aquilius turned to look Pierce in the eye. "I have also been reading W. B. Yeats. 'I do not love the ones I serve.' But I will serve."

Again they shook hands.

"Tomorrow you will be in Rome again, under your father's roof."

"I hope I can take him some presents—a flashlight, a cassette recorder?"

"We're past the deception. Take him a Fiat if you can fit it through the I-Screen."

"When can we go?"

"By tomorrow, I hope. Tonight we'll go back to the Transferpoint and arrange to go through the I-Screen. We'll need new clothes, money, and weapons."

"And how long will we be there?"

"I don't know. Not long. I've been under Briefing and Conditioning for two weeks." Aquilius would know that more than a month under B&C could be permanently damaging, even with Pentasyn to soften the effects.

"Will I also be Briefed and Conditioned?"

"No time. You haven't even completed your Training. I suggest we return to your room to pack."

"I have nothing I need to bring. The staff will store my clothes for me until I return."

Pierce nodded. "Then let us be on our way."

A few minutes later they were in a minivan owned by the Accadèmia, headed back to the Transferpoint. Aquilius said nothing, but looked out the windows with the all-observant eyes of a Trainable.

"The roads are somewhat better here," Pierce remarked.

"Somewhat. But ours are built to last a century; yours disintegrate in months."

The driver was listening to chatter on the CB radio. Suddenly the volume went up and someone began shouting incoherently.

The driver swore and glanced over his shoulder at Pierce. "Excuse me, sir, but they say a bomb exploded in the Transferpoint. The building is on fire."

Four:

The Transferpoint was surrounded by fire trucks; a helicopter fluttered overhead through the smoke. Pierce and Aquilius stood half a block away in the crowds, Pierce with his ringmike to his lips. The patch to New York was a poor one.

"The fire fighters think the bomb must have gone off right by the Ahania I-Screen," Pierce shouted. "No one's been found alive who was anywhere nearby. The whole lower level is on fire, all the I-Screens."

"*So Rome is shut down,*" Wigner replied almost inaudibly.

"Yes." He did not add what Wigner would of course know: several hundred million New Dollars' worth of equipment was lost, and could not be easily replaced.

"*You know the Hesperian embassy was under attack just before the bomb went off.*"

Pierce frowned. "No, I didn't know that."

"*They got a quick message through. Get this: Praetorians with Uzis were coming over the wall.*"

Pierce shook his head in disbelief. "If they'd been smart, they'd have timed it better."

"*No doubt. Listen, old son, get out to Fiumicino and grab a helicopter to Sardinia.*"

"We'll go to the city airport—quicker. But I've got a couple of things to do first."

"*You're in charge. I presume all your Roman gear's been lost.*"

"We'll scrounge up something in Sardinia."

"Any idea who's behind all this?"

"None. But they're certainly ambitious. Talk to you later."

Pierce switched off, then switched on again and tapped out a local number.

"Vido! This is your art-loving passenger from this afternoon," he said in Croatian. "Can you pick me up near the Piazza Navona in half an hour?"

"Of course, of course. Right by the taxi stand in the Via dei Coronari."

"Ciao."

Aquilius looked puzzled. Pierce smiled at him.

"A little errand before we get out to the airport."

They walked through the late-afternoon streets; Aquilius kept his eyes on the traffic honking past. Pierce hailed a taxi.

"Caesar was smart to keep wheeled traffic out of the city until nightfall," he said as they got into an old Citroen. "Though it's damned noisy all night."

"I liked it there. This Rome is too quiet."

"Does it frighten you?"

"No. I am only afraid of doing the wrong thing."

"When we get back to your world, I will be the one who does the wrong things."

"I don't like this, Mr. Pierce. First the emperor, then the Hesperian embassy, now the Transferpoint."

Pierce nodded. "Something nasty is happening on Ahania, and here. If we move quickly, maybe we can stop it from becoming even worse."

"Then why are you wasting time on this cabdriver, when we could be going to Sardinia?"

"My friend Vido may actually save us some time."

They reached the taxi stand in the Via dei Coronari. Pierce paid the driver and led Aquilius to the Piazza Navona, a block away. No cars were allowed in the piazza, and at this hour few people were about. The loudest sounds were the splash of water in the Bernini fountains, and the happy shrieks of two little girls chasing one another.

They walked about the piazza, drinking mineral water and eating sunflower seeds. Pierce wished the seeds tasted better. "I can almost see the stadium," Aquilius said quietly as he looked around the piazza. "We used to sit on the west side, about there—" He pointed to one of the close-packed old buildings that faced the elongated oval of the Piazza. "My father enjoyed—enjoys—the chariot races very much."

Pierce nodded. The stadium of Domitian had survived in the layout of the piazza, but its transformation must be deeply unsettling. He was pleased that Aquilius seemed calm: this detour was a quiet kind of test, and Aquilius had passed it well.

They went back to the taxi stand. After a few minutes the sleek Fiat appeared and stopped beside them. Pierce greeted Vido cheerfully as they got in.

"Business is over," said Pierce in Italian. "Let's meet this wonderful dealer in erotica."

"Who's your young friend?"

"A student with a great interest in classical art. He'll save me from buying imitations."

"No imitations, I promise," Vido guffawed.

They drove quickly north, into the suburbs where row after row of apartment buildings stood dark in the growing twilight. Their inhabitants were downtime now, living in prefabricated cabins or rudely built huts. The apartments gave way to villas, and Vido parked in front of one.

"His name is Signor Bruckner. They know me, so just say I brought you. I'll wait for you."

"Grazie, Vido."

They walked across the cracked sidewalk and rang the bell beside the steel door that shielded the garage. After a long wait, a voice came over a speaker: "Who is it?"

"Friends of Vido, and lovers of antiquity."

"Just a moment, please."

The steel door swung open; standing in the garage, just in front of a Mercedes 900 limousine, was a powerfully built man in an expensive Alfred Sung suit. He was in middle age, balding, and wore spectacles much like Claudio Grossi's. Pierce smiled at him and approached, hand held out.

"Signor Bruckner? My name is Gerald Pierce. This is my friend Achille Fabbro. We understand it's possible to buy certain collector's items here."

The man glanced over their shoulders at the Fiat, then grunted.

"All right. Come in, please."

The garage door swung shut behind them; they followed the man up a narrow flight of stairs to a large living room. The walls were hung with fine Greek tapestries and Roman portraits on wood. On a glass coffee table, a bronze dolphin rose from marble foam. Pierce estimated the value of the artworks in the room at well over two million New Dollars. Surprisingly, no one else seemed to be in the house—no maid, no cook, most importantly no guard. Only Bruckner's scent hung in the air, mingled with a very good Chanel aftershave.

"Please be seated. May I serve you some coffee, or a drink?"

"It is you who should be seated," said Pierce. He drew a Mallory .15 from his shoulder holster and aimed it at Bruckner's belly. "It is set for maximum impact, and I will use it without hesitation."

The man paled and sat down on the couch beside the coffee table, taking care to keep his hands visible. "If, ah, you want money, there is plenty. In the safe. I will give you the combination. Or some special artworks?"

Pierce sat down opposite him, ignoring Aquilius.

"I want only information. Who is your knotholer?"

"I don't understand the term."

"Don't insult me. You get your stock from Ahania, so you use an illegal I-Screen. Who runs it?"

"A man named Niccolo. I don't know his last name, or where he is."

"How do you get in touch with him?"

"I don't; he calls me when he has a shipment. It comes at night, in a truck, never the same one twice. Surely the procedure is familiar to you gentlemen."

"We are not competitors, not in that sense. But I would very much like to meet Niccolo."

"Ah—you are Federazióne police? I am eager to cooperate—eager. But you understand, he has covered his tracks very well."

"Have you ever known anyone who has undergone deep interrogation, sir?" Pierce asked.

"No."

"The process is painless, but the odds are that you will emerge psychotic. I am quite prepared to have it administered to you this evening."

Bruckner's face crumpled, and he began to cry. "I don't know, I don't know who he is or where he is. Please—take what you like, money, the dolphin—please, I don't know where he is."

"Come with us, Signor Bruckner."

Pierce and Aquilius escorted Bruckner back downstairs and out to the sidewalk where the Fiat waited. Aquilius got in next to Vido; Pierce and Bruckner sat in back.

"Aeroporto dell'urbe," Pierce said.

Vido, seeing Bruckner's red eyes and terrified expression, looked alarmed. "What's wrong?"

"A great deal, but nothing to concern you," said Pierce. "Just get us to the airport."

En route, he used the ringmike again to alert airport security. Overhearing him, Vido smacked the steering wheel with his palm.

"Please keep both hands on the wheel," the car said, in a calm female voice with a good Tuscan accent. Vido swore.

"Signor Pierce, can't we come to some understanding?" Bruckner pleaded. "I honestly do not know this Niccolo. Can I perhaps trade some other information?"

"I need to know who is going through to Ahania. And who might be shipping arms to Ahania."

"Arms, arms—I am a simple art dealer. I know nothing of weapons. I detest weapons. Vido, help me. Who has an I-Screen? Who ships arms?"

The driver glanced into the rearview mirror. "Tomasetti, maybe. He has a Screen, but he doesn't seem to sell anything anymore."

"Give me the address."

"Via Togliatti 45, in Ostia. Down by the docks."

"Very helpful. Anyone else?" Pierce asked.

Vido shook his head.

The Fiat drove through the night to the airport; Pierce asked Vido to turn on the radio, and they listened to news broadcasts about the bombing.

"Eighty-three dead," Pierce murmured. "We'll get them for that."

"Pardon me?" asked Aquilius.

Pierce switched to Latin. "In the Agency, our whole purpose is to protect civilized humanity against its enemies. We do not forgive."

At the airport, a squad of police met them. Pierce spoke briefly with their sergeant, who nodded, saluted, and then gestured to Vido and Bruckner to follow him. They entered the main terminal building and walked directly to an unmarked door.

"What will happen to them?" Aquilius asked.

"Deep interrogation."

The young Roman frowned. "But you traded other information. They gave you a name."

"Do you think I was underhanded?"

"Yes. Yes. This was not fair."

"It was not fair to kill eighty-three people either. I do whatever must be done."

Aquilius looked unhappy.

"Come, come," Pierce said cheerfully as he led the way across the terminal building. "On Ahania they would be tortured as a matter of law."

"Most of my texts," said Aquilius calmly, "like to argue that humanity has progressed since the days of the Romans."

"Do you think it has?"

"In some ways. Not many."

"I agree."

* * *

The Ostia *carabinieri* soon found that Vido had not lied about Tomasetti; at Via Togliatti 45, an old warehouse, an I-Screen had clearly been set up not long before. But it was dismantled now. The police reported only abandoned junk, an ancient IBM AT, and bloodstains on the floor. Evidently someone else had wanted to become a knotholer and had stolen Tomasetti's equipment. The identity of that person would take time to determine.

"It was a thought," Pierce said. He and Aquilius had not left the airport, staying instead in a VIP lounge with the local police lieutenant. "If Tomasetti had been in operation, we might have been able to identify the emperor's assassins. We might even have gone through the knothole directly to Ahanian Rome."

"Perhaps the assassins were the ones who took the Screen," said Aquilius.

Pierce nodded. "Perhaps. Most knotholers leave one another alone. The assassins might not want a Screen under the control of an outsider, even a sympathizer."

The police lieutenant, hearing a summons in his earphone, spoke briefly into his ringmike. He turned to Pierce and shrugged.

"Deep interrogation confirms Bruckner's story. He is a dealer in illegal art, nothing more. The cabdriver is his agent. We have descriptions of the trucks used by this Niccolo, including license numbers, so we will pick him up soon. But I doubt that he will be able to lead us far."

"Thank you. Then perhaps you could arrange an aircraft to take us to Sardinia."

Aquilius sat by a window in the Agency Learjet, watching the lights of Rome retreat into the darkness.

"Do you enjoy flying?" Pierce asked.

"Yes. I wish we could have made this flight in daylight. They flew us back from Sardinia to Rome on a beautiful day."

"Weren't you afraid? You were only, oh, three days from Rome, and flying thousands of meters above the Mediterranean."

Aquilius smiled. "They gave us plenty of tranquilizers."

The jet took them to the Venafiorita airport, just outside Olbia near the north end of Sardinia. When Pierce and Aquilius stepped down to the tarmac at nine-thirty that night, a Volvo station wagon was waiting for them. The driver was a tall woman in tight jeans and a black turtleneck sweater.

"Teresa Giuliani." Her handshake was hard and dry. "I'm from the reception center. They tell us you need some help."

"Yes." Pierce waved Aquilius into the front seat of the Volvo, while he climbed in back behind Teresa and stretched his long legs out sideways. "We are for some reason involved in a terrible mess downtime, and now here as well."

"We'll do what we can." The Volvo rolled through the gates, past saluting guards and out onto the *superstrada*. "You will have to discuss your plans with the director, Dr. Kallistis. We're not accustomed to sending people back to Ahania—only receiving them. I'm not sure we'll have everything you need."

"Will your people be able to supply us with Roman clothes and money?" Pierce asked.

"Clothes, yes, from the recruits." She glanced at Aquilius, as if she had suddenly recognized him. "Money will be harder. Most recruits bring very little."

Pierce nodded and closed his eyes. The pheromones of Teresa Giuliani were intensely arousing, but his enhanced senses and hair-trigger reflexes also made him almost useless as a lover: another reason to return to normal.

The Volvo drove swiftly through darkened countryside near the coast. The air was warm: Pierce smelled dust, unknown scrubby plants, and salt water. The road crossed Cabo Coda Cavallo, a rocky cape falling steeply into the sea, and turned south around the dry foothills of Monte Nieddu. At an unmarked side road Teresa turned off and drove down a series of switchbacks. At the bottom, Pierce knew, was a good harbor with only a narrow access to the

Tyrrhenian Sea. On the dry and rocky slopes above the harbor, prefab buildings rose in orderly rows. Down on the shore was a large floodlit building resembling an aircraft hangar and extending fifty meters into the water: the reception center and Transferpoint.

Security was tight all over the center. Squads of AID infantry tramped about with infrared visors pulled down over their faces, and guards stopped the Volvo three times before it reached the reception center.

Inside the huge, echoing building, Pierce saw that it extended well over fifty meters out onto the water. Its far end was open, and lights reflected off the polished steel of a large I-Screen mounted with its lower third submerged.

"It looked very strange," Aquilius murmured as they walked across a broad expanse of empty concrete to a two-story portable building set against the far wall. "We were sailing into an empty harbor, and suddenly—a strange circle with lights burning inside it. One boy thought we were going to Hell."

"Were you that boy?" asked Pierce.

"No. But the lights were a little frightening." He looked around almost fondly.

Inside the portable building was a warren of offices and store rooms. Teresa knocked briskly at a plain door and then opened it into an equally plain office whose every horizontal surface seemed piled with printouts.

"Dr. Kallistis."

He was a Trainable, of course, rather good looking with curly black hair framing a serene oval face. He shook hands and waved them into armchairs, cordial but businesslike and completely unlike the young aesthete who ran the Accademia in Rome.

"The Agency has asked us to supply you with all possible help. We will do so. Do you have any more news of the bombing?"

"Nothing. Perhaps the police will know more in the morning."

"Incredible that they could get so close, through all our security."

Pierce's eyebrows rose. "The attack probably came from Ahania. The embassy there was under attack just before the bombing. It seems likely that the attackers launched a bomb through the embassy I-Screen."

Kallistis's mouth turned down. "Then it's worse than I imagined. If some group downtime is that well organized, surely more than two of you should go through."

"In good time. We're simply conducting a reconnaissance."

"You will need to reach Rome quickly. At the moment we have no sailing ship available—one just left for Ostia this morning. We could recall it, but I think a helicopter would be more useful."

"Excellent. In fact, you should recall the ship anyway. It may be attacked by whoever's behind this."

Kallistis sighed and nodded. "It's almost a relief, dropping the cover. The Romans deserve to know the truth."

"Some already do," said Aquilius.

"Indeed." Kallistis smiled at him. "I take it that once you reach Rome you will be going undercover."

"Yes," said Pierce. "The helicopter will have to drop us off somewhere outside the city, so we can get in unnoticed."

"No difficulty. Dr. Giuliani will see to your equipment; I'm arranging for a helicopter from Olbia. Good luck." He shook their hands and remained standing while Teresa and the two men left his office.

Teresa led them into a large office. On a countertop, four technicians were unpacking a cardboard box.

"Your clothes." Teresa handed Pierce and Aquilius each a tunic of coarse wool—Pierce's brown, Aquilius's a muddy yellow. "A little small for Mr. Pierce, but the best we could do. And loincloths. Shoes. Cloaks. Belts and pouches. Knives. And the money."

Pierce stared unhappily at the pile of silver and copper coins. "Only a hundred *sestertii*? That's barely enough to keep us fed and housed for a couple of nights."

"It was all we could get on short notice. If you could

wait until tomorrow or the day after, we could find much more than that."

"I'm supposed to have a supply of Pentasyn as well," Pierce said.

She handed him a small plastic vial full of orange-and-yellow capsules. "A week's supply."

Pierce took it and studied the label. "More like two days' worth. The recommended dosage isn't strong enough. Not when you've developed a tolerance."

She looked at him with a mixture of surprise and distaste: what had he been doing, to develop a tolerance for Pentasyn?

"Would you like me to order more? That's the total supply in Olbia, but we could get more from Marseilles."

"We can't wait. How soon can we go through?"

"About twenty minutes. It will be just about two-thirty A.M. on Ahania."

"Good." Pierce stripped off his clothes and pulled on the scratchy Roman garments. At least they had found shoes big enough for him: sturdy, thick-soled, with uppers of leather strips. Aquilius, after a nervous glance at Teresa, also changed his clothes. Pierce was amused: most Trainables were fond of nudity, and had little reluctance in stripping in front of a woman. A Trainable endochronic, only three weeks away from his original culture, could be forgiven for a twinge of modesty.

"Before we go through," said Pierce, "I must make a few phone calls."

"Of course." Teresa Giuliani gestured to a nearby office. "Please."

The phone was an old Olivetti with a black-and-white screen. Since Pierce was not going to use video, that didn't bother him. He sent a quick message to his mother in New Mexico: *Delayed in Italy. Back soon, I hope. Love, Jerry.* Then he called Wigner again.

"Policy: how well armed can I be?"

"Where's the Mallory you took before?"

"Burned."

"Call the local carabinieri. *Take whatever you want. We're past playing games."*

"How long do we have?"

"I'd like you back in a week. We'll arrange for a pickup from Sardinia; all you have do do is beep us."

"For how long?"

"You're not back in a week, old son, we come looking for you. By November tenth we'll have a Screen working in Rome again."

"That's best case. They've given me only a couple days' worth of Pentasyn. Worst case: how long before my B&C burns me out?"

"Morrie Weissbrod lasted six months. Almost six months."

"Morrie's dead."

"True. But he was functional right up to the end."

"You're encouraging."

"Jerry—people need you."

"I know." It was one of the conditioning phrases Wigner sometimes invoked rather than waste time in tedious discussion. Pierce shrugged with good humor.

"Godspeed."

The call to the Olbia headquarters of the *carabinieri* was brief and businesslike. Their armorer authorized allocation of two Mallory .15 handguns, four recharges for them, and a thousand flechettes in twenty clips. As well, Pierce ordered four concussion grenades and a spetsnaz knife with four extra blades.

While they waited for the weapons to arrive aboard the helicopter, Teresa Giuliani showed Pierce and Aquilius the survival kit the reception center had cobbled together on a few hours' notice: in addition to the money and silver, it included a thumb-size radio homing beacon, four penlights, six gold rings, fifty razor blades and five handles, vials of medicines, a magnetic compass, and eight squares of silk.

"I could have used all this when I went through before," Pierce murmured to Aquilius. "It was a hard trip from Rome to the Alps, and a harder one back."

"What were you doing in the Alps?" asked Aquilius.

"Looking after the Agency's interests." Pierce smiled blandly at the woman. "This will be extremely helpful, Dr. Giuliani."

"If you're ready, the Screen will be operating in a few minutes."

"Very good."

She led them out into the hangarlike expanse under the high, arched roof. Floodlights marked the entry, and wavelets sparkled in the intense glare. Without warning, an old Sikorsky SH-60D Seahawk helicopter swooped out of the darkness and roared toward them. The pilot, a sallow young man in pale-blue Agency fatigues, put the helicopter down on its pontoons just a few meters from the little group. Squinting against the blowing dust, Pierce nodded his thanks to Teresa and gripped Aquilius by the arm. They trotted through the downdraft and clambered aboard into seats just behind the pilot. The roar of the engines was deafening, and seemed to bother Aquilius: the boy sat with his hands pressed to his ears and his eyes squeezed shut. Pierce saw the pilot's lips move as he talked via radio to the I-Screen team.

The helicopter lifted off again and rotated to face the I-Screen. At first, nothing changed. Then, within the polished steel circle, the air seemed to shimmer. The circle swirled with soap-bubble iridescence, and a moment later, as the colors vanished, the external lights disappeared. Beyond the I-Screen was a different darkness: the morning of May 23, A.D. 100.

Five:

The big Sikorsky crossed the Tyrrhenian Sea to the coast in less than an hour. The Italian pilot had been adequately briefed, but seemed a bit nervous to be flying through a night sky empty of radio traffic and homing beacons. After checking and packing the armaments that the Olbia *carabinieri* had sent, Pierce and Aquilius went up and joined him for a while, discussing possible landing sites.

"We want to be within walking distance, but not in a built-up area," Pierce said. A map of Ahanian Rome glowed on the navigation VDT; potential landing sites expanded on the screen to show fine detail, then shrank again.

Aquilius touched the screen at a point north of the city, near the Via Flaminia. The map flashed into fine detail of a region about five by eight kilometers.

"Our villa is here," he said. "It's called Vallis Viridis, Green Valley. We're only half a day's walk from Rome. Perhaps you could put us down there."

Pierce shook his head. "It's too open there, and look at all the villages nearby. Someone would be sure to report the landing. We need a place where we can land and disappear."

"That looks like your best chance," said the pilot. He pointed to the VDT, and the screen obligingly showed a narrow ridge in the countryside about fifteen kilometers north of the Aquilius estate. "Little village to the south; they'll hear us, and maybe see us, but we'll just be strange lights in the sky. You come down the hill at first light, get on the Via Flaminia, and you'll be fine."

"Good." Pierce nodded and went back to his seat while Aquilius kept the pilot company. Whoever was giving Uzis to the Praetorian Guard would soon hear of the strange lights in the sky, and might investigate, but by then he and Aquilius should be safely distant.

He was exhausted; the assassination of Domitian seemed to have happened both moments and years ago. Perhaps when they were on the ground he could catch a couple of hours' sleep, though insomnia was another hazard of Briefing and Conditioning.

The helicopter crossed the coastline where the Aeroporto Leonardo Da Vinci stood on Earth, at Fiumicino just north of the Tiber's mouth. A few tiny lights were burning in the streets of Ostia, and a few more to the east, in Rome itself. Night flight on the downtime chronoplanes could be unsettling: first the endless darkness, and then the faint, humble signs that people lived down there.

As the helicopter passed over Rome, Pierce wondered what the Romans would think of the distant roaring in the night sky, assuming they could hear it over the endless squeal and rumble of wagons in the streets. Another portent?

With no warning the Sikorsky began to descend. Pierce pinched his nostrils and blew, equalizing the pressure in his ears. The helicopter's floodlights swept over a steep hillside, pale-green grass a matrix for the darker green of olive trees. At the top of the hill, a clearing ran along much of the ridge. The pilot put them down with an efficient lack of ceremony. Pierce was surprised to hear the engines die; he had expected a quick drop under turning rotors.

"Don't worry," the pilot said; his voice seemed unnaturally loud in the absence of the engine noise. "I've never been downtime before. Wanted to take a quick look."

Pierce opened the door in the side of the helicopter. Warm, muggy air poured in. The pilot laughed.

"Smells like damned Sicily. *Roma antica*. You fellows are welcome to it."

"We'll see you again in three days?"

"I'll come through. If I pick up your homing signal, I'll come and find you. If the signal's not on, I go back through the Screen and try again two days later."

"Good." Pierce shook the man's hand; so did Aquilius, who then jumped from the doorway to the rocky soil of the ridge. Pierce used a penlight to guide them away from the drop zone and into a grove of olive trees. A minute later the engines came to life again and the helicopter rose darkly, in a storm of dust and leaves, into a starry spring sky. In seconds it was gone. When its clatter had faded away, Pierce and Aquilius heard dogs barking furiously down in the village, and a woman's shrill and frightened voice.

They walked a few steps to the southern edge of the clearing. Beyond it the ridge fell away steeply into darkness. A couple of orange sparks moved in the distance below: torches or lamps, burning in the village streets. Men called to one another while the dogs kept up their alarm.

"Welcome home," Pierce said.

"What now? They'll be up here soon."

"We go down the other side of the hill, then go around and pass the village before it's full light. We'll get on the Via Flaminia and reach your family's villa in time for *cena*."

"Very well." For the first time, Pierce heard him chuckle. "They will certainly be surprised to see us."

Aquilius turned and led the way across the clearing to the north. They began a rapid descent, guided by their shielded penlights along a narrow footpath. To the east the sky was beginning to brighten, with Venus gleaming above the sharp outlines of the Apennine peaks. Crickets clicked; frogs creaked. The air smelled of sheep dung and charcoal smoke.

Pierce paused to look out across the still-dark plains of Latium. "This is a beautiful world," he murmured.

"They are all beautiful."

"But you prefer this one?"

"I am glad to be back, but I am sorry for the people here. My world is doomed by yours. Your people have taught me Roman history that will never happen here."

"We lost our history, too. On Ulro and Urizen, my cognate—the person I was on those chronoplanes—was shot almost seven years ago."

Those worlds had not gained the accidental rescue of the I-Screen; they had plunged over the precipice into war, plague, and revolution, and had recovered only to be destroyed by Doomsday. Pierce had seen the report on his own torture and interrogation and execution, a trivial footnote in an encyclopedia of catastrophe.

"So you have a second chance at life, and you spend it risking death here."

"Some of us never learn," said Pierce.

The footpath reached a narrow gully and followed it west along a noisy brook until it reached a small stone bridge. Left would take them into the village; right would lead away from the Via Flaminia.

"Are we presentable enough?" asked Pierce. "Will they suspect something's wrong?"

"The only people who travel at night are farmers on their way to market, and those who guard them. Better to wait here until well after dawn."

Pierce nodded and climbed down the creek bank to get under the bridge. Aquilius followed.

"What happens once we reach Rome?" he asked.

"We ask questions. We watch. As soon as we know enough, we get back out where the helicopter can pick us up." Pierce leaned back against the stones, pulled his cloak tighter, and dozed off for a while.

It was full light when Aquilius touched his shoulder. They crept out from under the bridge and set off toward the village. The path, deeply rutted, led past small fields turning green with spring wheat. Cypresses lined the path and marked off many of the fields. Birds sang in the slanting light of the early-morning sun.

The village was a cluster of one- and two-story brick buildings that looked more like barracks than like farmers' homes. The dark-yellow stucco on the walls was marked with countless graffiti, mostly political: *Gn. Statilius S. is the best choice for aedile, Farmers support C. Albus, Vote for Honorius.* But Pierce also saw a symbol he had noticed often on his journey north from Rome to the Alps: a little fish, identical to that displayed by bumper-sticker Christians during Pierce's boyhood in New Mexico.

The air was thick with the smells of charcoal smoke and dung. In a smithy facing the village's single street, a wiry man pounded furiously on a red-hot iron rod, while another man threw firewood into a furnace. Women filled clay jugs from a lion-faced fountain nearby, and children ran about, giggling at the strangers.

Aquilius led the way to a *popina*, a little cookshop set in the first floor of a *taberna* overlooking the village street. A thin, acned girl stood behind a counter in which three kettles were set; beneath each, charcoal glowed in a bronze brazier.

"Two bowls of porridge," Aquilius ordered. "I'll have mine with olives."

"I'll have mine plain," said Pierce.

The girl took a few coins from Aquilius and ladled out two small wooden bowls of gray-brown porridge. She added a handful of black olives to one, and passed the bowls, with paddlelike wooden spoons, to the men. Aquilius stirred in his olives and ate with gusto. Pierce thought his porridge coarse and tasteless, but ate it anyway; he had eaten worse on his first trip to Ahania.

"What news from Rome?" Aquilius asked the girl.

"The emperor was slain in the Flavian Amphitheater—have you not heard that?"

Aquilius feigned surprise—rather poorly, Pierce thought. To distract the girl, he said: "The emperor Domitian, slain! May the gods preserve Rome. How did it happen?"

"Each traveler brings a different tale. Most say he was

struck by a thunderbolt out of a clear sky, just as the omens foretold."

"What omens?" asked Aquilius.

She looked genuinely frightened, but also excited. "Truly, the heavens have warned for months of great changes. We've heard of many omens, but last night was the strangest of all. A demon came close to here last night."

"A demon?" Pierce repeated incredulously. She nodded, almost complacent in her superior knowledge.

"We all saw its fiery eyes, up there." She pointed to the hill where the helicopter had landed. "And it made a terrible roaring. It came from Rome and returned toward Rome. I was very frightened."

"Indeed, it does sound frightening. We live in strange times," said Aquilius. "Perhaps it was a demon that slew the emperor yesterday."

"I do not know."

"Did the Christians foretell this death?" asked Pierce.

She looked anxious. "I have heard something like that. But that's just slaves' talk. I'm freeborn."

"And a credit to your father. Why would slaves talk about such prophecies?"

"Slaves talk about anything. We have a couple who talk nonsense all day long."

Pierce cleared his throat of the heavy porridge. "Are those slaves by any chance Christians?"

She looked scandalized. "In my family, we all respect the gods."

They handed back their bowls for a casual wiping, and said farewell to the girl.

"It's good to be home," said Aquilius cheerfully as they walked down the street. "Things smell right here. I know it's all unhealthy, but it still feels comfortable."

"That's why I wanted you to come with me. How did you read that girl's answers?"

"She knows a little more than she said, but not much. Her family slaves are probably Christians, and the family keeps it quiet."

"Christianity has made more progress than I'd realized. We used to think of it as a fringe cult among urban slaves, yet the *ichthyos* is on almost every wall here."

Aquilius smiled sourly. "Rome is always ready for a new sensation. Nero's persecution of them gave them notoriety. Even so, most still think of Christians as subversives."

"Do you?"

"Knowing what I do, of course."

From the outskirts of the village, the path curved southwest past small wheat fields, each fenced by stones. Where the land was infertile, it was put to some other use: a brickyard, a mill, a smithy and slagheap. Pierce noted that, as in his first journey on Ahania, people were always in sight. They washed clothes in a stream, herded sheep, chased crows, trotted along the road bearing wicker baskets of potter's clay or vegetables or even a whole slaughtered pig, its severed head staring blindly at the sky.

"Most are slaves," Aquilius muttered.

"How can you tell?"

The young Roman looked surprised. "From the jobs they are doing."

"Do their owners ever fear a revolt?"

"Once, the senate considered dressing all slaves alike. Then they realized the slaves would only draw courage from seeing their own numbers. Sometimes a slave will rebel, and even draw others into his folly. Most are too sensible. They know they could win freedom by good service; my father has freed scores of slaves, and he is not unusual."

"And if a slave murders his master, all the slaves in the household will be put to death," Pierce said.

Aquilius looked at him, squinting in the sunlight. "Mr. Pierce, after what I learned uptime, I understand how cruel slavery can be. But Rome cannot be supported any other way, at least until it gains uptime technology."

"Which will only create still more unemployed people, as slavery itself has."

"Your own world cares very little for such people."

Pierce laughed briefly. "True enough."

Not far to the west, a long row of cypresses marked the Via Flaminia. They cut across a field to reach it.

The highway was crowded. Like all Roman roads it was exactly 4.8 meters wide, enough to allow vehicles to pass one another. The pavement was made of large stones, each shaped to fit its neighbors tightly and showing grooves made by countless vehicles. Like teeth, the cobbles had pointed roots sunk deep into an underlying bed of gravel. On either side, a narrow gravel shoulder ran beside a gutter. Foot traffic stayed on the shoulder, while carts rumbled over the cobbles. Most were simple oxcarts carrying sacks of early vegetables or last year's grain; they moved at less than walking speed. Occasionally a two-wheeled chariot racketed past on iron-rimmed wheels, the standing driver shouting and swearing at anyone in his way.

The cypresses gave welcome shade; it was already warm and muggy. The two men walked steadily along the shoulder, occasionally passing other persons with a brief greeting or pausing to ask the latest news. Few knew much, beyond the fact of the emperor's death. One man said he had seen the Hesperian embassy in flames—"Such a pity, old Maecenas poured millions into that place"—but knew nothing about what had happened to the Hesperians themselves.

Late in the morning they came to a *mutationis*, a rest stop and changing station for official travelers. It was a tidy compound on the edge of a fenced meadow where horses grazed. The main building, built of bricks and faced with white stucco, had a shaded porch where two men sat on a bench munching bread. Each was dressed in a leather cuirass over a blue cotton tunic and wore a leather hat much like a twentieth-century British infantryman's round helmet. Between them were two leather shoulder bags, oiled against bad weather. They were postmen, members of the *cursus publicus*; their bicycles, two Norco mountain bikes painted glossy gold, leaned against the wooden porch pillars. Ten or twelve children clustered near the bikes, fascinated but afraid to touch.

"Hail, friends," Aquilius greeted them. "Are you coming out from Rome?"

"We are," said the younger of the two. He was a youth with a big nose and hard eyes.

"Please tell us the news. We heard the emperor was slain yesterday."

"You heard right," said the older postman; he had a ruddy, scarred face and greasy hair. "Saw it myself, I did, in the Flavian Amphitheater, just after *cena*. The *myrmillo* Astavius was just getting going with a useless *retiarius*, fellow who looked like he'd never seen a net before. All of a sudden, a thunderclap, with not a cloud in the sky, and then smoke and flames and everyone running for the exits."

"So much we've heard. And what has happened since then? Has the senate met? Who is the successor?"

"Trajan for sure," said the younger postman. "There's a fine general! We're bound north to send him the word of the emperor's death, and if he's as smart as he's supposed to be, he'll come south like old Caesar himself, with a good big army at his back."

"May the gods forbid another year of civil war over the succession," said the scarfaced man. "My father fought for old Vespasian," he said proudly. "He always bragged about that, helping restore peace after the year of the four emperors."

"Who has sent you on this journey?" Aquilius asked.

"General Drusus of the Praetorian Guard. Guess that tells you who the next emperor will be, eh? Can't stop a man with the Praetorians behind him."

"We hear the Hesperian embassy was burned," Pierce said.

The postmen looked at him and grinned. "A German, eh?" said the younger man. "Bet you're a Goth."

Pierce grinned back. "You win your bet. And what of the Hesperians?"

"They're said to be sorcerers. The Praetorians stormed

the embassy and slew them all. I hear the guards have some kind of new slings, throw little stones hard enough to kill a man. Make a great noise, too. But we haven't seen them."

"The Hesperians couldn't be much at sorcery if they're all dead," said Pierce with a broad, cold smile. The postman nodded and laughed, but the scarfaced one looked warily at Pierce.

"Will the consuls govern until Trajan arrives?" asked Aquilius, nervously changing the subject. Pierce made himself relax; if his anger was showing, he must conceal it.

"I expect so," said the younger postman with a cynical grin. "And the Guard'll keep them from doing anything foolish."

Pierce reflected on a hazard of Roman government: to prevent a return to monarchy, the Romans elected two consuls every year to govern them. Each could override the commands of the other, and so protect the rights of the senate and people. Since Julius Caesar, and especially since Caesar's nephew Augustus, the system had become a mockery. To give all the aspirants some experience, the consulship was now only two months long, and little more than a ceremonial post and a stepping stone to more powerful positions like provincial governorships. The current consuls were Cornutus Tertullus, an old man, and a young patrician named Plinius Caecilius—Pliny the Younger, nephew of the Pliny who had died in the eruption of Vesuvius. Technically, those two men were in charge of the government until the senate officially conferred power on the new emperor. As prominent members of Domitian's government, however, they were likely to be murdered. The Praetorian Guard would then proclaim its choice for emperor, and the senate would obey.

It had been a little simpler on Earth's timeline: there, Domitian's assassination had led to the short reign of Nerva, who in turn had adopted Trajan and put him in line for the principate. Here on Ahania, Domitian had named no successor, Nerva had died without becoming emperor, and Trajan would have to rely on courage and his legions to seize power without the aura of legitimacy.

"We must hurry," said Pierce. "A good journey to you both, and a good journey home."

"And to you," said the scarfaced man. He got up, stretched, and meticulously checked his bicycle. As Pierce and Aquilius walked back onto the road, they heard the jingle of the bicycles' bells. The mob of children ran shrieking after the two postmen, who were soon out of sight.

Back on the road, Pierce set a quick pace. Aquilius half jogged to keep up.

"Something is going very wrong," Pierce muttered.

"What?"

"Someone from Earth has converted the Praetorians to Christianity, and given them modern weapons. All our people have been killed, if the postmen are right. But why do the Praetorians want Trajan?"

They walked on through the morning and noon, when most travelers stopped for a siesta under the trees. Aquilius made no complaint about the pace; he recognized the country, and knew how close he was to the family estate. They no longer stopped to talk with northbound travelers, but by early afternoon they had begun to notice a change in the traffic. Many of the carts were *raedae*, bulky, bath-tub-shaped carriages drawn by mule teams. The drivers were clearly slaves of wealthy families, yet the carriages contained no passengers. Instead, sacks and bundles and chests were piled inside. Armed slaves stood at the rear of the carriages, looking as grim as the drivers.

Interspersed in this slow-moving traffic were smaller, lighter carriages, carrying well-dressed women and children and escorted by mounted slaves carrying pikes and swords. At any delay, the slaves would charge forward to threaten a slow-moving muleteer or even to run a cart off the road.

"I don't like the look of this," Aquilius said as a *mona-chus* clattered past; it was a two-wheeled cart, pulled by horses and driven by a woman wearing an elegant shawl. A teenage girl sat beside her, and no fewer than six mounted slaves rode escort. All looked frightened.

Soon Pierce and Aquilius came to a *mansio*, a travelers' inn. It was filthy and squalid; Pierce remembered riding past it during his trip north to the Alps, and the stink of the place was as strong as he remembered. The innkeeper, a short, fat man with an unfashionable beard, was wringing a chicken's neck in the foreyard of the inn.

"Hail, friend," said Aquilius.

"We're full up, young gentleman." He tossed the chicken's head in the direction of a dungheap and let the blood pulse into the dust at his feet.

"We don't seek lodging, only information." Aquilius spoke civilly, but Pierce sensed anger in the young patrician: innkeepers should speak more politely to their betters. "A number of well-born persons have been traveling north in some haste. Do you know why? Is it connected with the emperor's death?"

"I expect. Heard one rich bitch screaming at her slaves to go faster or they'd all be killed."

"She would kill them?" Pierce asked, not following the rapid country dialect. The innkeeper looked at him with contempt.

"No, *they* would kill them. Whoever it was killed the emperor. I reckon the emperor's men are dead or running. Always this way when the succession's not clear, and the new fellow wants to settle accounts."

"But where can they run to?"

The innkeeper's contempt grew tinged with amusement. "Perhaps to your homeland's forests, my German friend. But no place inside the empire will shelter them long if the new emperor's got a mind to find them."

"We hear the new emperor will be Trajan," Aquilius said.

"*I* hear the new emperor's already in Rome, and not Trajan."

"Who?" demanded Pierce. The innkeeper, sensing a dangerous urgency in Pierce's voice, shrugged.

"Haven't heard the name. Probably some adopted son of a great-nephew of Caesar's next-door-neighbor's whore." The innkeeper roared at his own wit, slapping the still-twitching carcass of the chicken against his leg. Blood squirted from the headless neck.

"Let's go," Aquilius muttered. "We must get to Vallis Viridis as soon as possible. It's a proscription."

Six:

At the twenty-third milestone north of Rome they turned east down a narrow, deeply rutted dirt road. The countryside here was orchards and vineyards, interspersed by tiny hamlets of wretched little huts, each with a rickety watchtower.

"These lands belong to our neighbor Calvus," said Aquilius. "This close to the highway, the fields are always in danger from travelers." Pierce nodded; he had seen many of the towers on his journey to the Alps.

At most of the hamlets the inhabitants watched them warily; the men all gripped hoes or axes, while the women and children kept back at a safe distance. They were slaves or migrant laborers, which meant little difference, and were clearly frightened of strangers.

Eventually they came to a larger hamlet, at the foot of a low hill crowned with an imposing villa. Here the slaves held leashed dogs that snarled and barked frantically, and some of the men had the look of overseers, not of slaves.

One man, wearing a leather cuirass over his tunic and holding a short sword, kicked the dogs into silence and marched up to Pierce and Aquilius. He was short and stocky, with grizzled hair and a deep scar across his nose.

"Get off this property, you two!"

"By whose right do you give us orders?" said Aquilius coldly.

"I'm the bailiff of Marcus Calvus Quinctius. Now go

on, *latrones*, get back to the highway and find someone else to rob."

One of the dogs broke loose and lunged at Pierce. He sidestepped it, gripped it by the scruff of the neck, and flung it into the air. The dog fell heavily, and limped away yelping.

The bailiff stared for a moment, then swore and brought his sword up for a blow. With the edge of his hand, Pierce struck the man's forearm and felt the radius and ulna crack. The sword clattered on the hardpacked dirt as the bailiff lost his balance and fell backward.

"We are peaceful travelers, friend," said Pierce. "Now we are going about our business. We wish you good-day."

The bailiff, holding his broken arm, squinted up at them. His face was pale from shock; he would not feel much pain for a few minutes yet. His mouth worked, but he said nothing. The slaves were very quiet as Pierce and Aquilius walked on down the road.

"It's unfortunate that he attacked you," Aquilius said after a few minutes. "Here in the countryside, any stranger is likely to be a robber. He must be new; the old bailiff would have recognized me. If the dog hadn't attacked you, I would have told the man who I am. We are not friends of the Calvus family, but we are neighbors."

"Why not friends?"

"Calvus is a client of Domitian. If he is in Rome, he has probably been arrested already; if he is here, they will come to get him very soon."

"I've read about this," Pierce said, "but seeing it is another thing. Does the new emperor really intend to kill all of Domitian's supporters?"

"Just the chief ones, the ones who might cause trouble later."

"Then you're lucky your family had no ties to Domitian and Vespasian."

Aquilius looked up at Pierce. "Perhaps. But we have ties to the Hesperians."

Pierce nodded. "Then we'll at least see that your family finds safety before we go into Rome."

"The innkeeper was right. No one is safe in the empire if the emperor wills otherwise."

"We'll see about that."

The road intersected a fence of whitewashed stones; beyond the fence, the land fell away east into a narrow, well-watered valley, as green as its name. The eastern side of the valley was thickly wooded with pine, though many patches had been logged and abandoned. In the valley bottom, wheat fields rippled with new green under the late-afternoon sun. And across the valley, grapevines followed the contours of the hills in orderly rows.

Pierce and Aquilius strode down the hill, following the road south along the western side of the valley. The land showed signs of long care.

"You don't seem glad to be back," Pierce said.

"Until three months ago, this valley was my Elysium, what you call paradise. I thought it would never change. Now I know better. A month ago, I persuaded my Trainer to bring me out here from the Accadèmia. We found this valley. It was all factories and workers' apartment blocks. No streams, no trees, the hills themselves were different. My family's graves were so much . . . archaeology."

Pierce touched his shoulder briefly.

"Now, what shall we tell my family?" Aquilius asked. "It will not be easy to explain time travel, or Doomsday, or even Training."

"No. For now, let us simply say that you and I have been visiting the Hesperians, and were allowed to return early. We arrived two days ago at Centumcellae, and came here on our way to Rome. We've heard alarming rumors about the emperor and the Hesperian embassy, and we're uncertain what to do next; perhaps your father can offer some advice."

"He may be in Rome," Aquilius said quietly.

"Do you have a town house there?"

"Yes, on the Viminal Hill."

"If we learn that your family is in Rome, we'll go straight on without resting. If they're here, we'll spend the night and then go on in the morning."

"What if my father forbids me? He's likely to say that Rome is dangerous, and he'll be right."

Pierce shrugged. "You'll come anyway."

"I can't. My father is—my father."

"Don't worry about it until the need arises. If he's worried about our running into the Praetorians, we can show him our weapons. That reminds me: do you know how to use a Mallory?"

"No."

Pierce pulled one out of his shoulder bag. It rested in his hand, a smooth weapon of white plastic looking something like a small Luger. He passed it to Aquilius.

"The button just above your thumb releases the clip. Right. And the dial next to it shows when the clip or the charger is almost exhausted. Each clip holds fifty flechettes, so you don't need to reload often. The charger lasts for three clips—maybe two at maximum impact setting. The flechettes are tipped with a shock-inducing drug. At impact 1 or 2, a hit anywhere will knock out even a big man. At impact 6 or 7, the flechette will go through a flak jacket and still have enough energy to penetrate the skin. If he's not protected, it'll hurt him badly. At impact 10 it'll go through a bronze helmet and take out the back of the man's skull as it exits. All right, slide the clip back in."

They paused in the dusty road. The only sound was the buzz of insects in the noon heat. Aquilius raised the Mallory and sighted carefully at a slender young pine tree twenty meters away.

"You're set for single fire at maximum impact. All right, squeeze the trigger gently."

The Mallory was almost silent; it made a faint kissing sound and in the same moment the trunk of the pine burst open with a sharp crack. The tree shuddered under the impact, which had taken out a third of the trunk's fifteen-centimeter diameter.

"Good," said Pierce. "Now watch what happens on automatic."

He took the weapon back, slid a switch, and aimed at the same tree. The first two shots severed the rest of the trunk, sending the top of the tree down with a rush of air through its branches. The stump, about five meters high, exploded again and again and again as Pierce lowered the barrel. The last three shots had left a meter of trunk gouged and splintered.

"Very impressive," said Aquilius. "It would be a popular weapon for the *bestiarii* in the games. You could blow an elephant to pieces very nicely."

Pierce looked at Aquilius and snorted.

They came in the late afternoon to a little village, much like the one ruled by Calvus's bailiff, except that this one was cleaner and better maintained. Its watchtower was of brick, with a wooden roof. The villagers looked almost as poor as the slaves of Calvus, but they seemed much less frightened.

"My father refuses to use slaves except in the household," said Aquilius. "He rents to free tenant farmers. Often he says slaves only ruin the land."

Pierce nodded. "This valley looks more prosperous than the country we came through. But how has your father escaped all these years if he's not a supporter of Domitian?"

"Mostly luck. We are of the senatorial order; our family is old and respected. My father attends the senate when he is in Rome, and honors the emperor, and otherwise tends to his land. He has asthma, so he cannot seek office even if he wished to. Even Domitian could find no reason to attack him. But if the emperor ever found himself short of money, he might accuse us of treason and confiscate our land. The Hesperians kept him rich enough to ignore us."

Pierce nodded. He looked about as they walked down

the village street, noticing an absence of fish graffiti on the walls.

A toothless woman, standing at a fountain with a clay pot, stared at them with amazement and then set up an ululating scream.

"It's the young master Gaius," she cried, putting down the pot and hurrying across the dirt road with her skirt gripped in one hard fist. She embraced Aquilius and kissed him noisily.

"Greetings, *nutrix*." He chuckled, hugging her in return. "Old Petronia, you're the best thing I've seen in days—in months."

Other men and women appeared in windows and doorways, or hurried toward the two men and the woman.

"Back from Hesperia so soon? What a wonder! Let me look at you—ah, you're pale. Did they not feed you properly?"

"I ate very well, and they looked after me quite hospitably."

"And you've come home at such a terrible time," Petronia went on. "Your father and the rest of the family have left."

Aquilius frowned. "No. Where have they gone?"

"The old master told that new steward of yours, that Sulpicius, they were bound for Capua."

"But why—"

"Indeed, why go where one has no friends or business?" Petronia grinned, showing her gums. Her voice dropped to a conspirator's whisper: "They've gone north, to seek Marcus Ulpius Traianus."

"Many are seeking Trajan today. Well, old nurse, is Sulpicius at least still at home?"

"No doubt. The old master took most of his household slaves with him, but the steward and a few others stayed on. Ah, and to miss your honored father by only half a day!"

"Dearest old woman," murmured Aquilius. "The whole village knows I'm here, and no doubt they know why my family's left."

"Some say your honored father fears the revenge of the Praetorians; I say he goes to appeal to the noblest of the great generals."

"Yes." Aquilius nodded. "Meanwhile, my companion and I must meet Sulpicius and make some plans. If the Praetorians, or anyone else, should come from Rome, can you and the others send them off again? Tell them I've gone away in search of my father in Capua?"

"Of course, little Gaius. What else do you think we'd do?"

The old nurse accompanied them through the village to the gate of a walled villa. A dog, looking much like a rottweiler, roared behind the bars of the gate until it saw Aquilius and began to howl and whimper in welcome. A slave with a broad knife stuck in his belt took one look at Aquilius, grinned, and let them through. The dog wagged his tail and licked Aquilius's hand.

"Good old Custos," Aquilius said, rubbing the dog's ears. "Just as noisy as ever. Greetings, Achilleus."

"Greetings, young master. This is a joyous surprise. Shall I bring Sulpicius out to greet you?"

"No, we'll find him."

The slave bobbed his head and pulled Custos back to his post at the gate. Aquilius led Pierce out of the gateway.

They entered a utilitarian garden of vegetables, including Hesperian potatoes and chilies, laid out around a circular fish pond. Three or four small huts leaned against the wall, quarters for slaves or storage sheds. A passable statue of Ceres overlooked the garden.

The path led round the pond to an imposing double door of carved wooden panels showing Roman soldiers defeating warriors in Gaulish trousers. Aquilius hammered happily on the door until the porter swung it open.

By the time they finally entered the house, every slave in it seemed to have greeted Aquilius with bows and kisses to his hands. Aquilius finally broke free, made his obsequies to the shrine of the household *lares*, and led Pierce through the atrium to a long, well-tended peristyle full of poppies and violets. A sallow man in a white linen tunic stood there, holding a wax-and-wood notebook in one hand and a stylus in the other.

"Welcome home, young master!" The man bowed.

"Hail, Sulpicius. I'm glad to see you. My friend Alaricus, a German, also back from Hesperia."

The slave studied him with intelligent eyes and seemed to respect, if not approve, what he saw in Pierce: a barbarian, but a capable one who had seen the fabled lands beyond the western sea.

"I hear my honored father and the rest of the household have left," Aquilius said.

"Only this morning, within an hour of hearing of the emperor's strange death and the burning of the Hesperians' embassy. Your father said he had urgent business in Capua."

"Sulpicius, the Via Flaminia is crowded with people fleeing a proscription. Did my father say anything about it?"

"Nothing, sir. But he did say, 'At least my boy is safely out of this.' Have you and your companion eaten, sir?"

"No. Ask the cook to bring us something. We'll eat here while we talk."

"As you wish, sir." But Sulpicius seemed to Pierce slightly scandalized that they should be willing to eat without even first washing the dust from themselves.

In very little time, cooks brought in trays of cold sausage, pickled cabbage, and a roast chicken that had probably been intended for Sulpicius. The steward persuaded Aquilius and Pierce to eat in the triclinium, where they could lie down properly for their meal.

The dining room, just off the peristyle, was small but elegant, with landscape murals on the walls and a magnificent mosaic of flowers on the floor. The square dining table was of some dark, heavy wood, thickly varnished, with a broad couch on each of three sides; the fourth side of the table faced the peristyle and allowed new dishes to be served.

Pierce found the ceiling uncomfortably low, and was glad to stretch out on one of the couches. Sulpicius took each course from the hands of the cooks, cut it into finger food, and served it first to his master and then to Pierce.

"Your revered father took the death of the emperor as a very bad omen for this house," Sulpicius said quietly when the cooks had left. "He learned of the attack on the Hesperian embassy, and realized that the two events must be linked, that enemies of the Hesperians have seized power. Having benefited so greatly from the Hesperians, we are a marked house."

"My father took most of the household slaves with him, it seems. The place is deserted. So quiet."

"Only six of us are here, young master. I plan to send away the cooks in the morning. Achilleus and I will remain."

"If the Praetorians come, what will you do?"

"Offer them hospitality, young master."

Pierce studied the slave with growing respect. The Praetorians would probably torture this man to learn his master's whereabouts, and Sulpicius must know it. Yet he betrayed no sign of fear.

"Were those my father's orders?"

"No, young master. He told me only to keep the cooks out of the wine."

Aquilius smiled in the deepening twilight. "I want all of you out of here before first light tomorrow. Old Petronia suspects my father went north, to find Trajan, and she's probably right."

"I suspected as much, young master, but I declined to voice my suspicions to your father. Clearly he would hope to evade pursuit by the Praetorians. If I were to be interrogated, I could tell them only what he told me."

"You will not be interrogated if I have anything to say about it. Follow my father north, or seek refuge with the shepherds up in the hills—go anywhere for now."

"The villa would be destroyed, young master," Sulpicius said quietly.

"Better to live to rebuild it, than to die in its ashes. I will not have you fall into the hands of the Praetorians."

"And yourself, young master? You surely cannot stay here."

"My friend Alaricus and I will leave soon after you do. We'll take a couple of horses and be gone before sunup."

"Where—"

"You cannot tell what you do not know, dear Sulpicius."

The steward nodded. "We shall be eternally grateful for your kindness and concern for our welfare, young master."

Aquilius nodded absently, chewing on a chicken wing and then throwing the bones to the floor.

"The wine we shall have to make a present of to the Praetorians. Did the family leave any valuables behind?"

"Very little, young master, except for a thousand denarii."

Pierce's spirits rose. What they had been given in Sardinia was scarcely a day's wages for a couple of common laborers; he had been resigned to robbing someone as soon as they reached Rome.

"We shall require seven hundred and fifty of them. Take the rest into your keeping, and use what you need to look after yourself and the others. With any luck, all will go well and you'll be back here with most of the money in a few days."

"As you wish, young master."

"Now go and make your preparations, or you'll get no sleep tonight. Off with you."

When they were alone, Pierce said to Aquilius in English, "Is he reliable?"

Aquilius looked surprised. "Of course. If he serves us well, we'll emancipate him and set him up in business."

"Your old nurse said he's a new steward; but you still trust him?"

Aquilius poured a little water into his wine and sipped it. "Mr. Pierce, he's been our steward for eleven years. To Petronia, he's a young upstart, but only to her. Now, perhaps we should discuss what we will do tomorrow in Rome."

Pierce nodded. His head hurt. "A quick and careful reconnaissance. Learn the news, find out who the new emperor is, and who his backers are besides the Praetorians. Find out if any of the Hesperians are still alive, and then get out of town and call for the helicopter."

Aquilius reached into his shoulder bag and pulled out a small battery lantern. He put it on the table and switched it on, creating a pool of warm white light. The cooks, across the peristyle in the kitchen, squealed with astonishment.

"A present for my father. I will not be returning to Earth with you, Mr. Pierce."

"Your Training is not complete yet."

"My Training can wait. I will have to follow my father and see to his safety."

"Your piety does you credit. But you may do him more good if you return with me to advise us on the best way to deal with the new emperor."

Aquilius smiled wryly. "My best advice is to stay away from the new emperor's missiles and machine guns."

Pierce rubbed his head and grunted. "*Damn*. Of course."

"I don't understand."

"That's why the Praetorians have sent for Trajan. They want to lure him into a battle against uptime weapons, and destroy his whole army. Then they'll have no serious opposition."

"That makes sense. Then if my father reaches Trajan, he will only be helping to draw him into a trap."

"Trajan may not be drawn. He'll have heard something of the Praetorians' weapons, and the way the emperor died."

"Even if he stays in Germany, the result will be the same. The usurpers will come to find him and anyone else who resists them."

"All the more reason to get back to Earth as soon as possible, and get some regular Agency troops down here. A couple of Gurkha regiments would do the job."

"What if they can't be sent? If no I-Screen can be built in time?"

Pierce rubbed his head again. The Briefing and Conditioning was beginning to hurt, but he didn't want to break into the Pentasyn yet. "If we must, we'll find every knotholer in Italy and use their equipment. I have to go to bed, Aquilius. I don't feel well."

"I understand. Come, I'll put you in my father's room."

Carrying the lantern, he led Pierce across the peristyle to a small cubicle painted red and gold, with a painted window that appeared to open on a seashore. The bed was a simple wooden frame across which leather straps had been interwoven. They supported a thin straw mattress: the Aquilii did not indulge themselves in luxuries.

Pierce pulled his cloak out of his shoulder bag and put it on; it would be his blanket. Aquilius wished him goodnight.

"What will you do now?" Pierce asked as he sank gratefully onto the bed.

"Plan for tomorrow, and see that everything is ready. I will rouse you well before dawn."

Pierce nodded and fell asleep. Only an instant seemed to pass before he heard Aquilius's voice again, low and urgent in the darkness:

"The Praetorians are here."

Seven:

As he sat up, Pierce's first feeling was relief that his headache was gone. A few hours' sleep had temporarily eased the pain of B&C.

"Where are they?" he murmured. The tile floor was cold under his bare feet as he groped for his sandals.

"Just entering the village. They're on bicycles. The men on night guard in the tower saw their headlamps and came to warn us."

Pierce reached in the darkness for his shoulder bag; Aquilius's penlight found it.

"Here's your pistol." He checked his own by touch. "How many?"

"They think ten or twelve."

"Will they come straight here?"

"I'm sure."

"Get the dog put away. Have you wakened the household?"

"Sulpicius has. I told him to get them out the back gate and across the stream as quickly as possible."

Pierce was moving into the peristyle. The air was chilly in this hour before dawn, but the sky was already lightening in the east. Overhead, the stars were growing pale. Village dogs barked close-by.

Pierce thought about the terrain. The dirt road through the middle of the village came directly to the front gate of the villa, and then meandered on into a meadow. Across the road was a cluster of mud-brick huts. Anyone roused by the noise of the soldiers could be in danger if the fight began in the road. The Praetorians would have to enter the villa and be disposed of there. The prospect of zapping some bad guys filled him with eager anticipation. This was what he did best; this was his contribution to staving off Doomsday.

Sulpicius appeared out of the darkness, his face a pale oval.

"Soldiers are at the rear gate, young master."

"How many?" Pierce asked.

"Four, I think."

"Good. Don't let them in, but keep the cooks and Achilleus in earshot of the gate, and make a little noise to keep their attention. Aquilius, you and I will deal with the ones at the front gate."

"The gate is locked," Sulpicius said. "They will have to break it down."

"Where is the key?"

"By the gate, hanging in a little niche," said Aquilius. "Are you going to let them in?"

"Yes."

Sulpicius vanished again. Aquilius led the way out past the fish pond to the front gate. Over the wall came the sounds of men and bicycles: the clack of kickstands, the shuffle of boots, the metallic rattle of firearms brushing against armor. Good: they were casual, careless, expecting to deal only with some frightened slaves and a family of helpless aristocrats. Pierce wondered if they had already murdered Calvus down the road.

"I'll play the house slave," he whispered. They approached the gate; the slave Achilleus had blocked the iron grille with boards, so outsiders could not see into the garden. "I'll let them in. You put yourself behind that statue. When I give the word, shoot the lead man and work back toward the gate. Is your pistol on impact 10?"

"Yes." The boy sounded very calm.

"Ever kill a man before?"

"I've seen it done hundreds of times. As you should know."

Pierce grinned at the insult. "Good."

Aquilius slipped behind the statue of Ceres, four or five meters into the garden from the wall. Pierce stood patiently on the path until someone began banging on the gate. He ran in place on the gravel for a moment, as if hurrying down the path from the main building, and then trotted up to the boarded gate.

"*Quis? Quis?*" he called out anxiously.

The answer was in Latin with a strange accent: "*Praetorii sumus. Aperiri!*"

Pierce found the heavy bronze key where Sulpicius had said it was. As he pulled away the boards, a flashlight glared in his face and he winced as a frightened slave ought to. He could smell the sweat of men preparing for a fight, or at least for a kill: it reminded him of the smell of the crowd in the Colosseum, and of himself. In the reflected light of the flash he saw glinting bronze, hard faces under horsetailed helmets, dark cloaks. The leader, standing half a meter away on the other side of the grille, wore Praetorian armor but no helmet. He was as tall as Pierce, with sandy hair and blue eyes.

One glimpse was enough. Four years earlier Pierce had seen the man's file: Dennis Brewster, DOB 6 December 1977, POB Tulsa, Oklahoma. Joined the White American Brotherhood 10 April 1997; arrested during the Wabbies' abortive putsch 26 October 1999; jailed in Fort Leavenworth; converted to the Church Militant, spring 2000; transferred to Church Militant Relocation Center, Dubrovnik, Yugoslavia, 17 August 2002. Deported downtime with six thousand other CMs, 1 October 2002. Suspected in two inmate killings at Leavenworth. IQ: 121. Psychiatric assessment: borderline paranoid, violent outbursts.

His presence answered one question but raised too many others. And, unless some of the others were also CMs, Brewster was too valuable to kill outright. No time to find out; Brewster would have to be spared.

The key turned and the gate swung open.

"*Salve, magister,*" Pierce mumbled as Brewster shoved through. The others followed close behind, two of them carrying Uzis at port arms. If they were Ahanians, they had been well trained. Pierce reached under his cloak and thumbed the Mallory's impact setting down to 3. As the last Praetorian came through the gate and passed him, Pierce aimed at Brewster and fired. As soon as the man was safely down, Pierce thumbed back up to 10, switched to automatic fire, shouted, "Now!" and shot the last man in line.

Flanked and enfiladed, the eight men dropped without firing a shot. Flechettes punched through armor with a noise like hammered nails, deformed on impact, and tore huge exit wounds.

Pierce moved quickly along the line of bodies, checking to see that all but Brewster were dead. Two required the coup de grace.

"Why did you shoot the first one?" Aquilius demanded irritably.

"Shh. I need him. He's a Hesperian. Help me drag him inside; then we'll get the rest of the Praetorians."

With Brewster unconscious in the atrium, they went to the rear of the villa. Sulpicius and Achilleus stood outside a little shed, each holding a short spear. The cooks, inside the shed, were sobbing quietly.

"Tell them the house is secured and you're letting them in," Pierce whispered. Aquilius nodded and went to the rear gate. After a short conversation he drew the bolts and stepped back without revealing himself. The four soldiers sauntered in, grinning; Pierce killed them all in two seconds. Aquilius swung the gate closed again and shot the bolts.

"Well done, Sulpicius," he said. The two slaves sagged back against the shed, staring at the four corpses in the dawn's growing light. "Come on, man, let the poor *mulierculae* out of the shed before they die of fright."

Pierce left Aquilius to calm the cooks down, and returned to the atrium. Brewster was still out. Pierce shouted for some rope, and Achilleus came running with the watchdog's leather leash. Once Brewster was securely bound, Pierce dragged him to the edge of the *impluvium*, the pool of rainwater under the opening in the atrium roof.

He forced Brewster's head under water for a moment. The big body convulsed; Pierce lifted him into the air and rolled him over.

The sky was brightening quickly now; Brewster's thin-lipped face was clearly visible. He coughed, banging his head on the tiles, and looked up.

"Hello, Dennis."

"Who are you? What happened?" His Oklahoma accent sounded incongruous coming from a man in a bronze breastplate.

"You were careless."

"Oh, Lord." Brewster's expression was anguished and baffled for a moment. Then he seemed suddenly to understand something, and smiled. "Dear Michael has tested me, hasn't he? He doubted my ability, and saw into the arrogance of my heart and soul, and now he's chastised me. Bless him."

Pierce paused for a moment. Every time he talked to a Praetorian, it seemed, the conversation went in an unexpected direction. "Are you happy to be in this predicament, Dennis?"

"I'm happy to be wherever Dear Michael chooses to send me, brother."

"Let's stop a moment, Dennis, and think: why did Dear Michael choose to send you and your men out here?"

"Why, to purge the friends of the idolaters. Now I see I was being tested, my pride was gettin' excessive, and I've been truly humbled. Praise God. Isn't that amazing, brother? Dear Michael has scarcely seen me in two weeks, and not at all since the crusade began, yet that man could look into my heart and see the pride and arrogance growing there, and with everything else he's got to worry about, he took the time to give me this lesson."

Aquilius came into the atrium, still holding his Mallory and looking excited but uncertain. The killings had finally sunk in on him. Brewster glanced at him and grinned.

"Hello, brother. Boy, you fellows sure nailed us good."

Aquilius frowned at Pierce, who only smiled and shrugged.

"Now, Dennis, there's more to this lesson than getting knocked out. Let's go back to the beginning and see where you went astray, all right?"

"Yes, sir. Uh, could I please sit up and get these ropes off? My arms hurt . . ."

"Let's just let them hurt for a little longer, Dennis. You just begin at the beginning."

Brewster obeyed, going back to the exile of the Church Militant while Pierce, silently recalling occasional reports on the colony, filled in the gaps.

The Dubrovnik I-Screen turned on twenty times that day in 2002, and each time three hundred members of the Church Militant were driven through at a run, dragging their few possessions in duffel bags. Stragglers were clubbed, then thrown through the next opening to be trampled by the following group.

Dennis Brewster was one of the first to go through, not long after Michael Martel and the Elders' Council. The shock of icy air numbed him at first, but the Elders quickly put him to work dragging the beaten brothers and sisters out of the way each time the Screen opened.

They had been exiled to Albion, over eight thousand years before Christ. The glaciers were in retreat but not yet gone, and the early-winter afternoon was bitterly cold. When he had time to look around, Dennis saw terrain utterly unlike that of Dubrovnik: scrub pines swayed in the wind, and where the Adriatic Sea had been, tidal marshes stretched far into the west under a dull gray sky.

Dear Michael had teams already erecting the tents the Agency had given them, and other teams were chopping down the pines for firewood. Sisters were drawing water from a nearby stream and making soup from dehydrated powders. Dennis had heard they'd been given only enough food to keep them for a week; after that, they would live off the land or die.

The short day darkened in a flurry of wind-driven snow. Six thousand people, less eighty who had died in the crossing, huddled on a thinly treed slope in prehistoric

Europe, singing the hymns that Dear Michael had composed: "Temper Me," "Oh Holy War," "Blood Brother, Blood Sister," "I Bring Not Peace But a Sword." No one led the songs; they sprang up as spontaneously as the icy wind, and spread from tent to tent, fire to fire. In their shoddy Agency-issue overcoats the Militants shivered, but rejoiced in their closeness and their strange new freedom.

Next morning a hundred more were dead; a gentle slope nearby became hallowed martyrs' ground as work crews hacked into the frozen soil to dig the graves. At noon the clouds parted and the sun shone brightly in a sky a deeper blue than any could recall on Earth.

That noon Dear Michael preached the Sermon at the Camp. He stood on a rocky outcrop, his glorious voice so strong that only a few on the edge of the congregation had needed to use their ringmike earphones. While the wind whipped his pale hair and reddened his cheeks, he spoke of the ordeal that God had now chosen as a means to strengthen His warriors, to prepare them for the coming glory. The idolaters, he said, had seen Doomsday on the dead worlds of Ulro and Urizen, but in their folly they had rejected the true message God had vouchsafed by that revelation. The Second Coming was now truly at hand, only two generations away, and many of them would live to stand in the ranks at Armageddon.

Before that moment at the climax of earthly time, however, they had been sent like the Israelites to dwell in the wilderness, to be tested and hardened. The idolaters in their folly had thought this exile was a punishment; they did not see how even in their blindness they did God's work and prepared for their own overthrow and damnation.

"*Amen,*" the great congregation murmured, and the sound muffled the wind itself.

In God's good time, Michael said, the Church Militant would return in glory and rejoicing to redeem Earth from her sin and folly and to prepare mankind for the onslaught of the Antichrist. No, they would do more: they would redeem even the suffering primitives of this and the other downtime worlds, bring them the saving news of Christ's birth, death, and resurrection, so that when Judgment Day came in 2089 not only Earth but all the chronoplanes would receive their Savior.

They stood helpless before God that day, strangers in a strange land that they would make their home. Here they would conquer the earth and subdue it, and here they would learn the lesson God had taught them through their sufferings on Earth: Christ's warriors would win through strength, a physical strength that was only the outward manifestation of the spiritual strength within. He who struck down Christ's enemy not only showed his spiritual strength, he increased it by the act. He who fell at the hands of Christ's enemies redeemed his spiritual weakness by the Christlike sacrifice of his life, by the total witnessing he made in the face of the idolaters. No one need fear for the souls of slain idolaters: they were already irretrievably in Satan's power, and the soldier of the Church Militant was only Christ's instrument in sending them to the damnation they had chosen when the way to salvation had been so clearly offered them.

The Militants were weak, but they would be strong. They were few, but they would be numberless. They were castaways in the wilderness, yet they would stand in Jerusalem to wrest it from the Jews and to sing God's praises.

That first winter tempered them: almost two thousand died of hunger and scurvy and diarrhea. But by summer the first crops waved in the sunlight, and babies bawled lustily in the hut villages. A hundred endochronics, frightened but capable hunters, were captured and taught simple English. In return they showed the Militants how to set snares, to drive aurochs into traps, to harvest the wild bounty of the hills and streams.

Brewster was a hunter that first year, coursing far to the north and east. By the second winter their villages were walled and secure, each hut with its big stack of firewood. Before the end of that winter, the first knotholers appeared.

They were Yugoslavs, unbelievers with no interest in the Church Militant but trade. Dear Michael and the Elders drove bargains with them, buying arms and medicine with the Church's hidden resources uptime. Then, inevitably, they fell under Dear Michael's influence, converted, and served the Church out of love and duty.

At unpredictable intervals the Agency surveyed the colony from the air, its blue helicopters chattering close overhead. Uptime contraband was carefully hidden: the rifles, the generators, the medical equipment. The Agency surveys showed only a hardscrabble colony of walled villages, small fields of grain, logged-off hillsides, and big graveyards.

In his sermons Dear Michael promised an early end to their exile. He began to disappear; rumors were that he had returned uptime to keep contact with Militants who had escaped the Agency's net. The ordinary soldiers of the Church, like Brewster, knew nothing of the Elders' deliberations or plans: their job was only to serve and obey.

Then, a year ago, he had been called into a special group. Fifty men and women assembled in a village of their own, ten kilometers from the main settlement. In the village were six men and two women whose job was to teach the fifty. The subject was Latin.

The tutors were prisoners, endochronics taken in a raid on Ahania. They were terrified, but at last came to accept their fate. In lessons that went on for weeks, the Militants learned to speak the Latin of the first century, and to learn something of life in the Roman Empire.

Dear Michael's purpose was of course clear to them, though still concealed from most of the Militants: to seize the Roman Empire, convert it to Christianity two centuries before Constantine's conversion, and to make it a power that even the International Federation and the Agency would have to respect. The IF's tyranny would be broken; the downtime colonies would win their independence as well, under the guidance of the Church. At last Earth itself would turn from idolatry and vain attempts to escape the wrath of the Lord, and prepare itself for the last days.

Brewster and the others would have followed Dear Michael anywhere, of course, but the thought of saving Rome itself, of embracing the first Christians and saving them from the persecution of the pagan emperors, made every breath as sweet and heady as wine. Soon, soon, they would be in Jerusalem. It was no matter that Domitian's brother Titus had overthrown it and turned it to rubble. He had only driven the Jews from it, as Christ had driven the moneychangers from the temple, and the Church Militant would rebuild God's City as an eternal hymn in stone.

Over a period of three months, in small groups, the fifty Latin speakers left their village. They crossed the tidal marshes, thick with mosquitoes, to a camouflaged shed on a quiet Adriatic inlet. Three young sailors ferried them across to Italy, and guides there took them west across the Apennines. In a quiet forest clearing, an I-Screen opened up; they stepped through into twenty-first-century Italy, and within hours stepped through again into Ahania.

"Dear Michael—that man is so smart," Brewster said. "He planned everything. He reached the Praetorians, got them on our side. Soon as we got through, they took care of us. Sure brushed up my Latin."

"And in exchange you helped train them in firearms," Pierce said quietly.

"Of course. And the faith." He shifted uncomfortably on the tiles. "Brother, may I please sit up? And undo this rope?"

"In good time, Dennis." Pierce took Aquilius aside.

"It's full light. What's being done with the bodies?"

"Sulpicius has called in some of the villagers to dig a grave, out across the stream."

"The armor, weapons—the bikes?"

"It will all be seen to. The bicycles will be melted down. The Uzis will be buried."

"The villagers seem practiced in this kind of business."

"Praetorians are no different from tax collectors."

Pierce nodded. His headache was coming back. He walked back across the atrium to his prisoner.

"Sit up, Dennis." He helped the young man pull himself up, and undid the leather strap. "Come and sit down." Dennis hobbled to a small stool, sagged onto it gratefully, and put his hands on his knees.

"You spoke about Dear Michael's perceiving your pride, and your own understanding of your errors is very encouraging. Very encouraging."

Brewster looked bashfully at the mosaic tiles. Pierce wanted to kill him.

"What I want to do now, Dennis, is to find the roots of that pride, the mistaken ideas that led you into folly. Do you understand that I sincerely have your best interests at heart? That I'm here to help you and guide you, not to punish you?"

"Yes, sir. And I'm grateful. Uh, sir, may I talk to my squad? Make sure they're okay? Before we go on looking at my mistakes. They sure don't deserve to suffer for my sins."

"Don't worry about them. Would you say your pride came from a sense of being in complete control in Rome?"

"Oh, no, sir. We sure *aren't* in complete control. Something went wrong just as soon as we got the emperor."

"What do you think it was?"

"No idea, sir. All I know is, my people was supposed to go into the idolaters' embassy same time they got rid of the emperor, but we didn't get the word until two, three hours later. And they gave us a tough fight. Now we've just got ourselves and some of the Praetorians to take over the whole city, a million people."

"'Ourselves'?"

"The Latin speakers."

"You see yourselves as the only important persons in this plan?"

"No, sir! Nothing like as important as the Elders or the Crucifers. But we're the only ones can talk to these people, to the Romans."

"Yet with all that you had to do, you were sent out

here. Doesn't that suggest the importance of this particular mission?"

"Yes, sir. Anybody supported Domitian, anybody friends with the idolaters, we have to remove. Can't give the idolaters a chance to get organized."

"Exactly. Their removal is vital to the plan, more vital than you may realize. Yet you had trouble with the attack on the idolaters' embassy, and we were afraid you'd have just the kind of trouble you've run into here. That's why they sent me out here, to see how you handled this."

Brewster's eyes gleamed with tears. "Sir, I have no excuse. I've put Dear Michael to extra worry and trouble, just when he doesn't need it, but I'm sure grateful he's lookin' after me even in this urgent time. I'm ready for chastisement."

Pierce wondered how much longer he could carry on the imposture. Brewster had simply assumed that anyone in Ahanian Rome who spoke English and knew his name must be a fellow Militant. The man had also assumed that his capture and interrogation were directed by Michael Martel; that rang true, given what Pierce knew about Martel. He had some general knowledge as well about the cult's background and beliefs, but much was bound to have changed during its exile downtime. At some point he was sure to say something wrong, something that would spark Brewster's suspicions. He wished he had thought to bring a few cartridges of interrogatory drugs; he could simply have injected the man and picked his brains systematically.

"Chastisement will come in due time, Dennis. I don't want simple punishment. You're too important. But I do want—Dear Michael wants—we want you to understand what mistaken attitudes have led you into this position. You've already done very well, touching on your pride in being named a hunter, and then a translator. You can see how the seeds were planted. Perhaps you can do this: Tell me what your thoughts have been for the last little while, especially since Domitian was removed."

"Yes, sir. I was just gettin' to that."

Good; they still believed in public confession. If he was lucky, he would learn all he needed. Then he could turn on the beeper in two days and the helicopter would come for him and he would be in Geneva. Pierce settled back and listened.

Eight:

"Sir, I think I know where I really fell into error."

"Yes?"

"About three weeks ago, at the demonstration."

"Tell me about it, Dennis."

"Well, Brother David got the message to General Drusus and he came out from the Praetorian camp to meet Dear Michael that night. You must've been there, but I didn't see you."

"Just tell me what happened, Dennis. As you saw it."

"Well, we get Drusus up on this hilltop, out east of the city. Him and fifty soldiers, his bodyguard. And Dear Michael—" Brewster was grinning, almost chuckling. "He had the whole show put together like the Fourth of July. Man, those endos started to doubt their idolatry about thirty seconds into the show. Flares, smoke grenades, weird noises on tape, and then Dear Michael walks out of the smoke with that PA loudspeaker built into his helmet? I tell you, sir, I was just about down on my knees, too. Couldn't blame the endos. And Dear Michael starts talkin' in Latin, oh, he speaks it so beautifully, I know it enough to know when somebody can really talk Latin. And old Drusus and his bodyguard just about have heart attacks when they hear that voice boomin' out."

"Get to the point, Dennis." Pierce was appalled: had it taken the Militants only three weeks to co-opt the Praetorian Guards, train them in modern weapons, and assassinate Domitian—all without the Agency or the embassy suspecting a thing?

"Yes, sir. Well, when the Praetorians said they'd follow the Lord's Word, I guess I just figured we'd won right there. And I kind of went slack. You think you can always scare the Romans into doin' what you want, you know?"

"Dennis, can you tell me why that's an error?"

"Well, sir, it leads to the sin of pride, to complacency and laziness, just like Dear Michael and Brother David always say. We got the Praetorians on our side, and I thought we'd be home free. Like, they got the power to decide who's emperor, and now we've got them in our pocket. But I forgot what Dear Michael always used to say back on Albion, 'Take nothing for granted—'"

Pierce knew that one. "—because Satan lies in wait for the self-satisfied." He allowed his voice to soar from a hiss to a roar of fury, and Brewster burst into tears.

"Oh Lord, oh Lord, forgive me my sins and my f-follies! And lead me b-back into Thy righteous ways."

Pierce stood over Brewster. "You thought that sixty million idolaters could be overcome with a few smoke grenades and a loudspeaker," he snarled. "You would have walked right into Satan's trap, Dennis, and led others with you. Dear Michael's plans could be ruined through such impious folly, and who would be to blame?"

"I would, I would! Oh, thank the Lord that Dear Michael saw through me and sent you to save me. Oh, sir, give me the chance to redeem myself. If you haven't eliminated these folks here, let me do it."

"These folks here are no longer your concern, Dennis. Now, I know you're a good man, and you've seen your errors. But you're not the only one who's made this mistake. It's like a virus, spreading from one person to another. Have you talked to anyone else who thought this plan would be easy to achieve?"

Brewster's face froze. He looked intently at Pierce, then at Aquilius, who had stood at the entrance to the atrium during the interrogation. Then he smiled, showing rotted teeth.

"All right, mister, just who are you?" Brewster demanded quietly. "Because you sure aren't one of the saved."

For an instant Pierce considered blustering again, bullying the man back into compliance. He decided against it.

"You must be Agency. Agency or IF, one of those Trainables. You must be."

"What makes you say that?"

"Only idolaters believe in viruses."

Pierce sputtered with laughter. "Oh, of course, and you people believe in scourges from God. Stupid of me to forget."

"So who are you?" Brewster's face went pale. "Where are my men?"

"Dead," said Pierce. "You know, Dennis, your sins of pride and arrogance really did get you into this mess."

"And I may pay for my sins. But we'll destroy you," Brewster said softly. "We'll find you and send you back to your master Satan. God is not mocked."

"God is mocked every time some little bully sets himself up as a messiah. Have you ever noticed, Dennis, how the God of the Bible resembles all the Michael Martels and Jim Joneses? He can build galaxies, but he'd rather worry about our sex lives, and He's got a neurotic need to be flattered all the time. Of course you think otherwise, but I'm sure we can agree to disagree."

Smiling, Pierce walked across the mosaic floor to where Brewster sat on the stool with his wrists lashed behind him. Without warning, Pierce swung his open palm into Brewster's face, putting all his strength behind the blow. The shock of it ran up his arm and almost blinded him: He could feel skin and muscle and bone yield and rebound under his hypersensitive hand. Brewster toppled off the stool and fell heavily on his side. The mark of Pierce's fingers flared white on his cheek, then reddened.

"You killed my people in the embassy, Dennis." Pierce

was aware of Aquilius stepping back involuntarily. "I don't care how crazy you are; you killed my people. Now, did any of them survive? Did you take any prisoners?"

Brewster's mouth worked for a time before he finally spoke. "No prisoners. We interrogated a couple before we killed them."

"I'll just bet you did. What's next on your agenda? After you've killed off enough of the endos to run this place?"

"Tell you nothing more. Oh, Lord, forgive my sins and errors. I have tried to walk in Thy path and to serve Thee in all things, and I have failed—"

Pierce growled in disgust. His head hurt, and Brewster's whining grated on his nerves. The interrogation would have to be suspended for a while, to let Brewster consider his options.

"Dennis, shut up for a minute. We're going to let you think things over. If you cooperate with us, you'll live. If you don't, you'll be just another martyr like those poor slobs you brought here to their deaths. I'm going to give you an hour or so."

He turned away from Brewster. "Aquilius, ask Sulpicius and Achilleus to put him somewhere—lock him in a storeroom, somewhere secure. Then we need to salvage some of the Praetorians' gear."

After the slaves had dragged Brewster into a room off the kitchen, they accompanied Pierce and Aquilius outside into the yard by the back gate. Through the gate they could look across the stream to where twenty men were digging furiously in the meadow. Some of the corpses were visible in the grass, naked and pale in the morning light.

Inside the gate stood the Praetorians' bicycles and piles of armor and weapons. Pierce picked through the armor, looking for usable equipment. Much of it was bloodstained or damaged: one bronze breastplate, exquisitely worked with images of Mars and Venus, had been conspicuously punctured in two places. Still, he managed to assemble a complete uniform that fit Aquilius as if tailored for him.

"Now what about me? Brewster's about my size."

"Don't try to imitate a Praetorian, Mr. Pierce. You're obviously a foreigner, just as Brewster is. Romans will take you for one of the Christians, but the Christians will soon realize you're not one of them."

"You're right. I'll stay a German civilian."

They went back into the peristyle and sat down to a breakfast of cooked cereal garnished with onions, olives, and garlic. Pierce found *ientaculum* marginally better than the porridge they had eaten yesterday. Sulpicius served them as he had the night before, seeming as calm as ever while the excited chatter of the gravediggers from the village floated over the back wall and into the flowered tranquility of the peristyle.

When the meal was done they bathed in a small, sparsely furnished room. The bath itself was a rectangular pool tiled in a mosaic of green, blue, and white: fish, water plants, and octopi, with a bright-pink nereid sporting among them. The cooks had been heating water for over an hour to prepare it; Achilleus looked after the two men.

"Have you seen *sapo* before, Achilleus?" Aquilius asked with a smile. He had brought some bars of soap as a present for his mother; now the bath smelled of lilac.

"No, young master, but I've heard of it. The Gauls use it to tint their hair, I've heard. It's supposed to be very costly."

"Not in Hesperia." Wallowing in one end of the wide, shallow pool, Aquilius soaped himself and scrubbed with a cloth. Achilleus looked doubtfully at the clumps of foam drifting about on the water. "When all this trouble is over, I think I'll start us making it. It's much pleasanter for bathing than oil."

He submerged, then stood up and stepped out. Achilleus rinsed him from a tall red-glazed jug, and then wrapped his young master in a large towel. "No oil, young master? It hardly seems worth the trouble of bathing if you're not to be rubbed down and oiled."

"Hesperia changes even the oldest habits, Achilleus. I don't even want oil on my hair." Sitting on a stool while a scandalized Achilleus dried and combed his hair, he switched to English. "What are we going to do about Brewster?"

"I'll interrogate him again."

"And if he doesn't talk?"

"He'll tell me what I need to know."

"And if he doesn't?" Aquilius persisted.

"We'll have to go into Rome to see things for ourselves."

Aquilius rubbed his lower lip. "I will be very happy if Brewster talks. My father will need me, and Rome will be dangerous."

Pierce nodded. The proscription would have the whole city in chaos. Better to walk into a well-ordered enemy fortress than into an anarchic city.

He stepped from the bath, feeling better with the last day's dust and grim washed from him. The bath towel was coarse and thin, but adequate. He was glad Aquilius had brought the soap; in his first trip to Ahania, he had ventured into public baths but had not enjoyed them. To his heightened senses, the scrape of a strigil over his oiled skin had been almost painful, and he had felt no cleaner afterward than before.

In his bedroom Aquilius changed into the Praetorian uniform. He emerged looking persuasively military. Pierce contented himself with his old tunic.

"Now let's go talk to Brewster again."

They took the Militant out into the peristyle garden and sat him on a stone bench with his hands still tied behind him. Pierce sat on a bench opposite. Brewster's cheek showed a darkening bruise.

"Dennis, I want to know just who's involved in the translation team. Each person's name."

"I'm not talking."

"That's all right." He thought for a moment. He had not seen the files on all six thousand exiled Militants, but he had those of the hundred or so elite firmly in memory.

Calmly, his eyes fixed on Brewster's face, he began to recite their names. Each time he saw the subliminal response, the expansion or contraction of the irises, the faint shift in muscle tone around the mouth, he knew he had identified another translator. All told, he found eleven through Brewster's responses to the names he spoke. One name in particular, Maria Donovan, had provoked an especially strong reaction: recalling her photograph, Pierce wasn't surprised. She was almost 180 cm tall, spectacularly blond, and the daughter of one of Martel's martyred early supporters. Pierce supposed Dennis had a crush on her.

"All right, thank you."

"I didn't tell you anything. I didn't!"

"We minions of Satan have our methods, Dennis. Now for the Crucifers. I'll bet they're really nice guys by now." He saw Aquilius frown, and explained: "Muscle boys. Goons. Martel's hit teams. Probably the guys who killed Domitian, right, Dennis?"

The instant's distraction was all Brewster needed. He launched himself headfirst off the bench and butted Pierce on the right cheekbone with startling force. The shock was aggravated by Pierce's enhanced senses, and he blacked out for a moment. Reviving, he saw Brewster freeing his hands from the leather strap and dropping Aquilius with a hard left to the jaw. Brewster spun and ran from the peristyle, crashing through the kitchen and out the back door.

The weapons are out there . . .

Pierce was up and running, reaching for the Mallory in his shoulder bag. In the tiny kitchen the cooks were screaming hysterically, clutching one another; they screamed louder at the sight of Pierce and the look on his face.

In the back yard Brewster already had an Uzi in his hands, and was efficiently slamming a clip into it. His face was oddly tranquil. He looked up and met Pierce's eyes. Then he began firing, from the hip.

On full automatic and maximum impact, Pierce's Mallory fired a spray of flechettes. A row of dust clouds puffed into existence along the wall behind Brewster; then the flechettes struck him and threw him backward. The roar of the Uzi cut off. Brewster struck the wall not far from the back gate, and bounced forward to fall face down in the dust.

The silence was broken first by squawking chickens, then by the cooks' renewed wails, and last by the shouts of the villagers out in the meadow. They came hurrying in, evidently more curious than afraid, and gaped at the torn corpse.

Pierce walked slowly out into the yard. When he glanced back, he saw the line of bullet holes the Uzi had gouged in the brick and plaster near the kitchen door. Another fraction of a second and the bullets would have torn him in two, and probably one or two of the cooks as well.

Aquilius, standing a couple of meters behind Pierce, spoke to the villagers: "Strip the body and finish the burial. When you're done, cover the grave so it looks undisturbed. If more soldiers come, and find this grave, they'll kill everyone in the village."

Pierce sat on a wooden bench outside a shed. Aquilius sat beside him, his face solemn and his cheek swollen.

"I should have seen him coming. I should have stopped him," Aquilius said; he sounded angry with himself.

"You couldn't have. We were slack; we should have checked his wrists." He drew a breath and let it out slowly. *Take nothing for granted, for Satan lies in wait for the self-satisfied.* The morning sun was warm on his face. Flies were already finding Brewster as the villagers, muttering to one another about the corpse's terrible wounds, stripped his body.

"If he'd only talked, the job would be over."

"Mr. Pierce, I want to find my father. Do you still need to go into Rome? Don't you know enough?"

"Almost. But we need to know just how well they're doing, what the population thinks, who's resisting—a day or two ought to do it. Then we'll head north and you can catch up with your family. It won't take you long on a bike." He rubbed his forehead.

"Aquilius, would the cooks have any dried apples?"

Before noon, Sulpicius had led the rest of the slaves and Custos the watchdog out of the estate and up into the hills on the east side of the valley. Achilleus had buried a few special family treasures under one of the sheds: the death masks of Aquilius's forefathers, a small and beautiful portrait of his grandmother, a dozen books.

Pierce chose two bicycles, sturdy Schwinn mountain bikes especially designed for the Roman market, and let the villagers take the others. A thought struck him, and he turned to Aquilius.

"Do you know how to ride a bike?"

"Of course! We all learned during our fourth week of Training. And I'd ridden a little in Rome."

They walked the bikes out through the front gate; Aquilius locked the gate and tucked the key into his bag. A few villagers stood nearby, Petronia among them. The old nurse marched up to Aquilius.

"You look more like a soldier than the Praetorian *latrones* did. You've defended the hearth of your forefathers, and I'm proud of you. You're as brave and handsome as your honored father." She kissed him noisily, making him blush, and whispered hoarsely in his ear. "Now, don't worry about the villa. We'll see that it comes to no harm, and if they send any more soldiers, we'll say you've gone away to Capua to join your father." She cackled.

Aquilius took her hands in his. "Farewell, Petronia. May we meet again soon, and happily."

They rode down another path, not the road they had taken from the Via Flaminia. It wandered west and south, climbing the side of the valley through groves of oak and pine, and then followed the ridgeline south.

"We'll meet the Via Flaminia at the fifteenth milestone," Aquilius said. "After that, we'll be in Rome within an hour. Unless we run into more Praetorians or Militants."

"I'm afraid we will," Pierce answered. He was thinking about Michael Martel emerging through the smoke of a fireworks display with his voice booming through a loudspeaker while the Romans bowed in awe, and people like Dennis Brewster waited to launch a massacre. Now the massacre was under way and they were hurrying into it.

Nine:

Once out of the valley, they found themselves in more densely populated country: farms, villages, brickyards, quarries, and sawmills. The hillsides were bare, dotted with stumps and gouged by erosion. Peasant girls, many carrying baby sisters and brothers on their backs, prowled along the roadside looking for anything that would burn; cooking fuel was scarce. Pierce recalled that the Hesperians had suggested burning coal, but nothing had yet come of it.

The narrow dirt roads were crowded with wagons drawn by donkeys or oxen; Pierce and Aquilius often had to get off their bicycles and walk around a line of slow-moving wagons hauling bricks or gravel. Peasants and artisans watched them with interest: bicycles were still a great novelty.

As they neared the Via Flaminia, Pierce pulled up alongside Aquilius. "I meant to tell you: You did well against the Praetorians."

Aquilius nodded, pleased and not trying to show it. "It was my first serious fight."

"Your father would have been proud of you. You were very calm and collected. How do you feel about it now?"

He thought for a moment, a handsome young man with sunshine gleaming in his black curls. "It was easier than I'd thought it would be."

"That was how I felt, too, after the first time."

"Next time I want to be closer. It's not really brave to hide in ambush and kill people who can't even see you."

"Bravery is like money. Spend it when you must, and save it when you can."

Aquilius looked offended. "That might impress a shop-keeper, Mr. Pierce, but I don't think of courage as money."

"I stand corrected."

"I do not mean to be disrespectful. You have not had the benefits of a Roman upbringing. Do uptimers feel sick after their first kill?"

"Often."

"I did not, and you did not. You enjoyed it?"

"I suppose I did. Yes."

They began a long glide down a hill, Aquilius ringing his bell to drive off a herd of goats while their herder, a dirty-faced boy, gaped at their speed and magnificence.

"Now you've killed many people."

"Depends on what you means by many."

"Do you still feel good?"

Pierce looked at him and grinned. "I call it zapping bad guys."

"Do you still feel good?" Aquilius persisted.

"Not as good, no. When I go back, they'll shoot me full of drugs and block this morning out of my memory."

Aquilius's jaw dropped. "You'll forget what happened?"

"Not entirely. But it won't seem very important."

"They have done this to you before."

"Many times."

"Uptimers are very strange."

"No doubt."

Pierce was both amused and alarmed. Downtimers often had a far more casual attitude to life and death than even the toughest twenty-first-century thugs. That was why Robinetti had called the Romans psychopathic, and he had not been the only one. Pierce wondered if the Agency would eventually use only downtimers for this kind of job. Probably not; prejudices died hard, and endochronics were endochronics.

They stopped at a *mansio* to rest. Aquilius's uniform

and their bicycles had a dramatic effect: the manager hurried to supply a table in the shade of a poplar, and a flagon of wine. Aquilius bought some bread and cheese, and a bowl of olives.

"What's the news from Rome today?" he asked.

The manager, a potbellied man in a greasy blue tunic, smiled nervously. "Much turmoil. You come from the north?"

"Yes. We've heard about Domitian."

"Indeed. Your comrades in the Praetorian camp are proclaiming a new emperor today, so I'm told."

"Trajan?" asked Pierce.

The manager shook his head and smoothed his thinning hair. "Someone I've never heard of, good masters. A person named Martellus. No doubt we'll hear more before long. Another flagon?"

"No." Aquilius tossed a handful of coins on the table and stood up. "We must hurry."

"I'll say this for the new fellow," said the manager. "He's a real Titus to the Jews."

Pierce, who had also stood, paused for a moment. "How so?"

"Why, the deified Titus razed Jerusalem, and this one's driving them out of their houses in Rome. About time, I think."

"Tiberius did the same," Aquilius said. "He sent four thousand to Sardinia."

The manager grinned. "This fellow's just killing them."

They pedaled out onto the road. In the early afternoon, most travelers had stopped to eat and sleep; Pierce and Aquilius had the road to themselves for long stretches.

After a few minutes they overtook a heavy ox-drawn wagon heading south. Three soldiers stood in the back, guarding a huddled crowd of women and children, most of them well dressed and with the bedraggled ruins of careful coiffures. Pierce met the eyes of one of the women, and realized they must be prisoners; he paused, gripped the side of the wagon, and let it pull him along on his bike.

"Hail, friend," he said to the driver. He was another

soldier, stubble-faced and squinting. "Who are these people?"

"Enemies of the new emperor, they tell me. Are you with that Praetorian officer?" Aquilius had dismounted and was walking his bicycle on the other side of the wagon.

"Yes; we're bound for Rome with dispatches."

"And we're bound for Rome with a lot of rich harlots and their brats," laughed the driver. His prisoners did not respond to the insult. The three soldiers in the back looked bored and tired. "They're friends of the Hesperians and the old emperor. Tried to run away when the fun started."

"How so, friends of the Hesperians?"

"They sent their children off to learn sorcery across the sea, or sold Hesperian goods." He looked again at the bicycles and cleared his throat awkwardly, sensing he might have offended dangerous people. Aquilius studied the prisoners' faces intently, but recognized none. Then he looked across the wagon at Pierce, who nodded and smiled.

"Are any of you women able to drive a wagon?" Pierce asked. They looked at him fearfully. Finally, one young woman, probably the slave of the older woman beside her, raised a timid hand. "Good girl!"

"What do you care?" the driver asked irritably. Pierce pulled his Mallory out and shot him at low impact. Two seconds later the three guards toppled over the back of the wagon. Pierce pointed to the slave woman.

"Get up here and turn this wagon around," he ordered quietly. "Head back north, or east. And good luck."

Round-eyed and terrified, the woman stepped up onto the driver's bench and grasped the leather reins. The two oxen reluctantly turned, aided by Aquilius.

The driver's mistress, a handsome woman with gray-streaked black hair, climbed up beside her maid. "You've done us a service." she said. "Give me your names."

"Another time, mistress," said Pierce with a smile.

"The men will be unconscious for about an hour. I hope that gives you enough time."

"We'll make sure it does. Come *on*, Vipsania, lay on that whip! Our thanks, gentlemen!"

Pierce and Aquilius waved, then dismounted and dragged the four unconscious men off the road and into the weeds growing between the gutter and a brick wall, where they would be less conspicuous.

"That could have been risky," Aquilius said as they headed south. "We were lucky not to be seen. Why did you do it? We might have gotten into a serious fight. The women are likely to be caught again anyway."

"I said we protect our own."

The crowded countryside, however industrialized, was still countryside; where the Via Flaminia entered the Aurelian Wall, Rome began. Aquilius stopped them a kilometer or so north of the Flaminian Gate. The road ahead was jammed with people, some trying to get into the city and others hurrying out of it.

"Why the crowds?" Aquilius asked a young man being carried in a litter by eight sweating slaves.

"The Praetorians are checking *every*one," the young man drawled. "Haven't you heard about the emperor?" He waved languidly as the slaves carried him north.

"We can't get into the city on bicycles anyway," Aquilius said to Pierce. "Not until nightfall. They'll recognize my uniform at once, and if they ask me what cohort I'm with, and I say the wrong thing, they'll arrest us."

"Would anyone recognize you personally?"

"My cousin Flaccus—but I doubt he'd be on guard duty. He's an officer."

"Then we'll talk our way through."

"And how shall we do that?"

Pierce shrugged and grinned. "I leave that to you."

Five minutes later they were at the gate, ringing their bells to clear a path through the crowd, and Aquilius was shouting for the officer in charge. A squat, bulging-eyed soldier stepped away from the five others who were blocking the gateway. He saluted Aquilius, who gave a perfunctory response.

"We have urgent news," Aquilius said quietly, forcing the pop-eyed soldier to lean closer. "Don't tell anyone, but there's been a full-scale massacre of our people up north. They walked into a trap. This German here brought word to me. We must get through to the Praetorian camp as quickly as possible."

"Who's been mass—"

"*Tst!* Hold your tongue if you want to keep it. Show no alarm. If your men get wind of this, or worse yet the civilians, we'll all be in the worst trouble of our lives." He grinned at the man. "Now show me a cheerful smile, and send us through. Very calmly."

"Who are you?"

"The emperor will be asking who *you* are, if you delay us a moment longer." Aquilius's smile faded just a little. Pierce stayed expressionless.

"Oh, well, then, go on through." The soldier forced a laugh.

"Good. We'll leave our bicycles here. See that they're not damaged."

They swung from their bicycles, and Aquilius led the way into the city.

"Very well done," Pierce murmured as they sank into the crowds. The Via Flaminia was now the Via Lata, Broadway, though it was little wider than most Roman streets. "One of the advantages of a coup is that no one really knows what's going on."

Aquilius looked pale. "I was sure he was going to stop us and demand answers."

"If he'd tried, he'd be dead." Pierce walked with one hand in his shoulder bag, fingers curled around the butt of the Mallory. "But you'd probably better get out of that uniform and back into your regular tunic."

Aquilius nodded. Pierce looked around as they walked down the narrow, flagstoned sidewalk, trying to gain a sense of the mood of the city. The usual late-afternoon bustle filled the streets: slaves on shopping errands hurrying in and out of shops, *tonsores* cutting hair and shaving people, idlers playing knucklebones on any clear patch of pavement. Merchants shouted at passersby, inviting them to see fine fabrics, good pots, rare spices, sizzling sausages. In a copyist's shop, fifteen slaves took dictation from a sixteenth as they wrote out some aristocrat's hendecasyllabic verses. Sunlight blazed on the many-colored painted stucco of the *insula* walls and on the graffiti that defaced them.

The little fish symbol was freshly scratched or painted almost everywhere, sometimes accompanied by the name *Christus* or *Chrestus*. Incongruously, posters had been plastered on many walls, drawing crowds who listened while some literate person read their text aloud; Pierce remembered the *dazibao*, the big-character posters that had been put up all over Shanghai in 2004 to protest the forced migration of a million Shanghainese to Vala.

"'. . . further proclaims that each soldier of the Praetorians shall receive a donative of eight thousand denarii,'" said the schoolteacher reading the poster. The crowd muttered, and someone said, "More taxes!"

"Not so," said the schoolteacher. He turned back to the poster, and went on reading in declamatory tones: "'The emperor, mindful of his people's needs, makes this donative out of his personal wealth. A gift of two hundred sesterii shall go to each Roman citizen living within the city, also from the emperor's personal wealth.'"

"If he's got that kind of money," a gap-toothed merchant said, "we'll see some fine games and shows." His grin settled on Pierce, and he gestured as if handling a sword. "Plenty of cold steel and hot blood, eh?" Pierce grinned back and sidled deeper into the crowd, where he could read the poster for himself.

The first part was a long and accurate account of the crimes and follies of Domitian, except that it claimed the Hesperians were *venerarii daemonem*, worshippers of demons who had goaded him into ever worse excesses and abuses. The Hesperians were a race of degenerate sorcerers, bent on corrupting and overthrowing Rome through trinkets and gewgaws, while using the Romans' own children as their agents. Now, at this moment of peril for the empire, the True God had sent priests to redeem Rome and return it to the *mos maiorum*, the old ways that had made her great. The new emperor, Martellus, was now both imperator and pontifex maximus, the supreme priest; into his hands the True God had placed divine powers to heal and slay.

In consequence of which, the Praetorians, seeing the manifestations of divinity in the person and acts of Martellus, had proclaimed him emperor and called on all Romans to acknowledge him as such.

Pierce and Aquilius made their way out of the crowd and continued down the Via Lata. A merchant intercepted them outside his shop, waving something silver.

"*Piscii, piscii*? Finely made, good sirs, of exquisite workmanship!"

They were silver pendants in the shape of fish, each on a silver necklace. Pierce laughed.

"Are you a silversmith or a fishmonger?"

"This fish won't smell, good sir, and it'll cost you far less than a real one. Five *denarii*, no more."

"Be off with you," Aquilius snapped, but Pierce touched his arm.

"We'll each take one." He counted out the coins while Aquilius looked annoyed, and then gravely hung one of the fish around his neck.

"You do the same," he said as the merchant went off after new customers.

"It's hypocritical and impious. I'm no Christian, Mr. Pierce."

"You're not a Praetorian either. We have an old saying: when in Rome—"

Aquilius snatched the necklace and tucked the fish inside his tunic.

They had gone perhaps three kilometers into the city when Aquilius led Pierce off the Via Lata and into a narrow lane running more or less east. It was almost a tunnel, with balconies and overhanging roofs blocking off the sky.

Washing hung from balcony railings, and drunks argued in storefront wine shops. Occasionally a woman looked down from her balcony at the handsome young Praetorian and his giant companion. But no one spoke to them; a kind of hush had fallen over the back streets of Rome.

As they neared the Viminal Hill, Aquilius paused by a fountain.

"This could be a mistake, Mr. Pierce. We're well known in our own neighborhood. If someone sees me, and the house is being watched, we could be taken."

Pierce nodded. "Give me directions; I'll take a look and be right back."

Aquilius had been right: The yellow-tiled house with its green-painted front was being sacked. The shops on either side of the front door were shuttered, and a line of soldiers and slaves straggled out the door bearing pieces of furniture, bags of smaller items, and even kitchen utensils. What looked like bullet holes pocked the plastered wall. Onlookers watched and joked, but none seemed willing to venture inside to join the looters. Pierce walked past on the far side of the narrow street and glanced casually through the door into the atrium. The place had been vandalized as well.

A soldier saw him looking. "Another enemy of the emperor," the soldier said cheerfully.

"Are they dead?"

"Just the house slaves. The old fellow wasn't in town. Cheap bastard he must be—this big fine house, and hardly a stick of furniture worth two sestertii."

"What if the new emperor's people want the house? Won't they want the furniture, too?"

"The new emperor is rich enough to furnish every house in Rome like old Nero's palace."

Pierce chuckled with the soldier, waved, and walked on up the street. At the first intersection he turned left and hurried back to Aquilius.

"They're in the house. The slaves are dead."

Aquilius went pale, and his eyes narrowed. His fingers gripped the pommel of his sword.

"They will pay. Oh, they will pay."

"More than you know, Aquilius. Now—where can we go? It'll be dark soon."

Aquilius seemed too angry to care to answer, but after a moment he turned north and led Pierce off the Viminal and into a low-lying neighborhood of decaying *insulae*. One apartment building had recently collapsed; a work crew was salvaging bricks and timbers, while local children scampered over the ruins looking for plunder. A whiff of putrefaction told Pierce that several bodies still lay under the fallen building.

"My father has a small *clientela*, mostly freedmen and men from the valley. I have little to do with most of them, but I know a few. We're going to find one of them."

The system, Pierce knew, had survived the empire's fall and would probably survive anything short of Doomsday itself. Every rich and powerful man in Rome attracted hangers-on, clients; in return for small pensions and gifts they provided an entourage, an intelligence network, a political claque. Each morning they would attend their patron, unless he himself was off paying respects to a still greater patron; the emperor himself was the the apex of a pyramid of influence, the patron of patrons, the godfather.

Aquilius's father, Pierce knew, had kept himself almost a recluse; yet even he had his connections. He would not have survived Domitian's long reign without them.

Between a wine shop and a *popina*, narrow stairs climbed up out of a passageway. Aquilius climbed slowly but confidently up the dark stairwell, while Pierce followed with his head low to avoid cracking it.

They emerged on the second floor and turned right along a wooden walkway overlooking a central courtyard. The building was superficially little different from tenements Pierce had seen in Mexico and Brazil. But the courtyard of a Mexican *insula* was common ground, a meeting place and playground for all its tenants, while here the courtyard was the private preserve of the wealthy renters on the ground floor. A couple of bedraggled cypresses reached for the sky; poppies bloomed white and blue in the flower beds. Cheap statues of Apollo and Venus stood on either side of a small fountain. Running water was a luxury not available to the upstairs tenants, Pierce knew.

Aquilius stopped before a door of rough-cut planks and knocked. A man's nervous voice replied: "*Quis?*"

"Marcus Verrus Tullio, it's Gaius."

Good, thought Pierce—he hadn't shouted out his full name. A place like this had no privacy and perhaps many spies.

The door opened; inside stood a small, frail man in a threadbare tunic that had once been white. His wrinkled face showed the signs of a recent attempt at a shave. He smiled uncertainly at Pierce, then pulled Aquilius inside and embraced him. Pierce followed and shut the door.

The apartment was a single room no more than three meters by five, with a ceiling too low to allow Pierce to stand upright. The only light came from a doorway opening onto a balcony overlooking the street. The floor was crudely tiled, the walls roughly plastered. The room was furnished with a tall Roman bed, a couple of low stools, and a small chest; out on the balcony a thin woman was cooking something in a small iron pot over a charcoal brazier.

"Antonia, look who's here!" Verrus drew Aquilius across the room, into the light. The woman looked up with real alarm on her pinched face. Her ankle-length *tunica recta* was patched and threadbare; somehow she reminded Pierce of his mother, when he had been a boy and she had been a single mother trying to keep him fed and presentable.

"Hush! Young master, please keep back away from the balcony. We're most honored by your presence, but it would be unwise for others to see you here."

"I understand, Antonia. We're sorry for intruding on you like this."

"Have you eaten?" asked Verrus. "We're just about to sit down to a small bite. My Antonia is a fine cook."

"We can't impose. But here—" Aquilius handed him

some coins. "Go downstairs to the *popina* and buy plenty of stewed rabbit, enough for all of us, and a jar of wine. And some bread. Good food in good company is a feast."

The little man was stunned by the quantity of money in his hand. "Of course, of course. Antonia, quick! Off downstairs with you, as the young master said. I'll look after the porridge."

Antonia's alarm softened somewhat. Taking the money from her husband, she dropped it into a leather purse on her belt and slipped outside. Verrus bowed and waved the two men into the stools, while he squatted on the balcony and fanned the charcoal.

"You return welcomed, but in an evil time," he said quietly; his voice was barely audible over the squalling of babies in the next apartment. "Have you been to your honored father's house?"

"My friend Alaricus has. He told me they've killed the household slaves. Now they're looting it."

"It is a frightful outrage. The best families in Rome are being slaughtered—it's like Sulla. Worse, it's like Nero. To proscribe a family as ancient and honored as the Aquilii—*infamia, iniuria*! And for nothing but showing friendship to the noble Hesperians. Young master, when I saw them break into your honored father's house yesterday, I wept that I could not attack them old and weak as I am."

"You are in danger also, Verrus. You're known as a client of ours."

"We are humble people, young master, of no consequence." He smiled weakly. "An old schoolmaster, married to a freedman's daughter. Indeed, if people see a young Praetorian officer visiting me, they may think us closely tied to this new emperor."

"Providing no one looks too closely at me," said Aquilius with a sour grin. "Verrus, we must ask a favor of you."

"After all the favors your honored father has bestowed on us, I shall be happy to do whatever I can."

"We need only spend the night here, and then to leave in the morning."

"But this wretched room is unthinkable for you!"

"More thinkable than a night in the streets, with real Praetorians roving about. We'll be quiet."

Verrus fanned the charcoal and thought. "Did anyone see you come in?"

"A couple of children across the courtyard. No one else, I think."

"Then we shall take the chance. In the morning, though, you had better leave well before dawn. This building is a rookery in the morning, prying eyes everywhere."

Antonia returned, shutting the door quickly behind her. She held a carved wooden bowl filled with a grayish stew; the aroma in Pierce's nostrils was pungent and savory. Tucked under one arm was a jar of wine, and under the other a large, flat loaf.

"Now we can celebrate the new emperor's accession properly," she said with an angry smile.

The food was good, though Pierce almost choked on the metallic taste in his mouth. His head was hurting again; sitting in the gloomy apartment, he was at least out of the glare of sunlight, but the smells of the building and the street below were overwhelming. Reaching into his shoulder bag, he opened the Pentasyn vial and quietly swallowed two capsules.

Verrus and his wife paid little attention to him, except to refill his bowl and wine cup. They asked Aquilius questions about Hesperia, but it was clear they had little real interest in it except as a source of marvelous devices. Aquilius, in turn, said little except that it was a land much like Rome but with many novelties. When he asked them about what had happened in Rome since Domitian's death, however, they became excited.

"The Praetorians have terrible new weapons," Verrus whispered as he shoved stewed rabbit in his mouth. "They look like ax handles, perhaps, but they make a thunderous noise and spit fire. Something comes out of them—someone told me it's like a slingshot, but no one ever hurled a stone like that."

"Where did you see them?" Aquilius asked.

"In your honored father's street. His slaves were killed with one. Just pulled out of the house, stood up against the wall in front of a soldier. He pointed it at them, and when it made such a noise I thought the slaves were jumping from surprise just as I was. Then blood gushed from their bodies though no one touched them with so much as a feather, and they fell dead in the street. Hundreds of us saw it."

Aquilius and Pierce exchanged glances. Pierce rubbed his face wearily. So they had indeed been bullet holes in the plaster. Another gift to Rome from her descendants. And Robinetti had thought the *Romans* were psychotics.

The next day or two would be very bad.

Ten:

Sundown was Roman bedtime. Pierce and Aquilius refused Verrus's offer of the bed and wrapped themselves in their cloaks on the wood-plank floor. It was hard, but Pierce had slept in worse places. Despite the rumble of iron-tired wagon wheels and the swearing of teamsters in the street below, he was soon asleep.

A thunderous explosion woke him and the whole city. While Verrus and Antonia called on the gods, Pierce went to the balcony door. It had been left slightly ajar, to give the room a breath of air.

The city outside was intensely dark, though the sky was strewn with stars. Pierce heard anxious voices calling from other balconies and windows; dogs yapped in the distance. In one or two windows across the street, lamps burned. Down in the street, a line of carts and wagons had stopped. Teamsters gaped upward.

The sky flared with light and a moment later another explosion echoed across the city. Pierce looked up in time to see glowing red streamers reach out into the darkness. A wavering spark climbed toward the zenith and exploded in blue flames.

"Fireworks," he said in English to Aquilius.

The young Roman stood beside him in the doorway, watching skyrockets splash and boom across the night sky. Before long, pale faces clustered on every balcony, looking up and gasping at each new bloom of burning light.

Verrus and Antonia had crept from their bed and now

stood behind Aquilius, who turned and smiled at them comfortingly.

"Don't be afraid. It's a Hesperian amusement, nothing more. But the Praetorians are using it to impress the people."

"An amusement?" Verrus looked appalled. "How can divine portents be an amusement?"

"It's true," Aquilius insisted. "They're not divine at all, Verrus. They're all based on something like Greek fire."

"No doubt you know best, young master." Verrus did not look persuaded. His wife looked up with a half-ecstatic expression on her face.

After half an hour the fireworks ended with a frenzy of multicolored explosions. Not long after, four men from the *cohortes vigiles* came tramping down the street with flashlights.

"All is well," one of them shouted. "The priests say the portents show heaven favors the new emperor Martellus. Rejoice, Romans!"

Pierce stepped away from the balcony. "They're doing quite well so far," he said in English to Aquilius. "Another few days and Martel may even have everyone behind him."

"I don't think so, Mr. Pierce. He won't have Trajan behind him."

"He'll get Trajan murdered, unless we can bring some of our troops here first." Pierce settled himself on the floor again. "Good night."

When he woke again, it was still dark. Verrus was touching his shoulder.

"It's time to go, Alaricus. Soon the whole *insula* will be awake."

"Thank you, Verrus." Pierce stood up and banged his head on the low ceiling. Again he felt better after sleep.

Aquilius had changed into his tunic the night before and was as ready to go as Pierce.

"You've greatly helped us, Verrus," he said. "We won't forget you."

"We have been honored by your presence. May we

meet again in happier times. Please give your honored parents the humble compliments of Marcus Verrus Tullio and his wife. And be very careful. The streets are full of brigands and *latrones*, not just the Praetorians."

"We shall," Aquilius promised him.

"Brigands and *latrones* are using the skies as well as the streets," said Pierce. "Don't let them deceive you, schoolmaster, or your good wife."

He smiled in the darkness at the sound of her indignant gasp. His mother had never let poverty frighten her into easy refuges; nor should this woman.

They slipped out the door and down the creaking stairs. At the bottom Aquilius guided them down a corridor, not out onto the street. They groped into a dark room that Pierce knew was the *insula* latrine. He found his way onto one of the stone seats arranged around the walls, and listened to the chuckle of running water below him.

Then they were out in the street again, heading east up the lanes of the Quirinal Hill. Near the top of hill they turned left on the Alta Semita, the High Path. It would take them northeast to the Nomentan Gate, not far from the Praetorian camp.

"If we can find my cousin, he may be able to tell us more about the takeover," Aquilius said as they dodged a wagon bound out of the city before sunrise.

"I want a look at the Praetorians' camp," said Pierce. "They've probably got most of their weapons there. The Agency will want as much detail as possible, so if your cousin can get us inside, good. If not, we'll spend the day looking around and then get out before sundown."

"Can we get past the guards again? It was easy with the bicycles and my uniform."

"Where lies fail, bribery usually succeeds."

The sun was rising into another lovely and cloudless spring day. The city was coming alive already: shutters banged back against walls, letting light and air into thousands of tiny rooms. Schoolboys were on their way to lessons, most followed by household slaves carrying their books. Women clustered around a bakery, buzzing to one another about the portents in last night's sky. But every now and then Pierce and Aquilius saw bodies sprawled dead in the street, a front door hanging half-torn from its hinges and the smell of smoke coming from inside. Onlookers, mostly young men in shabby tunics, stood chattering around the bodies.

"We'd better hurry," Aquilius muttered. "The gangs will be awake and back at work before long."

A few blocks farther down the Alta Semita, they met such a gang busily plundering a whole *insula*. They wore ordinary tunics, but had the look of soldiers—Praetorian *veterani*, Pierce suspected, men who had completed their basic sixteen-year hitch and were now enjoying four years of casual assignments before retirement. They were tossing people's clothing and furniture out of upstairs windows; some of the men wore gold necklaces that Pierce guessed had just been taken from their real owners. In several places inside the apartment block, women were screaming.

"More Hesperians?" Pierce asked one of the soldiers pawing through the loot on the sidewalk.

"*Iudaeii*. A whole building full of Jews."

"You're acting on orders of the new emperor?"

"*Certe.*"

"Look out below, Lop-ear!" a hoarse voice cried out cheerfully. The soldier Pierce had been talking to, whose left ear was missing, looked up, swore, and jumped out of the way. Pierce and Aquilius stepped back also as a body crashed from a fourth-floor balcony to the paving stones.

It was a girl not more than fourteen, naked, with her black hair done in ringlet bangs. Her throat had been cut. She had not been dead when her attacker had thrown her from the balcony, and now her dying eyes fixed on Pierce for a moment. He looked back with sorrow and compassion. Then she was gone.

"I'll kill that son of a *meretrix*," Lop-ear bellowed. "*Stultus! Ineptus!* Could've hurt somebody." Mocking laughter drifted down.

Aquilius paled; Pierce saw him reach for his shoulder

bag, and gripped him by the arm to hustle him on.

"That was infamous," Aquilius snarled. "He deserves death, he and all his accomplices."

"It's pointless. The building must be full of them. We could kill most, but for what? If the Militants know that someone's using Mallorys here, they'll hunt us down like rats."

"Let them try!"

Pierce kept them walking at a brisk pace, his hand still gripping Aquilius's arm.

"You saved the women yesterday," the boy said, "and used your Mallory."

"First, they were our people—families like yours, with Trainable children uptime. Second, it was outside the city; even if the soldiers report what happened to them, it'll be days before anyone realizes what happened." He grinned. "The soldiers might even make up a story about being waylaid by bandits. Better than admitting you don't know what hit you. But if we zap a whole mob of Praetorians, within a couple of kilometers of their camp, we'll have a real mess on our hands."

Aquilius looked angrily unconvinced. Pierce didn't blame him. The dead girl would be avenged in good time, but not until the Militants were neutralized. Then the Praetorians' turn would come.

The Praetorian camp was a square four hundred meters on a side, a walled encampment already over a century old. The Praetorians had once been generals' bodyguards; since Augustus, they were the emperors' private army, an evasion of the ancient law forbidding legions to be stationed within Rome. In the terrible year of the four emperors, before Vespasian had established the Flavian dynasty, the five thousand Praetorians had given the *imperium* now to this man, now to that, in return for bribes and privileges.

Martel had been wise, Pierce thought. He had gone straight to Rome's real masters and given them a bribe beyond their dreams: enormous power in this world and

salvation in the next. If Martel was not Roman, that made
no difference; Rome's first kings had been Etruscans. And
if he wanted to impose some strange religion on the empire, it was at least a religion that made a good show.

Pierce and Aquilius, part of the normal sidewalk traffic
across the street from the camp's western wall, casually
noted a few details. The sentries patrolling the top of the
brick wall were carrying AK-47s. From somewhere inside
the camp came the intermittent popping of rifle shots:
more Kalashnikovs, set on single fire. Pierce guessed the
Praetorians were being trained in their new weapons.

The sentries also had ancient walkie-talkies, or more
modern ringmikes, into which they self-importantly talked
at every opportunity. The western gate of the camp was
heavily guarded; only patrols were allowed to pass
through, or men in civilian tunics who were evidently
known to the guards.

"Looks as though most of their resources are right
here," Pierce murmured. "Now I really want a look inside."

"We could ask to see my cousin, but it could be very
dangerous."

"Indeed." Aquilius's cousin Flaccus might hand them
over to the Militants; if he was dead or imprisoned, anyone asking after him might be arrested on suspicion. But a
look inside might be obtained without ever entering the
camp.

Pierce looked through the curtain of painted wooden
beads that separated a *taberna* from the sidewalk. Even at
this early hour the place was full of drinkers. Nodding to
Aquilius, Pierce stepped through the beads. Aquilius followed. A few men looked curiously at them, then went
back to their wine and excited conversation.

With wine cups of their own, Pierce and Aquilius found
a corner and sat on a bench running the length of the
room. The other customers sat further down the bench, or
perched on stools, and were clearly off-duty soldiers: they
wore uniform-white tunics, but no armor or weapons except for sheathed knives at their belts.

"I'll thank old Domitian for one thing," said a soldier. "He kept good records on all his supporters, and especially those with children in Hesperia. Made our job as easy as killing ostriches in the arena. My squad alone must have finished off fifty or sixty yesterday, not counting the children. And the loot! Gold, silver, rubies, anything you like. Never seen a day like yesterday in my life."

"If your gang only got fifty or sixty, you'll have to work harder today to beat us," another man said with a laugh. "Our *decurion* kept tally. Seventy-seven adults and forty-two children in eighteen households."

"You lying pederast," the first man bellowed cheerfully. "Seventy-seven grandmothers sounds more like it."

"Some men are like that," Pierce murmured to Aquilius. "As soon as they've killed, they have to talk about it. I've never understood why."

Aquilius said, "Praetorians," very quietly in English, so that the wineseller and the other customers couldn't hear him. Pierce felt a faint alarm at the menace in the boy's voice. Aquilius was more than angry now: he was ashamed and eager to purge himself of it. "Praetorians. Raping and killing because a religious fanatic told them to."

Pierce said nothing at first, and took only a cautious sip of wine. It tasted horrible. He rubbed his bristling whiskers.

"*Salve*, friend," he said to the nearest drinker, a man who had so far been silent. "We're new in the city. Can you tell us what's happening?"

The drinker shrugged and smiled. "A change of government."

"You have the look of a soldier. Are you a Praetorian?"

"I am." He was a wiry, hard-faced man with bloodshot eyes. Pierce suspected he'd been up all night and was now enjoying a quick drink or two before going to bed.

"Are the Guards all behind this change?"

"No doubt of that. This is the best new emperor since

the divine Augustus himself. A great age is dawning for the empire."

Aquilius had regained his self-control. He got up, bought a pitcher of wine, and brought it back. Pouring the Praetorian's cup half-full, he topped it up with water from a jug on a nearby table.

"Astonishing," said Aquilius, "that Martellus and a hundred men could take Rome itself."

The soldier chuckled over the rim of his wine cup. "*Bene facis* for the wine, young fellow. But it was a few more than that. They say they have five thousand, as many as our own Guard. Not all have yet come here."

"Where do they come from? How have they achieved this miracle?"

"Martellus says they came from a land beyond the silk country, led by a sacred spirit. For my part, I don't care where they're from."

"You don't care that they're not Romans?"

"We decide who's Roman and who's not. Besides, this fellow's raised our pay to 1600 denarii—more than double what that *stultus* Domitian paid us. And a donative of 8000 denarii, five years' pay all in one lump! If he's not a Roman, send us more like him, I say." He laughed and drained his cup.

Pierce watched Aquilius's anger rising again.

"Praetorians are murdering people in their beds," the boy said coldly.

The soldier nodded, not at all offended. "The new emperor is smart. Give the old emperor's men time to catch their breath, and they'll be murdering *us* in our beds."

Pierce broke in, eager to avoid a quarrel. "Do you think he's divinely inspired? The *cohortes* last night were saying the lights in the sky were a sign from God."

The drinker looked serious. "The sign from God that I trust is his weapons. Ever seen what a *tormentum* can do? You stand off a hundred paces and kill a man before he even knows he's in danger. Only the first cohort's got them so far, but they're promising us more before long."

"So Marcus Ulpius Traianus had better stay with the legions in Germany," said Pierce.

"Ah. He's a good man, a fine man. If he's wise, he'll come over to Martellus. If he's foolish, he'll pay with his head. And his eternal soul."

"Then you have become a follower of Christus as well as a follower of Martellus."

The soldier grinned crookedly and pulled a chain out of the collar of his tunic. A small silver cross gleamed on the chain.

"He told us, in this sign we would conquer, and he was right. I used to be a Mithran, but I've seen the light."

Pierce, smiling back at the soldier, showed him the little silver fish on his own necklace. Aquilius unsmilingly did the same.

"Greetings, brother," Pierce said. "Please excuse my bad Latin. I am from the far north of Germany. I rejoice to meet a fellow believer. My friend and I have been uncertain whether the Praetorians had truly found Christus. Thus our questions."

"Well, well. More Christians than bedbugs in Rome these days."

"Yet tell me this, brother," Pierce went on. "Have all the Praetorians gone over to Martellus and Christus? Surely many must have been allies of Domitian and the Hesperians."

"Not many. A few. We've got rid of them. Anyone who owed anything to the old emperor or the sorcerers . . ." He drew his thumb across his throat.

From the corner of his eye, Pierce saw Aquilius slump a little. Asking specifically about his cousin would be pointlessly dangerous; Flaccus in any case was surely dead.

"And what of the sorcerers themselves?" Pierce asked. "Have they truly all been slain?"

"I think a few were saved for questioning. We'll get the rest soon—the ones out in the provinces, looking for more youths to kidnap. Have you seen their embassy since we sacked it? Martellus has opened it to the public.

The fruit trees have a good crop of heads." He roared with laughter.

"That must be a fine sight indeed," Pierce said gently. His head hurt, and the soldier's sweaty smell overwhelmed even the resinous aroma of the wine. "We shall go at once to see it. *Vale, frater.*"

"*Valete, fratres.* And thanks again for the wine."

Out on the street, neither man spoke for a time. At last Aquilius muttered: "A little longer and I would have killed him. But I'm beginning to understand some of the history I learned uptime."

"Then you're doing better than most of the human race. Actually, killing him would have been ungrateful after all the help he gave us. Only one cohort has firearms."

"Five hundred men is still a great many."

"But we know which cohort, and where it's stationed in the camp." The first cohort would be quartered near the center, alongside the commanding general's headquarters. An I-Screen could be opened up inside the general's tent if need be, or in the middle of the first cohort's barracks.

"What now, Mr. Pierce?"

Pierce thought a moment. "I want to take a look at the embassy, and then get out of town. Tomorrow night I'll beep the helicopter."

"And I will head north to find my family."

"It might be easier and quicker to come back with me, and then return with the troops."

Aquilius shook his head. "Too much could happen before then. I would rather stay here."

"I understand . . . but promise me something."

"Yes?"

"Don't kill anyone except to defend yourself."

"I promise. When the Militants are overthrown, then we will have our own proscription."

"That will be decided by our masters."

They were climbing through a labyrinth of narrow streets toward the Servian Wall, an ancient rampart that had once enclosed the whole city. Traffic thickened as they neared the Porta Viminalis, one of the few gateways through the rampart; many people were on their way to see the Hesperians' heads. At the bottleneck of the gateway itself they stood patiently waiting. Beyond were the gardens of Maecenas, the embassy grounds; Pierce could smell charred wood when the wind was right. He would do a quick survey as part of the gawking crowds, then slip away out the Tiburtine Gate to the countryside east of the city. Tomorrow he would be in Geneva, being deBriefed. Soon the Gurkhas would be showing the Romans and the Militants some real fireworks.

The blow from behind was quick and utterly unexpected. Pierce felt his legs crumple under him, but he was unconscious before he hit the pavement.

Eleven:

His eyes opened as he was already struggling to his feet. The same people were standing around him; the Servian Wall, stained with mold and weather, still loomed over them. But now the people were looking at him, showing concern or alarm or amusement. To Pierce they seemed like faces from a dream recalled years later.

His head and neck ached, and his legs were scratched and muddy. Something sticky trickled down his scalp.

"Two men," a woman told him. "*Latrones, raptores*. They struck you and the youth beside you. Ah, it's a terrible thing, all this crime in the streets."

Pierce looked around: Aquilius was gone. "Where is my friend?"

"The youth? He set off after them. Down there." She pointed down a dark lane.

Pierce swayed, touched his scalp, and looked at his bloodied fingers. His shoulder bag was gone: the Mallory, the survival kit, the Pentasyn, the beeper. He smiled and almost laughed. The Agency hit man, reflexes quickened, senses enhanced, armed with enough weapons to wipe out a legion—mugged by local talent.

"What did they look like? The men who robbed us?"

Everyone gabbled at once, each contradicting the others. Pierce nodded, smiled, held up his hands. Then he turned and headed down the lane. Each step made his head hurt. Careful: He might actually catch up with the robbers, and be knocked unconscious again.

The lane seemed to go on endlessly, two brick walls

interrupted by occasional doorways. Balconies overhead helped to block what little sky showed between the buildings. The lane itself was a strip of mud and garbage. It branched, branched again; he chose turns at random.

Eventually Pierce found himself in a little square, then in a wider street beyond it. He turned back, searching through back streets and alleys. The people there looked at him with indifference, as if tall men in bloodstained tunics often reeled past.

"Have you seen two men, running, with leather shoulder bags?" Pierce asked a boy. The boy shook his head and sidled off.

For the rest of the afternoon Pierce roved across the neighborhood. Once a patrol of the urban cohort stopped him, heard his story, and laughed.

"Big fellow like you, robbed by a couple of gutter rats? Ought to be ashamed of yourself."

Pierce nodded; they let him go. He found a square with a fountain and rinsed some of the blood out of his hair. The shock of cool water cleared his head a little; his fingers probed the lump on the back of his head. The actual cut was a small one, and had finally clotted over. He squatted by the fountain and thought.

He was half a kilometer or more south of the Viminal Gate, and not far from the Macellum Liviae, a big marketplace. Just beyond it was the Esquiline Gate through the Servian Wall, and beyond that the southern wall of the Hesperian embassy. The Praetorian in the wineshop had said the grounds were open; perhaps he could get into the building and find a beeper, a transceiver, something that the helicopter pilot could receive and recognize. Failing that, a weapon of some kind, or even a few coins. Aquilius had been carrying most of the money they had brought from Vallis Viridis; Pierce had only a handful of *sestertii* in a little pouch tucked under his belt.

Despite the growing ache in his head, he considered possibilities: Aquilius might have caught up with the robbers, retrieved the shoulder bags, and could now be hunting for him. Or he had been killed by the robbers. Or he had given up and, empty-handed, was now searching for Pierce.

The most consoling alternative was that Aquilius had retrieved Pierce's bag, left the city, and turned on the beeper. If the helicopter from Sardinia picked him up and took him back uptime, Aquilius could make almost as useful a report as Pierce himself. Then the Agency would send troops through to the Praetorian camp, occupy the whole city, and wipe out the Church Militant. In the process they would pick him up and get him to Geneva.

That seemed highly unlikely. He had better assume that Aquilius was dead, the shoulder bags lost forever, and start from there. If the robbers managed to blow themselves up with his explosives, that would be some consolation.

Pierce turned south through the Macellum Liviae, ignoring the merchants selling grain, wine, and fly-swarming meat. At the Esquiline Gate the traffic was heavy; again he had to wait to get through. But no one was mugged, and the people around him seemed cheerful and relaxed. A few looked curiously at him, and he heard a couple of giggling women speculate on whether he was tall in all proportions.

Once through the gate, he walked quickly along the south wall of the embassy. If the Praetorians had assaulted this wall, it showed no signs of it. But when he turned north at the corner, and found himself in the square facing the main gate, the violence of the attack was clear.

Bullet holes pocked the plaster and bricks, and the heavy wooden doors had been torn out—probably by a battering ram, though the Militants could well have supplied their allies with a couple of plastic bombs. Blackened footprints on the flagstones showed where men had run through fresh blood; Pierce thought of the two men, Fred and Howie, who had escorted him inside.

He joined the steady stream of people going through the shattered gate past a quartet of bored-looking Praetorians. Many of the sightseers wore their best togas, and a few were surrounded by retinues of clients and bodyguards. Scores had crowded around the fruit trees, confirming the rumor that the trees now bore heads. Pierce recognized several, including Robinetti's and that of a young woman, a data analyst who'd supplied much of the information for Pierce's Briefing.

Between the fruit trees and the main building, a crew of carpenters was noisily hammering a ten-meter wooden frame: it would be a cross, once erected, and would doubtless be overlaid with fine wood or even slabs of marble. Until Martel found time to build a proper monument to his victory, Pierce thought, the cross would serve quite well.

The embassy building itself was gutted. Maecenas's old belvedere tower was scorched and bullet-scarred. The original part of the palace had evidently been hit by grenades or mortars. The beautiful mosaic floors had been blasted in a dozen places, and wall paintings were blackened by smoke and blood. Many of the windows had had little panes of translucent glass; all were shattered.

Domitian's statue in the peristyle garden had been toppled and broken up. The wing beyond the peristyle had been systematically destroyed, demolished by plastic explosives and then burned to black rubble. The Praetorians must have had skilled help in the job. Nothing could be salvaged from it; anyone who tried would be seen at once by the gawkers or the scattered Praetorian sentries. In any case, the Militants had probably scavenged everything of value from it before burning it down.

Ah. Pierce almost swore out loud in anger at his own stupidity. The Militants would have beepers, transceivers, anything he liked; even the Praetorians had communications equipment. A ringmike or walkie-talkie wouldn't have the range to reach a helicopter off Sardinia, but the Militants' own equipment ought to be perfectly adequate for his purposes. And they would also have drugs like Pentasyn.

He turned away from the ruins and walked slowly out of the gardens, past the dangling heads and the excited sightseers. The beginnings of a plan were shaping in his mind.

From the once-beautiful gardens of Maecenas, it was a short downhill walk along the Clivus Suburanus into the stinking slums of the Subura. Pierce felt oddly comfortable there: The sheer numbers of people were a protection. He might encounter more muggers and street toughs, but now he showed no outward signs of wealth; he might be some rich man's German slave, on an errand after a recent beating by his master.

It was slow going, though. Little of the pavement was clear for foot traffic. Lacking sidewalks in this neighborhood, people spilled into the street not only to walk but to sell their goods and their bodies. Boys with painted faces looked at him with distaste and turned to gossip with one another until a likelier man turned up. Barbers trimmed their customers' hair and scraped their whiskers. A slave struggled through the crowds with a wicker basket full of live chickens on his head. Squads of bodyguards shoved through, clearing paths for their masters. A few idlers gaped uncomprehendingly at the printed posters the Militants had put up, but Pierce overheard no conversations about Martellus or the new ascendancy of the Christians. This was the Roman proletariat, too busy finding its next meal to worry about politics.

He passed through street after street after street of diseased beggars, gaunt whores, ragged children with the potbellies of near-starvation. The *insulae* here were even more decrepit than most, though here and there some great family's palace stood incongruously amid the neighbors' tenements. Pierce reflected that Julius Caesar, who had owned hundreds of gladiators, had lived in the Subura just as many American gangsters had remained in their familiar slums even as they became millionaires.

A funeral procession was leaving one of the richer houses, a yellow-tiled fortress. Among the line of mourners were men wearing clay masks: the death masks of the family's ancestors. The dead person would be entombed in the family vault, probably in one of the cata-combs or *hypogea* outside the city. Pierce smiled faintly to see many members of the procession carrying crude crosses; the family was almost surely not Christian, but was taking no chances.

At last he was out of the Subura and passing the Fla-vian Amphitheater where Domitian had died just three days ago. The sooty statues of goddesses and nymphs in the niches of the Amphitheater's wall gazed blandly out over the squalor of the Subura and the fifty-meter-tall Co-lossus. Across the wide street was a lower wall topped with iron spikes: The gladiators' school. A cheer rose from beyond it: The school contained its own arena, where the fighters trained. Pierce wondered if Martel planned to continue gladiatorial fights, or to ban them as the Church on Earth had done in the fourth century.

Well, with any luck he would never have the opportu-nity to rule on gladiatorial policy. Pierce walked round the Amphitheater to the south and climbed up the streets of the Palatine Hill toward the palace of Domitian.

Vespasian and his older son, Titus, had lived relatively simply while building magnificent forums and temples for the public. Domitian had relapsed into Nero's fondness for private luxury, and his palace reflected what could be done by a psychopath with delusions of divinity and un-limited resources.

The plans of the palace, and a few recent photographs, had been included in Pierce's Briefing. In the yellowing light of late afternoon, however, the palace seemed almost dreamlike: a man-made hill of gilded pillars, enormous tiled roofs, and marble walls. It had engulfed earlier pal-aces like that of Tiberius and Augustus, though it was far smaller than the Golden House which Nero had built, and which the Flavians had demolished to make room for their Amphitheater. No doubt intentionally, the architect Ro-birius had designed the palace so that all its north-facing windows and terraces overlooked the Amphitheater.

Pierce walked steadily across a flagstoned terrace to the north wall of the palace and a narrow, heavily guarded gate. Six Praetorians, all with Uzis, watched him approach.

"Greetings, brothers. My name is Alaricus. I am a German warrior. Tell me, if you will—among the followers of the emperor Martellus, is one a tall woman with yellow hair and blue eyes? And is her name Maria?"

The squad leader looked uncertain. "I've seen such a woman—a giantess, near as tall as yourself. She dresses like a barbarian, in trousers. Speaks pretty fair Latin, better than most of the emperor's people. What of it?"

Pierce clasped his hands prayerfully under his chin. "I am commanded to serve her."

The squad leader grinned. "I wouldn't mind serving her myself, for all that she's a head taller than I. Well then, friend, and who commands you to this pleasant duty?"

Pierce crossed himself. "The Father, the Son, and the Holy Spirit." A little awkwardly, the Praetorians repeated his gesture. "Far in the north I was given a vision," Pierce went on. "I have come south in search of her whom I saw in that vision. Is she not within this palace?"

"Well, I think so."

Pierce shouted "Alleluia!" and fell to his knees on the paving stones. "Here shall I wait until she condescends to favor me. Here begins my service to the emperor through his true servant Maria."

The Praetorians looked at him with a mixture of amusement, contempt, and anxiety. The squad leader shook his head.

"You can't stay here, barbarian. The emperor and his highest friends pass they way. Can't have you blocking traffic. Get on with you." He poked Pierce on the shoulder, not hard.

Pierce snatched the squad leader's hand in both of his and refused to let go. "Oh, friend and brother, I implore you! Only send a message to the lady Maria. Let her come to hear of my vision, and if she sends me away I shall go in all obedience. I ask nothing more."

Alarmed by the strength in Pierce's grip, the squad leader tried to free himself, failed, and glanced sidelong at his men. He would risk their veiled contempt if he stood here much longer in this demented barbarian's grip.

"Enough! Priscanus, get inside and find the lady Maria. Tell her we beg her presence for a moment only. Now let go, friend."

"Christ Himself shower blessings on you!" Pierce shouted, releasing the man. He remained on his knees, ignoring the pain. The Praetorians turned away and talked quietly among themselves.

The wait was a long one; sunset was red in the west before the soldier Priscanus returned. With him were two people, a man and a woman.

Bingo, thought Pierce.

The man was Willard Powell, who'd been one of Martel's closest associates before the deportation. He was a compact man of medium height, wearing a Roman tunic and a holstered pistol. Pierce noticed Powell hadn't shaved his sandy beard; he was very sensitive about his weak chin. His deep-set brown eyes studied Pierce with suspicion and little interest.

Beside him was Maria Donovan, whose name Pierce had mentioned to Dennis Brewster. Martel had made her one of his translators, and Pierce wasn't surprised to find her in the emperor's palace. She was a tall blonde in her middle twenties. Her father had been one of Martel's earliest martyrs, and she had grown up in the Church Militant. First as a mascot, then as a public symbol, she had enjoyed more freedom than most Militants. The Agency's psychological profile on her indicated a much tougher person than she appeared, but with a childlike faith in Martel's theology.

She was the first Militant Pierce had seen who paid no attention to Roman dress. Instead of a gown, she wore khaki trousers, calf-high boots, and an olive-drab shirt open at the collar. On each sleeve, about where a sergeant's chevrons would go, a cross was stitched in yellow thread: So she was a Crucifer, one of Martel's goons, as well as a translator. Like her companion, she wore a pistol, a Ruger .357. It did not seem outsize for a woman nearly as tall as Pierce.

He looked at her, smiled, and prostrated himself. "Praise Christ and His most noble servant the emperor Martellus! O lady, in the forests of the north I was granted a vision of your face. Angels commanded me to hasten south to this city, to serve and protect you. I now know they showed me a true vision, and I ask only to serve you."

Maria Donovan laughed—a musical, pleasant laugh. "Not so quickly, brother. Come, stand up. Tell me your name."

Pierce snapped to his feet. "I am Alaricus son of Thorus, my lady—a Goth."

"You speak good Latin for a Goth newly come from the forests."

"My lady honors me. I have been journeying almost four years, three years in the empire. Only three days ago did I reach Rome."

She frowned. "You say you had a vision?"

"Yes, my lady. It was just after my youngest brother was baptized—"

"Baptized? In the northern forests?"

"All my tribe are baptized, my lady." Pierce sounded surprised. "It is twenty years since the holy man came to bring us the good news of Christ's death and resurrection."

Maria Donovan turned to Powell, and said in English: "A Christian Goth? Willard, can you believe it?" Her voice had an east Texas twang.

"About time we found any kind of primitive Christian at all," said Willard. "They sure lie low."

She turned back to Pierce. "And how am I involved in this vision, Alaricus?"

"I was shown your face, my lady, and a voice spoke to me, saying, 'Seek the Lady Maria in the great city of Rome, and serve Christ through her. For she shall have need of a warrior in her battles for Christ.'"

"And you are a warrior?" She smiled, a little hesitantly.

Pierce stiffened a little, jutting out his chin. "We Christians in the north must be warriors, my lady."

"What are your weapons, Alaricus?"

"The short sword, the ax, the spear, and my bare hands, my lady."

"A boxer?"

"And wrestler."

"Show us how well you fight." She glanced at the squad leader. "Give him your sword, and pick one of your men to test him a bit. Nothing too rough."

The squad leader bowed his head and then handed Pierce a short sword. It was heavy but well balanced, with a grip a little small for Pierce's hand. One of the Praetorians, a rawboned man in his thirties with the look of a veteran, came to face him.

Without warning, the Praetorian lunged, bringing the sword up in a graceful rise that could have put its point into Pierce's throat. To Pierce the attack was lethargic and clumsy; he parried, then stepped forward and clapped the flat of his blade against the man's neck. Edge on, the stroke would have severed the man's jugular and vertebrae; instead, it knocked him sprawling. Pierce stepped back, wishing his head didn't hurt so much.

"Praise the Lord!" Willard exclaimed in English. "Maria, did you see that? The guy's really fast."

Maria called the squad leader over and spoke quietly to him. Pierce had no trouble overhearing: She wanted the remaining members of the squad to rush him from all sides, using the flats of their blades. The first man to hit Pierce would win a gold *aureus*.

The squad leader nodded, glanced at his men, and spun to face Pierce. The others fell into a pincer formation, closing in on his right and left.

Pierce stepped to his left, closing with the man on the right tip of the pincer. A kick to the groin doubled the man up; Pierce brought the pommel of his sword down the soldier's helmet with a clang, then shouldered him into the next man. As both went down, Pierce jumped past them to meet the squad leader. The two remaining soldiers were blocked by their leader for a few seconds. As the squad leader's sword approached, Pierce batted it aside, gripped the man's elbow, and flung him into the path of the remaining two. Three sharp slaps to face, neck, and armpit marked what would have been killing blows.

Willard clapped as Pierce took three steps backward and bowed to Maria Donovan.

"Well done, Alaricus," she said. "And you men, too, did well. You met a fighter trained in deadly skills."

"No wonder the barbarians conquered Rome," Willard murmured in English. "That's the pure Nordic showing here."

"He doesn't *look* very Nordic, but I like him. He's practically the first endo Christian we've found—"

"Come on, Maria—"

"Who hasn't converted in the last two days, and what's more he can take care of himself. I think he's worth using."

"Will Dear Michael approve?"

She laughed. "Approve a primitive Christian who can take out five or six Praetorians? Of course. Goodness, isn't this confirmation that Dear Michael's right? The early Church obviously isn't just a bunch of wimps."

Turning to Pierce, Maria Donovan said, "Brother Alaricus, we are pleased to see your skills. Come inside with us. We will share a meal and talk more about you."

"I shall do whatever my lady bids me."

To the Praetorians' surprise, Pierce hugged each of them in turn, and then followed the two Militants into the palace. He felt the old addictive elation: The bad guys were coming into range. An ancient spies' proverb said that if you live among wolves you must howl like one. He would howl until the time came to show his fangs.

Twelve:

Robirius, Domitian's architect, had been a master. Unlike the brick-built boxes of the *insulae*, light filled the palace. Every window seemed to open onto a different garden. Every wall not faced with marble was richly painted, and the floor of every room was a unique mosaic. Robirius had used poured concrete more than brick; walls were often curved, and some ceilings swelled into graceful domes pierced at the top to let in still more light.

The Militants were quickly making themselves at home. Workers in uptime civilian clothes were tacking wire screening over the windows to keep out mosquitoes. Generators were at work: Electric cables snaked along the corridors, and fluorescent lights glowed even in rooms where they weren't needed. Pierce heard the whine of an old-fashioned dot matrix printer, and telephones warbled incessantly.

Aware that Maria Donovan and Willard Powell were amusedly watching him, Pierce kept himself round-eyed and amazed. The act, he reflected, was easier than it should have been: The Church Militant was extremely well organized. The administrative infrastructure was already in place, complete with computers, filing cabinets, and desks. The Hesperian embassy had not been much better equipped, and it had operated in a windowless box rather than an imperial palace.

The halls were full of people, not all of them uptimers. Some were Praetorians, evidently advising their new masters on the resources of the palace and the city. Others looked like regular palace slaves, their faces downcast and frightened as they carried boxes of mysterious objects or trays piled with TV dinners.

Maria and Willard led him to a large room lined with bookshelves; the original scrolls were gone, replaced by loose-leaf binders, uptime books, and computer printouts. A small sallow man sat at a desk, watching a Polymath computer flicker at ten pages per second: Brother David Greenbaugh, a renegade Trainable. Pierce wished he could see the flickerscreen clearly, but Greenbaugh shut it down with a brief command and turned to face them.

"Actually found a Christian, have we?" said Greenbaugh dryly. He was still in his twenties but had lost much of his hair. Years of hardship on Albion had aged him as they had not aged Willard and Maria, making him seem very frail. But his eyes were those of a Trainable: quick, observant, hard and alive.

"He's a Goth named Alaricus," said Maria. Then, in Latin, she said, "This is Brother David, one of the emperor's closest advisers. Tell him your story, as you told it to us."

Haltingly, Pierce repeated his account of his vision and his journey south in obedience to it. Greenbaugh listened well, showing little sign of the Trainable's impatience with ordinary speech. When Pierce had finished, the first question came instantly:

"Who was this holy man who brought the gospel to your tribe?"

"We called him Christmanna. His own name, I think was something like Shimon or Shomanna."

"What did he tell you about himself?"

"Only that he had been sent by the Church of Rome to preach the gospel to the peoples of the north."

"Was he an old man?"

"I recall him as a young man, not tall, with a brown beard. But I was a very young boy when he came to us, and he stayed only two or three years."

"Did this Shimon preach to other tribes as well?"

"Yes, but only we listened. The Suebii nearly killed him."

"And why should your people listen when others did not?"

Pierce shrugged and grinned. "Perhaps Satan had preached to them first."

The interrogation went on, with Greenbaugh especially curious about the doctrines Shimon had preached. Pierce gave him a simplified version of Martelism, which sprang from Christ's statement that he had brought not peace but a sword.

"Shimon taught us that God had made us warriors, but we must choose whether to war for Christ or for Satan. Our chieftains chose Christ, and Shimon baptized them."

"What became of Shimon?"

"He went on to the east many years ago."

"And your people have had no contact with the Church since then?"

"You mean the Christians here in the south? No. We have been too busy converting our neighbors."

Greenbaugh smiled faintly. "And how do you convert them?"

"By the sword, of course."

"Very interesting," Greenbaugh said in English to Maria and Willard. "Could you follow that?"

"Yes," said Maria, and Willard nodded. "Isn't it fascinating! It confirms Dear Michael's revelations about the early Church teachings."

"It certainly does," Greenbaugh said. "The apostles here in the empire made a terrible mistake in preaching to the slaves. They should have gone straight to the army. This Shimon, whoever he was, understood that the true gospel would have to be taught to fighters. If the other apostles and missionaries had understood that, Rome would have been Christianized by now."

"But what happened to this fellow's people on Earth?" asked Willard. "Why didn't they convert all the barbarians?"

Greenbaugh shrugged. "Probably backslid. Without a

charismatic leader, the flock soon scatters. In any case, it won't happen this time around. We'll bring them into the fold; they'll be extremely useful."

"If they're all as good fighters as this one, we'll be truly blessed." Willard chuckled.

"That reminds me," said Greenbaugh, who then shifted to Latin: "Your tunic is bloodstained. Why?"

"This afternoon I was praising the emperor Martellus outside a house the Praetorians were purging of Jews. Someone struck me from behind and robbed me of what little I owned."

"And the Praetorians did nothing?"

"None were in sight at the moment. They came to my aid as I lay on the sidewalk, and when they heard my tale they sent me here."

That seemed to satisfy Greenbaugh. Before he could ask another question, Maria broke in.

"Brother David, what do you think of this man's so-called vision? Does it seem like a real revelation?"

Greenbaugh pursed his narrow lips. "Alaricus," he said in Latin. "How did you learn Latin?"

"I hired on as a boydguard for Gnaeus Ennius Minor, the son of the governor of Transalpine Gaul. The boy and his tutor taught me what little Latin I know."

Greenbaugh nodded. "Seems plausible," he remarked to the others. "His Latin's not very good, but he's got a patrician's vocabulary and he tries to pronounce words like a patrician." He smiled. "Sort of like a house nigger's English."

"Brother David," Maria said complainingly, "we're talking about a real live Nordic here, not some ape."

"Yes, Maria. But he is a barbarian, remember."

"He's a witness to Christ's Providence," Maria said intensely. "Our Pilgrimage was foreknown and Christ prepared the way for us, just as Dear Michael said. Oh, why should I feel surprised? Hasn't he been right every time?"

"Amen," Willard said. "Uh, Brother David, shouldn't we tell Dear Michael and the rest of the Elders about this?"

"Indeed. We'll put him on the agenda for tonight's meeting. Meanwhile, why don't you get him cleaned up and fed?"

Pierce allowed himself to relax slightly once they were out of Greenbaugh's sight. Trainables could pick up the subtlest nonverbal cues, and Greenbaugh might well have spotted some unconscious response or mannerism in Pierce and recognized him as a fellow Trainable. The renegade's long years among unTrainables, and the sudden transition to Ahanian Rome, had evidently blunted Greenbaugh's sensitivities. Even so, Pierce would avoid the man as much as possible.

But that computer would tell him everything about the Militants; if he could get access to it for even a few minutes, the Agency could wrap up this whole mess in a day or two.

Willard and Maria led him through more corridors and down a curving staircase of pink marble to the palace baths. They filled a series of rooms, paved with marble and decorated with statues and murals finer than anything Pierce had yet seen. The rooms all opened onto a garden; each room held a shallow circular pool of water about seven meters in diameter.

"The first pool," said Maria, "is tepid, the second is hot, and the third is cold. Scrub yourself with a sponge and this bar of *sapo*. We don't use oil, only this." She beckoned to an attendant, a little man with a big nose who seemed mortified at the sight of a woman when a man was about to bathe.

"Naso, give this man fresh clothing when he's finished, and take him to the servants' dining hall for something to eat."

"Certe, magistra."

"Alaricus, stay in the dining hall until you are summoned. The Elders will want to meet you tonight—including the emperor."

Pierce clasped his hands under his chin and looked alarmed. "My lady, this is too great an honor. I ask only to serve and protect you, and through you the emperor. Surely the emperor has weightier matters to attend to."

"Indeed he does. But if he chooses to see you, you will be ready."

"Yes, my lady."

They left him to Naso and the other attendants, who regarded him with cautious disdain. "Give me your clothing," Naso said in a voice not quite civil. "If the emperor is going to see you, we will make you as presentable as possible. Do you know what *sapo* is?"

"No."

"Our new masters are very fond of it. It's a kind of grease or tallow that makes a froth in water. No, don't laugh—try it and you'll see. It's not a bad cleanser, though it puts a dreadful scum on the water."

Pierce descended a flight of shallow steps into the *tepidarium*, the lukewarm pool. It felt wonderful; he settled onto the bottom, so only his head and shoulders were above water. The soap that Naso handed him was a slightly used bar of Ivory. He used it cautiously at first, even tasting it and then spitting while the attendants laughed.

"Everyone does that the first time," Naso said with a smile. "Don't use it on your hair; we have a different kind for that."

Another attendant, at Naso's gesture, climbed into the pool with a plastic bottle of Alberto VO5, poured a little in the palm of his hand, and rubbed it energetically into Pierce's hair. Pierce winced at the sting of shampoo on his cut scalp.

"Ah—did our masters do that to you?" asked Naso from the edge of the pool.

"*Raptores*. They took all I own except a few *sestertii* in a belt pouch."

"Well, you've done well to end up here, then, haven't you?"

"God has put me where He wants me."

"Oh, indeed, indeed. I must say God has certainly shown a changeable frame of mind lately. On the Ides of

May I was bathing the Lord God Domitian. Twelve days later I'm bathing a bloodsoaked German in the same pool. Another twelve days and who knows what might happen?"

"It's all in the hand of the Lord."

"That's exactly what makes me worry. Close your eyes and hold your breath." The attendant pushed Pierce underwater to rinse the soap from his hair, then pulled him up again. "Now please go on into the *caldarium*."

Another slave tended to Pierce in the scaldingly hot pool, while Naso continued to supervise. Finally Pierce plunged into the *frigidarium*, from which he emerged shuddering but refreshed. Naso handed him a large towel and a new dark-blue tunic.

"The fullers will clean your old one. Here's your belt and money pouch, and your shoes. They must have had to skin a couple of bulls to get enough leather."

"Only one; our bulls are very big. Is there a *tonsor* here?"

"I am he. Please be seated and I will shave you with a genuine Hesperian razor." He opened a small leather pouch and brought out a Wilkinson Rehonable.

Pierce gaped at him. "Do they allow idolatrous tools?"

"In grooming items our new masters seem most forgiving."

But he used no shaving soap, and the result was painful. Still, Pierce felt better for it. With his hair trimmed and combed forward, he looked a little more Romanized.

The sun was setting as Naso escorted Pierce down a series of staircases to a dark and smoky dining hall adjoining a kitchen. A taciturn cook handed him a bowl of stew that was mostly onions and garlic, with a few small bits of chicken. Naso ate the same, with gusto, and then led him back into a different part of the palace.

A broad terrace overlooked the Amphitheater and the slums beyond. Under the darkening sky, fires glowed in a hundred places. If anything, the noise in the streets below was louder than during the day.

"The Elders meet in there." Naso nodded toward a

doorway that gave onto what must be a large room. At the doorway four Praetorians stood guard with AK-47s. The windows had been screened; inside, electric lights glowed through the gauzy material of the curtains. Pierce could see the vague outlines of a long table and people sitting at it. A soft male murmur of voices drifted out into the warm evening.

Pierce drew a deep breath and let it out. With a clearer idea of just who was inside, and where, he might have been tempted to seize one of the Praetorians' weapons, break in, and kill as many of the Militants as he could. But Martel and his lieutenants protected themselves well; this was not the time or place for dramatics. He leaned against a marble railing, looked out over the city, and listened to Naso's whispered comments on the oxlike expressions of the Praetorians.

Time passed. Naso fell silent. The conversation in the room was too low even for Pierce's enhanced hearing. Mosquitoes whined about him. His head hurt.

Suddenly Maria's voice called out: "Bring in Alaricus."

"Good luck," Naso whispered.

The door swung open; another guard stood there, beckoning to Pierce. Beyond were the Elders of the Church Militant.

Six men, some in Roman dress and others in uptime clothes, sat around the table; in chairs along the walls were Maria and several others. They ranged in age from Greenbaugh's twenty-five to Elias Smith's fifty-seven. They had the look of men in power, a look Pierce had often seen, a look they must have had even on that first terrible night on Albion six years ago. They were masters, comfortable in their mastery. Pierce recognized them all, though he was struck by how much older they had become. The years on Albion had been hard on more than David Greenbaugh.

The one exception was Michael Martel. He sat at the head of the table in an uptime padded swivel chair, flanked by two Crucifers carrying Uzis, and he looked as splendid as he had back on Earth. He was tall and erect, broad-shouldered, with thick blond hair combed in the Roman style. His face was astonishingly beautiful, yet it showed nothing effeminate or weak: The underlying hardness in the man made his looks attractive to men and women alike. In the turmoil of the early years of the International Federation, when the Church Militant had first sprung from the ruins of the neofascist movements, Martel's physical presence had inspired mass hysteria. If his old fans could see him in a toga, Pierce thought, they'd go crazy again.

Smiling, Maria guided Pierce to stand at the opposite end of the table from Martel. Pierce immediately fell to his knees and lifted both hands.

"Praise God and His emperor! Allelulia!" he shouted.

"Stand, brother," said Martel with a slight smile. He leaned forward slightly, studying Pierce with interest. At thirty-eight Martel was too old to have been Tested, but Pierce suspected the man would have been Trainable.

"You are Alaricus the Goth. Sister Maria has told us how you came here speaking of a vision you had been granted, and a mission you had been given to serve the Church through her." His Latin was indeed as good as Dennis Brewster had said: He had caught the patrician cadence as Pierce had not.

"Yes, Emperor."

"And Brother David here"—Martel nodded to Greenbaugh, who sat at his right—"says you and your people were converted to the gospel by a missionary named Shimon. That you were taught to take up your sword in the cause of Christ."

"Yes, Emperor."

"We would like to know more, Alaricus."

The grilling began. Martel said nothing more, while Greenbaugh, Willard Powell, and the others took turns interrogating Pierce: where his tribe lived, who its chieftains were, how services were conducted, how the young were brought up in the faith. Powell was especially interested in the tribe's ability to make war: the number of warriors, their equipment, their tactics, their success against their enemies. Another Elder, Martin Armbruster, asked about the tribe's theology.

Pierce handled the questions slowly but without difficulty. His Briefing on Ahanian Rome had included a good deal of new information on the barbarian tribes of northern and eastern Europe; he even had a rudimentary vocabulary in three German dialects. Years as a senior Field agent had given him plenty of experience with false identities and cover stories. The questioning was far from intense: The Elders clearly wanted to believe him.

A silence fell at last. Martel looked around the table. "No further questions, brothers?" He seemed to nod at Pierce, but Pierce realized he was signaling someone at his back. An instant later he sensed someone stepping toward him. Crouching, Pierce spun to his right, and saw a Militant in Crucifer's uniform swinging a blackjack. The blackjack was already descending; Pierce clamped onto the Crucifer's wrist, pulled gently, and hauled the man off balance. The Crucifer reflexively put out his left hand to break his fall, while Pierce twisted the man's right wrist. The snap of his radius was clearly audible just before the man hit the floor.

"What'd I tell you?" Willard Powell exclaimed. "What'd I tell you? Isn't he something?"

"You are very quick, Brother Alaricus," said Martel. He seemed impressed despite himself. "You must be among the great warriors of your people."

"Emperor, you give me undeserved honor. I am much slower than most of my brothers and cousins. And it was just such an attack as this that put this wound in my skull today." He helped the Crucifer to his feet. "Brother, please bear me no ill will. I thank you for your sacrifice; may we stand together in battle for Christ."

"What's he saying, Brother David?" the Crucifer said through clenched teeth.

"He's apologizing for hurting you, Peter. Says he hopes he'll fight by your side some day."

"Praise God he's on our side," Peter said.

"Amen," said Greenbaugh.

"Well, Sister Maria," said Martel, "you've recruited a useful person. I'll assign him to you in whatever capacity you like. He'd be a good bodyguard, but perhaps you'll find other jobs for him."

"Maybe our first endo Crucifer," she said with a smile. "I can't wait to teach him something about guns." She turned to Pierce and switched to Latin. "The emperor has graciously accepted your offer of service. Henceforth you shall be my *satelles*, my bodyguard."

"Allelulia! Thanks be to God and to His emperor! Only tell me what I must do, lady."

"For now, come and stand beside me. When the meeting is over, we will assign you to a room and give you arms."

Pierce strode to her side, put his back to the wall, and folded his arms across his chest. He smiled proudly at the other guards and looked alertly about the room.

"Item six," said Greenbaugh. "The official accession to power. Brother Willard."

"We have a slight problem here, brothers. Uh, the Guards have proclaimed Dear Michael as emperor, all right, but the consuls and the senate seem to be stalling us. Officially, the consuls have to put the emperor's name to the senate for ratification, and the senate has to assign power to the emperor."

"Bad as the old days in Washington," said Martin Armbruster, triggering a laugh.

"I'm not arguing," Powell went on. "Problem is, we're going to have some trouble on our hands if we don't go through the motions. These people are amazingly like American idolaters—they don't care what you do to them, long as you do it properly. Now, we're the de facto government, but the mob could get nasty if it thinks we're not legitimate."

Elias Smith shook his head. "Brother Willard, we predicted the death of Domitian, we took out the IF embassy, we purged the Jews, we even put on the fireworks show last night. Doesn't that count for anything?"

"Brother Elias, it counts for a great deal. Even so, we've got a political hurdle to get over, and logistic hurdles after that. The senate only has to ratify Dear Michael, and that's the political hurdle. After that we've got to make sure the grain ships keep coming so all these people don't starve, and when all that's settled we have to get Trajan down here to settle that problem. But we can't do one thing until we've done the one before it. If we're not ratified, the governors in Egypt and North Africa will hold up the grain ships until they know who's really in charge here. If we can't feed Rome, we'll have riots on our hands. And if we have riots, Trajan could hold off until we're not a problem any more."

Another Elder, Matthew Knowles, raised his hand. "With all respect, Brother Willard, aren't you being awfully pessimistic? If we figure we can lick a couple of Roman legions, surely we can handle a few rioters."

"I'd like to think so, Brother Matthew. But just remember we've only got five thousand Praetorians and a couple thousand urban cohorts, plus maybe a thousand of our own people in combat-ready condition. This city's got over a million people, and a quarter-million are on the dole. They don't get their grain, they'll come looking for it. Maybe we could suppress them for a while, but don't forget the long-term political problem. When we're back in touch with Earth officially, the IF will try to discredit us any way it can. If they can blame us for food riots, or spitting on the sidewalk, they will. We've got to show them, and the people on Earth, that we're doing the Romans a lot of good. The legions are a simple problem compared to this one."

"So we've got to get the senate to ratify Dear Michael," said Elias Smith. "If the consuls won't cooperate, can't we have the senate appoint new ones?"

"We'd get ourselves into a premature civil war if we did. The original consuls could declare us usurpers, or recommend Trajan, and call on the senate to reject us. Now, I'm ready to do that if I have to, Brother Elias, but I'd rather do it nice and regular."

"So we have to work on these consuls a little," Smith said. "Especially Plinius. You know, on Earth Plinius persecuted the Christians of Bithynia in A.D. 113. The Lord took his life for it. Once we get him cooperating, we should send him to his reward a little early. Move we order General Drusus to seek out the consuls and bring them before this council."

"Second," said Knowles.

"Moved and seconded that General Drusus bring the consuls before this body," said Greenbaugh. "Discussion? Hearing none, I'll call the question. All in favor..."

Five hands went up. Martel, Pierce saw, did not vote. Maria jotted down a note in a steno pad. Reading over her shoulder, he saw that she and Powell were to be the ones to pass the word to the Praetorian general.

The meeting, closely following Robert's Rules of Order, went on to items seven, eight, and nine. Pierce listened and learned while pondering a frustrating question: How could he get to the consuls Plinius and Cornutus before the Praetorians did?

Thirteen:

Marie Donovan's Casio digital watch read 10:15 when the meeting adjourned after a brief prayer. Pierce's head hurt; he wanted to go to sleep.

"Come with me and Brother Willard for a moment, before we settle you in your quarters," she said. "We must have a word with Sextus Calpurnius."

"As my lady wishes."

Calpurnius was a centurion, the head of the Praetorian liaison group in the palace, with an electrically lit office not far from the north gate where Pierce had arrived that afternoon. Tall for a Roman, Calpurnius nevertheless had to look up to Maria and evidently didn't like the experience.

"The emperor commands that the consuls Plinius and Cornutus be brought before himself and his councilors."

Calpurnius looked at Powell and asked, "Does he wish it this night?"

"Perhaps the best idea would be to bring them to the palace tonight, to wait on the emperor's pleasure," said Maria with an edge in her voice. The Praetorian, still focused on Powell, raised his hand in salute.

"How long will it take to bring them in?" Maria asked. "And look at me when I speak to you."

Reluctantly and insolently, he did so. "Cornutus is at his country villa, outside Alsium; if I send some men tonight, they could have him here by tomorrow afternoon. Consul Plinius is in Rome, in his house on the Esquiline."

"Then go and collect him."

"If I may presume to advise, *domina*, the consul meets with the senate tomorrow morning. His absence might cause some confusion. Perhaps we might simply meet him after he leaves the senate."

Maria and Willard Powell looked at each other. "Makes sense," said Powell.

"Very well, Calpurnius. Ensure that a Praetorian escort is waiting for the consul at the senate. And get your men off to Alsium at once."

"Domina; dominus." Calpurnius bowed to Maria and Powell in turn. Maria nodded imperiously and left the Praetorian's office. Powell and Pierce followed.

In the corridor, Militants were still scurrying back and forth; hammering and sawing echoed off the marble walls. Maria led them into another section of the palace, far less ornate though still elegant: the staff quarters. Here fluorescent lamps gave way to bare electric bulbs, glowing at long intervals in the dark corridors. Maria knocked once on a door and then pushed it open.

The room inside was surprisingly large, illuminated by a single hundred-watt bulb burning above a table near the door. Extending into the darkness on all sides were tall shelves and racks, all bearing weapons: swords, spears, axes, daggers, shields, and helmets. Farther back in the darkness, Pierce could see and smell firearms—AK-47s, Uzis, and the special tang of AB-4 from Spanish wire-guided missiles.

Even more interesting to Pierce was a shelf of communications gear, some of it certainly scavenged from the Hesperian embassy. He saw several beepers and made a note to steal one at the first opportunity.

A hard-jawed Militant in khaki trousers and shirt stood behind the table. "Sister Maria!" he boomed with a gap-toothed grin. "An' Brother Willard. How are ya? What can I do for ya?"

"We've got a new recruit, Kelly. He's an endochronic named Alaricus." She gestured toward Pierce, who smiled and nodded at the mention of his name. "Dear Michael's assigned him to me as bodyguard. We'll get him qualified on firearms in the next few days, but for now we just need a sword and dagger. *Gladius et sica*?" she added to Pierce. He nodded.

"Awright," said Kelly, scratching his chest. "Got a nice little number here, good edge, nice balance." He lifted a scabbarded sword from a peg and tossed it to Pierce, who caught it and drew the blade. Kelly had been right: The blade was a passable form of steel, scrupulously kept sharp and free of rust. The hilt was iron, the grip and pommel brass' shaped to resemble a snake's body and head. It was a well-designed killing tool and beautiful as well. If Signor Bruckner, the art dealer in uptime Rome, had survived deep interrogation he might have paid fifteen thousand New Dollars for it, in expectation of a five-thousand dollar profit.

The dagger, while not as beautiful, was a serviceable weapon. It reminded Pierce of his lost Spetsnaz knife with its spring-loaded blade. If the men who mugged him had fooled with it, triggering the spring, one robber might well have killed the other. It was a cheering thought.

"And here is your insignia." Maria pinned a very ordinary uptime lapel button to his tunic. It was white, with a yellow cross like the ones on her sleeves. "It will be your pass anywhere you go. Tomorrow or the next day we'll begin your training with *tormenta*," Maria said as she signed for the weapons and led Pierce and Powell outside. "For now we'll show you your room."

"Is it next to my lady's?" Pierce asked.

"Of course not, Alaricus."

"I am your bodyguard; I must guard you in your sleep as well. I care nothing for a room. Only give me a cloak, and I will sleep in your doorway, my lady."

Maria looked startled and a little amused: "Makes sense, Maria," said Powell. "If you're trusted him with your life, I suppose you can trust him with your virtue as well."

"I suppose so." She switched back into Latin. "Come on, then. We'll see if we can find you a mattress, anyway."

Her room was actually a suite, complete with a toilet, on the second floor overlooking a tiny garden. Pierce insisted on exploring the suite carefully, looking out the window to ensure that no one could enter by climbing vines. Satisfied, he accepted a well-woven cloak of gray wool and allowed himself to be stationed in the recessed doorway between the suite and the corridor, with a thin straw mattress. Powell said good-night. Maria stood in the doorway as Pierce settled himself. He felt a strong sexual tension between them: a message of pheromones and gesture and eye contact.

"Good night, Alaricus. I believe God has sent you to us as a sign of our success."

"My lady, it is you whom God has sent. Sleep well; I shall pray for you."

"And I for you." The door swung shut, leaving Pierce curled up on his mattress with his new sword in his hand. He heard her throw the bolt on the door. Good. Quite apart from what B&C had done to his sexual competence, he had had a long enough day as it was. The fluorescent lights and the comings and goings in the corridor did not trouble him at all; exhausted, he fell asleep.

Sometime long before dawn he woke. The palace was still, the corridors empty at last. Pierce got up, stretched, and went down the hall to the nearest latrine. Someone had put up a digital clock on the wall outside it; it was not quite three A.M. He had at least two hours before the palace would begin to stir itself.

He found his way to the north gate; two Praetorians were asleep there, and two others played knucklebones by the light of a battery lamp.

"And who are you?" one of the sentries asked with a grin.

He tapped his button. "Alaricus, bodyguard of the lady Maria. I am on an errand; you are commanded to secrecy. You saw no one, heard no one."

"By whose command?"

"The emperor's."

Pierce walked on swiftly into the noisy, torchlit darkness of the Rome night. He was soon outside the Amphitheater, slipping between one cart and another in search of one of the *pervigiles popinae*, all-night bars that catered to whores, criminals, and young aristocrats.

He could hear it before he saw the two oil lamps burning above its door: a crowd of drinkers, some city people and some peasant farmers stopping for a quick cup of wine before going on to the markets. Pierce walked in, covering his insignia button with his cloak.

At one table, four or five men were bawling a song while two whores screamed at each other. Two toughs were playing dice on the bar at the back. The place stank of bad wine and vomit.

The *popina* was lit only by a few candles and oil lamps, but Pierce's eyes soon adjusted. He wanted a city man, reasonably well bred, and not too drunk. Soon he spotted a balding man of forty or so, dressed in a threadbare blue *synthesis*, a light tunic and cloak worn for formal dining. Evidently he had come from some dinner party to this place. His face was flushed, but he seemed in control of himself.

"*Salve, amicus,*" Pierce said, sitting at the man's table. The man slowly turned his head to look at Pierce.

"What do you want, German? Looking for a roll in bed?" His voice was clear and vibrant, reminding Pierce of recordings he had heard of Dylan Thomas.

"Looking for the consul Plinius Caecilius."

The man burst into laughter. "Don't look for him here. He's very proper, our consul."

"I must speak with him. Can you tell me where he lives?"

"On the Esquiline. Among other places here and in the countryside."

"What street? What house?"

"Ironmongers' Street. Everyone knows the house."

"I'm a stranger to Rome."

"Indeed. Well, go along to Ironmongers' Street and look for the house with the most clients waiting outside."

"I must see him now. Show me where the house is."

"Go out in the streets? At this hour? I'm not that drunk, thank you." He cleared his throat and recited: "'A man who goes out to dinner without having made his will is liable to a charge of carelessness.' And a man who leaves a *popina* at this hour would be convicted on that charge."

Pierce smiled. "You quote Juvenal."

"None has a better right; I *am* Decimus Iunius Iuvenalis. And why would a German barbarian recognize my work?"

"Men are not always what they seem, or you would not need to write satire. I am a great admirer of yours, though from your works I would not have expected to find you, of all people, in such a place as this."

"Ah, my friend..." Juvenal sadly put a hand on Pierce's shoulder. "In such times as these, one must find consolation where one can. Sleep itself is denied us by the horrors of the day. Better to drink here than to weep one-self dry in one's own wretched little flat. Mm? Which reminds me: I need another cup of wine."

"Take me to the consul's and I'll buy you a flagon."

"If you plan to murder the consul, please don't. He's a good fellow, and he has troubles enough, what with the sorcerers and Christians and portents in the sky."

"The consul is in grave danger. I must warn him."

"Good luck to you, then. And to our beloved consul." The poet was drunker than Pierce had thought. He began to fall asleep. Pierce gripped Juvenal by his arms and lifted him to his feet. Tossing the man's cloak over his shoulders, Pierce guided him to the street.

"Now. Show me."

They lurched through the night streets, Juvenal humming songs and pausing once to vomit in the gutter. Pierce kept his sword in his hand and the occasional passersby kept well clear of them.

"It's all to do with these foreign Christians, isn't it?" Juvenal demanded suddenly.

"Yes."

"I knew it. I knew it. One superstition or another—
Chaldeans, Commagenians, Hesperians, Phrygians,
Isaics, Jews, Christians—all the same, mm? Selling the
blessings of their gods for a fat goose and a slice of cake,
promising youthful lovers and big inheritances, if only
their believers will befoul themselves in some obscene
rite, or crawl naked on hands and knees into the frozen
Tiber, or slice their own testicles off. And then they suddenly go for our throats, murder the emperor with witch-
craft—mind you, he was no real loss—and seize power.
But who would have thought it would be the Jews? Mm?"

"It's not," Pierce said. "Martellus is murdering the
Jews. He hates them more than Tiberius did."

"They're all the same," Juvenal insisted. "Sectaries,
quibbling over fine points of nonsense and superstition.
Foreigners."

Pierce said nothing at first. His Briefing had made him
aware of Roman anti-Semitism in general and Juvenal's in
particular, and it was no more palatable in Latin verse
than in English prose. The image of the Jewish girl, flung
from her balcony to die in the gutter, flashed in his mind;
he felt a sudden, pleasant impulse to break Juvenal's nose.

"What was it," Pierce said calmly, "that Pliny the elder
said? *'Vicendo victi sumus; paremus externis.'*"

"'By conquering we are conquered,'" Juvenal repeated. "'We serve the foreigners.' All too true. Who
conquered the Greeks?" he demanded loudly. "We did!
And who runs Rome? The Greeks!"

"At the moment, it's the Christians," Pierce answered.

"Superstition. No respect for the old ways. We're cor-
rupted by peace and wealth; we need a war to restore our
virtues."

> *"Nunc patimur longae pacis mala, saevior armis*
> *Luxuria incubuit victumque ulciscitur orbem,"*

Pierce recited. "Now we suffer from long and evil peace:
Luxury, worse than war, avenges a conquered world."

"You lack breath control, and your accent is vicious, but I am flattered nonetheless."

"Your prayers for war may be answered sooner than you think."

As they climbed up the streets of the Esquiline Hill, Pierce began to worry. It must have been close to four o'clock; he would have little time to talk to Plinius and then to return to the palace before he was missed.

At last they came to Ironmongers' Street, and to a private house on a corner. Holding the poet upright with one hand, Pierce pounded on the door with the other. Dogs began barking at once; then came the sleepy swearing of the porters, roused from their pallets just inside the door.

"Is this the house of the consul Plinius Caecilius?" Pierce shouted.

"Be off—he doesn't receive visitors until the second hour after sunrise."

"This is an urgent message from the emperor Martellus. I must see the consul at once."

"Fifty *sestertii.*"

"A typical rich man's porter," Juvenal snarled, "buying his freedom out of the purses of his master's clients."

Pierce pulled his money pouch out of his tunic. "Eighteen *sestertii,* all I have in the world. Take it."

"You were going to buy me a flagon of wine," Juvenal complained.

"When you're sober enough to enjoy it."

Pierce could hear bars being lifted from the door. It swung open a crack, and a flashlight half blinded him. The porter's hand snatched the pouch. Pierce pointed to his button, and the door opened a little more.

"The consul's not going to be in a sweet mood, I can promise you that," the porter growled.

Pierce clapped his drunken guide on the shoulder. "My thanks."

Juvenal sagged against the wall of the house. "I'll just recover my strength for a moment. A pleasure to be of service."

Pierce turned and slipped through the door, which

groaned shut behind him. Someone had finally silenced the dogs, but the household was clearly awake and alert. The porter led him a few steps into the atrium, and showed him a stool.

"Stay there. I'll call the master."

The flashlight made a moving ellipse of light that suddenly vanished as the porter turned a corner. Pierce was left in the darkness, aware that other porters and two dogs were waiting not far away. He looked up at the stars through the gap in the roof above the *impluvium*. Still dark, but it must be close to four-thirty.

The porter returned, his flashlight aimed to show the way to his master. Gaius Plinius Luci Filius Caecilius Secundus paused, a dark figure; the flash swung into Pierce's face.

"You bring a message from Martellus." Plinius's voice was strong and calm, the voice of a man born to power and privilege.

"Not one that he wants sent, master. You should absent yourself from Rome. The Praetorians have orders to bring you to the palace immediately after you meet the senate in the morning. They've already sent men to Alsium for Cornutus."

"Why?"

"To force you to recommend Martellus to the senate. The Christians are afraid of an uprising if he is not confirmed as emperor."

"You wear the sign of the Christians on your tunic. Why do you bring this message?"

Pierce smiled in the darkness. "Do you know much about the Christians, master?"

"Until this happened, I knew them only as another burial society. An eastern superstition."

"Christians are quite as contentious as other men, master. Not all of us support Martellus in this matter. Better to support a true Roman as emperor, than a usurper who will lead us from the old ways."

"Your cult refuses to honor the gods and the emperor—"

"Even when the emperor is a supposed Christian. I will not tire you with an account of our inner quarrels. I only ask that you find business out of the city, as soon as possible. The senate will understand."

"And if this is a provocation, a trap?"

"Ask your man to put his Hesperian light on my face." It dazzled him again. "I am Alaricus the Goth, bodyguard of the lady Maria of the Christians. I put my life in your hands. If you distrust me, or if the Christians try to punish you for evading them, tell them who it was who warned you. They will kill me out of hand."

"And if you deny you warned me?"

"I am an unknown man; you are the consul. Who will be believed?"

"Or I could simply put you to death right now."

"You could, master, though I would defend myself as best I can and some of your slaves would die with me. I would rather be allowed to leave; I must be back in the palace before I am missed."

The dark outline of Plinius moved slightly. "You may go."

"Thank you, master."

Pierce stood, bowed, and turned toward the door. Someone opened it for him. As he stepped through, he heard Plinius's clear voice behind him:

"Tell my *clientela* I will not be receiving their *salutatio* today."

Juvenal was still there, slumped against the stucco wall. Pierce shook him.

"What was your message for Plinius?" Juvenal mumbled.

"An appeal to support poets more generously. Where's your house?"

"My house is a humble *cenaculum*, a one-room flat under the tiles of an *insula* owned by Plinius himself. So you might say he supports me already."

"I'm bound back to the palace. If it's on the way I'll take you home."

"You have my eternal gratitude, O literate German. Like that? Mm? Two oxymorons in one sentence. Eternal gratitude and literate Germans, contradictions in terms."

Juvenal guided him several blocks west to an *insula* not far from the Amphitheater. The poet swayed in the doorway.

"Perhaps we'll meet again. if you do not find me at home on the fourth floor, seek me in the local wine shops. Or waiting for my daily little gift from one of my patrons."

"Farewell, Juvenal. You've served your people better than you know this night."

"It occurs to me that you've yet to tell me your name, my friend."

Pierce was already gone, running through streets beneath a paling sky.

Fourteen:

The cooks were the only ones up when Pierce returned to the palace. He went into the servants' dining hall and demanded breakfast; the cooks gave him a big bowl of hot cereal laced with honey. He wolfed it down and asked for dried apples. A junior cook gave him a double handful out of a wicker basket. Pierce ate some and stored the rest in a fold of his tunic.

Back outside Maria Donovan's door, Pierce settled himself on his straw mattress and picked cereal grains out of his teeth with his dagger. He was relatively safe, thanks to the Militants' own efficiency. They had destroyed the Hesperian embassy and slaughtered all the uptimers in Rome; anyone who turned up claiming to be a Christian Goth must therefore be what he claimed, especially if his theology was so close to the Church Militants'.

But he could make a misstep, as he had by mentioning viruses to Dennis Brewster. At the first hint of suspicion from the Militants, he would have to vanish. Better yet, he should vanish while they still trusted him, preferably with some kind of beeper.

Pierce considered branching choices. The Militants had brought considerable stores of uptime goods, including drugs; that was a major reason for his embarking on the masquerade. In the convoluted theology of the Militants, viral diseases were divine punishment for minor or major sins. Bacterial infections, however, were natural; antibiotics and painkillers were acceptable treatment for them. Pentasyn had originally been a painkiller, and a good one,

159

before the Agency had discovered its usefulness in reducing the symptoms of extended Conditioning. Somewhere in the palace, therefore, was a pharmacy that would include Pentasyn or some of its analogs; even aspirin would help a little.

Martel would have a treasury as well—all of Domitian's wealth, plus that of the rich families slain in the proscription. A pouch full of *aureii* and *denarii* could keep Pierce fed and sheltered for a few weeks anyway, until the Agency finally came to the rescue.

It seemed likely, however, that the Militants were still using knotholers, bringing in supplies from uptime. If he stayed in the palace he could find out where the knotholes were, and might be able to use them to get uptime on his own. It would not be easy, but it might enable him to be deBriefed weeks earlier, and to prod the Agency into moving against the Militants. What he had already learned about them would make the Agency's counterattack far more effective.

Remaining in the palace would also enable him to sabotage the Militants whenever the opportunity arose, and if Aquilius were to fall into the Militants' hands, Pierce would be in a position to help.

So staying would be a calculated risk, but one worth taking. As he dozed off, Pierce admitted to himself that it was also fun, in an ugly kind of way.

The snap of the bolt being thrown roused him instantly. When Maria emerged, he was standing in the doorway, his mattress rolled up to one side.

"My lady."

She was dressed in khaki and olive drab again, her blond curls just touching her collar. "Good morning, Alaricus. Did you sleep well?"

"I did, my lady. How may I serve you this morning?"

"Have you eaten?"

"Yes, my lady."

"Well, come along with me to the superiors' dining hall. We generally have breakfast together and talk about

what has to be done. Then we'll see what happens next."
She smiled dazzlingly at him.

The superiors' dining hall must have been used for the
emperor's inner circle. But the couches on which they had
dined had gone, replaced by folding wooden chairs. Slaves
were whitewashing a pornographic mural from one of the
walls. The room, which opened onto a large garden,
smelled of coffee and frying bacon. In the next room
Pierce saw a small squad of cooks, obviously Militants,
working over a series of propane stoves. Attendants
brought in platters piled with bacon, scrambled eggs, uptime oatmeal, and jugs of coffee. The aromas were overpowering to Pierce's sense of smell.

Maria greeted the dozen or so men and women in the
room before joining Willard Powell and a couple of other
men. Pierce did not recognize them; they must have been
rank and file before the church's deportation to Albion.

Maria said a brief prayer as an attendant brought her a
mug of black coffee. Then she sipped it, brightened, and
joined the conversation. Pierce stationed himself behind
her chair, arms folded, his eyes moving restlessly around
the room. The table talk was casual at first, but Willard
soon grew serious. "We've had something kind of strange
happen. Seems that a couple of days ago a Praetorian
came into the city from the north; told the guards some
soldiers had been massacred and he was on his way to tell
us. But he never turned up. The guards passed the word to
their officers, and it got to Sextus this morning. I asked
him if any of the proscription teams were still in the field,
and he said plenty, but he'd check 'em off as they come
back in. If anyone's missing, we'll know before sundown."

"No idea what happened to the Praetorian?" Maria
asked.

"Nope. He was with a barbarian of some kind—the
guy who'd told him about the massacre, supposedly. No
sign of either one."

"Smells fishy to me," said one of the other men. "I bet
the guards just got somebody's story all turned around.

No way anybody's going to massacre a squad of Praetorians carrying Uzis."

"That's probably true, Brother Lyle. Or the Praetorian was a deserter trying to cover his tracks. We'll learn the truth if the Lord wills it."

"Amen," said Maria. "Have they brought in that consul yet—that Plinius?"

Willard looked at his wristwatch. "It's only seventwenty. These folks get up early but they don't have much sense of time. Sextus sent off his men to the senate, but I don't know when Plinius will be finished there. Might be before eight, might be ten."

"We'll make him see the light," said the man called Lyle.

"I sure hope so," Willard answered. "These pagans can be the most pigheaded, stiff-necked, crazy folks I ever saw. I was along on a proscription the night of the twenty-second, right after the action against Domitian. Don't remember the people's name, somebody on the list Drusus gave us. Some old fat *paterfamilias*, all alone in his house. He'd sent everybody away, even the slaves. He's sitting there in his garden, just waiting for us, and we tell him to stand up. 'You can kill me where I am,' he says, and he lifts his chin up like this, so we can cut his throat. So we did."

Just the way Cicero had greeted the assassins sent by Augustus, Pierce reflected. The old Roman ways weren't as obsolete as Juvenal thought. Though they soon would be if their upholders went on allowing their own throats to be slit.

The conversation swung off into shop talk: how well the telephones worked inside the palace, and how poorly on the radio link to the Praetorian camp; how rapidly the endos were accepting the new state of affairs; whether motorcycles would be available within the next week.

"Anyone heard how they're taking this uptime?" Willard asked.

"All pretty quiet," said Lyle. "They're just saying terrorists bombed the Rome Transferpoint. Nothing about what's happening down here. Course they're doubtless working like demons to hit back at us."

"They're not expecting three cohorts with machine guns and mortars and Mallorys," Willard grunted, wiping a slice of toast around his plate. "Plus the population on our side. I expect we might see a couple hours of fighting when they come through, but we'll let 'em see how bad it's going to be, how many endos they're gonna have to kill, and then they'll see the light."

Pierce knew better. AID would kill as many endos as necessary to prevent the establishment of an independent state downtime. Let the Militants get away with secession, and scores of other groups would try it. The International Federation would drown in a flood of revived nationalism. Then recruitment of endo Trainables would become impossible, and the drive to understand and prevent Doomsday would stop.

But Willard had said three cohorts; the Praetorian in the wine shop yesterday had said only one cohort had firearms. That suggested plenty of weapons but not enough trainers. The longer AID hesitated, the harder the struggle would be to regain power.

"I'd be happier if we could link up with the primitive Christian communities," Lyle sighed. "Sure can't understand why they haven't come forward yet."

"Well, I'm going to have to hurry," Maria said, finishing her coffee; she had eaten nothing. "Got to take *my* primitive Christian here to his first shooting lesson."

They all glanced up at Pierce, who nodded and smiled blankly before resuming his endless survey of the room.

"Come, Alaricus," Maria said. "We're going to study the *tormentum* this morning."

"As my lady bids."

A team of eight slaves carried Maria in a litter, while Pierce walked alongside through the streets. "I would rather walk," she told him, "but the Elders say the Romans would be shocked by the sight of a woman in trousers."

"It is unusual," Pierce said.

"Not to me. I am as much a warrior as you are; I can't fight in a skirt. So I'm confined to this absurd *lectica*."

The morning was well advanced by now, and four Praetorians ahead of the litter had to force a path through the crowds. People in the streets watched curiously, evidently wondering who was concealed behind the drapes of the litter. Pierce kept his sword out, watching for any hostile expression or gesture. He overheard scraps of conversation, a few having to do with *Christiani*, and twice he heard Plinius's name.

They ended up at the Praetorian camp; just over twenty-four hours had passed since he and Aquilius had walked past the gate they now entered. From not far away came the sporadic rattle of small-arms fire.

Like any camp of the legionaries, this one was laid out in rigid geometry. The *porta principalis sinistra*, the gate facing the city, led the party to the *via principalis*—thirty meters wide, and dividing the elite first cohort from the rest of the Guards' quarters. The atmosphere was as familiar as the layout; the camp reminded Pierce strongly of the U.S. military bases he had served in as a T-Colonel during the bad old days of the Emergency. He saw little overtly military activity around the barracks, only the familiar fatigue details: cooking, cleaning, hanging out laundry.

Pierce noted the quarters of the tribunes and prefects, and the *tabernaculum* where the Praetorian general, Drusus, lived. They passed row on row of two-story brick barracks, coming finally to a wide road that ran just inside the eastern wall of the camp.

A crude firing range had been set up here, with man-shaped targets—cheap plaster statues—standing before bales of hay; the rangemaster obviously did not want ricochets off the brick wall behind the targets. Ten Praetorians in full uniform were standing at firing posts, each with an AK-47. Each soldier had a Militant coach standing beside him, monitoring the way he locked, loaded, unlocked, aimed, and fired. Judging from the fragments on the ground, a lot of statues had been consumed.

Maria descended from her litter and led Pierce to the

rangemaster's shed. A Crucifer, uniformed just as Maria was, stood up to greet them. He was a crewcut young man with frostbite scars on his cheeks and nose.

"Morning, Brother Jeff. I have another pupil for you. Praise God, he's an endo Christian from Germany, name's Alaricus. Dear Michael's very pleased with him and wants him to be my bodyguard. We need to give him a quick course."

Jeff stared coldly at Pierce, who smiled back and folded his arms across his chest.

"Hail, Alaricus," Jeff said in bad Latin. "Have you seen what a *tormentum* can do?"

"I have heard, brother."

"Watch these men. *Iaculari!*"

A ragged volley of single shots went off. Plaster exploded on some of the statues, though no one hit what would have been a vital organ. The level of marksmanship was dismal: The Praetorians would have to spray a target to hit it. Pretending to be startled, Pierce grunted and shivered, then recovered himself. Maria smiled and patted his arm.

"You have seen the wrath of God in the hands of His servants," she said. "Do not be afraid."

"No, my lady."

In English, Jeff asked, "What you want to start him with, Sister Maria—handgun?"

"I think so."

"Makes sense. He's bodyguardin', he's gonna be in close most of the time. We'll get to long arms in a couple days."

The rangemaster handed Pierce a Smith & Wesson Model 14 .38 Special—a snubnosed police revolver that must have been at least twenty years old. With some help from Maria, Jeff explained how it worked; Pierce nodded blankly. Then he was shown how to strip it and reassemble it. After watching Pierce do it twice, Jeff turned to Maria.

"Catches on quicker'n most."

"I'm not surprised."

The morning wore on through a series of explanations

and drills, while Pierce's ears rang from the AK-47s going off alongside. The Praetorians' accuracy improved, a little. Not until late in the morning did Jeff finally allow Pierce to load the pistol, aim it at a statue, and squeeze the trigger.

The head of the statue shattered. Pierce grinned and shouted, *"Allelulia! Praise God!"*

"Well done, Alaricus!" Maria looked delighted. "Again!"

With both hands wrapped around the grip, Pierce lowered his sights and fired again. A chunk erupted from the statue's chest. Again: the stomach. Again: a miss. Again: the right leg shattered halfway up the thigh and the statue toppled over.

Jeff's coldness melted. "Praise Jesus, we got us a live one! Sister Maria, this boy was *made* to use a firearm. Alaricus, reload and let's see you do that again."

His shooting was less accurate this time, so that Jeff and Maria could give him advice and point out his errors. But by the time they stopped near noon for *cena*, a mob of Praetorians was watching and cheering every shot.

Jeff stood by the litter as Maria climbed into it. "Sister Maria, you get Kelly to issue this boy a good weapon, not some old Saturday-night special, hear? Maybe even a Mallory. And you bring him back tomorrow with plenty of rounds. He's gonna be worth a platoon all by hisself." Jeff grinned as he patted Pierce's shoulder. Pierce patted him back, then turned and trotted away alongside the litter.

Almost as soon as they went through the gate back into the city, something seemed wrong. Noon was the end of the working day for most Romans; they would eat *cena*, have a nap, and then go to the baths later in the afternoon. But the streets seemed quieter than usual, the shops almost deserted. At the Viminal Gate, where he and Aquilius had been mugged in the crowd, no one at all was passing in either direction.

The four Praetorian escorts marched steadily down the Vicus Patricius, only rarely having to warn someone out of the way. Maria's eight litter bearers moved at a smooth shuffle, while Pierce strode just to the right of the litter.

The street took them down past the ruins of the Hesperian embassy and on into the Subura slums. Now the looks of bystanders were indeed hostile; teenagers gestured obscenely while old men and women looked sidelong and spat. Pierce looked up nervously at the overhanging balconies. Someone could tip a heavy potted plant off a railing, or launch a few roof tiles.

"Christiani!" The cry was a mocking warble. Out of a cross-street to the right came a swarm of street kids, boys and young men in ragged tunics. They carried rotted vegetables and chunks of bricks.

"Praetorians! Fall back on the lady!" Pierce shouted. They obeyed instantly, swords out and shields up as turnips and onions sailed toward the litter.

Pierce shoved his way between the litter bearers, under the litter to the other side of the street. Two hardbitten men with long daggers were within five steps of the litter.

The distraction would have worked beautifully, Pierce thought as he lunged forward. The assassin on his left took the sword just below the sternum; the man grunted, the wind knocked just out of him by the force of the thrust. When he looked down and saw the blade in his chest he tried to draw breath to scream, failed, and sagged. Before the man could fall, Pierce swung him into his accomplice, knocking the second man off balance. Yanking his blade free, Pierce let the first man drop to the pavement. He seized the second man's wrist, pulling the dagger away, and ran him through.

The crack of Maria's Ruger echoed off the *insula* walls. Seeing no one else threatening on this flank, Pierce ran back around the litter, which the bearers had quickly lowered to the pavement. Maria was on her feet amid the bearers and Praetorians. One of the street kids was shot, writhing in a pool of blood and muck while a severed artery spouted from his throat. The others were running for their lives back up the alley.

"Anyone hurt?" Pierce asked. One of the Praetorians had been hit in the face with a half brick, but was still on his feet. No one else was injured. Pierce turned to Maria. "My lady, the litter is too dangerous. Let two of the bearers carry it while the rest of us surround you."

She turned on him with a snarl, shoving her pistol into his face. "Where were you? *Timidus!* You ran just as they attacked!"

"My lady—" With his bloody sword he pointed over the litter at the two dead assassins. "These two were the real *homicidii*. The children were a distraction."

"Oh—" She looked appalled. "Oh, Alaricus, forgive me! You saw the true threat. Truly, Satan lies in wait for the unwary. The Lord's Providence sent you to us."

"My lady, I praise God for granting us victory. Now quickly, let us get back to the palace."

The Praetorians kept a box formation around most of the bearers, who were closed in around Maria. Then came two bearers with the litter, and Pierce covering the rear. He looked at the shot boy, still shivering and pulsing his short life away while people watched from balconies. *You'll be avenged*, Pierce silently promised him.

The party moved several blocks in silence: A kind of bubble enveloped them, within which the slumdwellers would not stay. From the balconies, wrinkled old women peered down with index and little fingers extended to ward off the evil eye.

When they were at last out of the Subura and hurrying between the Amphitheater and the gladiators' school, Pierce moved up to join Maria. She smiled shamefacedly at him.

"I owe you my life."

"No, my lady. Had I not been there, God would have slain them with some other instrument."

She touched his arm. "Your humility is an example to us all, Alaricus . . . But why would they attack us?"

"Many Romans hate Christians, my lady. They think we hate mankind, that we disturb the state by not worshipping the gods and the emperors. They even think that Christianity leads to atheism."

She looked shocked. "Why?"

"To the Romans, all religions but their own are superstition, crazy and foolish ideas about false gods. The Romans think people believe in superstition only because they are afraid not to believe. They say that once you recognize how foolish your ideas have been, you reject all belief in gods and sink into atheism."

She nodded. "In a way they're right; it's just that *they're* the ones who are superstitious, not us. We will have to work hard to show them the light."

"Yes, my lady."

"But the people who attacked us were—criminals, *nefarii*. They wouldn't care about religion."

"My lady, the Romans think themselves the only truly religious people in the world. But I suspect they attacked us not for our religion but for the death of Domitian. Many of the common people liked him because he gave such good games and shows."

Maria listened thoughtfully. "You're a godsend in more ways than one, Alaricus. We thought only about the *honestiores*, the rich and powerful friends of Domitian, not about the *humiliores* in the slums. I will mention this to the Elders."

"My lady, please do not tell them I advised you; I am only a simple bodyguard."

She smiled fondly at him. "Don't worry, Alaricus. I won't embarrass you."

The guards at the palace gates had an urgent message for Maria. A special meeting of the emperor and the Elders was under way: The consul Plinius had disappeared after sending the senate a warning to confer no powers whatsoever on the self-proclaimed emperor Martellus.

Fifteen:

Six Crucifers, all carrying Uzis, were patrolling the terrace outside the meeting room; no Praetorians were in sight. One of the guards held up a hand to bar Pierce as Maria was going through the door.

"Elders and Crucifers only, Sister Maria."

"This is my bodyguard, Brother Elliot. Where I go, he goes."

"Sorry, sister. Those are our orders."

Maria glared at him, then turned and gripped Pierce's wrist. Together they barged into the meeting room.

Greenbaugh looked up annoyedly. "Didn't they tell you, Sister Maria?"

"Brother Alaricus goes where I go, Brother David. He's already saved my life today."

"Praise the Lord. But you're safe here, even without him."

Pierce agreed. Four Crucifers, all with Uzis, were stationed around Martel at the head of the table. Six others stood by the terrace doorway and the inner door. He wondered what had provoked the increase in security.

"With respect, Brother David, I think he might be of some help." She described the attack on them in Subura, and Pierce's remarks on anti-Christian attitudes.

"Please let him stay. We need his perspective on what's going on."

"I don't—"

"He may stay." It was Martel. He smilingly waved off

Maria's thanks. She went to her chair by the wall; Pierce
stationed himself beside her.

"Just to bring you up to date, Sister Maria," said
Greenbaugh. "This morning Plinius sent word to the senate not to recognize the emperor. Then he disappeared.
We're questioning some of his house slaves, but I don't
think we'll get anywhere with them. The Praetorians have
brought in the other consul, Cornutus, but he says he
won't do anything until he's talked things over with
Plinius.

"What's more, Brother Dennis and his men have vanished completely. Several of our people have been har-
assed in the streets today. And now you've brought us
news of an attack on yourself. Obviously we're facing
some opposition, maybe more than we'd expected. We're
discussing how to overcome that opposition."

Maria nodded but said nothing. The discussion had
clearly been going on for some time. Pierce gathered that
most of the Elders and Crucifers wanted to crush the opposition as quickly as possible; a minority wanted to wait,
to let more opponents show themselves.

"Brothers and sister," said Elias Smith, "this is a society completely dominated by class. The ruling class calls
the shots and everybody else has to obey. It looks pretty
clear to me that all the aristocrats are against us, even the
ones who didn't like Domitian—even the ones who didn't
like the so-called Hesperians. So they're stirring up the
ordinary people against us. We were on the right track
with the proscription, but we didn't push it hard enough."

"We still are pushing it, Brother Elias," Willard interrupted. "This is more than a handful of aristocrats we're
up against."

"Mr. Chairman," Elias said to Greenbaugh, "please remind Brother Willard that we operate by rules of order
here."

"Brother Willard will wait until recognized before
speaking," Greenbaugh mumbled.

"Now," Elias went on, "think about this opposition.
One of our teams has gone missing; is that really serious,

or has Brother Dennis simply found he had more work than he counted on out there in the countryside? Sister Maria is attacked in a horrible slum by some criminals; we're glad she escaped, but is that evidence of resistance? A few other people are insulted in the marketplace. The only real resistance has come from a couple of pagans at the top of the totem pole. Once we show *them* who's boss, the majority will come around."

"Sister Maria," said Greenbaugh.

"Thank you, Mr. Chairman." Maria Donovan's eyes glistened; her beautiful features looked tense to Pierce. He wondered if she was on the edge of falling ill. "I have to take exception to what Brother Elias says. First of all, we've eliminated at least five hundred major Romans, not counting their families and the Jews. I agree they should have been eliminated, but we're going to need the ruling class. If we wipe it out completely, how do we govern? Secondly, the attack on me wasn't just some casual mugging. They were waiting for us, and the whole neighborhood knew it. Nobody warned us. They just got out of the way and watched. To me, that means a lot of these people don't yet see us as a way to be saved."

"They'll see it clear enough when they realize they *need* saving," Elias said with a wet-lipped grin.

Maria was about to answer when Martel raised a pale hand. The Elders and Crucifers seemed to freeze in their places, their eyes on him.

"Mr. Chairman. We have two problems here, not one." Martel paused, steepling his fingers before his mouth as if deep in thought. "Popular resistance was expected, and we've worked out a strategy to minimize it. I'm concerned about attacks on our people, yes, but God made us to be attacked, and to be strengthened by attack. The pagans will come around soon enough. Remember—the old emperors ruled this city with five thousand Praetorians; we have that five thousand, plus over two thousand of our own, and plenty of equipment. Civil disturbances are not a worry.

"But the second problem does concern me. If the senate refuses to legitimize the change of government, we don't have just the city against us; we have the empire, fifty or sixty million people. Even then we could win. It would take time but we could win.

"We don't *have* time, brothers and sisters." His blue eyes, deep-set and intense, swept their faces. "The Federation will be upon us any moment. We have all agreed that they will accept us if the cost of fighting us is too high. As it would be with fifty or sixty million people behind us." They all nodded.

"But if they come through and find us fighting in the streets, and the provinces in revolt, they will rightly consider us weak—and then they'll come in and destroy us."

The room was absolutely silent.

"They will destroy us, that is, if we act foolishly, or if we fail to act at all. Because we would be telling God we aren't wise enough to deserve His blessing and His covenant.

"So we *must* win the approval of the senate. We *must* be legitimized by these pagans before we can win their souls for Christ. It wouldn't be enough to force the senate; the people would still have to be won over, and we don't have the time. But the people can make the senate act."

"How, Dear Michael?" asked Greenbaugh.

Martel smiled dazzlingly. "We're not the first to face this problem, brothers and sisters. Most of the cities and empires of ancient times were ruled by aristocrats. They kept the ordinary people in their place, just as the Romans do. But sometimes a leader would arise. A man who'd win the support of the people against the aristocrats. A man who gave the people what they wanted.

"The aristocrats didn't like these fellows much. They never do. When a man gained power from popular support, the aristocrats called him a tyrant, didn't they? And that was an ugly name. No one wants to be a tyrant.

"Well, brothers and sisters, a better name for such a man is plain old 'leader.' He's a man with the confidence of the people, and no one better stand in his way. That was the foundation of the late lamented United States of

America, and the other Western democracies."

Martel's eyes flashed. "And why did those countries fall, brothers and sisters? Not because the people failed; the so-called leaders failed. They didn't have the will to be tyrants, even when the people *demanded* it of them. They prattled on about the Constitution, about democracy, about the rule of law, when what their people wanted was action. And we've seen, yes, we've seen the folly of that lack of will. We, especially, have paid a heavy price.

"I suggest to you that God has been teaching us, and teaching us well. He taught us what happens when leaders grow weak. Now He wants to see if we've learned our lesson. We've eliminated our rivals, yes, we've purged the Jews, yes, we've proclaimed Christ crucified and risen again, yes, yes. And I know God is pleased with us, pleased with how we're standing up to the test. So He wants to see now if we have the will to lead these wretched pagans out of their idolatry and win them for salvation."

"Amen," the Elders chorused.

"Here is how we will do it," Martel went on. "Tomorrow we will hold a great celebration in the Colosseum. We'll bring in the common people of Rome, and show them what we showed the Praetorians. Brothers and sisters, we'll show them Heaven and Hell; we'll show them divine providence. We'll win the people to our side, and then the senate will follow. The aristocrats will have no choice, unless they want the people rising up against them. And *then* the Federation will have no choice but to accept us and recognize us."

They all nodded and murmured assent, pleased to be given a goal.

"Brother Willard," Martel said, "please take charge of this event. We'll be using some of the same effects, and the same holo and audio equipment. How soon can you set it up?"

"Most of it by tonight, Dear Michael. The rest overnight or first thing in the morning. We've got to get word out about this celebration, and that'll take a while. Can we figure on late afternoon for this?"

"It's in your hands." Martel waved, dismissing the subject. "Do whatever needs doing."

"Yes, Dear Michael."

Martel still had the floor, but he said nothing for a time. Then he looked up at the Elders and the others assembled before him.

"Have you ever known divine guidance to fail us?" he asked with a faint smile. "'Where two or three are gathered together in My name,' He said. And He is here among us, hearing every word, guiding our thoughts and words. Let us pray."

Pierce folded his hands and prayed with the rest of them; his head hurt, and it was a relief to close his eyes. He would have to find the Militants' pharmacy pretty soon.

The meeting adjourned, but Martel beckoned to Maria to stay on as the Elders left. Pierce saw that the Crucifer bodyguards stayed as well.

"Come and sit," Martel said, gesturing to the chairs just vacated at the table. "You also, Alaricus. We all owe you our thanks for saving the lady Maria today. Tell me what happened, as you saw it."

Pierce swallowed, as if nervous. "As we came back from the Praetorians' camp, Emperor, I saw the streets seemed very quiet, almost empty. When the children attacked us, I thought it must be a distraction. So I looked the other way and saw the two men. That is all."

"Alaricus, the man Shimon who converted your tribe— he preached that skill in combat is a sign of special blessedness."

"Yes, Emperor."

"We also preach it, because it is true. Sister Maria has said that you have learned to use a *tormentum* faster than any Roman has. And that, too, suggests that you have been chosen for a special mission."

Pierce nervously crossed himself; so did Martel and

Maria, more slowly. The Crucifers, however, remained alert and on guard.

"We have been surprised by one thing since we came to Rome," Martel went on. "We proclaimed the rule of Christ, and many people have said they are Christians. Some even wear a fish like yours, or a cross. But they have all converted since the death of Domitian. We are glad to welcome them into the fold, if they are sincere, but we are worried by the absence of those who were Christians before we came. Can you help us?"

"In any way I can, Emperor."

"First, why have the Christians not come forward?"

"Ah, that is easy, Emperor. To be known as a Christian under the old emperor was to be doomed to die. Anyone accused of belief in Christ was forced to make sacrifices to the Roman gods; anyone who refused would be put to death."

"So your master, the provincial governor, did not know you were a Christian?"

"No, Emperor. I attended him and his family when they took part in their rites, but I made no sacrifices."

"And did you know other Christians?"

"I heard of some, but I did not know for certain. I did not want to seek out Christians who might come under suspicion; then I, too, would come under suspicion."

Martel looked pleased; a conspiratorial glint shone in his eye. "You are wise for such a young man, and you know your enemy. Here is what I ask of you, Alaricus: Can you seek out the Christians of Rome for us?"

Pierce's jaw dropped. "I—I will gladly try, Emperor, but if they have hidden from Domitian and the urban cohorts, they can surely hide from me. I scarcely know this city."

"I understand. But you have been specially favored by Jesus, and I think He will guide your feet as He guides our thoughts."

"And if I succeed, Emperor, what shall I do then?"

"Bring their leaders to me. Tell them that they should not be afraid, that a place of honor has been prepared for them." Martel's powerful eyes focused intensely on Pierce's. "They must understand that, Alaricus. We are saving our fellow Christians from centuries of oppression and persecution. And when our enemies rise against us, as they did today against the lady Maria, we will need true Christians at our side."

Pierce nodded. He could well believe that part of the Militants' purpose in mounting this coup had been the prospect of meeting genuine primitive Christians, and saving them from government persecution. He recalled the mention of Plinius: On Earth, in the year A.D. 112, Plinius had been sent to Asia Minor by the emperor Trajan as an imperial commissioner, and had executed many Christians. It had been government policy, not a whim; Christians were antisocial, subversive, and superstitious, as much a threat to peace and order as bandits.

But having endochronic Christians at his side would also give Martel a political boost when the coup became known uptime. Plenty of Christians, especially in North America, would support Martel for that reason alone. The Agency had minimized contact with Ahanian Rome precisely to avoid political embarrassment about primitive Christianity. Martel understood that and was determined to exploit it. He could hardly do otherwise: A Christian sect ruling ancient Rome, but unable to produce any endo Christians, would be in trouble.

From Martel's point of view, Pierce reflected, an alliance with endo Christians could succeed even if the uptime public remained ignorant of it. The old Chinese general Sunzi had said that the supreme military skill is to defeat the enemy without fighting. AID might keep the lid on the coup, but the Agency itself would know how strong Martel had become and might come to an understanding with the Militants rather than risk an all-out battle.

Or so the Militants might reason. Pierce knew better.

"How shall I carry out this task and still guard the lady Maria?" he asked.

"Within the palace, her fellow Crucifers shall guard her whenever you are away. She shall leave the palace only when you are available to protect her. No, Maria, don't be angry," he said in English. "You look tired; a little rest will do you good, and Alaricus will probably need only a day or two. After that, you'll be free to go anywhere you like."

"Thank you, Dear Michael. But now I'm worried that Alaricus could be in danger if he goes out alone looking for Christians."

Martel smiled and chuckled softly. "I think we've seen that Alaricus can look after himself very well." He sat back and clapped his hands.

"Good," he said in Latin. "I have kept you from your *cena*. Go and enjoy your meal. Take whatever you think you will need, Alaricus, and then go at once to seek our brothers and sisters."

Pierce rose. "I go gladly, Emperor. Keep me in your prayers, and I shall succeed."

"In nomine patris et filius et spiritus sanctus," Martel murmured, crossing himself again.

Pierce escorted Maria to the dining hall, where the murals were now completely whitewashed, and left her to her meal. Then he went to the servants' mess hall, where the cooks gave him a kind of vegetable stew.

"Would you like some more dried apples?" asked the junior cook.

Pierce slapped his stomach and laughed; the dried apples he had tucked in his tunic this morning were still there. "Two double handfuls," he said, "but put them in a sack."

She found a simple string bag and handed it to him. He tied it to his belt and went to the palace baths.

"Not *more* blood?" Naso protested. "And all *over* that fine new tunic! Your old one is clean, but if you come back in this condition a third time, I shall protest to the emperor himself."

"You will have to wait until *I* have protested first." Pierce pulled off the tunic and loincloth and took the bar of soap Naso offered him.

"No wounds this time. You're learning quickly how to

take care of yourself in Rome. What happened?"

"A scuffle. While I think of it, can someone clean my sword?"

Pierce sank into the lukewarm bath as Naso drew the sword from its sheath and made a face.

"*Foedus!* Disgusting." He handed the weapon to a slave, who hurried off with it.

"The emperor has given me a task, Naso, and perhaps you can help me."

"If I can, master."

"The city is full of new Christians, but he wants to meet those who were Christians before he and his people came to Rome. Do you know of any, or where I might search for them?"

"Perhaps among slaves and foreigners, master. I'm sure I have no idea; this is the palace, after all."

"The old emperors executed Christians who refused to abandon their beliefs, isn't that so?"

Naso smiled cynically. "Not many ever died that way, master. Pull them up before a magistrate and ask them to sacrifice a cock to Jupiter, and the bird was dead before the magistrate had finished his speech. That's enough of the tepid bath, master, move along, please."

"Keep me company." Pierce went into the next room and stepped gasping into the hot pool. "Are there any places the Christians are supposed to frequent—a neighborhood, a market, one of the public baths?"

"Master, I would gladly tell you if I knew. Many rumors come to me, but nothing of the Christians just lately. Would you like a scrub brush?"

After a plunge in the cold pool, Pierce dried off and dressed in his old tunic. Naso bustled off to look after a group of Militants, while the slave who had taken Pierce's sword returned with it.

"If you seek Christians, master, try the baths of Scribonius Tertius, near the Campus Martius. Tell the *balneator* that Terentius sent you."

The words were a murmur; the slave bowed and slipped away. Other attendants came to shave Pierce's whiskers and comb his hair. When they were done, he asked Naso for a personal bath kit.

"Want a proper bath, do you, with oil and a good strigilling? I'm not surprised; this *sapo* just isn't the same, is it?" Rummaging in a closet, he produced a small flask of oil, a comb carved from a seashell, and a curved blade of bronze—a strigil, for scraping oil and dirt from a bather's skin.

Pierce thanked him and tucked the kit into his shoulder bag. Then he returned to Maria's room. She looked wan and exhausted when she opened the door, and he smelled vomit on her breath: a delayed reaction to the brawl, Pierce suspected. He felt ill himself, though the bath had eased his now-permanent headache.

"My lady, I am sorry to disturb your rest. But the emperor has given me this task, and I must hurry. Can you help me obtain what I need?"

"Gladly."

"First I must go to the armorer, the man who gave me this sword. I would like to have a *tormentum*."

She looked taken aback. "You're good with it, but are you sure?"

"My lady, I will be alone in this great city. Even if I do not use it, it will give me confidence."

"Very well. What else will you need?"

"Some money—a few *denarii*, nothing more."

"That I can give you myself." She went to a box on the small table by her bed and took a fistful of coins. "Will this be enough?"

Pierce estimated the handful at forty *denarii* or so. "More than enough, my lady. What I do not spend I will return to you."

"Of course." She sat on the edge of her bed, rubbing her temples. Pierce felt a sudden burst of joy.

"My lady, are you ill? Can I do anything for you?"

"No—it's just a headache."

"Surely some potion would help."

"I'll be fine, Alaricus. Just as the emperor said, I only need some rest."

"But you're not well, my lady! I can't leave you in this condition. Let me send for a *medicus*."

"No... perhaps you can do this for me. In the hall of the fish murals, there is a room where we store our *medicamenta*." She took a steno pad from the table and scribbled on it, then ripped the page out and handed it to him. "Give this to the person on duty, and bring me what he gives you. Then I'll go with you to the armorer."

"I go at once, my lady."

Once outside her room, Pierce struggled to keep himself from breaking into a run. He had planned somehow to find time to prowl the palace until he found the pharmacy; now Maria had sent him straight to it.

The pharmacy was a small room on a dead-end corridor; a counter sealed off most of the room, whose walls carried shelves right up to ceiling. The pharmacist was a gaunt middle-aged man who lacked three fingers and, like Brother Jeff the rangemaster, carried frostbite scars on his cheeks. He read the note from Maria: *Dear Brother Samuel, I've got another of my migraines. Please give this man some painkillers for me. Thanks, Maria.*

"Do you speak English?" Samuel asked. Pierce looked blank. The man sighed. "Of course not. Wish she'd said what kind she wants."

Pierce burst into rapid Latin, knowing the man wouldn't understand but would catch the key word: "My lady asked me to bring her some *medicamenta* for her headache. *Medicamenta*."

"Medicaments, yes, I got that. Uh, *quis medicamenta?*"

"She wanted a *medicamentum* called P-penta—? Pentasum?"

"Pentasyn?"

"Ita est!" Pierce nodded. "Pentasyn, Pentasyn."

"Ah, okay, my friend. Just a minute."

Samuel went to a shelf near the back of the room and took down a small yellow cardboard box. He counted out some capsules and shuffled back up to the counter. "Ten caps ought to do it." He started to write instructions on an envelope, but Pierce shook his head fiercely.

"My lady asked for twenty," he said in Latin, *"Viginti, viginti."* He opened his hands twice.

"Ah, twenty. She wants twenty caps? Boy, that's some migraine." He went back for more and then finished his written instructions on the envelope before putting the capsules into it.

Pierce took the envelope and smiled gratefully, *"Gratiam habere! Bene facis."*

"If that means thank you, you're welcome."

Pierce had two of the caps in his mouth within a minute of leaving the pharmacy. Eight more went into his belt pouch, under the coins Maria had given him.

"Pentasyn?" she said when he handed her the envelope. In English, she mumbled, "I'd have been happy with a few old aspirin. Well, Brother Samuel knows best." She took a capsule and washed it down with water. "Now let's go get you a weapon, Alaricus."

Sixteen:

The *insula* stairs were narrow and rickety and stank of urine. Pierce came out onto the fourth-floor landing and drew a deep breath. Below was the courtyard, a rectangle of pounded dirt and broken pots with only a few weeds growing in it. Ragged laundry, attached to poles extending from every balcony, dried slowly in the muggy afternoon heat.

To live under the tiles of an *insula* was not a figure of speech: These cubicles' ceilings were the tiles themselves. In winter the rooms must be bitterly cold; now they were suffocatingly hot. Pierce heard squalling babies behind many of the cubicle doors, and the balcony itself was the playground for a dozen filthy toddlers. Rats scuttled past Pierce's feet.

A shopkeeper on the ground floor of the *insula* had given Pierce directions, so he turned right and walked along the balcony past four doors before knocking at the fifth.

"*Quis?*"

"Alaricus—your traveling companion of last night. I've brought your payment."

The door opened; Decimus Iunius Iuvenalis, the greatest poet of imperial Rome's Silver Age, stood crouched defensively with a knife in one hand.

"It is you. What do you want?"

Pierce held out the flagon of wine he had bought from a good shop on the Esquiline. "I promised you this. May I come in?"

"Of course, of course." He smoothed the rumpled fringe of hair around his bald spot. "You find me unready to receive visitors."

The cubicle was sweltering; its tiny window faced west, making the room that much hotter. Sunlight threw a painful glare over everything: the rough plank floor, the rotting plaster, the stains from countless leaks, the shabby bed and stool, the chamber pot, the little trunk serving as a table and writing desk. Book scrolls were piled under the bed, perhaps because they could be protected from leaks there. Pierce thought of a line from Juvenal's *Satires*: "Poverty has no greater misery than that it makes men ridiculous."

Juvenal produced a couple of earthenware cups from a shelf and pulled the cork from the flagon. While he seemed nervous and agitated, his hand was steady as he poured two generous drinks and handed Pierce one of them.

"A pity I have no water to mix with this, but we will have to make do, won't we? I drink to your health and prosperity, my literate German friend."

"And I to yours." To Pierce's enhanced sense of taste, the wine was sour and musty. "What news have you heard today?"

"Only what I overhear from my neighbors' conversations; I have been unwell today. The consul Cornutus is rumored a prisoner of Martellus. The consul Plinius has urged the senate not to confer the *imperium* on Martellus. Plinius is believed to have left the city, some say to his villa in Tuscania, some say to the dungeons of the emperor's palace. An Amazon who serves Martellus was attacked in the Subura at noon, and they say she slew ten men with a *tormentum*. Martellus plans a great assembly of some kind tomorrow afternoon in the Flavian Amphitheater. Other than that, there is little news."

Pierce smiled. "Have you made plans for dinner yet? If not, I would be grateful for your company. And before that I would like to visit the baths."

"I would be honored to accompany you, but I fear—"

"I must insist, dear Juvenal, on paying for everything. It's you who honor me."

"Before such a gracious offer, I am helpless." He drank the wine in his cup and poured himself another. "More? Not yet? Well, then, it seems your visit to the consul was a helpful one."

"All thanks to you and your knowledge of this great city."

"Your kindness embarrasses me. Any Roman would have shown the same courtesy."

"Any well-bred Roman who believes in the old ways."

"Well, yes." His bloodshot eyes focused sharply on Pierce. "If I can be of any further service . . ."

"The pleasure of your company is service enough. As a stranger to Rome, I am fortunate indeed to have crossed your path. Let us finish this refreshment and then seek out the baths."

"Of course. I know of a very pleasant establishment not far from here—"

"Do you know the baths of Scribonius Tertius, in the Campus Martius?"

Juvenal's face fell. "Indeed, but it's quite a distance from here, and not quite the place for gentlemen of quality like ourselves. It's frequented by slaves and freedmen and low sorts."

"No doubt it is," Pierce agreed genially as he allowed Juvenal to pour him some more wine. "Still, it would amuse me to see the place. And afterward, I shall let you find us the best *taberna* in the city for our meal."

"Ah. Well, I believe I know a most suitable place. It's—"

"Surprise me with it, dear Juvenal. Now, if that flagon is truly empty, let us be on our way."

"Of course. Only let me put on my toga and gather my bathing kit."

Pierce had obtained a toga of his own from the stores in the imperial palace. He had taken care to choose one that was not too elegant, but it still looked much better than

Juvenal's stained, patched garment. Nevertheless, the poet wore his with style and dignity.

"We Germans never feel quite comfortable in a toga," Pierce said. "I wish I could look like you."

"Allow me, dear Alaricus: a fold here, and here—tuck it in a bit here." He stepped back. "Much better. If you weren't so tall, no one would take you for anything but a young fellow of the equestrian order."

"I have no intention of disguising myself, only of conforming to proper behavior."

"Then you are fated to be part of a small minority in this city, my friend."

Pierce laughed. "I am undeserving to be the sole audience of such wit. Come, let us be on our way."

They made their way through the Forum; Pierce remembered the chaos here in the minutes after Domitian's death. Now it was simply another late afternoon in the center of the city, with crowds milling about in search of gambling or gossip. Once out of the Forum, they were soon on the Vicus Iugarius, a street curving around the south slopes of the Capitoline Hill. It turned into the Via Tecta, a long, straight street running northwest past the senate.

"In Egypt I yearned to be back here," Juvenal said. "Oh, Alexandria is a fine city, some of their poets aren't bad at all, but the climate! And the dreadful food!"

"You were there in the army?"

"A tribune of the III Cyrenaica. Not much work to do —stopping the occasional riot, escorting the governors, that sort of thing. I had hoped for a military career, but it's all politics. The commander didn't like me, especially when I complained about some irregularities in the men's pay. Before I knew it, he trumped up some charges against me. Nothing that would stick, but enough to encourage me to resign. So I returned to Rome eight years ago, and misfortune has followed me ever since. My two children died, and then my beloved wife. My kindest patron died also, and his son has no interest in poetry at all. So I scrape along, teaching a little rhetoric, writing a bit of verse now and then."

"A bit of verse? Your satires are known all over the world."

"And I am not a *sestertius* better off for it."

"A sad comment, when *Omnia Romae cum pretio*—Everything in Rome is costly."

Juvenal smiled, showing bad teeth. "You have read me too well. I was wrong. Bread and circuses are cheap, the bribe we pay ourselves not to tear the city down about our ears. Now, enough of this lamentation. What interests you in the baths of Scribonius Tertius?"

"Someone told me it was an agreeable place, with a good library."

Juvenal's eyebrows rose. "Indeed? It's a well-kept secret, then. I know it only by repute, as a place frequented by slaves and foreigners, especially Jews. Ah, perhaps you enjoy staring at circumcised men?"

"Not in the slightest. Dear poet, humor me in this. I am new here, and I wish to see all sides of this great city."

"You will soon be tired of the foreigners' side of it, I assure you."

"I've heard it said that he who is tired of Rome is tired of life."

"A nice line; whose is it?"

"Oh, it's just a saying in my homeland."

"Perhaps I can find a use for it."

Here and there along the streets they saw men slapping up posters announcing tomorrow's great assembly in the Amphitheater, and handing out free bright-yellow tickets for admission. Pierce admired Willard's efficiency; organizing a event for fifty or sixty thousand people, on twenty-four hours' notice, was no small achievement. Doubtless that was why Willard was one of the Elders: Those who could not satisfy Martel's demands would not last long.

"Shall we get tickets?" he asked Juvenal as they read a poster."

"I have no interest in games and shows."

"Martellus promises no games; look at the poster. 'A

great assembly of the senate and people of Rome, to witness the miraculous powers of Christ acting through the emperor Martellus.' Surely it will at least give you good material for a lampoon or two.''

"I came near enough to grief that way with the late Domitian; I shall not mock this new pretender."

"As you please."

The houses and apartments were lower in this part of the city, and Pierce could see Domitian's Stadium over the rooftops to the east. That was where Aquilius's father had enjoyed going to watch the chariot races; one day it would become the Piazza Navona, where Bernini's fountains glittered in the sunlight and little girls squealed as they chased one another. Pierce wondered where Aquilius was.

The baths of Scribonius Tertius stood in a relatively empty part of the city; the Campus Martius, a broad field running down to the Tiber, lay just across the street. Men were riding horses or driving chariots in the distances, while others nearby ran races or wrestled, or practiced military drill.

Pines grew along the sidewalk, giving some shade to the entrance of the baths. A porter at the gate charged them half an *as* apiece. Pierce and Juvenal went through a courtyard into a changing room where they stripped and got out their bath kits: oil, combs, strigils, and towels. They put their clothes into their shoulder bags and kept them close at hand; too many thieves prowled the baths.

"That's excellent oil you have there," Juvenal remarked.

"Please share it with me."

Once oiled, they joined the dozen naked men who were exercising in the courtyard. Some wrestled, while others played a ball game called *trigon*.

"Not a circumcised man among them," Pierce observed. The poet muttered unintelligibly.

With another man they set up the threesome needed for *trigon*. Standing in a triangle, they tossed a small, hard leather ball back and forth, often feinting a throw in one direction before hurling the ball in another. A missed catch cost the player a point: The winner was the man with the lowest score. The game was enjoyably innocent; Pierce found himself relaxing for the first time in days, with Pentasyn in his blood and his enhanced reflexes making the game even pleasanter.

When the game broke up, Pierce did some stretching and calisthenics while chatting casually with the other bathers. Most were hard-bitten men with scars and missing fingers or toes. A few seemed to be slaves, clerks to rich men, and two of those were Blacks. They talked about the price of vegetables, rates of pay for construction workers, and good brothels. No one mentioned Martellus, Christianity, or anything to do with politics.

"Where is the *balneator*, Scribonius Tertius?" Pierce asked.

"He wanders about," one of the men answered. "Sometimes out here, sometime in the *piscina*, sometimes in the sweat bath or the library. You'll know him when you see him. A fat one-eyed fellow.

Pierce and Juvenal went on into the *piscina*, a long, narrow swimming pool about a meter deep. The water was scummed with oil, and the floor of the pool felt slimy. Even so, it was pleasant to swim a few laps. After quick dips in the baths and a few minutes in the sweat room, the two men scraped each other clean and toweled off.

"So far I find this a tolerable place, but nothing out of the ordinary," Juvenal commented.

"Go and examine the library; we'll meet again in a little while. I'll be interested in your opinion of it."

"It will be my pleasure, especially if any of my works are in it."

Pierce bought a snack of honeycake and walked about the courtyard until the fat man, one eye clouded white by cataracts, appeared.

"*Salve*," Pierce greeted.

"*Salve*. Have you enjoyed your bath?"

"Very much so. A young fellow named Terentius recommended this place to me."

Scribonius Tertius's round face was almost unreadable, but Pierce saw the involuntary revelation of interest and anxiety.

"A welcome customer. I am grateful that he spoke well of this humble establishment."

Pierce found his fish pendant in his shoulder bag; knowing he would be going naked, he had taken it off before reaching Juvenal's room. Holding it cupped in his hand, he let Scribonius glimpse it.

"I am looking for people who have worn this symbol in their souls for more than a few days."

"May I ask where you spoke with Terentius?"

"In the baths of the imperial palace, where he works as an attendant."

"Then you serve Martellus."

"I do."

Scribonius waved him into a marble bench in the shade of the courtyard wall, and shouted to an attendant to bring wine.

"The new emperor proclaims himself a Christian, but many have their doubts," the *balneator* said. "They think it's only a ruse, a trick to make them come forward and expose themselves to death."

"Why would they think so?"

"It stands to reason, does it not? The Christians are a tiny group in this great city. For every Christian, a thousand people honor the gods of Rome. Why should anyone risk the support of the thousand for the praise of one?"

"If he thought he could convert the thousand with the help of the one . . ."

"My friend, such a man would be foolish, or else truly blessed. The Christians are slaves and freedmen and foreigners. Most are Jews, and many have been slain in the last few days. I do not think the gentile Christians will put their lives in this stranger's hands. Least of all when he behaves more like Titus to the Jews than like Christ to his disciples."

"You sound as if you know a good deal about this sect."

"A man who keeps a public bath learns a good deal about everything. And keeps most of it to himself."

"Then let me draw upon your knowledge, friend. If Martellus were sincere, and wished to save the Christians from persecution, how could he prove his good intentions?"

"By ceasing to murder Jews," Scribonius said instantly. "And by ceasing to murder Romans who served Domitian. By allowing all religions to worship in peace. Then, perhaps, the Christians might announce themselves."

"And if I were to announce myself a true Christian in the service of Martellus, what would be your advice to me?"

"To keep your mouth shut, young friend. Even if your master has only love for Christians, many Romans do not. He cannot be everywhere to protect the faithful. Someone attacked some followers of Martellus in the Subura today, and died for it; since then, at least five people have been killed for wearing that pendant you showed me."

Pierce nodded. "Your advice is wise. I will show the pendant to no one else. And I promise you that no harm will come to Terentius or yourself."

The fat man's one good eye fixed on Pierce. "You are an unusual young man. You look like a German, talk like a drunken patrician, and behave like a senator."

"And work for a Christian whom other Christians don't trust."

Scribonius chuckled and poured him some more wine.

"Am I right in saying that a man like yourself welcomes powerful patrons?" asked Pierce.

"You are indeed. No man has too many friends."

"Then count me as one of yours. If you find yourself in need of help or advice, I hope you will call on me at the palace of Domitian. My name is Alaricus; I am the *satelles* of the lady Maria—the woman they call the Amazon."

"Not a lady who needs a bodyguard, if the stories I hear of her are true."

"Even Amazons need friends."

"Not an interesting library, I'm afraid," Juvenal said as they walked back into the center of the city. The sun was down in the west. "It has Aristotle on comedy, too much Menander, a very many books about Greece and Asia and their cults, but few of the great Romans."

"But you yourself have said '*omnia novit Graeculus esuriens*,' 'the hungry little Greek knows everything,'" Pierce teased him. "Why bother, then, with Roman works?"

"You provoke me, Alaricus."

Pierce patted the poet's shoulder. "Only to stir your digestive juices before a fine meal."

He noticed, without mentioning it to his companion, that the fish graffiti on the walls had often been scratched over, or turned into obscene priapic sketches. Scribonius had been right: A lot of people didn't like the Christians.

The *taberna* Juvenal had chosen was near the Forum, with a terrace overlooking a little garden and the tiled rooftops beyond. They were dining late; the sun had just set when they entered, and most of the remaining customers had settled down to drinking. Pierce let Juvenal order for both of them as they reclined on couches at a terrace table already much used.

"I noticed that your conversation with Plinius led to surprising results," Juvenal commented as the waiters brought a tray of appetizers including hard-boiled eggs, olives, and a kind of salad of lettuce and mint. "What may we expect from your visit to the baths?"

Pierce shrugged. Juvenal squinted at him in the light of the lamps hanging beside the table.

"What is your occupation, friend Alaricus?"

"I turn my hand to whatever comes along. Like you, I served once as a soldier."

"And you still do. Your bearing gives you away, and your way of looking at everything. What I do not know is who your master is."

"You do not need to know."

Juvenal smiled. "I have been instrumental in your comings and goings, have I not? If you are taken and tortured, whose name will spring first from your lips? No, my friend, I think I should know your motives a little better than I do."

Pierce looked him in the eye. "I am a supporter of Marcus Ulpius Traianus."

"Ah, I knew it!" Juvenal murmured excitedly, glancing from the corner of his eye at the nearest drinkers. "A German newly arrived in Rome with plenty of money, meeting with consuls, bathing where brigands and cutthroats are known to gather—just as a pretender tries to make himself emperor. Such skill in intrigue speaks as well for Trajan as his military achievements. Well, I shall gladly support you."

"I knew you would. Decimus Iunius, I put absolute confidence in you. And the general will be grateful for your help."

Pierce fell silent; the attendants had returned, throwing the leftovers to the tiled floor and setting out plates piled with roasted chicken, pork, and kid. As Juvenal's fingers plucked now at one plate and then at another, Pierce went on:

"My task is to weaken the pretender, so that he cannot resist Trajan. If Martellus learns about me, of course he will kill me out of hand."

"You honor me with your trust, dear friend. Call upon me for whatever service I can give."

"I shall. Now, enough of business; let's enjoy this meal."

Through the main course—slices of roast boar, baked potatoes, and an almost-Chinese dish of chicken, nuts, and vegetables—they talked about literature and music. *Secundae mensae*, the dessert, was a platter of raisins and dried fruit. Juvenal apologized; later in the summer, the fruits would be fresh.

"As long as the wine is old, who cares about the age of the fruit?" Pierce asked.

"Well put. Now, can I do anything else to aid you in your work?"

"A great deal. You go everywhere; you know the common people and the wealthy alike. You observe them acutely. Continue to do so. Listen to the conversations in the street, and in the atriums of your patrons. Sense the mood of the people, and let me know what it is. I shall pay you well for this service."

Juvenal waved the idea away. "It will be a pleasure. And how shall I report to you?"

"I will visit you from time to time. If I miss you, I'll leave a message in the *taberna* on the ground floor of your building."

"Very well. And now that that is settled, what now? Another bottle?"

"Alas, not tonight. I must bid you farewell for now. Perhaps we can meet the day after tomorrow. Until then, you will need some expense money." He gave the poet ten *denarii*, more than enough to support him for several days.

"You are too generous."

"A German vice that Romans must endure with their famed stoicism."

Juvenal grinned. "You are like the *eiron* in a Greek play—a fellow much more than you seem."

"On the contrary, I have much to be modest about."

They walked companionably to Juvenal's *insula* and said good night. As he returned to the palace, Pierce wondered whether Juvenal was indeed a supporter of Trajan; his nonverbal responses had seemed sincere, and Trajan was the logical man for the poet to back. But Juvenal's streak of weakness and self-contempt might betray his ideals. If he decided Martellus was going to win after all,

he might denounce Pierce for the sake of a few *denarii*—
or just the freedom to go on starving in his room under the
tiles.

It was a risk Pierce was willing to run; if Juvenal tried
it, Pierce would charge the poet with admitting to Trajan-
ist sympathies, and had no doubt that the Elders would
believe their pet Christian over an unknown pagan. And
that would be the end of Decimus Iunius Iuvenalis.

Seventeen:

"You're to report to the emperor in his meeting room," the decurion told Pierce at the north gate of the palace.

"I go at once."

The guards on the terrace took his revolver before admitting him to the meeting; obviously Martel was not relaxing security even for endo Christians sent by divine providence. Maria Donovan, in her usual chair by the wall, smiled at him as he crossed the floor to stand by her side. Pierce scanned the Elders around the table, trying to sense their mood.

Willard was chairing the meeting tonight. He nervously stroked his sandy beard, and his eyes moved restlessly from one face to the next: doing his own readings, Pierce decided, and feeling less secure than he liked.

"...think we ought to develop a fallback plan if this rally in the Colosseum doesn't work," David Greenbaugh was saying. The Trainable was clearly exhausted, his face pale and slack. "We're making an appeal to the general population, but we have to remember that those people are all clients of one aristocrat or another. There's a chance that the aristocrats will tell their people to stay away, to reject the emperor. And that'll just make the senate more stubborn than ever."

The others said nothing: Old Elias Smith, a tough survivor of jails, riots, and deportation, seemed half-asleep. Matthew Knowles and Martin Armbruster sat purse-lipped and anxious, understanding Greenbaugh's argument but not certain whether to back it.

Martel broke the silence. "What kind of plan would you suggest, Brother David?"

"Well, Dear Michael, we're going to need the aristocrats to help run the empire. We've been purging the old emperor's people, and the aristocrats who benefited from trading with the IF. That's a lot of people, and we've certainly put the fear of the Lord in the rest of them. If they don't think they have a chance under a Christian emperor, they'll turn to Trajan. So we should develop some positive contacts with reasonable people in the elite—both the senators and the equestrians. When they see the light, we'll bring them on side. That's how Augustus did it when he set up the principate, and so did Caligula and Nero and Domitian. These aristocrats are always fighting each other, and there's sure to be a faction that'll be glad to back us up if it means they can get rid of their enemies."

Elias's hand went up. "With respect, Mr. Chairman, Brother David's argument goes against the policies Dear Michael has established. We heard last night how these ancient aristocracies always hated popular leaders and called them tyrants. I'd be glad to see them all humbled. And that's what's going to happen after tomorrow in the Colosseum."

Knowles nodded. "Mr. Chairman, I seem to recall reading somewhere that they had to keep promoting people into the aristocracy because it would've died out anyway. Let's not worry too much about them; if we get the majority of people with us, we can pick and choose the best of them to take over administration."

Greenbaugh looked angry. "Mr. Chairman, that's all very well as a long-term policy once we're firmly in control. But I'm talking about getting through the next few days and weeks, with the International Federation likely to pounce any moment now."

Martel nodded, smiling. "We're looking at both sides of a single answer, brothers. We need to win the support of patricians and plebeians alike; support from one will encourage support from the other. After the rally tomorrow, we'll have both. We've got Cornutus locked up in the basement, and he's changed his mind about resisting us. So Cornutus will endorse me as emperor, and the people will swing over to me after they hear that and see the show we're going to put on for them. That'll bring the aristocracy into line."

"But what about Plinius?" Greenbaugh asked. "He's still loose, and he could cause a lot of trouble."

"We'll find him." Martel looked almost smug. "And if we don't, it hardly matters. His term as consul is only two months, and it ends on June thirtieth. By then we'll be firmly established, and I'll appoint the next two consuls."

"Any further discussion, brothers?" asked Willard. "Then let's move on to item four, the program for tomorrow."

Knowles raised his hand at once. "Mr. Chairman, we've got these *lusiones*, these fake combats, scheduled before Dear Michael speaks, and that worries me. It seems just as bad as the pagan emperors to be holding fights."

"If Dear Michael would take the chair for a moment, I'll answer Brother Matthew's concerns," Willard said. "Now, I know just how you feel, Brother Matthew. But these *are* just pretend combats, with wooden swords. No one's going to get hurt, well, maybe bruised a little. And we've got to fill those seats. We get fifty thousand people in there, we've got five percent of the whole city. So we put on a show; no harm in that."

The debate sputtered on a little longer, but Knowles finally acceded. Willard resumed the chair and ran them briskly through the rest of the agenda. Pierce listened with interest.

"Last item," Willard said somberly. "Brother Dennis and his team are still missing. We've had patrols out in the area he was last reported in, and they can't find hide nor hair. We know they were in the villa of somebody named Tertius, and then they went on to a place called Vallis

Viridis, but they never got there. The local people say they don't know anything about it."

"Who were they after in Vallis Viridis?" asked Armbruster.

"A senatorial family named Aquilius. Close ties to the IF; their boy got sent uptime for Training. But the whole family's gone. Supposedly to Capua."

"We'll turn 'em up eventually," said Elias Smith. "And Brother Dennis, too."

"Further discussion? Motion to adjourn?"

They prayed briefly before pushing back their chairs and dispersing. Martel caught Pierce's eye and beckoned to him and Maria. When everyone but the guards had left, Martel asked:

"What success, Alaricus?"

"A little, my lord. I believe I have found a place where Christians sometimes gather. They know I am interested in contacting them; now I must wait a little. I think they are frightened."

Martel leaned back, smiling. "Well done! How soon do you think they will come forward?"

"Perhaps a day or two, my lord."

"Good. But they are foolish to be frightened of us."

They'd be foolish not to be frightened, Pierce thought.

"My lord, the man I spoke with seemed worried about the disappearance of Plinius and the senate's refusal to grant you the *imperium*. I think the Christians fear being accused of treason if they support us."

Martel nodded. "They will learn courage. Thank you, Alaricus. Pursue your contacts, and persuade them to come forward and join us."

"I shall, my lord."

In English, Martel said to Maria, "He's doing pretty well, isn't he? Seems to have made more progress in half a day than we have in weeks."

"I'm real proud of him, Dear Michael."

"You have a busy day tomorrow; you'd better get some sleep."

Outside on the terrace the guards returned Pierce's pistol. Maria grinned as he replaced it in his shoulder bag.

"Did you need it?"

"Not yet, my lady. But if we go to the Praetorian camp tomorrow, we may need it very much."

"We'll be going early, and leaving early. I have much to do at the Colosseum."

"The Coloss—ah, the Flavian Amphitheater? Of course, my lady. I am looking forward to that. People are talking eagerly about it in the streets."

"They'll be talking about it for years."

Outside her door, Maria said, "Are you sure you're comfortable there in the doorway?"

"Very much so, my lady."

"I think I'd feel safer if you slept inside the door."

"Oh, no, my lady. If anyone got through the door, it would be much harder to defend you."

She almost pouted. "I'd still like it better."

"My lady, I do not just sleep in the doorway; I patrol all the corridors nearby. I cannot do that if I am locked inside your rooms."

"Very well; I won't argue. Good night, then. We'll be up early tomorrow."

"Yes, my lady."

Pierce smiled faintly as he heard her slam the bolt home. Under other conditions, it would be amusing to let her seduce him; but he needed freedom tonight.

For an hour he sat silently in the doorway, while the palace staff wound down the night's activities. At last the only traffic down the corridor was a Praetorian watchman who plodded by every fifteen minutes or so. After a couple of circuits the Praetorian paused and nodded to Pierce.

"You're the German who shoots so well," he said in a whisper.

"At the camp? Yes, they showed me how to do it."

"They gave me a *tormentum*, too, but I don't like it." He pulled back his *sagum*, a dark-gray cloak, to reveal a holstered Beretta. "Too much noise. I get into any trouble, I'll use my sword. Then everyone sleeps peacefully," he added with a grin.

Pierce grinned back, a comrade in arms. "Especially the one who gets the sword in his belly . . . I hear that the consul Plinius has disappeared."

"So they say. We've got the other one, old Cornutus, in a cell downstairs."

"A cell? The consul in a cell?"

"The old fellow tried to escape when we put him in an apartment. So he's down in the basement, just out of reach of the emperor's wine."

"Wine! You make me thirsty just to talk about it."

The Praetorian winked and sidled closer. "These people don't seem to care much for it, so a few flagons have gone missing. Fine stuff, even wines from Chios."

"No! Here, tell me how to get there, and I'll pay you two *denarii*."

"Three."

"Done."

When the watchman went on his way, Pierce slipped from the doorway and headed down a nearby flight of stairs. The air chilled at the bottom: This part of the palace was underground. Corridors led in different directions, illuminated by occasional battery lamps. The watchman's directions were good, and Pierce made his way easily to the wine cellar. It was a long room with an arched brick ceiling; amphorae, tall ceramic containers, stood three deep along the walls. Above them were shelves holding smaller flagons. Judging by the gaps, more than a few flagons had been taken recently. At the far end of the cellar, a corridor led into darkness. Pierce stepped cautiously into it, sniffing for the scent of a man, and soon found it.

The door was thick, with a gap of about ten centimeters at the bottom where a gutter ran out to a drain in the corridor. Kneeling, Pierce put his face close to the gap. The stink of old urine and excrement was dizzying.

"Cornutus Tertullus," he said quietly.

"What is it?" It was an old man's voice, but not a frightened one.

"I am a friend. Last night I warned Plinius to leave Rome."

"They told me he was here in the palace."

"They lied, Consul. He's gone; before he left, he sent word to the senate to reject Martellus as emperor."

Pierce heard a sudden intake of breath. "This Martellus is worse than Sejanus, then. He is a usurper."

"Tomorrow he plans to display you in the Amphitheater, and to use your endorsement to persuade the senate to accept him."

"They said Plinius would be there, too, and that he supports the usurper."

"As I said, Consul, they lied. I must go now; think well about what these people want of you, and what history will say of your actions."

"I shall indeed. Whoever you are, I thank you."

"The senate and people of Rome will thank you tomorrow, Cornutus Tertullus. *Vale*."

"*Vale*."

Pierce went back through the wine cellar, picking up a bottle of Chian wine as he went. If nothing else, Juvenal would appreciate it.

Returning upstairs, he walked quietly to Brother Kelly's armory. The door was held by a simple padlock; Pierce unscrewed the hasp with the dagger Kelly had given him, let himself in, and found the shelf with the communications gear. A moment later he had a beeper tucked into his tunic. He went out, replaced the hasp, and returned to Maria's door. Now, at least, he had a way to signal the helicopter when he was ready to run. It made him feel pleasantly secure.

In the morning, before dawn, Pierce and Maria crossed the city to the Praetorian camp. Their escort was a squad of urban cohorts, none with firearms but formidable nonetheless.

The long stretch of clear weather seemed about to break: The stars were lost behind an overcast, and dawn when it came was a gray murk. Mist swirled through the streets, mixing with the smoke of countless charcoal fires to form an eye-stinging smog.

Pierce felt better than he had in days. A few more caps of Pentasyn had dulled the symptoms of B&C, leaving his senses sharp. The beeper was safely tucked in his shoulder bag. He had slept well after returning from the palace basement, and looked forward to the day.

Striding along beside him, Maria seemed equally cheerful. "This will be a great day in the history of Rome, Alaricus. Today Rome becomes truly a Christian empire."

"But it is already, my lady."

"We have a Christian emperor; by tonight we will have a Christian city. You will see marvels, miracles."

"I have seen marvels ever since I was granted my vision of you, my lady."

She touched his cloaked shoulder. "You are a fine man."

Brother Jeff the rangemaster was up and busy when they reached the camp. His men were setting up new targets, and a fresh crew of trainees stood stamping their feet in the dawn chill.

"Morning, Sister Maria." He smiled at Pierce. "*Ave*, Alaricus."

"Well," said Maria in English, "we got our boy his own shooting iron, Brother Jeff." She reached into Pierce's shoulder bag and brought out the revolver. Brother Jeff looked at it and nodded.

"Not bad, but I think he can handle a Mallory."

"Well, let's see him try."

The rangemaster brought out a Mallory .15, a twin of the one Pierce had lost. Pierce listened attentively as Brother Jeff explained the difference between bullets and flechettes, between low and high impact.

"This *tormentum* is very quiet, but very powerful. I will show you." At impact 10, Brother Jeff exploded the head of one of the statue targets.

"But I didn't even hear it!" Pierce exclaimed. "May I try this wonderful weapon?"

With the familiar grip in his hand, Pierce had to force himself to shoot awkwardly at first. Brother Jeff pointed out his errors; he nodded, and shot more accurately. While the Praetorians potted away with AK-47s, he smashed target after target. Brother Jeff stood beside him, barking out impact numbers: *"Duo! Sex! Decem!"* while Pierce's thumb rolled the knob to the correct setting before firing.

At last the rangemaster turned to Maria. "Sister, if you don't believe now that marksmanship is a God-given skill, I don't know what it would take to convert you."

"I've seen the light," she said with a smile. "You know I practiced with a Mallory once for three weeks and couldn't hit a blessed thing with it. Too light—I'd keep twitching my hand and putting the flechettes all over. But he's got a steadier hand than those statues, doesn't he?"

"Alaricus," said Brother Jeff in solemn Latin, "I declare you a qualified marksman. And I hereby give you this weapon and its ammunition." He handed over two clips.

"You are too kind," Pierce protested. "This is too fine a weapon for me."

"You deserve better than this piece of iron." Brother Jeff smoothly unloaded Pierce's revolver and put it into a wooden crate with an assortment of other handguns. "When you have the time, come back and I'll see what you can do with a rifle."

The Mallory had a nylon holster that clipped to Pierce's tunic belt. It felt good, almost too good: He would have to control the urge to massacre the Elders as he had the Praetorians at Aquilius's villa.

They returned to Domitian's palace, once again passing between the gladiators' school and the Amphitheater. It was late morning, and people were already milling about. Scalpers hawked the yellow tickets that had been given away free, while vendors peddled snacks to people waiting for the Amphitheater gates to open.

"We're going to have a lot of people today," Maria said.

"Not all of them will be friends, my lady. I hope the Crucifers are prepared."

"We will be."

Palace cooks were sent over to the Amphitheater to feed the Militants, Praetorians, and slaves working to set everything up. Maria's job was to oversee the security for Martel and the Elders; they would be seated on the *pulvinar*, just where Domitian had died less than a week ago. Maria watched a crew of slaves installing a four-strand barbed wire barrier around the *pulvinar* and the seats immediately above it. Martel and his entourage would be entering through the imperial gate; onlookers would be able to see him, but could not approach closer than twenty meters.

On either side of the barbed wire, Praetorians would stand guard; they would be armed only with swords and spears, however. Pierce approved: The Praetorians had already shown they could be bought and sold.

"When the emperor arrives, Alaricus," Maria said apologetically, "I will have to take your *tormentum* also. I hope to make you a Crucifer someday, but for now you must yield your weapon."

"I understand, my lady. As Shimon told us, 'Satan lies in wait for the unready.'"

"O Lord," Maria said softly in English, her eyes fixed on Pierce's. "Dear Michael's very words. If ever I doubted, I repent."

Pierce was not concerned about giving up his Mallory when the gathering began. He had no intention of killing Martel; unless the Agency was on the brink of stepping in, an assassination would be pointless and probably suicidal. One of the Elders or Crucifers would take over, and would have time to reorganize. And even if he could wipe out all the Elders as well as Martel, someone like the Praetorian general Drusus might seize power. That would only complicate the Agency's efforts to reestablish itself.

The walkie-talkie on Maria's hip crackled into life. She lifted it to her lips while Pierce looked appropriately startled.

"Sister Maria? Brother Joe. Uh, I'm supposed to get the combat show organized, but I got held up here in the palace. Brother David said maybe you could go over to the gladiators' school and make sure everything's set."

Maria scanned the barbed wire. "Sister Maria here. Okay, Brother Joe. You owe me one."

"Thanks. Blessings."

"Come along, Alaricus; we have to talk to the *lanista* at the gladiators' school."

The school was just across the plaza from the Amphitheater, a walled compound of low brick buildings and a miniature stadium. The porters at the gate were squat, powerful men—probably ex-gladiators who had earned their freedom and stayed on in the management end of the business. They stared up at Maria with a mixture of astonishment and lechery on their battered faces.

"Is Lucius Scaurus here?" she demanded.

"He is," said one of the porters.

"I am on the emperor's business. Take us to him."

They pulled the gate open; Maria strode in with Pierce behind her. He saw a dusty practice ground surrounded by shedlike buildings, one of them obviously a gladiators' barracks. The porter led them through the practice ground and past a long, low shed divided into barred cages. Men, filthy and beaten, crouched there under a roof too low to allow them to stand, *noxii*, common criminals who had been condemned to death in the arena. Unarmed, they would be slaughtered by gladiators as a lunchtime amusement before the afternoon's serious fighting began.

Without even a glance at the captives, the porter escorted Pierce and Maria to the little stadium, whose wooden seats rose ten meters. A passage under the stands brought them into the first row of seats, three meters above the arena. In the walkway between the stands and the arena itself, over twenty men and a few women stood watching a practice combat between two Samnites—gladiators with the weapons and armor of Rome's ancient enemies.

In the stands sat perhaps fifty men, some of them well-dressed and affluent; the rest were obviously slave attendants. They watched the practice with interest and knowledgeability, cheering at a good blow or parry and jeering at slowness or caution. Their shouts died away as they noticed Maria. The watching gladiators looked up, and then even the combatants. Silence fell.

A breeze sprang up, bringing with it a smell of putrefaction. Pierce detected it first, but a moment later Maria's face tightened with disgust.

"I wish to speak with Lucius Scaurus," she called out.

A gaunt, hard-faced man wearing a toga over a red tunic stood up from a seat in the first row. "I am he. May I have the honor of knowing who addresses me?"

"I am the Domina Maria, representing the emperor Martellus."

Scaurus's hard face creased in an obsequious smirk as he hurried over. Slaves scuttled after him, bearing parasols and fans.

"Please, my lady, be so good as to seat yourself." His attendants began to fan Maria, stirring the humid, stinking air. "May I offer you the poor hospitality of my school—a cup of wine, a morsel of bread or fruit?"

"*Benigne dicis*; no, thank you. I need only to make sure that everything is ready for this afternoon's gathering in the Amphitheater."

"You see our men practicing now, my lady." He gestured expansively toward the men in the arena. "Get on with it, you *agrestii*! Louts!" The combatants resumed, but no one paid much attention to anything but the tall blond Amazon. "These are not our best, mere *paegniarii*. They fight with wooden swords and whips, like little boys. Surely you will want some proper fighters?"

"No. The emperor was very clear on that. He wants no bloodshed in this gathering."

Scaurus shrugged and threw his hands in the air. "I obey, of course. But please do not forget that the gladiators of my *familia* are the most renowned in the empire. That fellow there, Astavius"—he pointed to a squat man in the helmet of a *myrmillo*—"was in the arena at the very moment the thunderbolt slew the evil Domitian, fighting at the specific command of the emperor."

Pierce recognized him: The man had been fighting a *retiarius*. Then, just beyond the man, he saw a young woman standing by the arena fence. Her dark hair was pulled back tightly into a long ponytail; she wore a leather breastplate over a white tunic. She was the gladiatrix Pierce had seen weeping in the *spoliarium*, the morgue under the stands of the Amphitheater. In the light of day she was even lovelier than she had been by lamplight.

Evidently bored by the rehearsal of the *paegniarii*, the woman looked up at the stands; her eyes met Pierce's, and she recognized him at once. He looked back impassively.

"Indeed," Maria said uninterestedly. "Scaurus, what is that smell?"

"Smell, my lady? Oh—the *carnarium*?" He grinned, showing dead front teeth. "That's the pit where the dead beasts go after every *venatio* in the arena. And the slain *noxii*, if their wretched families don't claim the bodies. The pit's just beyond the walls." He pointed toward the east.

"Dear Lord," Maria muttered in English. Then, in Latin: "A new era has dawned in Rome. Do not expect to send more men to their deaths in the arena."

The *lanista* looked astounded. "Surely I misunderstand my lady. The people expect it. The people demand it."

"The emperor Martellus demands otherwise." Maria looked disapprovingly at Scaurus. "In any case, you need not concern yourself with that for a time. Only bring in your fighters this afternoon, and make sure they give a good performance."

"Of course, my lady." Scaurus and Pierce sprang to their feet as Maria rose and headed for the exit. Pierce felt the eyes of the gladiatrix on him as he left.

"Disgusting," Maria said as they passed out through the gate. "This is almost a perversion of the faith. We fight for the glory of God and the spread of the gospel. If we die, we redeem our sins; if we kill, we serve God's will. But these—these creatures fight and die for nothing. For an afternoon's amusement, and to fill a pit with rotting flesh."

"My lady, you speak the truth. The emperor will make the world a better place by forbidding these shows."

He wondered what would happen to the *noxii*. Perhaps, if he was not to be paid for killing them, Scaurus would simply have them clubbed and pitched into the *carnarium*.

The *lanista* had been right, though. Deprived of their games and shows, the people of Rome might well become combatants themselves.

Eighteen:

The procession from the palace began with the lictors, a dozen officials bearing the *fasces*—bundles of bound rods that symbolized the Roman state. Seeing this familiar vanguard, the crowds flanking the Amphitheater plaza set up a cheer that soon died away. Next should have come a contingent of boys, sons of the city's greatest families; instead, two cohorts of Praetorians marched stolidly into the plaza.

Pierce and Maria watched from an archway on the second story of the Amphitheater, where they could survey almost the whole length of the procession as it came down the Palatine Hill. Maria carried an AR-20 sniper's rifle; through her ringmike she kept up a steady exchange of comments with her security team, scattered on rooftops and balconies along the procession route and around the plaza. Pierce had little to do except to watch the marchers and the spectators.

Obviously the crowd was surprised and disappointed by the appearance of the Praetorians. The appearance of a hundred Crucifers, all carrying Uzis and wearing uptime camouflage uniforms, stirred some interest; so did the ordinary Militants who followed, dressed in red choir robes and singing Martel's hymns.

When it became clear, however, that the procession had no gladiators, animals, or dancers, the crowd began to shift uneasily. Pierce felt a sting of alertness: Riot was in the air.

At this point the procession should have displayed

images of the gods, nymphs, muses, and graces; instead came a small band playing for the choir, followed by more Crucifers escorting the Elders, and a lone man carrying a white flag with a yellow cross.

"Here he comes," Maria murmured into her ringmike. "All stations, full alert."

Martel appeared, seated on a litter carried by ten Crucifers and escorted by Praetorians. He was dressed in a white toga over a purple tunic, and his golden hair gleamed in the late-afternoon sun. The Praetorians had organized claques in the crowd, and Martel's arrival sparked new cheers and a flutter of hundreds of white handkerchiefs.

The procession circled the Amphitheater in a brassy uproar of cheers, screams, and hymns. Maria and Pierce kept pace, walking almost half a kilometer along the circumference of the Amphitheater so they could keep the emperor in sight. As Martel passed, many in the crowd surged across the plaza to the nearest entrance and swarmed up into the seats. Maria led Pierce up the tunnel to the emperor's gate; it was walled in marble, with a ceiling painted in purple and gold. They stationed themselves at the side of the gate, about a third of the way up the north side, where they commanded a view of most of the spectators.

"Alaricus, remember that you will be in the presence of the emperor. I must ask you to give me your *tormentum*."

Good; she hadn't forgotten. He handed the Mallory over without a word. Pierce had known security chiefs with far more experience who had slipped up on just such details.

Martel, the Praetorians, and the Militants came in through the emperor's gate as the band played a fanfare; his descent down the steps to the *pulvinar* caused more cheers and fluttered handkerchiefs. A few spectators pushed up against the barbed wire and recoiled; their neighbors laughed.

"Everything's going fine," Maria said to her security team. "Keep your eyes open, people."

Pierce thought it was going rather poorly. The Amphitheater was crowded, true, but the mood of the crowd seemed a mixture of curiosity, hostility, and bafflement. After the procession, they did not know what to expect; many had doubtless been deeply offended by the neglect of the gods and the absence of gladiators.

The overcast had deepened during the day, and the Amphitheater lay in a shadowless, chilly late-afternoon twilight. The arena was bare, devoid of the usual scenery used in the combats. Across the smooth-raked sand a troupe of silver-armored *paegniarii* marched to salute Martel. He returned the salute with a smile and they fell upon one another, slashing with whips or stabbing with wooden swords. With every blow they cursed and shrieked; Pierce recalled old samurai movies.

The crowd watched with a kind of sour good humor, calling out sarcastically: "Look out, Cupid, my grandmother's fighting you next." "Hit him harder, he's still asleep!" But before the troupe had finished and marched out, fires were burning here and there in the stands—a sign of boredom here, Pierce decided, as at uptime Mexican bullfights.

The curtain-raiser was over. Martel stepped to the edge of the *pulvinar*; as he did so, Willard—a few steps behind him—spoke into a ringmike to technicians below the stands.

Martel raised his hands above his head, and his voice, enormously amplified, boomed out across the arena and up into the highest seats.

"People of Rome."

His answer was a sudden intake of breath, a gasp from fifty thousand people.

"People of Rome," Martel repeated. "I greet you in the name of the Father, the Son, and the Holy Spirit. I am Martellus, sent by God to bring Rome a new age of blessedness and joy.

"Many of you already know that in the reign of Tiberius a man was crucified in Judea: Jesus Christus. The Jews who killed Him mocked Him as King of the Jews, but He was far more than that; He was Lord of the world. He died on the cross, was buried, and three days later He rose from the dead to speak with men before He ascended into Heaven."

Watching the crowd just beyond the barbed wire, Pierce thought the sound system was impressing the audience more than Martel's words. The sermon went on, a potted resume of Martel's version of Christianity, until he got to the cover story.

"We are, the Church Militant. In a faraway land we were told by God to make our way to Rome, and to make the empire blessed. First we came secretly, and revealed ourselves only to a few. They saw the truth we brought, and begged us to save all Rome from the pit of damnation."

Suddenly the floor of the arena boiled with lurid orange flames that seemed to climb out of an abyss. The sound system exploded with a clap of thunder. The crowd screamed, almost as loudly as when Domitian and his entourage had been murdered.

"There is Hell," Martel roared, and the last word echoed over and over. "Look upon it, O Romans, and think that you may find yourselves burning in it at the very moment of your death. There will all sinners be cast by a wrathful God, while the saved will sit in Heaven as you sit here, watching the eternal sufferings of the damned."

Pierce was impressed. The holoprojection was extremely good, and the computer graphics, based on Hieronymus Bosch's vision of hell, were suitably monstrous—especially when blown up to a gigantic scale to make them easily visible to the upper seats. The sound system now drowned out the crowd with howls and maniacal laughter and screaming feedback.

Again Martel raised his hands, and the vision vanished instantly. The loudspeakers carried instead the choir singing "I Bring Not Peace But a Sword," Martel's most rousing hymn. The crashing chords, the military beat, and the subsonic thump in the synthesizers all combined to produce a different kind of emotional stress from that of the vision of hell. As the hymn neared its end, another holographic image began to form in the air over the Amphitheater. It loomed almost as high as the Colossus's fifty meters.

The image was a cross, on which Christ was nailed. He hung at an angle, as if about to fall upon the spectators, and blood—luridly red—dripped liquidly from his hands and feet and side, falling and then disappearing.

"Now, Romans, look upon the Son of God, who died to save us all from that fiery pit," Martel roared. Then, modulating his voice to an echoing whisper: "Look upon the blood that cleanses all sin. Only wash yourself in that blood and accept Him as your personal savior, and you shall walk hand in hand with Him through the golden streets of Heaven, for all eternity."

The image faded away. By now darkness was falling fast, and some people had run screaming for the exits. Praetorians turned them back with clubs and spear butts.

"In the midst of the darkness of this world," said Martel gently, "He brings us . . . *lux*." Floodlights mounted at the very top of the seats came on, bringing daylight to the whole Amphitheater. The spectators sighed in wonder, and Pierce heard one cry out, "Brighter than Domitian's chandelier!" The lights died away again, except for three focused on Martel.

"In that light, Christ sees all our sins and all our virtues. We cannot hide; we cannot lie. We have only to say, 'Lord, I accept you as my personal savior. Lead me into your paths, and spare me from the fires of damnation.' And we shall be saved."

He fell silent, and the fifty thousand, now sitting in darkness, murmured anxiously.

"Yes," Martel went on, "we shall be saved even if we are put to the sword, even if we are condemned to be devoured by the beasts in the arena. And I have come to you, O Romans, to bring you good news. Jesus loves you, and wishes you all to dwell in Heaven with Him for eternity. That is why He has sent us here, to bring you salvation and peace.

"I acknowledge Jesus as Lord of the world, O Romans, and He has sent me here to serve as His vicar. I am to serve Him as emperor, so that all may come to salvation. Not only Romans—but Rome itself. For I was given a vision, O Romans."

A third holoprojection blazed above the arena, almost too bright to look upon: a burning cross, thirty meters high.

"And Jesus said to me, 'In this sign you shall conquer.' O Romans, in this sign we shall conquer all the world, from the frozen sea of the north to the frozen sea of the south, from the western islands to the silk land. That is the task that Jesus has given me, and that I took up gladly. I am emperor of Rome, but I serve a greater Lord, and I bid you to follow me in that service."

The Praetorians and the claques set up a cheer, and the rest of the crowd raggedly echoed. To Pierce they seemed bemused, almost dazed by Martel's show. People milled about, as if sitting still were now impossible, yet no one could move far. The choir and band struck up another hymn, with the nervous chatter of fifty thousand people as a kind of *basso continuo*.

Off to the eastern side of the stands, just beyond the barbed wire, Pierce saw more-purposeful movement: a handful of cloaked men working their way through the crowd toward the wire.

"My lady." He pointed.

"Sector one east," she murmured in English into her ringmike. "Do you see four or five men approaching the wire at about the thirtieth row? Keep an eye on them."

She touched Pierce's arm, a little longer than she needed to, and said, "Come."

They moved along a walkway toward the wire. The cloaked men were scattered and moving slowly, but they seemed to be converging on a point between the twentieth and thirtieth rows.

The hymn was over, and Martel resumed his place.

"People of Rome," his voice boomed out, "Roman law is the splendor of the world, and we are respecters of the law. God has sent me to rule as emperor, and your own great men have acknowledged me. The general of the Praetorian Guard, and all his noble warriors, support me."

Gaius Vitillus Drusus, gleaming in gilt armor, stepped forward into the spotlights and saluted Martel.

"*Ave, Martellus Imperator*," Drusus cried, his hoarse voice echoing, and the Praetorians chorused, "*Ave, Martellus Imperator.*"

"And the consuls also endorse me, Romans. Behold Cornutus Tertullus, whose nobility and achievements are known to you all. Welcome, consul."

The man stepping uncertainly into the spotlight was tall for a Roman, stooped and bald. His toga was dazzlingly white.

"I am the consul Cornutus Tertullus," he said, clearly expecting his voice to be amplified as it was. "Last night I was taken into custody by armed men, brought to Rome against my will, and shut up in a stinking cell in the palace."

"Uh-oh," said Maria.

"They told me the consul Plinius Caecilius supported this usurper, but in fact he has gone into hiding. Romans, I cannot speak for the Praetorians. But my fellow consul and I must under the law advise the senate on who should succeed to the *imperium*. I will not recommend—"

Someone finally cut the sound system; Cornutus hesitated for a moment, and then continued in a bellow that carried extremely well:

"I will not recommend that this foreigner be granted the *imperium*, even if the Praetorian Guard has been deceived by his tricks and illusions."

He turned and stepped from the spotlight. Only the people in the lower seats had heard his last words clearly, but many began chanting: "Cornutus, Cornutus!" It changed to "Cornutus, Plinius, Traianus!"

Pierce wasn't watching the *pulvinar*; the cloaked men were nearing the wire, while Maria's security people drifted down the steps. The Militants sitting inside the wire seemed oblivious of what was going on.

Martel was back in the light, hands raised while the uproar in the stands gradually died away. Cornutus was being hustled through the emperor's gate by four Crucifers.

"Romans!" Martel roared. "I half expected such a betrayal by a man who gave me his word. Those who grew rich and mighty under the evil Domitian are not happy; let them suffer, if the Roman people prosper. And you shall prosper. I hereby proclaim a donative to every household in this city of five hundred *sestertii*, to be paid within a month."

Applause answered him, but it was far from unanimous. Pierce heard someone cry: "The empire is worth at least a thousand *sestertii!*" while others laughed.

Six cloaked men were just beyond the wire now; suddenly they charged it, the first three flinging themselves across it to make a bridge for their companions. Those men cast off their cloaks and drew swords, shrieking furiously as they charged the nearest Militant spectators.

Security men converged instantly, rifles and pistols out and firing. Pierce sensed something wrong: The cloaked men were almost thirty rows above the *pulvinar*, and surely they meant to attack Martel and not a random handful of his followers. He turned and looked elsewhere.

Everyone in the stands was watching as gunfire slaughtered the six men. Martel had turned and was squinting against the floodlights to see what was happening.

"Emperor, get out of the light!" Pierce bawled. Leaving Maria, he raced down a flight of steps. In the shadows outside Martel's circle of light, various figures jostled: Praetorians, Cornutus, Willard, and others. Pierce crashed through them and pulled Martel back.

The arrow came out of the darkness below the *pulvinar*, from the walkway inside the arena fence. It whispered only centimeters past Martel and Pierce and vanished again into darkness. A woman screamed in the stands, struck by the shaft intended for the emperor.

Three Crucifers leaped down into the walkway, just as Pierce had in the moments after Domitian's death. Pierce heard the thump of a second bowshot, a gasp, and then the sounds of struggle.

"Got him!" someone shouted in English.

"Don't kill him!" Willard yelled back. "Get him back to the palace! I'll interrogate him myself. Anybody else down there?"

"No, Brother Willard."

The whole Amphitheater was in confusion now. Martel's people and hired claques were shouting his name, while others jeered or chanted Trajan's name. Pierce saw fistfights breaking out in places.

"My lord," Pierce said to Martel, "we must take you to safety. More killers may lurk here."

In the dimness outside the spotlight, Martel's beautiful face was unreadable.

"I thank you, Alaricus. The Lord was guiding your footsteps tonight." Then, in English: "Willard, end this farce. I'm going back to the palace to find out who that assassin was working for."

"Yes, Dear Michael." Willard growled into his ring-mike; a few seconds later, three skyrockets soared into the darkness and exploded in bursts of yellow and white. While the spectators stared upward, Martel strode quickly to the emperor's gate with Pierce at his heels. Crucifers fell in around them; Maria joined them at the gate.

"Dear Michael, the Lord is still looking after us," she said as they clattered through the echoing tunnel.

"I want to know who that assassin is," Martel snapped. "All our security arrangements, and someone with a bow and arrow gets into range without anyone even noticing. And the whole event ruined."

Pierce could smell Martel's rage and saw Maria's shoulders slump. She would be in disgrace; he would have to exploit that somehow.

And why didn't you let the guy take Martel out? That would be Wigner's instant question. He knew his answer: *For the same reason that I didn't kill Martel myself. It would be meaningless unless the Agency was ready to take over*. And whatever else the assassin might be, he sure wasn't Agency. The distraction had been a clever and gallant improvisation by someone with no previous experience with barbed wire; an Agency attempt on Martel would not have been made with a bow and arrow. This was strictly a local effort, and if it had succeeded, it would only have thrown the Militants into temporary turmoil before launching a still worse terror than before.

Skyrockets flared and boomed overhead, outlining the Colossus as Martel and his retinue walked quickly back up the hill to the palace. Martel said nothing more; Willard and Maria kept up a steady exchange with their people in the Amphitheater, where half the spectators were watching the fireworks and the other half were chanting for Trajan.

"Get our people outa there," Willard was barking. "As fast as possible, everybody outa there and back into the palace or the Praetorian camp. I don't want anybody hurt, you understand?" Then, to himself, he muttered, "Lord preserve us, what a mess."

Once Martel and the Elders were safe inside the palace, the others went back into the streets to oversee the retreat of the Militants and Praetorians. Pierce stayed close to Maria, who kept her security people in a protective ring around the Militants as they headed for the exits and streamed out into the plaza. The fireworks were soon over, and some of the spectators began to riot in the darkened stands.

Maria and Pierce found themselves face-to-face with Drusus in the plaza.

"General, have your men clear the Amphitheater," Maria ordered.

"It'll mean bloodshed, my lady."

"I hope so. These animals need to learn who their master is."

She was shuddering with rage and shame, but turned to Pierce with his Mallory in her hand.

"Here. You deserve it more than I."

"My lady, you are too harsh on yourself. We must rejoice that the emperor was spared."

"Spared to bring blessings to these brutes." She gestured angrily toward the Amphitheater looming above them, where the Praetorians were already at work under rekindled spotlights. "They don't deserve salvation; better to toss them into the *carnarium*."

The crowds remaining in the stands were now fleeing the swords and spears of the Praetorians, hurrying down the *vomitoria* toward the palace. Few stayed around; they vanished into the darkness, some chanting for Martellus and others for Trajan. At last Maria ordered her people back to the palace. Drusus returned to report the Amphitheater cleared, twenty-three spectators killed, and two Praetorians slightly injured. She thanked him and led Pierce away.

Martellus had ordered the palace guards to escort Maria and Pierce to Martel. The way led through an enormous peristyle garden, now illuminated by electric lights, where Maria once again demanded Pierce's Mallory. Then they entered the throne room.

It was part of the palace Pierce had not yet seen, and its magnificence, enhanced by candles and lamplight, made him pause at the entry. The room was vast and high, its fifteen-meter ceiling inlaid with gold and silver geometric patterns and its walls rich with frescos. Gilded statues of the gods, each over ten meters high, stood in gigantic niches along the walls; busts in marble and silver flanked the pillars that upheld the ceiling. The polished marble of the floor gleamed like the surface of a reflecting pool; the windows were screened by finely embroidered curtains.

At the far end, a raised platform of gold-inlaid marble supported a throne; Martel sat there, resting his chin on his fist, while the Elders stood flanking him. Maria and Pierce paused before the platform and looked up.

"Sister Maria." Martel's voice was flat, expressionless. "You were responsible for security, and I want to thank you for your actions tonight."

"Oh, Dear Michael, don't thank me! We nearly lost you!"

"Not until God wants me; but we know He helps those who help themselves, doesn't He?" Martel smiled faintly. "We've interrogated the assassin. You'll be interested to know he's a Jew. Says his grandfather and uncles died at Masada, and he was looking for revenge. Typical."

"That explains why it was such a treacherous attack," Maria said furiously. "Now I blame myself for not purging the Jews more completely."

"Christ's enemies are infinitely guileful and deceptive," Martel said, shaking his head. "But we've been blessed with another lesson in preparedness."

"Yes, Dear Michael."

"The Elders and I have discussed this evening. We had hoped to swing the people over to us, and we've succeeded to some extent. That consul—there's a pagan who'll never know redemption. And the assassination attempt only made us look stupid."

"But the show was magnificent!" Maria protested. "Even better than the one we gave Drusus. That'll be what they remember."

"Perhaps. But we put on the show for Drusus in the hills, not in the Colosseum. The Romans are accustomed to spectacles there. Sometimes they flood the arena and hold sea battles. Domitian had that enormous chandelier for night games. We underestimated our audience."

He sat upright, folding his hands in his lap. "In any case we're still in charge, but we need more popular support. I want every possible endo backing us. The Agency will be on our necks any day now."

"I'll do whatever I can, Dear Michael."

"For the time being, Maria, you'll stay in your quarters. It's Alaricus I need."

Pierce had been looking about the throne room, but he fixed his eyes on Martel when he heard his name. Martel switched to Latin.

"Alaricus, the Lord guided you again tonight."

"Amen, my lord."

"I would like to make you a Crucifer, but for that you would have to speak our language. Nevertheless, I give you all the privileges and rights of a Crucifer, including the right to bear a *tormentum* in my presence."

"I am honored, my lord." He took the Mallory back from Maria, who met his eyes with a curious expression: pride, affection, and resentment seemed to blend in it.

"The Lady Maria will remain in the palace to attend me for the next few days," Martel went on. "In the meantime, I will have great need of your help.

"Alaricus, bring me the Christians, and bring me the consul Plinius."

Nineteen:

Again Pierce slept in Maria's doorway, but not easily: She wept for almost an hour, quietly but audibly; then she prayed aloud for a time. Pierce's head hurt. He took two Pentasyns, drowsed for a time, woke with his head hurting again, and finished the capsules off. Sometime during the day he would get some more; for now he needed sleep.

Early in the morning he woke, went to breakfast, and slipped out into the city. Here and there a few slaves were sweeping up the debris of the night: potsherds from shattered *amphorae*, broken bricks, discarded clubs. To Pierce it looked like the remains of a series of brawls rather than a full-scale riot, but it was bad enough. The Militants' grip on Rome was weak; they would have to clamp down very hard, or let go altogether.

The *insula* of Verrus and Antonia was teeming with people by the time Pierce reached it. Pierce looked up and saw the schoolmaster's little balcony; he crossed the street and leaned against a colonnade pillar. A few children gaped at him, and other idlers kept their eyes on him as well. He ignored them.

After a few minutes he saw Antonia look down into the street. He looked at her with a faint smile, but did not wave or call out to her. She stepped back out of sight, and soon appeared on the sidewalk, gripping a faded blue wool shawl. Looking straight ahead, Antonia walked down the street; Pierce followed.

The next apartment block had a colonnade that sheltered a number of shops and sidewalk vendors. Verrus and six young pupils occupied a patch of sidewalk—a typical middle-class Roman classroom. Verrus looked up while the boys chanted lines from the *Aeneid*, and saw his wife. Then he looked over her shoulder and saw Pierce. Antonia turned abruptly and went back, brushing past Pierce with her eyes modestly downcast.

"Stop, stop!" Verrus commanded. "Cassius Minor, recite the lines for the others so they can hear it again. I'll be right back."

Pierce stopped by one of the colonnade pillars and looked out across the street. Verrus stood beside him.

"*Ave*, Verrus."

"What do you want?"

"Only to know where Aquilius is. We were separated not long after we left you."

"I have no idea. This is very disturbing news."

"Indeed. I feel responsible for him. Verrus, if he comes to you again, tell him I've been looking for him. I'll be back here in a day or two. He can leave a message with you?"

"Of course."

"Then I will see you again, tomorrow or the next day." Pierce handed him twenty *denarii*, nodded, and walked across the street.

The city was fully awake now, the shops crowded, the colonnades busy with people. Pierce made his way north to the Campus Martius, taking his time and eavesdropping where he could. Many people had been to the Amphitheater the night before and eagerly told others what had happened. Pierce watched one teenager scratching a graffito on a wall: a fair rendition of the Christ holo. The boy seemed to have been genuinely stirred by what he had seen, but his companions joked and laughed about it.

At the baths of Tertius, Pierce paid his two coppers and went inside. An attendant directed him to a tiny office off the exercise yard, where the *balneator* was working on his accounts.

"Have you spoken to your friends about the matter we discussed?" Pierce asked.

Tertius looked levelly at him. "I have. But it was before last night. After what happened in the Amphitheater, my friends may be frightened again."

"My patron is more eager than ever to meet your friends. He offers them his full protection."

"Come back here tonight, just before sundown," Tertius murmured. "You can meet some of my friends. But you must come alone."

"I understand. I cannot expect you to trust me if I do not trust you."

The man smiled a little as he stood up, ending the interview.

"The issue is a difficult one, as we shall explain tonight."

"Until then."

Munching dried apples, Pierce walked back into the center of the city. The urban cohorts were conspicuous, as were the Praetorians who guarded the Forum, the Capitol, and other important buildings. Rome seemed busily tranquil, but Pierce sensed more trouble. A populace accustomed to spectacles had been surprised but far from staggered by Martel's holos and fireworks. It had also been scandalized by his neglect of the gods and their proper rituals. Now the Romans were trying to decide what they thought: in conversations at neighborhood fountains, in arguments in the marketplace, in fistfights and stabbings in the *popinae*.

Pierce reached Juvenal's apartment building late in the morning. He did not wait for the poet to look out the window and perhaps spot Pierce in the milling crowds below; instead he again climbed the urine-stinking stairs.

"A bottle of Chian wine, courtesy of a friend of mine."

Juvenal's face creased with a smile. "Splendid. Splendid. Shall we sample it?"

"Hide it, and save it for a special occasion. I hope you're free for a quiet meal?"

"Indeed, if you'll wait until I put on my toga. You are wearing yours, by the way, with more grace."

"A good student tries not to shame his tutor."

As Juvenal dressed they chatted about the show in the Amphitheater, which the poet had pointedly avoided, but about which he had heard a great deal.

"Most of the people in this neighborhood are angry about a rumor that Martellus plans to ban the gladiatorial shows. It's all very well to look at the underworld, or giants hanging crucified in midair, but the ordinary people want to see a bit of action—some good fellows with sharp swords."

Pierce nodded. "It holds the empire together. Like the chariot races."

"Oh, well, some may like chariots. But you're at the mercy of your horse, and the other fellows' abilities. In the arena, you live or die by your own abilities."

"As many do outside the arena."

Juvenal smiled sourly. "Many, but not all. Come, let us be on our way."

A few blocks away, on the Esquiline Hill, they entered a *thermopolium*—a large dining room filled with trestle tables where customers, all men, sat on benches to gulp down bowls of cooked cereal or stewed vegetables. A slave led Pierce and Juvenal through the room to an east-facing colonnade above a small but elegant garden. Four tables, each with three couches, stood in the shelter of the colonnade; none were occupied.

"This place caters to rich and poor," Juvenal said as he reclined on a wide leather-covered couch. Pierce joined him on the same couch: Custom demanded it, and it made conversation harder to overhear.

"Consider us rich," Pierce said. "Order a proper *cena*."

As if he had memorized the menu, Juvenal rattled off his order to the attendants. The first course, an appetizer of mushrooms in honey, arrived almost at once.

"Have you heard anything about the consul Plinius?" Pierce asked.

"Who remembers Plinius? It's Cornutus who gained all

the glory last night. Imagine the whole Amphitheater filled, and magical means to make one's voice like thunder—and then giving the floor to Cornutus Tertullus, one of the dullest orators ever to bray under a Roman sky."

"Plinius," Pierce insisted.

"The manager of my *insula* sent a slave off to Laurentum today with the month's rents. Plinius keeps close track of his accounts."

"So he's at his villa on the coast."

"Unless he trusts his freedmen more than he used to." Juvenal made a face. "You know, Alaricus, in the days of the deified Augustus, literary men could turn to a Maecenas for patronage. Now a rich man like Plinius sets up as a poet and patronizes himself while real poets starve." The stewed onager arrived, and Juvenal dug his spoon into the steaming bowl.

"Is he any good?"

"As a poet? He's horrid. Some of his letters, I'll grant you, have a passable style. When not congratulating himself, or reporting the compliments others have paid him, he shows some powers of description and even some wit. But his precious hendecasyllables—well, this is a poor topic for table talk."

Now the courses arrived all at once, their smells making Pierce dizzy and a little nauseated. Roman cuisine was fond of sweet and sour, honey and vinegar in the same dish, and a fish sauce called *garum*—stinking worse than Vietnamese *nguoc mam*—was doused over peacock and roast pork alike.

"How do you read the people's mood today, after the display last night?" he asked.

Juvenal laughed, an unpleasant wheezing noise. "Like that of a man who's drunk too much and gorged on tainted meat. Speaking of which, you've scarcely touched your wine."

"Is Martellus stronger than he was, or not?" Pierce demanded.

"Oh, stronger, I suppose. Now he's got at least some of

the people, as well as the Praetorians, and the senate will consider that. But the walls are covered with pasquinades mocking him; I gather he made a terrible speech, very short, so everyone's calling him the Laconian. Against him he has the aristocrats, and some of the people, and the priests."

"And Trajan."

Juvenal looked serious. "Now for the important news. This morning, when I went to give the morning salutation to one of my patrons, another client told me that Trajan is already well south of Mediolanum with two legions."

"Impossible! How could a Roman army in Germany already be informed of Domitian's death—and be across the Alps and south of Milan?"

"It appears he was planning to overthrow Domitian already, and began his march at the beginning of May. He should be at Rome within ten days—perhaps even sooner."

Pierce said nothing. The news made a depressing kind of sense. Only Agency support had kept Domitian in power for the last four years, while he grew steadily more despotic and irrational. Many Romans would have yearned for Trajan, and he would have sensed his own growing insecurity: As the likeliest successor to Domitian, Trajan would also be Domitian's likeliest menace, someone to be eliminated. If Trajan had decided to strike first, he understood the empire.

Pierce wondered what the Agency would have done if the Militants had not intervened. Domitian had been increasingly unpopular uptime; perhaps Wigner would have shrugged and allowed Trajan to take over. Or he might have sent Pierce downtime again to keep Domitian going for a few more months.

If Aquilius had gone north, Pierce reflected, he might by now have reached Trajan's army. If so, and Trajan believed his warning, the army might save itself by halting for a few more days. If Trajan pressed on, he was certain to be destroyed.

"Why so silent, my friend?"

Pierce shrugged. He couldn't pin his hopes on Aquilius, who was probably dead in some pauper's grave outside the walls, or on the convenient arrival of the Gurkhas and Cubans. All he could do was to stay alive and try to undercut Martel any way possible.

"Nothing," he said to Juvenal. "Once more I am grateful for your friendship."

They parted as the city began to settle into its afternoon siesta. Pierce returned to the palace and sought out Willard; he was in the terrace meeting room, talking to Greenbaugh while the Trainable watched a computer flickerscreen. Both men looked up as a Praetorian ushered Pierce in.

"Hail, Alaricus," Willard said, standing up and taking Pierce's hand. Pierce looked respectfully baffled by the flashing computer screen, which was feeding Greenbaugh data on existing and anticipated combat supplies. "What can I do for you?"

"I have learned more about the Roman Christians, my lord, but I do not want to trouble the emperor directly. May I tell you instead? And Brother David?"

"Of course."

"I have been invited tonight to a meeting. They asked me to come alone, and I agreed as a sign of trust."

Willard nodded eagerly. "Praise Jesus—a meeting with true Christians. Some of them must have known Peter and Paul. Brother David, can you imagine that?"

Greenbaugh paused his computer and nodded. "We live in great times."

"This is welcome news, Alaricus. The emperor will be pleased."

"That is all I seek. May I now attend on the lady Maria?"

"You may," said Greenbaugh. "The Lord go with you."

"And with you, my lords."

As he walked out of the meeting room, Pierce heard Greenbaugh saying in English, "The Lord moves in mysterious ways, putting that young man at the service of a spoiled brat."

"Well, he's doing Dear Michael more good than he's doing her," Willard said.

Pierce knocked softly on Maria's door. "My lady? It is Alaricus."

"Come in."

The room was flooded with sunlight; palm fronds just outside the window rustled in a light breeze. Maria sat on the edge of her bed, one of Martel's books open beside her. She looked depressed and tired. Pierce greeted her and told her his news about the Christians and Plinius.

"I'm glad to hear it," she sighed. "At least someone here is accomplishing something."

"My lady, are you unhappy?"

"The emperor, Alaricus, is punishing me. I was in charge of his safety last night, and I failed. So I sit here while everyone else gets on with the job."

"He is kind and merciful, my lady. Soon you will be back in his favor. I will remind him that I was sent to serve you."

Her blue eyes brimmed with sudden tears. "What a kind and loving man you are. Come and sit beside me. I've been so lonely—I need someone to talk to, someone who understands me."

He read her carefully, everything from the dilation of her pupils to the tone of her skin and the scent of her pheromones. She was out to seduce him; he wondered about her motives. Was it simply a spoiled girl's secret revenge, a way of asserting herself over Martel's authority? Or was she planning to form some kind of alliance with him, to bind him into a sexual clienthood and manipulate him in her struggles with the Militant hierarchy? Nothing in her dossier indicated any sexual experience at all, but her dossier was six years old.

Pierce sat on the edge of her bed. "My lady, I have a thought. No one else knows about Plinius. Suppose we went to arrest him and bring him back to the emperor as a surprise. Surely he would forgive you then."

Her eyes, which had been fixed on his, lost their focus for an instant. She smiled hesitantly and then threw her arms around his neck.

"*Ita est! Ita est!* Alaricus, it's a brilliant idea."

After that the seduction went much as Pierce had expected. They made love silently and aggressively, enjoying each other's bodies. Pierce's enhanced senses obliged him to hold back, which only encouraged her. When they were finished and lay exhausted in each other's arms, Maria whispered:

"When shall we leave?"

"I should be back from my meeting with the Christians before midnight. We could leave a little before dawn. Laurentum is not far, just a little south of Ostia. We should be back with the consul well before nightfall."

"What if he betrays us as Cornutus did?"

Pierce chuckled softly. "Then the emperor will soon be obliged to appoint two new consuls, who will understand what must be done."

"So the sooner we have Plinius, the better. Good. And what an adventure it will be," she added with a mischievous smile. "What a gift for Dear Michael."

They discussed the plan for a while, lying naked on her high bed in the sultry afternoon; then Pierce left to make arrangements in the imperial stables. First he went to the pharmacy and obtained another ten Pentasyn caps; the pharmacist refused to give him more.

"She's going to be slaphappy if she goes through 'em at this rate," he said to himself in English. Pierce looked blank, shrugged, and left. He swallowed four of them as soon as no one was looking, but even that amount only dulled the ache. Extended B&C, he reflected, was like having one's pupils dilated and going out in bright sunlight; the intensity was exquisitely painful. The Pentasyn worked like dark glasses, muting the increased sensory input but never blanking it out altogether.

The stables, on the southern edge of the palace, were

relatively quiet at this hour. Pierce found the stablemaster, a Sicilian with a squint and the predictable name of Strabo.

"The emperor has given me an urgent and secret mission," Pierce told him quietly. "I must have three horses saddled and ready by the first hour before dawn tomorrow."

"As the emperor wills."

"No one must know of this. If all goes well, your reward will be a fine farm in Campania, and a million *sesterces*."

Strabo's jaw dropped. "I will mention it to no one."

"In the name of the Father, the Son, and the Holy Spirit."

The sun was low in the west when Pierce returned to the baths. At this hour the customers had all gone home and the door was shut; Pierce pounded until a slave unbarred it and let him in.

"My master awaits you in the library," he said. "Please come this way, sir."

They crossed the exercise yard to a narrow two-story building. Tertius's office was on the ground floor; they passed it and climbed a flight of creaking wooden stairs to a second story overlooking the tiled roof of the baths. The slave led Pierce along a walkway to a door and told him to go in.

Pierce found himself in an airy room with four windows in the long south-facing wall and floor-to-ceiling bookshelves on all the other walls. Apart from a few stools and benches, the room was unfurnished. Pierce glanced at the tags hanging from the scrolls: plays by Menander and Plautus, philosophical treatises by Epictetus and Pythagoras, the *Natural History* of Pliny the Elder, *The Jewish War* by Josephus Flavius the historian and turncoat.

"Welcome." Tertius was sitting at the far end of the room among four other men. All were old, with white hair and beards. They wore shabby togas with no sense of style, but all struck Pierce as powerfully intelligent. Whatever else Tertius and his companions might be, they were men of character.

"Come and sit with us. I have told my friends about you, but perhaps you can explain in your own words what you seek."

Pierce walked down the long room and bowed before sitting in a backless chair. "I thank you gentlemen for troubling to meet with me. I am Alaricus, a Goth in the service of the emperor Martellus. He is eager to meet with genuine Christians and to make them part of his government."

A dark-eyed man, very old and frail, smiled crookedly through his wispy beard and spoke in a whisper: "Has he not found enough Christians in the last week, declaring themselves in the Forum and every street in Rome?"

"I said genuine Christians, honored sir. Those who know that the Son of God died for our sins and rose from the dead. Those who have risked and suffered martyrdom for the sake of Jesus."

"My name is Ioannes Marcus," said the dark-eyed old man. "I am a Christian. But I am also a Jew, and this Martellus has slain thousands of Jews. Many of them were Christians also. Why does your Martellus slay his fellow believers?"

"He believes that the Jews crucified Christ and rejected his message of salvation," Pierce said expressionlessly.

Marcus looked surprised. "Crucified Christ. Does he suppose the Romans had nothing to do with it?"

"I cannot speak further for the emperor on this subject. I can tell you, however, that he urgently desires the support of true Christians, and he intends to make the whole empire Christian."

Marcus chuckled and stroked his wispy beard. The setting sun, shining through the windows, turned his wrinkled face to bronze. "And this Martellus has already tried to convert the Gentiles through a display of miracles in the Amphitheater, has he not? He has shown fifty thousand Romans a vision of Hell, and the image of Christ on the cross."

"He has."

"And perhaps the Gentiles are foolish enough to believe him, but what of us? I was a small boy at Golgotha, but I remember it perfectly. They drove the nails into Jesus's wrists, not His hands; and into His ankles, not His feet. In the vision of Martellus, where was the peg between Jesus's legs, to support His weight? Why was the vision's beard short and brown, when Jesus's was long and black?"

"I cannot answer your questions. I am a simple Goth, a servant doing my master's bidding."

"And we are simple Jews, doing *our* master's bidding. We have tried to bring the good news of Jesus to Jews and Gentiles alike. And our master has warned us, as we warn others, to know the signs of the end of the world. He told his disciples on the Mount of Olives, 'Do not be misled. Many will come in my name, saying, "I am he," and will mislead many. And if anyone says to you, "Behold, here is the Christ," do not believe him; for false Christs and false prophets will arise, and will show signs and wonders, to lead the chosen astray.' That is what He told his followers, and so have I written it for all Christians to read."

Pierce stood up without willing it. His voice was hoarse: "You are Sanctus Marcus, the author of the gospel."

"You are too kind to call me saintly, but I have indeed written a little book on our master. Please sit down, Alaricus. You are too tall, and my neck hurts when I must look up at you."

"So you see the visions of the Amphitheater as the signs and wonders of a false prophet," Pierce said, obeying the old man.

"Of course. We're very excited, for it shows that tribulation will soon come, and then our master will return in glory."

"And you have no interest in coming forward to support the emperor Martellus."

Marcus smiled. "Our master told us to render unto

Caesar that which is Caesar's, but he said nothing about anyone named Martellus."

"Even if you could preach to him and his followers, and show them the true faith?"

"They have clearly had some exposure to the gospel," Marcus said, "though in a distorted form. Even you, a Goth, recognized the verses of my little book. It is up to the individual to grasp the message or to reject it, and to face the consequences. Is that not freedom? To choose between known consequences? We have chosen eternal life; Martellus and his followers have chosen eternal damnation."

The library was growing dark. Tertius had already lighted an olive-oil lamp and now lighted two others. Ioannes Marcus looked tired.

"What shall I tell the emperor?" Pierce asked.

"The truth, I hope. Perhaps he will reconsider and repent of his crimes."

"Or he may search you out and destroy you as a menace."

"With your help, he will not need to search far."

"I will tell him nothing of this meeting, but he may discover you through other means."

"This, too, our master warned us of: We shall be delivered up to the courts, and flogged in the synagogues, and stand up before governors and kings. Brother shall deliver up brother to death, and fathers shall deliver children, and children their fathers. It has happened already, and will happen again."

The old man's eyes were suddenly bright with tears. "At least I shall not deliver up my children and grandchildren, Alaricus. For they have all, all been slain this week by the Praetorians."

Twenty:

Once again Pierce stood in the terrace meeting room, facing the emperor and the Elders. But tonight Maria was not in her chair against the wall.

"Emperor, the man who was to lead me to the Christians did not appear at the place we were to meet. I have failed, but I will persist."

Martel, looking abstracted, nodded. "Keep on, Alaricus; the Lord will guide you."

"Shall I take on other tasks as well, Emperor?"

"Not for now. When you are in the palace you shall guard the lady Maria, but you are free to come and go in your search. You may leave us now."

Pierce bowed. As he left, he heard Greenbaugh say, in English, "Back to the agenda. Item seven: Looks like the Agency has closed our knotholes."

Already out the door, Pierce paused to look in his shoulder bag while trying to overhear the Trainable.

"... means we haven't got all the weapons we'd like, but we planned for it and we have enough for three cohorts and our own people. I've ordered our reception teams to pull back and keep the knothole sites under surveillance. Anyone comes through who looks like Agency will wake up with Satan."

Elias's voice interrupted: "They'll more likely come through where we're not expecting them, David."

"We're expecting them almost everywhere, but plenty of locations in uptime Rome just can't be used. That's one reason why we're here. As long as they don't seize Dear

Michael or the rest of us, it doesn't matter; we have our communications net set up and our forces on alert. When the Agency sees what the story is here, they'll have to negotiate. But we expect to have some bloodshed before they see the light."

Pierce nodded to the Praetorian Guards and left the terrace. At least the Agency was doing something. He considered simply vanishing, and waiting for the helicopter to move in and pick him up. For the time being, however, he was probably safer right where he was, and in a position to do the Militants some harm.

Maria's room was lighted by a single small battery lamp beside her bed. The glow made the murals seem more deeply colored than in candlelight. She welcomed Pierce with an embrace and a kiss that was both hard and yielding.

"You've just come from the emperor?"

"Yes, my lady."

"No—now, when we're alone together, I am only Maria."

"Yes—Maria. I told him I had failed to meet the Christians. He told me to keep on, and sent me here."

"Of course. This is where you should be." She put her arms around his waist and nuzzled his throat. "We must be up early. Come to bed."

"The guards will expect to see me in the doorway."

"So they shall—in a while."

In darkness she opened to him, held him, and shuddered wildly in his arms. Then they lay together while her fingertips caressed him.

"Do you think we have done wrong, Alaricus?"

"No. Many Christians show their love for one another this way."

She giggled. "You don't know how right you are. But where I come from, some of us feel ashamed of it."

"Christmanna—the man who converted us—said nothing of that. God made us to lie together and give one another pleasure."

"Amen. If only some of my people believed it. You must tell no one about this, Alaricus. Or Dear Michael will punish us terribly."

"Why should the emperor care if we comfort each other?"

"The emperor believes this is a sin. And sometimes it is, when the people don't care about each other and when they give each other sickness this way. But you and I care, and we won't make each other sick."

"Yes, my lady."

"Hold me until I fall asleep, and then go out to your place in the doorway. And wake me a little earlier than you need to."

She was soon asleep. Moonlight fell through the screened window, giving Pierce plenty of illumination as he gently rose and dressed and stepped silently into the adjacent toilet. On a little shelf he found Maria's Pentasyns and took two. That left four more; if she suffered no more migraines she would not notice the loss of two capsules, and he might well be able to replace them in the next day or two.

Soon he was settled on his thin mattress in the doorway, his cloak around him. The Praetorian who had told him about Cornutus passed by, waved silently, and walked on. Pierce dozed off.

The sky was just lightening as they rode from the palace next morning. The day would be fair: A few clouds blurred the stars, but they would soon burn away under the sun.

Pierce was grateful that the Romans had quickly adopted the Hesperian invention of the stirrup, but the saddle was uncomfortably small and his tunic rode up. The horses were sturdy, short-legged beasts whose iron shoes rang loudly on the paving stones.

Pierce and Maria rode down the Nova Via to the Amphitheater plaza, not far from the Colossus. Just to the south was the Vicus Patricius, which led to the Porta Ostiensis—the gate to Ostia and the sea. They rode down

the street, under the aqueduct of Nero, and around the
eastern end of the Circus Maximus. The street was
crowded with wagons rolling into the city, but the horses
had no trouble finding room along the sidewalks. The third
horse trotted peacefully behind Pierce, roped to his saddle. Maria rode close behind, one hand on her holstered
Ruger .357. She still wore uptime combat clothing, but
had at least put on a Roman cloak that made her look like
an ordinary horseman.

Traffic around the Porta Ostiensis was heavy: Through
this gate came all the goods from the port of Ostia, including the grain shipments that kept a third of the city eating.
The guards were urban cohorts, too concerned to keep
traffic moving to look closely at two riders whose horses
wore imperial insignia on their bridles. Pierce breathed
easier when they were outside the walls and trotting
past the huge pyramidal tomb of Cestius.

Maria brought her horse up alongside and smiled at him
in the brightening dawn. "This is what I wanted," she
said, reaching out to touch his arm. "We're doing something, just the two of us, for the glory of God."

Pierce smiled and nodded, saying nothing. He felt an
urge to tell her about Saint Mark and his lost grandchildren, not out of cruelty but because the interview in the
library had disturbed him and he needed to share it. No:
Describing the old man's tears would only rattle her, perhaps force her into a defensive shell. He would lose his
influence over her, to no advantage. The story of Mark
would have to wait until the deBriefing.

The horses moved at a steady pace, enjoying the cool
spring morning. The road was lined with pines and cypresses; beyond were cow pastures and small farms.
Clusters of houses, temples, and shops were almost con-
tinuous: This was a densely populated region. At a *mansio*
at the sixth milestone, they stopped for a moment while
Pierce bought bread and a small pot of honey. They ate in
the saddle; Maria was too noticeable to be allowed to
enter a shop, and Pierce did not want some enthusiastic

mailman to hurry into Rome with reports of a blond Amazon riding toward Ostia.

Before the sun was very high they reached the eleventh milestone and turned southwest down a narrow road. The soil was sandy, but the horses were not much slowed. On either side the woods closed in.

"How do you know where to go, Alaricus?"

"Everyone knows where the consul's villa is, my lady." Especially, he thought, if they had Plinius's collected letters Briefed into memory; the consul had described both the route and the estate.

"No more 'my lady,' if you please, my lord. I am Maria and you are Alaricus."

"Yes—Maria."

She smiled and leaned over, grabbing Pierce by the neck and pulling him close for a kiss.

As Plinius had described, the road sometimes widened into sheep pasture or meadows full of horses or cattle. Herders, mostly teenage boys, waved as Pierce and Maria passed. This was more peaceful country than around Vallis Viridis, country where shepherds had no fear of brigands. Pierce suspected that the reason was the power and ruthlessness of the local landowners; they were the seeds of the feudalism that would eventually supplant the empire.

Well before noon they came in sight of the sea, deep blue and dotted with the sails of ships. The road descended in switchbacks out of the wooded hills to a coastal plain dotted with villas and hamlets. The air smelled of salt, and at times Pierce and Maria could hear the thump of surf against low cliffs. The peasants working in the fields gaped at Maria—she had discarded her cloak by now—but answered courteously when Pierce asked directions to Plinius's villa.

When they reached it, Maria said, "Oh, my goodness," in English. The villa's red-tiled roofs rose above a brick wall and beautifully trimmed box hedges that might have come from an English country garden. Servants in blue-

and-gold tunics sat dicing at the gateway; their spears and daggers were as elegantly serviceable as their uniforms.

"Hail," said Pierce. "We come from Rome to speak with the consul on a serious matter. Will you announce us?"

The guards' leader, who was doubtless a retired legionary, shook his head. "The consul's not in residence. We don't know where he is."

"Please don't waste our time," Pierce said calmly. "We come from the emperor Martellus."

"You may come from Iuppiter Maximus et Optimus, but the consul is not in residence."

Maria looked impatiently at Pierce and put her hand on the Ruger. He shook his head at her.

"In that case, my friend," he told the veteran, "be so good as to tell the consul's steward we wish to leave a message."

"You can leave it with me," the veteran grunted.

"And I could leave my head with you, too"—Pierce laughed—"for the emperor would soon enough relieve me of it. It must be the steward; the message is highly confidential and urgent."

The veteran squinted up at the riders for a moment, then pursed his lips and nodded to the youngest of his men, who slipped through a side gate into the grounds of the villa.

Ten minutes passed in casual conversation with guards; then the boy returned. "They're to meet Lucius in the garden. We're to keep their horses here."

"Very well," snapped the veteran, glad the decision was out of his hands. "In you go, then, you and your giantess with the huge tits."

"Watch how you speak, fellow!" Maria said as she dismounted. In boots she was head and shoulders taller than the tallest of the guards. They looked startled and a little amused by her outburst. Pierce saw them winking and smirking at one another as they opened the gate.

"The Romans are very frank of speech," he murmured as they passed through the gate. "Any person who looks different, or behaves strangely, they criticize outright. It took me a long time to become deaf to their fescenninity. Quarrels are useless, least of all with insolent servants."

Maria nodded angrily.

Through the gate, they entered an estate that reminded Pierce painfully of the Hesperian embassy. On their left was a pillared portico leading to the interior of a sprawling mansion, much of it two stories high, its walls painted in white with blue and gold trim. To the right a gravel drive, lined in close-trimmed box and rosemary, extended to unseen stables. The thump of surf was just audible beyond the mansion.

A slave led them down the drive and through an archway into an ornamental garden. A vine pergola extended across it, giving shade to paths and benches. On either side stood mulberry and fig trees, flourishing in rich and well-tended soil. Directly ahead, to the west, ran a long arcade; beyond it was a terrace overlooking the sea and linking the mansion with a smaller building.

"It's beautiful," Maria whispered in English. Pierce said nothing. He looked at his left at a chest-high wall; beyond it, he knew, was the villa's kitchen garden. If they were to walk to the terrace and turn left, they would find themselves at the door to an indoor heated swimming pool. The various courtyards, dining rooms, bedrooms, the gymnasium and kitchen and slaves' quarters—all were as their owner had described them in a letter to a friend named Gallus. And to support this casual splendor, Pierce reminded himself, Juvenal and thousands of other tenants lived in wretchedness.

Standing under the pergola was a wiry little man in a blue toga, holding an accounts book of wood-and-wax tablets under one arm. He frowned at Pierce and Maria as they approached.

"I am Lucius, the consul's steward. This is most unusual," the man fumed, giving them no time to introduce themselves. "If you have some message for the consul, please give it to me and waste no more time. If the consul should favor us with his presence, I will make the message known to him."

"We have it on good authority that Plinius is here," Maria said. "Please do not try to deceive us; you will only make matters worse."

"I cannot make my master appear out of thin air."

Pierce touched Maria's arm. "We will give him the message ourselves," he said, leading her toward the arcade and the terrace beyond. Lucius looked terrified.

"I shall call the guards! Making yourselves free on the master's property! We'll soon see about that! Guards! Guards!"

"What are you doing, Alaricus?" Maria demanded as they stepped through the red-painted wooden pillars of the shaded arcade onto the sunlit terrace. Down a steep, rocky slope was a narrow beach and the sea. Pierce looked out at the horizon and wondered what was happening uptime on Sardinia.

"I saw him glance toward the little building," Pierce lied. "Let us look inside it."

With Lucius sputtering and shouting at their heels, they reached what Pierce knew was Plinius's private suite. Its curving west wall, behind a pillared overhang, was mostly windows made of leaded glass panes the size of a man's hand. This was the sun parlor, and in it, seated in a backless chair of bronze and leather, was a heavyset man in early middle age. He was reading out loud from a scroll and looked up only when Pierce pushed open the door.

"*Ave*, Plinius Caecilius," Pierce said with a smile. "May we intrude on your studies?"

Plinius stood up. He was dressed in a simple white tunic, and his black hair was tousled. He was rather round-faced, with a small mouth and a large nose. His eyes held a poised intelligence, and despite his bulk he carried himself with the same aristocratic grace that Aquilius had. "You are welcome to Laurentum, friends. Ah, Lucius, there you are. Please bring our guests some refreshments."

"My lord, these persons intruded on your privacy without invitation or permission. They claim they have some message from Martellus."

The gate guards had arrived by now, daggers and spears ready; Plinius looked at them and made a brushing gesture. "Thank you, boys, but you're not needed. Go back to your post. Lucius?"

The steward bowed, looking anxious. "The refreshments will be here in a moment, my lord."

Plinius turned to Pierce and Maria and gestured to a bench by the windows. "Please seat yourselves. If you come from Martellus, you must have had an early start from Rome."

"Indeed, sir," Pierce agreed. He introduced himself and Maria. "We learned that you were here, and decided we must urgently invite you to return to Rome. Your presence is needed."

"May I ask why?"

"The city is restless. Serious riots could break out. The emperor is maintaining order, but the senate has not yet conferred the *imperium* upon him. His position is most awkward."

Plinius nodded gravely, but a faint smile tugged at the corners of his mouth. "I understand my colleague the consul Cornutus denounced Martellus in the Amphitheater, in a voice like thunder."

"Your understanding is correct." Pierce was impressed with Plinius's intelligence service. "In that, he was following your reported advice to the senate. But now it is essential that you return and lend your support to the emperor before Rome plunges into civil war."

"This Martellus is not even a Roman citizen," Plinius said. "And neither are you two, I suspect, though your Latin is excellent. Nothing in law or tradition permits such a usurpation. We face not civil war but a legitimate attempt to repel a foreign invader. Martellus commands many magical powers, but I do not think he can stand against the whole empire. Ah, thank you, Lucius."

The steward, accompanied by two worried-looking slave women, entered the sun parlor bearing a silver tray with a silver pitcher of wine and three exquisite cups. The women set up a collapsible table for the wine and small bowls of olives, onions, and flat round loaves of bread like pita. Conversation ceased while the servants passed food around and then departed.

"So you see I cannot oblige you." Plinius spat an olive pit onto the tiled floor. "My duty is to Rome, not to your master. I have advised the senate of my opinion and withdrawn here to await events."

"You're coming back to Rome with us," Maria said. "Freely or not, as you wish."

Plinius smiled, showing yellow teeth. "You tell me I am free to choose slavery. I suppose you will threaten me with that odd weapon on your hip."

"No, sir," Pierce said. "If we must we will drug you and carry you slung over a horse's back. You will be unharmed, but it will not be a triumphal entry into Rome." He paused. "And we cannot guarantee the safety of your wife and household."

Plinius looked grim. "So I am to be the utensil by which your master legitimizes his usurpation."

"You are a man of wisdom, Plinius Caecilius," Pierce said. "The transfer of power is always difficult when an emperor leaves no successor. Rome rules the world because it understands power. You are among the greatest men of your age because you, too, understand power. You gain nothing, and Rome gains nothing, if you do not recognize the new reality."

The consul laughed and crunched on a pickled onion. "My friend, you sound like every opportunist who ever hoped to wear a toga with a senator's purple stripe." He clapped his hands. "Very well! I recognize when I am beaten. We shall leave at once."

Lucius was hovering just outside; Plinius called him in and rattled off a series of orders. Then, rising, he led them down the arcade to the main house. His wife, Calpurnia, a plump woman with an ornately curled coiffure, stood with her maids in a long, pillared inner room. Plinius embraced her, murmured in her ear for a long moment, and then turned back to Pierce and Maria. He did not introduce them: A nicely calculated insult, Pierce felt.

At the gate, Lucius was waiting with a donkey cart laden with wicker boxes: The consul did not travel light. Plinius was delighted with the horse Pierce and Maria had brought, and climbed eagerly into the saddle.

"My lord, surely you need a proper armed escort," the head of the gate guards said.

"I have it." Plinius nodded to Pierce and Maria. "Now let's be off."

The afternoon was warm. It was pleasant to let the horses amble at a pace the donkey cart could match, and to enjoy the woods and meadows. Plinius chatted about the progress of the crops and the history of the region, but said nothing about politics. In exchange Pierce talked about conditions in Germany. Maria listened for a while, but then grew bored and kicked her horse into a trot.

"Germany sounds exactly as my friend Cornelius Tacitus has described it," Plinius remarked. "The finest historian of our age, the greatest since Thucydides. My uncle and I are fortunate to be mentioned in his works; it is a guarantee of immortal fame."

"Your own letters assure you of immortality," Pierce said.

"You know my letters? I am twice fortunate."

"They are read and discussed in Transalpine Gaul as well as here."

"That is most gratifying. And now, my friend, can you tell me why, having encouraged me to leave Rome, you now demand my return?"

"When I came to your house that night, I told you that the Christians have many factions, and not all want to see Martellus in power. Your message to the senate was a serious blow to him, but he has recovered. The Praetorians are still strongly behind him, and many of the populace were impressed by his show in the Amphitheater. If he continues without further challenge, he will soon win over the senate, one man at a time if necessary."

"Or he can simply execute Cornutus and me, and appoint new consuls."

"He must not be made to feel that desperate. Martellus wants to be seen as the legal emperor, not as usurper."

"And what service may I now perform?"

"Come before Martellus. Tell him you have reconsidered, but that you must confer with the senate and with the popular assemblies as well."

"The assemblies? They have no real power. To hold Rome, one must control the Praetorians, the armies, and the aristocracy—not the people."

"As one who understands Roman politics, you can assure him that such consultation will help to strengthen his support among the common people and therefore among the three real powers. You might tell him that *vox populi, vox Dei*—the voice of the people is the voice of God. The true purpose of all this will be to delay."

"Just as Fabius Maximus Cunctator delayed Hannibal until he had no hope of victory."

"Precisely."

"So I will find tedious problems on the road to the official granting of the *imperium*. Very well. We were doing more than a little of that with Domitian for years." Plinius smiled faintly. "Is your Amazon companion your ally in this?"

"No, sir. In fact, if you had compromised me in her hearing, I would have had to kill her."

"*Eheu!* I suspected as much. This plotting and counterplotting is just like Domitian."

"It will be much less necessary under Trajan."

Maria had paused to let them catch up. While she was still out of earshot, Plinius murmured, "One thing all Christians seem to believe—that tomorrow will be better. Very strange, when fortune rules our lives and each day brings us closer to death. And as for *vox populi, vox Dei* —that's positively blasphemous."

"My superiors could not agree with you more," Pierce answered with a smile.

But he felt cold anxiety: Fortune ruled his own life, and every hour brought him much closer to death.

Twenty-one:

They reached the Ostian Gate not long before nightfall. Maria warned the Praetorians at the gate not to mention who was with her and Pierce; but they recognized Plinius under his hooded cloak, and Pierce was sure the news would be all over the city within hours. They made no objection to the donkey cart, which by law should be barred from the city until dark.

Pierce felt terrible. In the course of the day he had consumed all of his capsules, but they had given him only brief respites. Even the fading sky of twilight hurt his eyes, and he ached as if brutally hung over. Yet somehow the pain did not mask the sensitivity that caused it. He could smell the faintest scent, hear the softest whisper, see the flies buzzing on the meat in a butcher's stall a hundred meters away. He yearned for sleep, but first he would need to raid either Maria's store of Pentasyn or Brother Samuel's pharmacy.

At this hour the city was relatively quiet, with most people indoors and the market carts not yet free to crowd the streets with their noisy night traffic. The three riders and the cart made good time, and reached the Palatine Hill while sunset was still red in the west.

"I'm worried, Alaricus," Maria said as they dismounted at the stables. "What if Dear Michael is still angry with me? And with you?"

"Don't worry, my lady—Maria. He will be overjoyed."

She paused for a moment and looked deep into his

eyes, anxious and needing reassurance. He smiled and lightly touched her hand.

Plinius walked between them into the palace, looking surprisingly fresh and alert after the long ride. He seemed impressed despite himself by the fluorescent lamps, the warbling telephones, and the strangely dressed Militants striding so confidently through the halls.

A Crucifer told them the night's meeting was being held in the throne room; Pierce felt alarm, and forced himself to ignore his headache. Why would the nightly meeting be held there?

Four more Crucifers, backed up by six Praetorians, guarded the immense six-meter doors. One was Brother Kelly, the armorer, who seemed surprised to see Maria. He slipped into the throne room and returned almost at once.

"He wants to see you, Sister. Right now."

Maria and Pierce crossed themselves while Plinius adjusted his toga, and they walked in.

The room was as vast and intimidating as before, but now Pierce sensed an unusual mood in the people who sat and walked about under the high ceiling. Martel sat on Domitian's throne, with David Greenbaugh sitting beside him at a flickerscreen. The Trainable's face reflected the rapid flash of data from the screen; occasionally he muttered something to Martel or the Elders sitting below the emperor's raised marble platform. Facing the emperor and Elders were dozens of Romans: soldiers, senators, tribunes. Pierce looked for Cornutus but didn't see him; the consul had vanished after his speech at the Amphitheater.

"What have we here?" Martel called out in English, looking up at the newcomers.

"Dear Michael, we have brought the consul Plinius Caecilius to speak with you."

Silence fell. The Romans turned and stared, some grinning maliciously and others looking horrified. Greenbaugh looked up from his computer.

Plinius raised his hand in salute. "Hail, Martellus."

"I am to be addressed as *imperator*."

"And so shall I address you when the senate confers upon you the powers of *imperium*. I intend to urge the senators to do so."

Martel leaned back on his throne, surprised and evidently pleased, while the Romans murmured to one another. "This is welcome news, honored consul. What has changed your mind?"

"I have had time to reflect, Martellus. To consider the realities of the day. When your servants here came to see me at Laurentum, I was ready to return."

"How did you know he was at Laurentum?" Martel demanded in English.

Maria smiled nervously. "Alaricus heard a rumor. I decided to follow it up. I hope I haven't angered you by sneaking off like that, Dear Michael. But I wanted to help you, and this seemed like a mighty good way to do it."

Martel's face showed nothing for a moment. Then he smiled. "You're forgiven. You're a good and faithful servant, Sister Maria, and I'm well pleased with you. As are we all," he added, and the Elders all nodded and murmured "Amen." Pierce thought Greenbaugh and a couple of the others looked annoyed at Maria's return to grace.

"Alaricus," Martel asked, "why did you turn to Sister Maria with this rumor?"

"I serve the *domina* Maria, Emperor; naturally I turned to her with my news, and sought her advice."

"You have done well. In time I am sure you will bring forth the Christians as you have brought forth the consul. Now, Plinius Caecilius—when may we expect you to go before the senate with your recommendations?"

Plinius launched into a long explanation of how he proposed to approach the senate, what he wished to tell the popular assemblies, and what the precedents would be for his arguments. Martel listened politely for a time, then raised a hand to silence him.

"Consul, I leave the matter in your capable hands; follow the procedures you think best, and accept my gratitude for your support. But we have an urgent issue before us tonight. News has just come that Marcus Ulpius

Traianus has marched into Italy with two legions. He is now near Trasimenus, and could be at the gates of Rome within four or five days."

Plinius was visibly startled by the news. "Does the senate know this?"

"Those present here tonight know it; the senate will be officially informed the day after tomorrow, when Trajan's head is displayed in the Capitol. You have arrived, dear Plinius, as we are discussing the means by which Trajan will be destroyed tomorrow."

"Do you have an army in the field?" Plinius asked incredulously.

Martel smiled. "None of our men are more than fifty miles from Rome, but tomorrow by noon Trajan will face the greatest armed force this world has ever seen. We have means of transportation that make the Hesperians' bicycles look like a peasant's oxcart. Tonight we are making our plans and giving instructions; tomorrow before dawn we leave for Trasimenus."

"I confess myself astounded by this news," Plinius said. "A single courier can cover five hundred miles in a day and night, by changing horses every few miles. But an army?"

"I wish we could bring you with us, Plinius, but you will be needed here. Someday soon, though, you will travel from Rome to your ancestral home at Comum between sunrise and sunset. Now forgive me, but we must turn to other matters that do not concern you. Sister Maria and Alaricus, please arrange for the consul's accommodations and refreshments, and then return to attend us."

Leaving the throne room, they took Plinius to a lavish apartment not far from Maria's. A dozen slaves welcomed the consul.

"Why should I not simply return to my own house?" Plinius asked.

"The emperor will need you close at hand for advice and consultation," Maria said. "We don't want to lose you again."

Plinius's calm expression did not betray the contempt he must have felt for such a thin excuse. "Very well. Perhaps, young lady, you might return to Martellus while I keep Alaricus with me for a moment. I would like him to convey some messages to my household."

"Of course." Maria looked at Pierce and her smile vanished. "Alaricus, are you ill?"

"I have a slight headache, my lady."

"You look feverish." She touched his forehead. "No fever, but you're clearly not well. Would you like something for it?"

"Perhaps my lady would send me to the pharmacy for one of the sovereign remedies you have there, such as the one I obtained for you."

"Of course. She scrawled a note and handed it to him. "give that to Brother Samuel in the pharmacy."

"Bene facis, domina."

When she had gone, Plinius dismissed the slaves and took Pierce onto a small balcony overlooking a garden; across the way was Maria's own apartment.

"What am I to make of Martellus's boasts?" Plinius asked quietly.

Pierce rubbed his temples. "He can probably make good on them. If he takes a cohort or two of Praetorians armed with *tormenta*, Trajan's men will be slaughtered."

"And at Trasimenus, of all places."

Pierce understood. The Carthaginian Hannibal had destroyed a Roman army at Lake Trasimenus two centuries earlier; now another foreign invader threatened to destroy Rome itself.

"Have we chosen the wrong side, Alaricus?"

"No, Consul. And it would not matter if we had."

Plinius snorted with amusement and took Pierce by the arm. He looked into Pierce's face. "A man of principle, masquerading as a spy. You are like the *eiron* in a Greek play, a man who is more than he claims."

"And Martellus is a *miles gloriosus*, a braggart soldier."

Plinius laughed. "You're no Goth, Alaricus; you're too well educated. You're a Hesp—"

Pierce's thumbs were at the consul's throat. "Hush," Pierce said softly. Plinius nodded, startled by the strength in Pierce's hands and the coldness in his eyes.

"Your pardon, good friend. I forgot where we are."

"I must leave you now. If you need to send a message to your household, or to anyone else, go to the palace baths and ask for a young slave named Terentius."

"Good luck, Alaricus."

"I will need it," Pierce mumbled.

Samuel the pharmacist doled out six Pentasyns while Pierce thought seriously about killing him to obtain the rest of the supply. With an effort he only nodded and turned away.

Two capsules brought some relief. He sat in a darkened doorway for a few minutes, enjoying the absence of pain. Soon he would have to rejoin Maria, but he was only a short distance from David Greenbaugh's office and its computer. At this hour the palace was relatively quiet; the Romans were off to bed, and the Militants had gathered in their dining halls for supper and gossip. He would never have a better chance.

Greenbaugh's office had a cheap combination padlock on it; under Pierce's fingertips, the tumblers fell with easily detectable clicks. The fluorescent lights were still on, and the computer was flickering to no one. Pierce realized it must be linked to the one in the throne room; he would not even have to outwit the machine's defenses. He sat back and watched page after page of data flash past.

It was discouraging news. One of Martel's knotholers, located just north of the city wall, had actually moved ten big Fiat trucks downtime, along with ample supplies and gasoline. Martel could easily move a cohort of Praetorians—or Crucifers, if he wanted the Militants to enjoy all the glory of destroying Trajan. Worse yet, the location of the motor pool meant he would have no hope of reaching it, penetrating its defenses, and sabotaging the trucks.

Greenbaugh's computer also told him what weapons and ammunition they could take to Trasimenus: plenty of automatic rifles, grenades, CS and CN tear gas, more T-60 antitank missiles, even two flamethrowers. Pierce shook his head, wishing Aquilius had somehow reached Trajan and warned him off.

He got up and was heading for the door when he heard footsteps in the corridor. They stopped; the missing padlock must have been noticed. Pierce stepped to the side of the doorway, behind a filing cabinet, and waited. The door opened. A young Militant poked his head in.

"H'lo?"

Receiving no answer, he stepped back and shut the door. Pierce waited a minute; two minutes; five minutes. Then he stepped through the door, slipped the padlock onto the hasp, and walked out into the corridor without bothering to check first. If the kid had decided to watch the door, Pierce would bluff his way out of it somehow, playing dumb.

No one was watching. By the time the palace security people came to check—if they did at all—they would find only a locked door and an undisturbed office.

His head was not throbbing quite so badly as Brother Kelly admitted him back into the throne room. Most of the Romans had left, and the discussion between Martel and the Elders was in English. He found Maria seated off to the right of the Elders, and stationed himself beside her. She smiled quickly at him, and he smiled back.

"So we leave here at four A.M.," Greenbaugh was saying. "The first two maniples of the first Praetorian cohort will be here, armed with AK-47s and Uzis. We'll have Alfa and Bravo platoons of the Crucifers, and twenty palace servants as ammo carriers. Arrival time at the motor pool will be 4:45 to 5:00. Departure at 5:30. ETA at Lake Trasimenus will be 9:30 to 10:00, assuming no major delays. By noon we have Trajan mopped up, and we're home for supper."

The Elders laughed. Martel grinned. "Tell me, Brother David, can we arrange a triumph for tomorrow?"

"Uh, I don't think so, Dear Michael. But if you want to spend tomorrow night outside Rome, we could bring you in on the morning of June third, put on a real show. If Plinius gets the senate to ratify you tomorrow, we've got a real one-two punch. You're the emperor, Trajan's history, and you've got the whole empire in your hands. By the middle of June the whole city will be baptized, and most of the empire by the end of the year."

"If the International Federation gives us that long, I'll be surprised," said Martel.

"Dear Michael, I'm beginning to let myself think that the Iffers have given up already," Greenbaugh answered. "In their shoes, I'd've sent in whatever I could find, soon as I could—even a couple of dozen *carabinieri*. But I think the Lord has put a cold hand on their hearts, made 'em think about what they could be getting into. They're thinking about the political backlash, thinking about all the good folks they haven't managed to deport yet, who might decide we're in the right and the Iffers are in the wrong. And the longer the Iffers delay, the harder it's going to be for them to do anything at all."

"Five or six months from now," said Elias Smith, "we'll have schools in every town, no more slavery, no more gladiators, no more superstition. After what the Iffers allowed, we'll look like guardian angels."

"Amen," the other Elders murmured.

"Amen," Martel echoed. "But I'm not sure we'll move all that fast, Brother Elias. It took the original Church Fathers three hundred years and more to stop the gladiators. We may find the games are a way of strengthening our support while getting rid of our enemies."

Willard nodded and laughed, stroking the beard over his weak chin. "We can throw the *Jews* to the lions!" he guffawed.

Martel joined in the merriment, then stood up to end the discussion. Pierce observed that Robert's Rules of Order did not govern meetings in the throne room.

"It's getting late, brothers and sisters," he said. "We have a date with destiny tomorrow morning. I wish you all a good night. Sister Maria, will you lead us in prayer?"

Maria sprang to her feet, hands clasped before her face.

"O Lord," she said, "bless us who give our lives to Your service, and guide us to victory tomorrow when we go into battle for Your sake and the salvation of all mankind."

"Amen," everyone chorused, even the Romans who had understood nothing of their new masters' conversation.

Pierce escorted Maria back to her apartment. She was exhilarated. "We're going, Alaricus! Dear Michael is allowing us to go into battle with him against Trajan. Aren't you excited?"

"It is a wonderful honor, my lady."

She shut the door behind them and shot the bolt. "In here, I am not your lady but your lover."

He smiled and took her in his arms, wondering what he might be able to do to sabotage the expedition.

Twenty-two:

Six hundred Crucifers and Praetorians marched in step through the night streets of Rome behind Martellus and the Praetorian general Drusus, who rode horses. Every tenth man carried a battery lantern, illuminating the pavement of the Via Lata. Pierce, walking with Maria not far behind Martellus, looked up and saw pale faces gazing down at them from tenement windows and balconies: They looked frightened, and no one cheered.

The marchers passed through the Flaminian Gate, where the guards clashed spears against shields in salute, and continued about a kilometer north before turning east on a side road. Within a hundred meters they came to a walled estate and halted in a field beside it. The sky was just turning gray. Pierce saw dark figures push open tall twin gates in the wall, and a moment later truck engines roared to life.

The Praetorians, standing nervously in the trampled field, shouted in surprise at the noise. Headlights flared beyond the gates, and the first truck rolled out.

Maria squeezed his arm in the darkness. "These are wagons that go by themselves," she said. "Don't be afraid of them, Alaricus."

"Not with you beside me, my lady." He allowed himself a moment's regret: If he had known of this knothole's location, he could have risked a return uptime after the mugging. And if the Agency had known it, Rome might now be ruled by a Cuban *comandante* of Agency infantry.

The trucks, he saw, were standard Italian Army Fiat

troop carriers, with camouflage paint and rolled-back canvas tops—the kind of vehicles soldiers had been calling cattle trucks since World War II. Pierce wondered how much of a bribe it had taken to get such vehicles; whoever had taken the bribe would regret it.

Martellus dismounted from his horse and climbed onto the running board of the first truck. Two Praetorians held their lanterns beside him, so everyone could see the emperor and Drusus at his side. Willard Powell, rubbing his beard, stood close-by; he handed Martel a bullhorn.

"Romans!" Martel shouted. "Today we ride faster than the wind, and we strike more terribly than the thunderbolt. No charioteer has ever traveled the Via Flaminia as we shall. Be brave and steadfast. By noon we shall win the greatest victory Roman arms have ever gained. For the glory of Jesus, let us go forward!"

A ragged cheer answered him, and then a louder one. Martel and Drusus got into the cab of the truck, while Willard hopped in behind the wheel. Crucifers began helping the Praetorians into the trucks and getting them settled. Pierce and Maria clambered into the second truck, standing just behind the cab while Crucifers and Praetorians crowded companionably in on the benches running the length of the truck bed.

As the loading was going on, four men on motorcycles roared out through the gate and disappeared into the darkness: a vanguard, Pierce supposed, to clear the highway of peasant carts and foot traffic. Martel had thought of everything.

With a blast of airhorns the convoy got under way. The trucks lurched back to the Via Flaminia and swung north, each filling most of the roadway. The Praetorians shouted and swore as they saw how fast they were going, and then began to enjoy it.

Pierce, standing beside Maria, enjoyed it much less: The wind and dust stung his eyes, and the exhaust from the lead truck made him cough. The uneven road surface jolted the trucks and forced everyone to cling to a handhold. Maria bumped into him from time to time, or steadied herself with a hand on his shoulder. He moved a little farther away; he did not want Crucifers gossiping about Maria Donovan's interest in her endo bodyguard.

The trucks were soon going seventy kilometers per hour—not much compared to an uptime *superstrada*, but dizzyingly fast for the Praetorians. Occasionally the lead truck braked to avoid hitting some stupefied peasant and his sheep, or a team of slaves manhauling a wagonload of bricks. But the motorcyclists had done a good job of clearing the road.

Mist rose with the sun, and the air was colder than usual. Where the road ran close to the Tiber the fog was thick, but the hilltops stood above it like islands under a clear June sky. Pierce saw that many peasants were standing beside the road, or off in the fields, watching the convoy pass. He wondered what they made of it—whether they even connected it with the advent of Martellus, or saw it as just another mysterious portent.

The Via Flaminia was growing familiar to Pierce by now, but Maria was fascinated by everything; evidently she had seen little outside Rome since her arrival on Ahania. Looking at the dirty-faced peasant children who watched the convoy pass, she said to Pierce, "Soon they will all be in school, learning Christianity, learning how to read and write."

"Even they?" Pierce said.

"Give us the children, and we'll never lose them when they grow up."

He nodded. That was, after all, very much the policy of the Agency for Intertemporal Development.

Whenever the convoy reached a town or village, each truck slowed to a crawl. Twice they had to leave the road because it ran through a narrow gate, and detour around the walls of the town along some mule track. When they could drive through the streets, the people crammed onto balconies and rooftops to watch them pass, or ran before the lead truck—like young men in Pamplona, thought Pierce, running before the bulls. The bystanders sometimes cheered, but most simply watched in amazement.

The convoy stopped only twice that morning, each time to let the soldiers get off to eat from their backpacks and to relieve themselves. They did not stop at a *mansio*—Martel must have sensibly expected the Praetorians to get drunk if they got the chance—but in empty, misty fields where the only people were shepherd boys. Hearing the animated chatter of the Praetorians, and the quieter talk of the Crucifers, Pierce noted their growing seriousness: They were nearing Lake Trasimenus, where this outing would become a battle to the death.

The countryside grew drier and more rugged, the villages poorer. Hillsides were covered with pine stumps and scrub, and the occasional small herd of goats wandered across them. In the valley bottoms, mist clung despite the heat of the sun on the hilltops.

At the crest of the hill, the motorcyclists were waiting. Martel's truck, traveling some distance ahead of the convoy, braked to a halt. Pierce saw Martel, his blond hair gleaming in the sun, descend from his truck and speak with one of the motorcyclists. Then he climbed gracefully to the top of the truck cab and lifted the bullhorn to his face.

"Romans! Christians! Our scouts report that Trajan's army lies not far ahead, marching toward us along the shores of Lake Trasimenus. We shall smash into their vanguard, and then turn aside, off the road to the left, so that the invaders are trapped between ourselves and the lake. Obey your officers! Use your *tormenta* carefully, and only on the enemy. Remember that in the sign of the cross you shall conquer. I bless you all in the name of the Father, and the Son, and the Holy Spirit."

The soldiers set up a cheer; Martel's truck moved forward again.

They were descending into the valley of the lake, which lay wrapped in mist. Trasimenus was broad and shallow, its shores a muddy tangle of reeds and drowned trees. To the left, rocky, barren hills rose steeply. Pierce studied the terrain carefully. The land just beside the road was fairly level; it would not be hard for the convoy to leave the pavement, parallel the marching column of Trajan's soldiers, and then drive them into the lake.

Now they were alongside the lake and rolling through a thick fog; the sun's disc glowed in the grayness overhead, but Pierce could scarcely see the trucks ahead and behind. The lake was invisible on the right, and the hills on the left.

Maria, beside him, tightened the chin strap of her helmet—an uptime model, recently declared obsolete by the Yugoslavs. She checked her Ruger and patted her ammunition belt, slung over one shoulder. Pierce could smell her fear, but a glitter of anticipation brightened her eyes. He felt a sour sympathy for her: She was a killer like himself, a guardian of her people. She had chosen the wrong people to guard.

The convoy crawled along for several kilometers, each driver watching for the truck ahead to swing suddenly off the road. The mist was still thick, though occasionally it cleared enough to provide a glimpse of the gray surface of the lake, or of the bare brown hillsides rising less than a hundred meters to the left of the road.

Suddenly Martel's truck sounded its airhorn, shifted gears, and accelerated into the mist. As it disappeared, Pierce heard shouts and the popping of rifles. He drew his Mallory.

The taillights of the lead truck glared close ahead, too close, and Pierce heard brakes screaming as he and Maria were flung against the cab. Farther back in the convoy came the crunch of collisions. Through the mist, Pierce saw Crucifers pouring out the back of Martel's truck.

"Not yet!" Maria screamed in English to them. "Get back in!"

A *pilum* struck the top of the cab, only an arm's length from Pierce; the barbed, meter-long iron head, set in a wooden shaft almost as long, caromed off the truck and clattered on the pavement.

"Get down!" Pierce growled to Maria, pressing down on her shoulder. "They've outflanked us."

Arrows whirred into the trucks, many falling among the

unshielded soldiers. Uzis rattled, the noise sounding distorted by echoes from the unseen hillside nearby.

"What's happened?" Maria demanded as they crouched behind the cab.

"They must have seen the scouts. They knew we must be coming, and they've set up an *insidia*—an ambush. Now it's we who are caught between them and the lake."

Maria grimaced. "It doesn't matter. We'll still beat them."

Another spear struck, this one pinning a Praetorian through his leg to the bench he sat on. His eyes wide with surprise, the soldier tried to stand up but toppled over. The weight of his body pulled the spear out of the bench. He writhed, gasping, on the truck bed while his comrades hoisted shields over their heads.

Pierce thumbed his Mallory to maximum impact, stood up, and found a target in the mist—and another. The flechettes struck through armor with the sound of hammered nails. Pierce ducked down again. Other soldiers were firing into the mist, screaming and swearing.

Martel's amplified voice rose above the noise: "Christians! Get down and form ranks. Prepare to attack!"

Pierce almost swore in English. Martel's command would only encourage the ambushers: They had the range of the convoy, and now the soldiers would be exposed to more spears and arrows.

Still, the men obeyed. Pierce fell in between Maria and Brother Kelly, the Militants' armorer. Arrows and slingstones fell all along the line, dropping men where they stood. The Crucifers, in standard uptime camouflage battledress, were terribly vulnerable. The Praetorians, at least, had brought their shields and now formed "turtles" —close-packed groups with shields fitted together above their heads.

Pierce snapped off a few flechettes whenever the mist cleared enough for him to see an ambusher, but Trajan's men had chosen their spot well: The hillside here was steep, with plenty of rocky outcrops to give cover. Visibility was no more than twenty meters, and most of the ambushers were well beyond.

Pierce's respect for Trajan rose. The general had not planned on a battle here, but he had improvised brilliantly. Martel's motorcyclists, spotted at a distance, must have warned him that he was dealing with Hesperians or someone like them; perhaps he had already heard something of Martel's coup. Knowing that the mist would offer concealment until noon or later, he had moved his legions off the road and onto the hillsides—laying the same ambush that Hannibal had used to destroy fifteen thousand Romans under Flaminius not far from here. He had doubtless left a decoy force on the road, with a barricade of some kind to block the attackers' progress.

Trajan's men might have panicked at the trucks if they had seen them, but they had only heard a strange roaring noise in the mist. The pop and chatter of small-arms fire might unnerve some, especially those who saw their comrades fall beside them, but Pierce was sure most of Trajan's men would keep their discipline. If Trajan actually had two legions, Martel's eight hundred soldiers were charging against ten to eleven thousand veterans. This would be a real battle, not a massacre.

Martel roared out again, almost singing: *"Parate! Prepare! Oppugnate! Attack!"*

Maria's voice, a powerful alto, rose in Martel's hymn "I Bring Not Peace But a Sword," and other Crucifers took it up. Then the line trotted forward off the road, scrambling through brush and up the slope.

In a leather helmet and breastplate, his arms and legs exposed, Pierce felt hideously vulnerable. Maria beside him wore a lightweight bulletproof vest as well as her helmet, but she, too, would be easy to bring down.

More slingstones fell around them. Pierce strode up the hillside, looking as far ahead as he could. A *veles*, one of the legionaries' light auxiliaries, popped up from behind a bush, not thirty meters away. Pierce could see his face clearly under the iron skullcap; the red leather of the boy's studded jazerant tunic made him a good target as he whirled his sling. Pierce shot him and he fell, blood gushing from his mouth.

As they climbed, the emperor's troops saw Trajan's men more clearly, and few ambushers survived. Crucifers and Praetorians began cheering and quickened their pace up the hillside. The mist was brightening, thinning. Bodies of legionaries and *velites*, ripped by bullets and flechettes, lay everywhere. Pierce saw a dead Praetorian and took the man's shield.

"We're winning!" Maria shouted in his ear. "Praise Jesus, Alaricus, we're winning!"

"The worst is still to come," he said. "We've been fighting no more than a few hundred men. The main force is somewhere up there."

Her smile vanished. With her fist to her lips, she barked into her ringmike: "Willard! We may be getting into a trap. Where's Trajan's main force?"

Pierce didn't hear the answer, or need to. Martel's forces were emerging from the mist onto the brown, treeless upper slopes. Less than a hundred meters ahead was the ridge of the hill. Something like a dark cloud suddenly rose above it into the bright blue sky. Pierce grabbed Maria and pulled her toward him as he raised his heavy shield over their heads.

The cloud was a volley of arrows. One struck Pierce's shield, with enough force to stagger him. Crucifers dropped all along the line. Uzis and AK-74s answered the arrows, but found no targets; Trajan's archers were shooting from behind the ridge.

"Oppugnate!" Martel's voice boomed.

"I don't *know* who's holding our right flank!" Maria yelled into her ringmike.

A stone the size of a man's head dropped into the line a few meters to their left and bounced crazily down the slope into the mist. Then another fell, crushing two Praetorians under their shields. Trajan must have a couple of onagers in action: simple but effective wheeled catapults.

"We've got to fall back and regroup," Maria said. Pierce shook his head.

"They'll drive us right into the lake. We must go forward and take the ridge before they come over it and down upon us. If we can kill enough of them, perhaps we can drive them off. It's our only chance."

She nodded, and fire burned in her eyes. "Oh, Alaricus, I love you."

He said nothing, but began walking quickly up the hill as arrows snapped through the air. Maria kept pace under his shield, shouting to the others to advance. The Praetorians, understanding their predicament better than the Crucifers, hurried forward, firing almost at random.

Trajan's first cohorts made it to the ridge just before Martel's men: a solid line of hundreds of shields, blazing in the noon sun. From the rear ranks came a hail of spears, while those in the front rank held theirs leveled. A *pilum* glanced off the curved face of Pierce's shield, knocking him off balance. Maria steadied him, then lifted her Ruger and began firing steadily and carefully.

Others were shooting, too, and holes appeared in Trajan's line. Someone fired off a T-60; it killed scores further down the line. Pierce brought up his Mallory and squeezed the trigger.

With adrenaline acting on tripled sensory input synthesis, he fought in a slow-motion dream. The shields of Trajan's legionaries fell, regrouped, and advanced again. Just over that hill, Pierce knew, were ten thousand men pushing forward, frightened no doubt by the terrible noise beyond the ridge but moving anyway through sheer discipline. A wall of dead men began to block Trajan's attack, and it was easy to pick off targets as men broke ranks to clamber over their dead comrades.

But the legionaries could not advance far. More T-60s smashed into them, sending oily clouds of black smoke into the air that must have looked as terrifying as they sounded to the rear ranks of Trajan's forces. The roar of small-arms fire was constant. Dust thickened in the still air as men crashed to the ground and rolled dead down the hillside toward their slayers. The air had smelled of dust and sweat; now it stank of excrement.

Pierce and Maria, crouched behind their shield, fired and advanced. Gradually they found themselves among the dead and dying of Trajan's front ranks, while other Crucifers and Praetorians advanced also. A slingstone or two still fell, but the legionaries' organization was crumbling: Those still standing in the front ranks could not pull back into the solid mass of men.

Kneeling on a legionary's bloody corpse, Pierce realized that they had taken the ridge. The far side of the hill was a dusty, crowded mass of men, a forest of spears with here and there a clearing for an onager or a squad of *velites*.

Maria pulled a grenade from her vest, yanked the pin, and hurled it. It exploded well behind the front ranks, who seemed to implode back into the vacuum she had created. A Crucifer off to the right opened up with a flamethrower. The screams of burning men, shrill and desperate, sent a visible tremor through Trajan's forces. The rear ranks could now see what was happening, and began to break and run.

"We must move to the right—to the emperor," Pierce shouted. Maria nodded and gestured to a squad of Crucifers to follow them.

Pierce knew that Trajan had one hope left: to turn Martel's right flank, take pressure off the center, and then, perhaps, drive the Crucifers and Praetorians back down into the mist and the lake. The right flank must be strong enough to blunt any such attempt.

Martel, Drusus, and Willard were in the thick of the battle, just below the ridge beside two platoons of Crucifers and some Praetorians, firing AK-47s over a rampart of legionary corpses. Martel, shouting orders into his ring-mike, seemed serenely happy.

The emperor and his men were all the right flank there was. The hillside to their right fell away into a little draw; legionaries were already coming around the shoulder of the hill and running down the draw.

The Crucifers who had followed Pierce and Maria were armed with AK-47s and grenades. Throwing themselves flat, they opened fire on the legionaries and killed at least ten in thirty seconds. The survivors, startled and frightened, pulled back.

Martel stood up and waved his men forward. Cheering, the Crucifers and Praetorians swarmed forward across the hundred meters of dust and corpses to the legionaries' line.

His golden hair in the sunlight blazed like a halo around his head, and the whole line of his soldiers roared when they saw him. Charging forward, the emperor's troops came well over the ridge and saw Trajan's men finally break.

Pierce and Maria kept pace with Martel, rounding the shoulder of the hill and making sure no legionaries tried to get through the draw again. Pierce saw that this would be no rout; while the front ranks were pulling back in a disorderly mass, their officers quickly rallied them into formations and marched them down the hill and into the shelter of a wooded streambed at its base. Beyond the stream, not far up the slope of the next hill, a small tent was pitched. Pierce saw horsemen riding to it and away again: It must be Trajan's headquarters.

Martel had won, but Pierce saw that it would be no massacre. Trajan's men were retreating in good order, even as sharpshooters picked them off. They would shelter under the trees as they had hidden themselves in the mist that was finally burning off, and escape into the hills. Eventually Martel might force Trajan into a trap or onto his own sword, but not today.

Martel himself must have realized that; he ordered one last barrage of T-60s and then halted the advance.

The hot afternoon air was full of flies buzzing and men weeping. Both sides of the hill were strewn with corpses, armor, weapons. Praetorians and Crucifers slumped where they stood, suddenly exhausted. After a few minutes, some stood up again to loot corpses.

"Praise God, who has given us this victory," Maria said. Her face was yellow with dust, her uniform dark with sweat and men's blood. "Come, Alaricus, let us pray with the emperor."

Nodding wearily, Pierce followed her across the battlefield. He wished he could find a private moment to swallow his remaining Pentasyns. Others were converging on Martel also, singing hymns and cheering and firing off rifles in celebration.

"Hail, Emperor!" Maria cried. "Oh, Dear Michael, what a wonderful victory! God is pleased with us."

"Indeed." Martel smiled out across the battlefield. "And I am pleased with you, Maria. You and your men stopped the enemy like—like Horatius at the bridge. And you, Alaricus the Goth, did well also. You have been a great soldier for Christ."

A Praetorian officer, his Uzi slung over his back, turned his attention to Pierce. He wiped sweat from his balding head and grinned, glad to discover an old companion in arms.

"Alaricus the Goth! You used to call yourself Alaricus Rufus the Gaul. You brought us the news of Domitian's death before you went into the Hesperian embassy. And now we are well met again."

Twenty-three:

And why didn't you shoot Martel during the battle, the phantom Wigner asked in Pierce's mind, *or just after, when the Praetorian blew your cover?*

If Martel had been killed, Trajan would have run us all right into the lake, Pierce answered. *And if I'd killed him after the battle, the others would have cut me down where I stood. And then what good would I be to you?*

What good are you now? the phantom Wigner inquired.

He had come back from Trasimenus tied and blindfolded in the back of Martel's truck, with the boots of four Crucifers planted on him. Occasionally his guards had spoken to him, always in English: "Hey, pagan, I'm going to kick your nuts up between your ears." And then they had done so, while Pierce silently said mantras and kept himself as relaxed as if he had understood not a word. He had prayed loudly in Latin until they had gagged him.

The convoy had returned to Rome at dusk, and he had been carried in some kind of a litter from the motor pool outside the Flaminian Gate to the palace. Now, still blindfolded, he was tied to a wooden armchair in what was probably the room Cornutus had been held in: It had the same reek of excrement and wine.

"Well, let's not waste any more time, my friend," Willard said in English. He was not the only Militant in the room, but the only one who had spoken so far. "It figures that we'd miss a few Iffers, and you're one of them. All we want to know is who you are and what you thought you were doing."

Pierce answered in Latin: "Brother Willard? I don't understand. Why have I been beaten and imprisoned? Am I being tested? Have I failed the emperor in some way?"

"Y'know, I thought you talked funny Latin. House-nigger Latin, Brother David called it. Pretty much what a Trainable would speak, I guess. What are you, one of their recruiters?"

"Please, brother, I don't understand you. Please tell me what I've done wrong."

Out of the aching darkness Willard's hand smashed into Pierce's blindfolded face.

"It ain't funny any more, boy. You talk Trainable Latin. You know how to use a Mallory. You're packin' a beeper and a bunch of Pentasyn capsules, and Sister Maria figures you must've stole 'em from her or the pharmacy. You don't need Pentasyn unless you've been Conditioned and your nervous system can't take it anymore. You said you just got into Rome, but you know your way around and you even found ol' Pliny. Maybe you're just an innocent old Christian Goth like you told us, but I think you're an Iffer and I intend to beat the truth out of you or send you to Satan in the process."

The beating went on for a long time. Sometimes Willard or one of his unspeaking associates hit Pierce hard enough to knock him and the chair over onto the slimy floor. At one point, without warning, someone popped a can of soft drink that had been violently shaken and held it to Pierce's nose. The fizzing liquid—Coca Cola Classic, from the taste—shot up into his nostrils, choking him. A favorite interrogation method of Mexican police, Pierce reflected while his body heaved and shuddered. When he could breathe and speak again, he prayed in Latin. They hit him some more.

Finally they were gone. Pierce hadn't noticed; he felt as if he had dozed off and wakened to find himself alone, lying on his side and still tied to the chair.

Had he lapsed into English? Had he admitted anything? No: His Trainable's memory had recorded every moment, every question, every kick and blow. He had spoken only

Latin, answered questions only in Latin. He had denied ever seeing the Praetorian before. He had said the Pentasyns were kept for Maria, who had sent him to the pharmacy for them. He had found the beeper in one of the palace latrines. Willard hadn't believed a word.

Breathing hurt. His hands, lashed tightly to the arms of the chair, were numb and doubtless swollen. Clotted blood stopped his nostrils and gummed his eyelids; his lips were puffed and split. Willard's assistants, like the Crucifers on the truck, had kicked him in the crotch and kidneys; Pierce had felt the warm gush of urine, no doubt mixed with blood, early in the beating.

He cried for a while, in painful, hissing gasps. When they killed him it wouldn't be much different from this: dark, silent, but free of pain and thought. He would be no different from the legionaries he had killed at Trasimenus, from the little Jewish girl hurled into the street. So be it. The trick would be to deny Martel any satisfaction, to remember that no matter how long the pain went on, it would end soon; and if he denied Martel even a vestige of the truth, he would slide into the darkness a winner.

At some point he slept, and woke to footsteps in the wine cellar. Strong hands lifted him, still tied to the chair, and carried him out of the cell, through the cellar, up stairs. No one spoke to him. He sensed empty nighttime corridors, a coolness in the air. Then the echoes changed, and he was outside, in a large walled space— a garden?

"Remove his blindfold," Martel said in English from a little distance. Rough hands yanked the cloth away. It was night, cool and thick with mosquitoes. Battery lanterns burned not far away, reflecting on walls of mirror-polished marble. They enclosed a long oval garden whose shape had gained it the nickname of the Hippodrome. Domitian had built it as a retreat for walks and private discussions, ordering the walls to be polished so that no assassin could slip up to him unnoticed.

Pierce was aware of men standing close behind him. A few meters in front of him, sitting on a bench, was Martel. He wore a toga and cloak, and rested his chin on his fist.

"They say you answer to no English, so I will humor you," Martel said in Latin. "Your behavior is a credit to you and your masters."

"Hail, Emperor," Pierce whispered.

"The game is over. Do not annoy me by pretending. Speak in English or be silent. I would have liked to know who you are and what you thought you were doing, but I can live in ignorance. Whatever your name, you are hereby *damnatus ad gladium*, my friend, condemned to the sword, and you will go into the arena to die very soon. The people of Rome will want their amusements, and I have decided to obey them with a celebration of my accession. Lucius Scaurus!"

"My lord emperor!" Pierce recognized the voice: the *lanista* who ran the gladiators' school across the plaza from the Amphitheater.

"This person is now in your hands. He'll be executed during the games three days from now. I realize that a *noxius* condemned to the sword is ordinarily butchered by a gladiator, but in this case the man is to be allowed to defend himself—with only his bare hands, however."

"As you command, my lord emperor."

"Do you understand what is going to happen to you, Alaricus?" Martel asked. "You're going to die, and your body will go into the *carnarium* with the other offal, while your soul goes to eternal damnation. You had your chance for everlasting life in Jesus, and you rejected it. You have brought this on yourself."

Pierce said nothing. Martel's beautiful face was impassive. At length a little smile tugged his lips. "I'm looking forward to watching them drag you out through the *Porta Libitinensis*, Alaricus."

Pierce said nothing. Martel nodded and Pierce felt himself lifted and swung around. Two strong slaves, he saw, held each arm of the chair. They carried him out of the garden and through corridors and courtyards to the Via Nova, the street leading down to the Amphitheater plaza.

Scaurus walked alongside Pierce, saying nothing until

they were well away from the palace. Then he looked curiously at Pierce.

"Just the other day your mistress was telling me the games would soon be no more, and now here you are. *Fortuna* governs the lives of men, doesn't it?"

"Yes." His own voice sounded strange and thick in his ears.

Scaurus grunted and nodded. "They've beaten you. We'll have our doctor look you over, see what can be done for you in three days. If the emperor wants you to defend yourself, you have to defend yourself even if you're not allowed a weapon. The spectators don't enjoy a one-sided fight. Fellow can't fight well, tie him to a stake and cut his throat, I say."

Pierce said nothing. They crossed the plaza; the high marble walls and arches of the Amphitheater glowed in the light of the full moon, and the gilded Colossus gleamed. The doors of the gladiators' school swung open before them, and Pierce saw himself being carried forward into darkness.

He woke with morning light in his face. Straw prickled underneath him; women's voices were singing a plaintive song, and the smell of putrefied meat was almost as strong as the stink from a nearby privy. He was lying in a pile of straw in a kind of cage—part of a low-roofed shed, divided into compartments by iron bars, and with its long east wall also made of bars rather than bricks. He had noticed it when he and Maria had visited the school, and had wondered what would become of the condemned criminals if Martellus banned the games.

They had put irons on him: leg cuffs joined by a half meter of strong chain, and the same on his wrists. He still wore the tunic he had worn at Trasimenus, filthy with caked blood, dried urine, and the slime of the cell in the emperor's wine cellar.

Cautiously Pierce sat up. His head ached; everything ached. Delicately, painfully, he pulled up the hem of his tunic and pulled aside his loincloth. His genitals were purple-black, his scrotum swollen to twice its normal size. A bloody discharge from his penis had left a sticky mess on his bruised thighs.

Slowly and methodically he examined the rest of his body. The Crucifers had known their business: They had broken blood vessels almost everywhere, but no bones.

The metabolic acceleration sparked by Briefing and Conditioning would hasten his healing; when they took him into the arena, he would be in relatively good condition apart from the universal ache of too many weeks under B&C. Until then he would only feel as if he were dying.

Sagging back into the prickly straw, he looked outside the shed. It faced east across a small patch of mud to a larger, better-built barracks. Chickens pecked in the dirt. Beyond the barracks, Pierce could see part of the arena where he and Maria had sat not long ago. The shed itself, divided into six small cages, held twice as many men. Only Pierce was alone; the other cages held two or three apiece. All were chained like him. None showed any interest in the others.

Somewhere off to his left, women were singing: probably kitchen slaves, preparing a meal. Despite his aches, and the stiffness of his jaws, Pierce was ravenous. He realized how much weight he had lost when he looked at his irons: The cuffs were small, yet they fit snugly over wrists and ankles.

The sun rose until his cage was in shade. Occasionally a slave hurried past on some errand, but no one showed the slightest interest in any of the prisoners. Near noon, a handful of men strolled past; they were squat, muscular, with dull eyes and calm expressions: barley men, gladiators. One of them, Pierce saw, was Astavius, who had been in the arena when Domitian had died. The gladiators looked dispassionately into the cages and walked on. Pierce wondered if one of them would be assigned to fight him.

A few minutes later a young woman came by. Like the men, she looked uninterestedly into the cages; but when she saw Pierce she paused. It was the gladiatrix he had seen twice before.

"You were with the foreign Amazon," she said. "And before that I saw you in the *spoliarium* after Eros died."

"Was that his name?" Pierce's voice was a rasping whisper. "I was sorry to see you grieve. You must have been very fond of him."

"He hoped to receive the wooden sword of freedom someday soon and then he was going to buy me from Scaurus. *Eheu*, he let his guard down. Why are you in here, and not watching from the stands?"

"I seem to have annoyed the new emperor."

She laughed, her black ponytail swaying. "That's the spirit! A true gladiator knows the value of a joke."

"I'm no gladiator. The emperor wants me in the arena with my hands and nothing more."

"The spectators won't like that. They want to cheer for a Samnite, or a Thracian or Gaul—you know, properly dressed and armed—not just a beaten dog."

"Perhaps the spectators will intercede with the emperor for me."

"I doubt it. This fellow seems to follow his own whims. One day he forbids the shows; the next he's ordering a big one."

"You're probably right. Will you be fighting?"

"No; I fought last winter. Twice a year is all for me."

"Then why were you in the tunnels under the stands?"

"Sometimes we have to help with the animals and scenery—you know, open doors in the animal runs, put the scenery on. At least we young people do. The older gladiators don't have to."

Pierce nodded. Most of the fights he'd seen before Domitian's death had employed painted backdrops that obscured some spectators' view; for one combat, a small grove of false trees had been set up on the sand. The Romans needed adornment even in a fight to the death.

"My name is Alaricus."

"Sabina. Were you fornicating with the Amazon?"

Pierce smiled; it hurt.

"Was she any good? Did she betray you? Is that why you're here?"

"No, I'm not here because of her." Although she had been coldly, murderously angry there on the battlefield, as Praetorians held Pierce and Willard found the beeper and the Pentasyns.

"Well, I wish you luck."

"For me that means a quick death."

"I know."

She was gone, walking with a swagger most Roman women would be scandalized by. Pierce estimated she was seventeen or so, a mix of toughness and naïveté. He found himself oddly grateful for her attention.

A woman slave came by the cages not long after, tossing flat loaves of bread through the bars. Pierce got two, each no larger than his hand and too hard to tear. He snapped them into pieces and soaked each fragment in his mouth until it was soft enough to swallow; chewing was too painful.

When he was finished, and still hungry, he dozed for a time. Cheers from the little arena woke him: A practice bout must be on. One of the *noxii* began to scream, over and over again, until his cagemate beat him unconscious.

Pierce felt a little better; he hauled himself to his feet, feeling nauseated, and staggered the three meters from one end of the cage to the other. Grasping the bars, he gave them a tentative shake. They were thicker than his thumb, set with three crossbars, and embedded in concrete. The lock on the gate was crude but adequate. With a crowbar, he could probably bend the bars or break the lock in thirty seconds; but he might as well wish for an I-Screen.

The rear wall was brick, showing vestiges of plaster and the despairing graffiti of men about to die. The floor of pounded dirt was stone-hard. The roof of the shed was made of heavy beams overlaid with thick boards, low and accessible but impossible to breach. Without some kind of tool, wall and floor and roof were invulnerable.

His only chance for escape would come when they

took him out of the cage. Unless Martellus wanted him to fight in chains, they would free him, march him into the pens under the Amphitheater, and then drive him into the arena. If he could wrest a sword from someone, he might just cut his way out of the arena and into the tunnels, but the Crucifers would have their guns trained on him.

So the only real chance would come when they took off his irons. If that happened in the arena, he was doomed. If it happened anywhere else, he might just break free and escape: to Juvenal's, to Verrus's, to Plinius's house on the Esquiline or even his estate at Laurentum.

Steady on, old son, the phantom Wigner cautioned him. *You've been professionally beaten, you look as if you've been dragged through a slaughterhouse face first, and you have neither weapons nor money. Your best efforts would probably just get you killed in the Subura instead of the arena.*

And maybe I'd take a couple of Praetorians with me, Pierce answered the phantom. *Or Crucifers.*

He shuddered through the night, covered with nothing but his stinking tunic and a little straw. The *noxii* sobbed, quarreled, and buggered each other.

Next morning, very early, Sabina appeared. She squatted down comfortably outside his cage.

"You look better but you smell worse," she said. "I'll be seeing you in the arena after all. Scaurus says I'm helping with the backdrops, and then in the *spoliarium* to keep the trophy hunters out."

An idea occurred to Pierce. He analyzed it as he lurched a little closer to her and sprawled on the damp straw. Licking his cracked lips, he spoke very softly, so the *noxii* couldn't hear. "How would you like to be free and rich, Sabina? The richest woman in Rome?"

She smiled. "Does the emperor need a wife?"

"I'm a dead man." She nodded, her intelligent brown eyes reflecting no undue sympathy. "I have no hope of escape, but perhaps a hope of revenge. I'm a Hesperian. My people will soon return to Rome to overthrow Martellus and put Trajan in power. Even if I die in the arena, if you can help me my people will pay you more than you can count."

Sabina chuckled. "And Scaurus will flog me more times than I can count."

"Scaurus will know nothing about it."

"He will if I tell him."

"That's for you to decide. You have the power of life and death over me. I will tell you what I want. You can tell Scaurus if you like. But if you don't, and you help me, you will never want for anything again."

"I don't believe you, but I'll do it anyway. If I can."

Pierce frowned in surprise. "Why?"

"Hesperians wouldn't trouble with a nobody like me. But in the *spoliarium*, when poor Eros was lying there, you touched my shoulder and looked at me, and I saw something in your eyes. You understood what I felt."

He nodded slowly.

"Tell me what you want."

"There's a storeroom off the tunnel from the *Porta Libitinensis*," Pierce said. "Behind some boxes, I think there is a metal tube, wrapped in cloth."

That afternoon he had violent diarrhea, making the cage stink worse than ever. Near sundown, Maria and two Crucifers arrived with Scaurus escorting them. They all looked distastefully through the bars at Pierce.

"His bowels have turned to water," Scaurus observed cheerfully. "Happens all the time, even with the gladiators. Tomorrow night we'll have a big feast for all the fighters, and most of them will spend the night in the privy."

Maria nodded absently and spoke to Pierce in Latin: "I wish they'd let me interrogate you, Alaricus. Brother Willard's too gentle. But I'd have pulled the truth out of you."

"Perhaps too much truth, my lady."

Hatred burned in her eyes. "You presented yourself like an angel, but now I see you as you really are."

"My lady—I did find the Christians."

Maria sneered. "Another lie."

"I met Sanctus Marcus, my lady. He who wrote the gospel. He is a very old man, but he was at the crucifixion of our Lord."

Now her face was pale.

"He says Martellus is a false Christ. And he is very sad, because the Praetorians have murdered all his children and grandchildren. He is a Jew, of course."

The other two Crucifers evidently understood Latin, so they looked astounded as she suddenly flung herself against the bars, reaching toward him with clawlike hands and screaming *"Liar! Liar! Liar!"* in English. By the time she remembered her Ruger and tried to draw it, they had gripped her arms and pulled the pistol away from her. Then they drew her away from the shed, while she went on screaming and Scaurus looked both amused and alarmed.

Pierce sagged back into the stinking straw, furious with himself. For the sake of upsetting her, he had risked his life. Worse: He had risked his one hope for vengeance.

Twenty-four:

During the night Pierce heard the gladiators carousing in a building near the practice arena. Following tradition, Martellus as giver of tomorrow's show was laying on a banquet for his fighters. Some would be gorging on what might be their last meal, and drinking themselves sodden; others would eat little and drink nothing. Around midnight the party broke up as gladiators staggered back to their barracks—or, as Scaurus had foretold, the privies. Pierce saw the occasional beam of a flashlight and heard snatches of English: Evidently some of the Militants had joined the party.

The night was cold and misty. Pierce lay curled on his side, straw pulled up around him from warmth, and listened to the clank and squeal of iron-shod wagon wheels on the paving stones of the Amphitheater plaza nearby. The other prisoners snored or wept. They were sorry wretches; two were clearly schizophrenics, the other four slow-witted bumpkins who scarcely understood what was happening to them.

Sabina's voice murmured out of the darkness: "Sst, Alaricus—you awake?"

"Yes."

"I got into the tunnel today. The metal tube is right where you said it was."

Pierce sat up slowly. His wrists and ankles were sticky with blood from the chafing of the iron cuffs. "Good. Will you be able to get it out?"

"I'm not a weakling."

"And you can get into the arena?"

"Of course. You just have to stay alive until I can get the tube out to you."

"Good. Good." He slumped back into his straw. "Sleep well, Sabina." He was asleep before she replied.

At dawn, slaves opened the cages and hauled out the prisoners. Guards with spears shoved them down the muddy lane to the school's bathhouse, where slaves doused the *noxii* with buckets of water. Pierce felt far from clean, but the crude bath revived him.

Around them, the school was tense and excited. Gladiators who were scheduled to fight moved gravely through the lanes, first to breakfast, then to a bath, and last to be dressed for combat. Others talked together in eager undertones. Pierce and his fellow prisoners were ignored; they stood under guard outside the baths while trainers and fighters shouldered past them. Sabina was nowhere in sight.

The sun was well up now, though Pierce shivered in his soaked tunic. His enhanced senses exhilarated him: the blue of the sky, the intricate texture of a brick wall, the oddly delicate fingers of one of his fellow prisoners— everything was rich and intense. The ache of B&C was still there, but he shrugged it off. If this was the last day of his life, he would enjoy whatever it had to offer.

After an hour or so, a slave sauntered up to the guards. "These *damnati* are to go over to the Amphitheater now."

"About time," the guards' leader muttered. "All right, boys, let's go."

In a ragged clump, the prisoners shuffled through the school, out the gate, and across the plaza toward the Amphitheater. They entered the gladiators' gate, on the east end of the building, but were quickly shunted into a side corridor lighted by a single olive-oil lamp. "You can sit down if you like," the guards' leader said.

Overhead, the cheers of the crowd came faintly. The fights had begun not long after dawn and would continue until noon; then many people would go home for lunch, unless the execution of the *noxii* promised to be amusing. Pierce considered overpowering the guards and making a break, but rejected the idea. The four guards carried razor-sharp spears, and while they seemed relaxed and mild, they never took their eyes off the prisoners. Even if Pierce could get away, he was crippled by his chains and by exhaustion. They could cut him down before he even reached the plaza.

He slumped against a wall, put his head on his knees, and thought, working through all the possibilities. It would be a near thing at best. He would have to move fast, trusting that the T-60 was in operating condition, and get off the missile within a couple of seconds of shouldering the launcher. Otherwise the Crucifers would see what he was trying to do, and they would blow him to bits before he could fire.

The morning passed. At last the guards said, "All right, boys, time to meet the gladiators."

A couple of the *noxii* burst into screams and tried to break free. The guards clubbed them half-senseless with the butts of their spears, then shoved them along with kicks and blows. Pierce said nothing. He got up and walked silently before the guards, through a maze of stone corridors that gradually climbed into light.

The sun blazed off the sand, forcing Pierce to squint. A sardonic cheer roared up from the crowd. When his eyes had adjusted to the glare, Pierce looked up and saw the seats of the Amphitheater climbing up and up, a hundred meters to the awning masts, and almost every seat taken. How many? Fifty, sixty thousand?

The last gladiator of the morning was being dragged out feetfirst by slaves dressed as Mercury, while Black boys hastily raked the sand and a Roman band played Arablike music. In the center of the arena six posts stood in a circle, each about one and a half meters high; not far away from them was a squat gladiator in silver-plated armor and the helmet of a *myrmillo*: Astavius, the fighter Pierce had met in the arena just after Domitian's death.

The guards marched their prisoners across the sand and

backed them up against the posts. Each man's elbows were pulled back and roped together behind the post, so that the chains on their wrists lay tight across their chests. As the guards tied Pierce, he felt a wave of nausea: They were going to butcher him after all. He would have no chance to stay alive, to use the T-60.

Frantically he tugged at the rope holding his elbows, but it was far too strong. He tried to pull his wrist chains, hoping to break a link, and failed.

"*Romans.*" It was Martel's voice, amplified and echoing. "*For your noon enjoyment I offer you something a little different.*"

Pierce turned his head and saw the emperor, standing on the repaired *pulvinar* and speaking into a ringmike. His toga was dazzling white in the sunshine. Behind him sat various Militants: the Elders, Maria, a few others. They looked uncomfortable, facing south into the hot sun; Pierce wondered how they had enjoyed the morning.

"*First, each of these* noxii *shall die in a different way. Watch closely.*"

Without much ceremony, Astavius clumped up to one of the prisoners, touched the shivering man's belly with the point of his sword, leaned back, and swung it in an irresistible sweep. Pierce, only a meter away, could scarcely hear the victim's scream over the roar of the crowd. The disemboweled man took some time to die; Astavius, his silver breastplate splashed crimson, went on to the next one, swung again, and beheaded him.

The crowd seemed to enjoy it. Within a few minutes Pierce was the only prisoner still alive.

"*Now,*" Martel said. "*This last fellow is a Hesperian, and a clever tool of Satan. We're going to play a game with him, and see how long he can evade the swords of Astavius and the others. The man who slays him will earn a thousand* aureii *for ridding Rome of a viper.*"

Pierce turned his head toward the gladiators' gate and saw four more armored men marching toward him. Each carried a short sword but no shield.

Astavius stood before Pierce, watching Martel for a

signal. "This is foolishness," Astavius muttered. He had an oddly high voice for such a burly man. "The people want a proper fight or a proper execution, not this running about."

"How can I run in chains?"

The gladiator frowned at him. "I'm supposed to strike them off. This is a kind of thing that can ruin a man's reputation."

"I'll tell the emperor that when we meet next."

Astavius suppressed a laugh. Martel called out: *"Myrmillo, free this wretch from his shackles."*

The gladiator obediently inserted a key in the cuffs of Pierce's leg irons and twisted. Each cuff popped open. The four other gladiators stood close around Pierce.

"I don't want to kill you boys," Pierce said as Astavius worked on the wrist cuffs.

"Don't worry, you won't," said one of the gladiators.

"I will, if only to buy a little time. Just put on a bit of a show, chase me around, and you'll be richer than Martellus himself."

They looked at one another as Astavius cut the rope around Pierce's elbows. *"Dementia,"* one of them said.

"Very well, gladiators," Martellus roared over the sound system. *"At the count of three: one, two, three!"*

Astavius's helmet had broad wings and a hinged faceplate with a grid over the eyes. Pierce's fingers stabbed through the grid, then gripped the faceplate. The blinded gladiator, reflexively jerking backward, needed only a light shove to be thrown flat. With every muscle aching, Pierce lunged forward, stepping on Astavius's armored chest and springing out of the circle of swordsmen.

Somewhere far away was the roar of the crowd, but for Pierce the only reality was the quartet of men turning to attack him. He skipped away, edging toward the *Porta Libitinensis*, with the swordsmen close behind him. At the posts, Astavius writhed among the corpses.

A tall, wiry swordsman rushed Pierce, his mouth wide in a scream drowned out by the crowd. The point of the sword rose in an arc toward Pierce's belly; he stepped aside, gripped the man's wrist, and broke it as he had broken the Crucifer's arm before Martel and the Elders. Pierce pulled the sword from the man's limp hand, shoved against another attacker, and stepped back to gain some room.

Where was Sabina? He parried a lunge from one of the three remaining gladiators, then sliced the man's thigh open to the bone. The gladiator's cry, muffled by his faceplate, was almost lost in the roar of the crowd.

Far more cautious now, the two remaining men circled Pierce. Careful: disable them too soon and Martel might simply order the Crucifers to open fire. The noise of the crowd made it hard to focus. The two men were closing in from opposite sides, each preferring a shared reward and life to spend it in.

"I told you!" Pierce shouted. "Take your time. I just need a little more time!"

They ignored him, their eyes implacable behind their faceplates: boys of nineteen or twenty, their only purpose in life to kill. Pierce chose the shorter one, rushed him, and knocked his sword aside. In the same motion he cracked the boy's head with the flat of his blade.

"Alaricus!"

Sabina's shrill voice made him turn. She was sprinting from the *Porta Libitinensis*, carrying the T-60 in its cloth wrapping. He ran to meet her, took the T-60, and unrolled it.

The last gladiator hacked at him. Pierce dropped and rolled, clutching the missile. The sand felt like broken glass under his skin.

He came to his feet facing north, with the *pulvinar* about thirty meters away and off to his left. The last gladiator was close behind; he had punched Sabina, who lay sprawled near the *Porta*. Pierce put the launcher on his shoulder and swung round, trying to hit the man with the missile, but the gladiator dodged away and lunged in—

—and snapped backward, half his face exploding in a red spray. It was clearly the effect of a Mallory at maximum impact; the Crucifers must be shooting at him already. He swung back, pulling the launcher closer, and saw the Crucifers crowding around Martel with their guns out and Maria in the forefront. But they were looking up in the stands, not at Pierce; he followed their gaze and saw a short, dark-haired, boy in a plain toga, holding a Mallory in both hands and firing down at the *pulvinar*: Gaius Aquilius Faber.

Putting his eye to the sight, Pierce found the crowd of Militants: Willard with his beard, Greenbaugh's sallow face, Elias Smith clutching a bleeding arm, Maria pumping shots up at Aquilius, Martel pointing back at Pierce and shouting over the PA system:

"The Iffer, you fools! The Iffer, down there!"

The missile shuddered on his shoulder and struck almost instantly. Pierce dropped, hands pressed to his ears, and rolled. Debris pattered down around him—fragments of marble and brick, scraps of leather and fabric, part of a silver platter, an uptime boot with a foot still in it.

Pierce got up, looked for the *Porta Libitinensis*, and staggered toward it. Sabina had recovered, and ran toward him, her brown legs flashing. He felt her strong, narrow hand grip his, pulling him toward the safety of the tunnel. He managed to focus on her and saw her laughing.

At the blood-smeared entry to the gate of the dead, Pierce stopped and turned. This time, no soldiers prowled the *pulvinar* looking for survivors. The whole north quadrant of the stands was emptying, except for the dead and wounded. In the rest of the Amphitheater the crowds were struggling for the exits also, though some stood peering at the smoke and ruin in the emperor's box. Pierce could not see Aquilius.

"Come on," Sabina said. Her voice seemed to come from far away. He obeyed, lurching forward into the gate dedicated to Libitina, the goddess of the dead.

Twenty-five:

They hid in the *spoliarium*, sitting in darkness that smelled of the corpses around them. Sometimes they heard shouts and footsteps in the distance, but no one entered the room of the dead, even to take relics from the gladiators. Sabina held him in her arms and stroked his head, murmuring in a country dialect he could barely understand. He enjoyed her nearness and dozed a little.

The tunnels at last fell silent except for the scrabble of rats. Sabina pulled him to his feet and led him back out to the tunnel. No lights burned. The underworld of the Amphitheater seemed deserted, though in the distance Pierce could make out some kind of intermittent noise: gunfire. Sabina turned right, away from the arena. Slowly they groped their way to the outside.

Night had fallen, and no lamps burned in the entrances. The plaza was dark, though Pierce could see people running across the pavement. Occasionally someone shouted, but the words were blurred.

"Where shall we go?" Sabina asked.

"Anywhere. It doesn't matter."

"Not back to Scaurus."

"No . . . to the Campus Martius."

The streets were silent and empty, with even the all-night *popinae* shuttered.

"Do you know Decimus Iunius Iuvenalis, the poet?"

Sabina looked up at him. "Who?"

"A silly man, but a friend of mine."

"No, I don't know any poets."

"They have their uses." Pierce hoped Juvenal was safe and drunk somewhere.

They went by a roundabout route, avoiding the gunfire around the Palatine. Why would the Militants be shooting? Or were the Praetorians and Crucifers debating who should be the successor to Martellus?

At the door of the baths of Tertius, Pierce pounded slowly. He seemed to have gone through so many gates, so many doorways, looking for shelter, for safety for himself and his people. And on the other side were only danger and blood . . .

The gate swung open. Tertius himself stood there, with three frightened slaves carrying cudgels. The *balneator* held up a lamp and recognized Pierce.

"Come in."

Pierce staggered and almost fell as he crossed the threshold, but Sabina and Tertius caught him.

By lamplight they bathed him, oiled him, rubbed him down with strigils. They put ointments on his cuts and sores, and bandaged them in gauze. Then Tertius guided him to a small room upstairs, near the library, and left him and Sabina to rest. He lay in her arms, waking often from grim dreams into the safety of her embrace.

Early the next morning he woke for good, with sun streaming through a window and Sabina snoring beside him. He lay for a long time without moving, luxuriating in the heat of her body, the softness of her breasts, the tickle of her pubic hair. Outside, in the courtyard of the baths, the slaves were singing as they swept.

Another sound intruded, faint but growing louder. Pierce heard it before the slaves did, but soon they had fallen silent to listen for it also: a low, wavering drone. He eased himself out of Sabina's arms, got up, and walked naked to the room's single little window.

It faced south over the roof of the baths and across the city. The sun was just up, gilding every eastern wall and roof. Off to the west, low in the sky but appearing to climb as they grew nearer, a cluster of glittering dots approached Rome. They were in V formation: eight huge Sikorsky

B-450 troop carriers, flanked by four Bell A-90 gunships. All were painted Agency blue and white.

"What is it?" Sabina asked sleepily from the bed.

"Our friends have finally arrived. Come and look."

She stood naked beside him, on tiptoe so she could see. "*Iuppiter optimus!* What are those?"

"Flying machines—like ships that sail through the air, full of soldiers."

They were circling the center of Rome now, the troop carriers staying well out while the gunships swooped in on the Palatine Hill and Domitian's palace. Smoke shot up, and seconds later they heard the thump of explosives.

"They'll wreck the palace," Pierce sighed. "But I don't really mind, as long as they wreck the Praetorians' camp as well."

"And Scaurus's school."

"Yes; they'll get around to Scaurus eventually."

The detonations were coming faster now, a stuttering rumble; black smoke rose in a straight column into the still June morning. The slaves in the courtyard were chattering anxiously to one another. Pierce saw the Sikorskys curve in, losing altitude as they converged on the palace. He supposed they knew their targets from interrogation of the Militants' knotholers; what he himself had learned was irrelevant.

"Come back to bed," said Pierce.

The battle lasted all morning, but by noon the center of Rome was silent under a pall of smoke. Pierce and Sabina breakfasted late with Tertius, who had given them new clothes: a fine linen tunic and wool toga for Pierce, an ankle-length dress for Sabina that she was delighted to try on.

"Surely, though, it's too early to venture out," Tertius said. "These terrible portents—"

"All will be well," Pierce told him. "Tell Ioannes Marcus that his children and grandchildren will be avenged."

"That will not console him. He is not a vengeful man."

Pierce nodded and looked away, embarrassed. These early Christians reminded him of the Navajo back home in New Mexico: people for whom vengeance, the premise of his soul, was a meaningless idea.

"We will see you soon, Tertius. Again, our thanks for your shelter."

"We never know when we might shelter an angel unaware. Until we meet again, Alaricus."

Pierce and Sabina walked through almost-deserted streets, back into the center of Rome. The gunships, their work done, circled overhead not far above the rooftops; Pierce saw their pilots, in white helmets and sunglasses, gawking at the sights of Ahanian Rome.

"Are we going to meet your friends?" Sabina asked.

"Eventually. First I have to find another friend."

They reached the *insula* of Verrus and climbed the dark stairs to the schoolmaster's little cubicle. His wife, Antonia, answered their calls. Her eyes were red and wild.

"They went to the Amphitheater together, and they haven't returned. Not a word, and the world ending all around us! Curse the day my poor husband ever gave you shelter, you and that foolish boy."

Pierce's face darkened. He took Sabina's hand and pulled her away, while Antonia shrieked and wept and half-naked children stood on the walkway and gaped at her.

Up on the Palatine, the palace was burning. Agency troops and urban cohorts seemed to be cooperating in putting the fires out, but Pierce thought not much of the palace was likely to survive. The Amphitheater plaza was sweltering in the midafternoon heat. Agency troops in camouflage fatigues—mostly Cubans, with a platoon of Dutch—were patrolling the area, waving off sightseers who had ventured too near. Pierce and Sabina walked toward a squad of Cubans who were enjoying the shade at the foot of the Colossus. Their sergeant, a big Black man, approached menacingly.

"*Buenas tardes, sargento. Me llamo Geraldo Pierce;*

soy agente de la Agencia del Desarollo Intertemporal. Bienvenido a Roma.'"

"What you doing here, man?" the sergeant asked in good English. Pierce politely switched languages.

"Looking for a colleague of mine. He disappeared when Martel was assassinated yesterday; I think he might be in the Amphitheater."

"In there? Nobody in there but some prisoners and corpses."

"We just need a few minutes to check."

"Sure, man."

Sabina was impressed as they walked through the emperor's gate and out onto the blasted terrace. Empty, the Amphitheater seemed even larger. The marble railing and floor of the *pulvinar* were stained black with soot and blood. In the arena below, a few hundred people sat or stood in the blazing sun: members of the Church Militant, and perhaps some Praetorians. A platoon of Gurkhas stood guard in the lowest row of seats.

Further up in the stands, crows flapped and cawed as they pecked at the corpses still unclaimed. Pierce led Sabina halfway up and then turned right, toward the east. The Militants had sprayed this whole section with gunfire, and almost twenty bodies lay sprawled across the seats. Crows squawked and flew off as Pierce and Sabina came near.

Neither Aquilius nor Verrus was among the bodies. Relieved, Pierce led Sabina out the nearest gate and back into the plaza. The Cubans were still there, taking pictures of each other with the Colossus in the background.

"I need to talk with the commanding officer," Pierce told the sergeant.

"He's got his headquarters up at the Forum. You know where that is?"

A command post had been set up in a colonnade on the edge of the Forum; a Cuban named Robles was in charge. He welcomed Pierce with cautious courtesy, unsure what to make of a gaunt, bandaged man in a toga who spoke flawless Spanish.

Pierce told him only that he had been in Rome at the time of Domitian's assassination and had done what he could to learn who was behind it. He was now looking for a number of Romans who had helped him.

"Their names don't mean anything to me, Mr. Pierce, except for Plinius. We got him out of the palace and sent him home. The Agency said to make sure he was safe. But we'll look for your friends. Ah, can I offer you a drink, a meal?"

"Later, thank you, *commandante*."

Less than an hour later they were knocking at the door of Plinius's house on the Esquiline, while dogs barked frantically inside. A porter peeked through.

"The consul's not receiving clients today. Go away."

Pierce recognized the porter's voice from the night he had come with Juvenal. "I'm Alaricus, a close friend of Plinius Caecilius, and the consul wants to see me very much. I'm the man who brought him back from Laurentum."

The door swung open. "Enter, master. We will tell the consul you are here."

They waited in the atrium while Sabina stared, awestruck, at the size and magnificence of the house. Before long a slave hurried in and invited them to the peristyle garden.

It reminded Pierce of the garden in the Praetorians' observation house, across the square from the Hesperian embassy. But this garden had been lovingly maintained, with trimmed hedges, immaculate flower beds, and fountains filling the air with light and music.

"Alaricus himself!" Plinius rose from a bench, his arms spread wide in a parody of an orator's gesture. "Risen from the dead, it would seem."

Two other people, who had been concealed by a hedge, stood up: Verrus and Aquilius. Pierce burst into delighted laughter and strode forward to embrace them both.

"And this is the girl who brought you the T-60," Aquilius said. "Robbing me of my chance to win fame as a tyrannicide. I owe you my thanks; they would have killed us in another instant."

Sabina blushed, a gladiatrix turned into a shy girl. Plinius drew her to a bench and called for wine.

"We have much to tell one another," he said. "Come and sit, Alaricus, or whatever your name is. 'Pirrus,' Aquilius calls you. I am showing you poor hospitality."

They sat in the fragrant garden, shaded by a fig tree, while Aquilius told Pierce what had happened: how he had caught up with one of the *raptores*, retrieved his own bag, and then fruitlessly continued the chase to get Pierce's. He had returned to the Viminal Gate, found no trace of Pierce, and like him had wandered the nearby streets. Finally he had returned to Verrus's flat.

"But he said he hadn't seen you." Pierce was annoyed with himself: He was proud of his ability to detect lies, and the schoolmaster had completely deceived him.

Verrus looked amused. "Persons in my circumstances, sir, become adept at dissimulation."

Plinius chuckled. "Yes, it's hard to be a client, always agreeing with thick-witted patrons—eh, Verrus?"

"Not in the case of your clients, I assure you, my lord."

"I decided you had probably gone to spy on the Praetorians or the Militants," Aquilius went on. "Then I saw you outside the Praetorian camp, with the Militant woman, and thought that perhaps you had changed sides. I apologize for my lack of faith, Mr. Pierce. I know your culture chiefly through its historians. Changing sides is very common among people in your profession."

Pierce smiled, though his head hurt. He wished he had asked Robles for some Pentasyn.

"Then I saw you again at the Amphitheater, when you saved Martel's life. I urged Verrus that if you came looking for me, he was to tell you nothing. After that I kept close to the palace, waiting to see if I could kill Martel."

"But you also came to see me," Plinius said to Aquilius. The consul seemed to relish Pierce's look of surprise. "He had the same purpose that you did, Alaricus—excuse me, Pirrus. And he seemed very relieved to learn that you had already advised me to reject Martel and leave Rome. That suggested you were still loyal to your own people. I confess, I would not have followed your advice unless Aquilius had appeared soon after. You were an unknown barbarian, but Aquilius—well, I served under his father."

"You never thought of going to find your father?" Pierce asked.

"I thought of it, yes. But then I decided I could protect him better here, by killing Martel." He looked sober. "If I had known how close Trajan already was, I would have gone north after all, to warn him."

"Don't blame yourself, boy," Plinius said. "You can't change the past; what's done is done. In any case, Trajan is still alive. My servants tell me his legions are up the coast, near Centumcellae. No doubt he'll be welcome in Rome."

"More than welcome," Pierce agreed. The Agency would be glad to make Trajan emperor—though whether Trajan himself would enjoy being a puppet remained to be seen."

"I have to tell you, Mr. Pierce, that I won't be going back uptime," Aquilius said in English.

"Why not?"

"Rome needs me more than the Agency does. We can't be protected by lies about Hesperians any more. We will have to learn how to live with you without being destroyed."

Pierce nodded, slumping a little. Aquilius, Sabina, Verrus, Plinius: each of them beautiful, complicated people trying to live difficult lives. And now he had made their lives still more difficult. The Militants and their rogue emperor had been only a nuisance, a minor hitch in the great plan to save the chronoplanes from Doomsday. Emperors and peasants, Neanderthals and physicists, all were servants of the plan whether they liked it or not. As was he himself. He protected his people, even if it meant he must sometimes kill them.

One of the gunships rumbled past overhead. The Romans looked up—Verrus with awe, Sabina with alarm,

Plinius with curiosity, Aquilius with calm resolve. They were his people, Pierce thought, and he loved them but he could not stay with them. Soon he would go back through the I-Screen, to the deBriefing that would restore his senses to tolerable dullness. He would confront Wigner at some point and demand to know why the counterattack had been so delayed. Wigner would give him some nonsense about logistics, priorities, political dilemmas.

It hardly mattered; after his deBriefing, they would put in some more blocks so that he wouldn't be angry about it—about the death of the Jewish girl, about the grief of Saint Mark, about the horror that the twenty-first century had visited on Ahanian Rome.

Sitting in the peristyle of the consul Plinius, Pierce rubbed his face and then touched Sabina's hand. She looked at him, her dark eyes full of trust. Eros the gladiator had been a lucky man until he'd let his guard down. Pierce would miss her, until they blocked that, too.

For a while, he would even miss Maria.

About the Author

Crawford Kilian was born in New York City in 1941 and grew up in California and Mexico. After graduating from Columbia University in 1962 he returned to California, served in the U.S. Army, and worked as a technical writer-editor at the Lawrence Berkeley Laboratory.

In 1967 he and his wife Alice moved to Vancouver, British Columbia, where he has taught English at Capilano College since 1968. In 1983 the Kilians taught English at the Guangzhou Institute of Foreign Languages in the People's Republic of China.

Crawford Kilian's writing includes several science-fiction novels, among them *The Empire of Time, Icequake, Eyas,* and *Lifter*. In addition he has published children's books, an elementary social-studies text, and two nonfiction books—*School Wars: The Assault on B.C. Education* and *Go Do Some Great Thing: The Black Pioneers of British Columbia*. He is the regular education columnist for the Vancouver *Province* newspaper.

The Kilians live in North Vancouver with their daughters, Anna and Margaret.